The Treasu

M000299579

A Supernatural Mystery Adventure

Guardians of the Dharma Series

Book 1

The Treasure

of the

Pandavas

By Author Victor Cosmos

Edited by V.L.Murray

Cover Design by Snir Alayof

Victor Cosmos

ISBN: 978-1-7352101-3-1

Dedication

This novel is dedicated to the Dharma Warriors of the past, present and future.

Victor Cosmos

Contents

The Treasure of the Pandavas

Victor Cosmos

Chapter 1 - The Inheritance

Diana Warwick sat in the large, crowded lecture hall, discreetly suppressing another yawn behind her hand. She glanced guiltily around the room to see if anyone had noticed, but their eyes were all glued to the podium. Relieved, she straightened her back into an attentive posture. The annual seminar organized by the London School of Economics always invited a keynote speaker of the highest stature, and this year was no different. The Irish-American, Dr. Robert Frawley, was one of the leading mathematicians in the world, and a Nobel Laureate, and Diana had studied his work often in the pursuit of her Master's degree. Speaking slowly and clearly, Dr. Frawley said, "As you may know, before the introduction of the concept of zero, it was cumbersome and hence difficult to calculate very large numbers using Roman numerals. What you may *not* know, however, is where and when the concept was first introduced." Smiling, Frawley paused for a sip of water. "We should thank the great Indian mathematicians who introduced these concepts and shared them with humanity, without need for a patent, for they made mathematical calculations much easier and more precise, paving the way for modern mathematics to influence science. Without this influence, many spectacular

1

inventions, we now take for granted, would not have been possible."

He looked at the awed audience and took another sip. In the silence, Diana heard the buzz of her cell phone vibrating in her purse. She immediately reached under the table and pulled it out, noting the text message icon dancing across the screen. She quickly browsed through her mobile message inbox. The text, a rather vague comment, was from her father, *"Diana, please call, when possible. It's important."*

A premonition passed through Diana. Was this related to her grandmother? She looked at her watch fingering it nervously. Dr. Frawley had been speaking for fifty minutes. Surely the hour-long seminar would soon be over.

She texted back: *"Will call in a few minutes, in middle of something."*

She instinctively put her right hand on her forehead and tried to make sense of her premonition.

"Actually," Dr. Frawley emphasized, "many Greeks of classical antiquity used to travel to India's famous universities—including Takshashila and Nalanda—to learn Sulba Shastra, the science of mathematics. In the 6th century BCE, the famous Pythagoras was the first to bring Indian mathematics to the Greek world, and together with mathematics, he also introduced the ideas of reincarnation and ethical vegetarianism. But what became known as

Pythagoras' Theorem had already been explained in the *Baudhayana Sutras* before the 8th century BCE.

He paused again, this time to allow the enraptured students a few seconds to digest this new revelation. Running his thumb along each finger as if counting, he continued. "Albert Einstein once said, 'Indians taught us how to count, without which no worthwhile scientific discovery could have been made.'"

Clasping both his palms together, he said, "What we call the Arab numerals are in fact Indian numerals; the Arabs themselves call it Al-Hindi—that which has come from India. Arab traders brought them from India to Europe. Interestingly, the Catholic Church opposed it, referring to it as the devil's work. However, vast numbers of open-minded and knowledgeable Europeans embraced it whole-heartedly, as it was superior to Roman Numerals."

After what seemed like an hour, Dr. Frawley glanced at his watch and said, "Alright, that's all the time we have for today. Those of you interested in learning more about this subject can read my books or go to my website for a list of additional resources." Frawley smiled. "I understand this is your last day at college before the term break. I hope you enjoyed the lecture, and I wish you all a happy winter holiday and a memorable New Year. I hope to see you all at future conferences."

Diana joined in the enthusiastic applause as the Head of the Department of Mathematics took the microphone to thank Dr. Frawley for closing out the term with such an interesting lecture. As a group of eager students gathered around Frawley, hoping for further discussion, Diana grabbed her purse, and with a quick wave to some colleagues, hurried out of the lecture hall, as her high, stiletto heels clicked on the floor in a quick rhythm.

* * * *

Swiping her phone lock open, Diana tapped her father's name in her favorites on her phone. Andrew Warwick answered on the second ring.

"Diana, we need to talk." His voice sounded raspy.

"Dad is everything alright?" She adjusted her long hair to hear well.

"It's about your grandmother," he said. "I'm afraid she's not well. Diana, she wants to see you."

My premonition was correct. Clearing her mind and adjusting her voice, she said, "Okay, Dad, I understand. I shall leave London tomorrow morning—early. Tell her not to worry; I'll be there, soon."

"Thank you, sweetheart, I am so relieved to hear that. I'll see you tomorrow. All of the family will be there."

Diana walked out of the LSE building and onto Houghton Street, hurrying toward the bus stop. The bus was crowded, but she barely noticed. She just stood there, immersed in her thoughts. Her conversation with her father had left her with an unsettled feeling in her stomach. Grandmother Eleanor had always been a bit dramatic, but she wouldn't insist on Diana coming home early unless it was very important. Diana had always been very close to her grandmother. In fact, Diana, her parents, and Grandmother Eleanor had all lived together at the Warwick house in Leeds. Being an only child, Diana had always been the darling of the family.

The Aldgate stop was approaching, indicated by the electronic board inside the bus. Diana pressed the red button so the bus driver would know to stop. He slowed down, and the bus halted at the precise spot. Diana stepped out and walked the remaining few blocks to her flat.

Her flatmate, Ana, was already home when Diana walked into the apartment. "How was your day today, Sweet D?" Ana said cheerily, as she moved her legs in a smooth dancing motion to the soft tune being played in the background. Seeing Diana's pale face, Ana said, "What happened? Why do you look so stressed?"

Diana tried to smile, but didn't quite succeed. "I spoke to my dad. He said my grandmother is ill and she wants to see me right away. I'm off to Leeds early tomorrow morning."

Ana's face fell and she stopped dancing. "I'm so sorry!" She walked over and gave Diana a quick, warm hug. "I'm sure she'll recover soon. She probably just misses you."

"I hope so." Diana slumped into the couch, her heart aching with grief and fear. "I can't imagine losing her."

"Don't even think like that. Everything will be fine." Ana smiled again as she resumed her slow rhythmic dance motions. "I am off to the pub to meet some new friends; why don't you come along? Maybe get your mind off things for a bit?"

This time, Diana blushed. Ana's enthusiasm for life was inexhaustible, but she was cautious, too, and she had never gotten into trouble of any kind.

"No thanks, Ana. You go and have a good time. I have to pack, and if I can sit down for an hour or so with my class notes, so much the better."

Ana's pretty face flashed a grimace. "Work, work, work! You should learn to relax." Her smile turned bright again. "But okay, I understand. You take care, and let me know how your grandmother is doing."

After some time, Ana grabbed her red evening bag, from the table, which accentuated her red and black patterned dress and short, black boots. She threw Diana a mischievous smile on the way out.

After Ana left, Diana sighed, glad to be alone with her thoughts. Her stomach began to grumble and she realized how hungry she was. She prepared herself a quick meal of salad, multigrain bread, and a glass of chilled apple juice. She sat at the kitchen table dangling her legs, munching and sipping absentmindedly. After eating, Diana checked her black suitcase a second time to make sure she had everything she needed then sat down at her desk and flipped open her laptop. She sent an e-mail to her office, informing them of the family emergency, and purchased train tickets online. Then with a sigh, she slipped into bed, switched off the light and was asleep within seconds.

It seemed like no time at all had passed when Diana's alarm went off at 6:00 a.m. She jumped up to silence it, afraid it would disturb Ana. Carefully moving around the apartment, Diana was able to get ready and leave the flat without making much noise.

When she arrived at the station, the train to Leeds was waiting with doors ajar on Platform 4. She quickly purchased a sandwich, boarded the train and saw an empty seat near the window. She collapsed into it and closed her eyes, trying to relax as the train sped toward Leeds.

Diana spotted her father's black Jaguar as soon as she walked out of the Leeds Central Train Station. He waved as she headed toward him. He warmly hugged his daughter, then opened the car boot and slid her black bag inside. Diana held onto her laptop and climbed into the car. The Jaguar slowly glided into the traffic.

Diana could not restrain herself anymore. "How is Grandmother doing, Dad? What did the doctor say?"

Andrew looked straight at her. "Well, you know she caught a bad cold about a month ago and she never fully recovered." He sighed, throwing his head up in a gesture of helplessness. "But you know how your grandmother is, she insisted on going around Christmas shopping. Last week she got a fever, and then she had to rest like never before. The doctor said a new strain of flu attacked her immune system after the cold, and he gave her some antibiotics and vitamins, the usual. There is not much to be done; he says we can't expect much better at her age, especially with her heart condition. The fever has gone down, but she is getting weaker and weaker by the day."

Diana swallowed a few times before she was able to speak. She looked at her father. "Maybe she should go to the hospital? They could give her respiratory support, just until she gets better?"

Her father shook his head. "She refuses to go." He gave Diana a sideways look. "I'm afraid she's given up, sweetheart. They're saying it's a one-way street at this point. She's very tired and has been in a somber mood." He paused, glancing at his daughter again. "She keeps saying her time has come to leave this world and she wants to say goodbye to each and every family member."

Andrew's voice quivered and she could see how much his mother's illness had affected him. He pulled to a stop at a traffic light and wearily passed a hand over his eyes. He reached for his daughter's hand and gently squeezed it. "Diana, the only thing we can do is try to make her happy and comfortable, and hope she will be inspired to get well again and continue to live, if only for our sake."

Diana nodded in agreement and wiped the tears from her eyes. As Andrew turned the Jaguar onto the A61 motorway, he and Diana caught up on other things—her classes at the LSE, her part-time job at the Financial Services Authority, and the goings-on in the Warwick home. Finally, he exited the motorway at AL Woodley Lane and headed toward Sand Moor Golf Club, next to the Eccup Reservoir. The Warwicks' home was in between the two.

* * * *

As they pulled into the driveway in front of the large Victorian Mansion, Vanessa Warwick, a woman in her fifties, with short brown hair, dressed in a white suit and blue-patterned blouse rushed out to greet her daughter. She had been eagerly waiting for her arrival. Her eyes were swollen red with dark circles beneath them. She was deeply attached to her mother-in-law and had been taking care of her for several years.

She grabbed Diana in a tight embrace. "Come, darling," she whispered, "get inside. Grandmother is waiting for you. I just talked with the doctor and I'm afraid there might not be much time." She took her daughter's hand and together they walked into the old house and up the stairs into the master bedroom. The room was filled with flowers, and a small group of relatives. Diana's aunts, uncles and cousins, stood at the foot of the bed where Eleanor Warwick lay, propped up by pillows.

Vanessa watched as her daughter stared at her grandmother, obviously startled by the change in the once vibrant woman. She was very pale and her eyes were closed, but she was smiling serenely. When Andrew entered the room and quietly closed the door behind him, Vanessa realized the last member of the family had finally arrived. She glanced at the others but had no heart to smile at anyone. Everyone appeared to have the same bereaved and uncomfortable look, as if feeling impotent in the face of the inevitable.

Vanessa softly walked to the bed, and sat down. "Eleanor," she whispered, "Diana has come to see you." At first there was no response, and everyone held their breath for a moment. Vanessa tried again. "Eleanor? Diana is here, do you want to talk to her?"

* * * *

This time Eleanor opened her eyes, ever so slowly, and began moving her lips, whispering something indistinct. On the other side of the bed, Diana moved closer, leaned down, and gently hugged her grandmother. She seemed so frail, so much weaker than the last time she had seen her. An awful fear began to engulf her. Sweat oozed from her hands, but then Grandmother smiled gently and seemed to gain some strength from her presence. Eleanor lifted a bony hand and whispered a little louder, "Diana, my child, come closer and sit next to me."

Diana obediently moved, grasped her grandmother's hand, and softly replied, "Grandmother, please don't worry. You will be all right. We'll take care of you."

"I would love to stay," her grandmother rasped, "and be with you for many more years, just for the sake of your affection and the happiness of your company, but I feel my time has come and there is something I really need to do before I go. Listen carefully and please do what I say. Will you?"

Her throat constricted with emotion, Diana was only able to nod in agreement. The others in the room were out of earshot and so no one could overhear their conversation.

"This is a family secret I have been carrying since your grandfather George died. I wanted to tell you many times but kept waiting for some reason, but now is the time to bring it up, without any more delay. Many years ago, I tried to tell your mother and father, but they were not interested enough to hear or do anything about it."

Eleanor paused and closed her eyes again, and for a moment Diana thought she had fallen asleep. But then her grandmother opened her eyes once more. She whispered, "Diana, I am bequeathing to you the Rockforth property, and something else, something very important that is kept safe in the Royal Bank of Scotland at Dunbar, near the castle. Now, please open the top drawer of my night table. There is a wooden box. Take it out."

Diana's hands were numb as if frozen. *What is this about?* But with her grandmother's eye contact and encouraging smile, Diana reached over to open the drawer and pulled out the small wooden box.

"Open it, sweetheart," whispered her grandmother.

Diana gently opened the box. Inside was a key. It had the number seven engraved on it.

"It's a safe deposit box key, Diana. Promise me you will do what I say." Her chest movement slowed, she paused a moment as if to catch her breath, and seemed to strain her voice.

The Treasure of the Pandavas

"You know, my dear, your grandfather George lost his parents in the war." Diana nodded, leaning forward. "Well, after their deaths, George's grandfather, Edward, gave him this key and told him a story. It started with Edward's own grandfather, Arthur. Arthur became distraught after his wife's death and entrusted his young son, Jonathan, to his sister, Elizabeth, before embarking on a life of travel and exploration abroad. One day, Auntie Elizabeth received a package from Arthur, along with a letter saying he had stumbled upon something very valuable and needed someone in the family to help him." The old lady paused again, rubbing her eyes as if exhausted, and apparently oblivious to her granddaughter's wide-eyed expression.

"Elizabeth could not find anyone who was willing to go, and Arthur never returned. At first, Edward was too afraid to investigate. He thought that it must have been some cursed treasure, for in those days treasure hunting was a common occupation. Eventually, he decided to find the treasure himself, but unfortunately he died in Jerusalem before he could uncover anything. Even your grandfather, who wanted to go, was unable to fulfill his dream, because he could not leave his business and family, and he had no brothers or sisters to whom to entrust their care, even for a short time."

The old lady's shoulders sagged and she closed her eyes. "Now it's up to you. Promise me you will find Arthur's treasure and clear his name, my child. We owe it to him."

Diana nodded in agreement, knowing it made her grandmother happy. She wanted to ask what Arthur had been accused of, why someone had to clear his name, but she could not form the words or muster the courage. This time, the silence was even longer. Diana didn't know what to do. She could only wait, more worried than ever. Lost in her thoughts, she stared at the frail, old body of her grandmother, lying in the bed.

Eleanor suddenly opened her eyes and spoke forcefully. "There is something else you need to know, my child. Your grandfather, George, spent many summers at Rockforth, and he loved to carve wood. He personally made the desk in his room...." Her voice trailed off as she smiled wearily and closed her eyes again with a soft sigh. Still at a loss for words, Diana could only reach out for her grandmother's hand and hold it tight, in empathy.

* * * *

The next few days passed with no improvement in Eleanor's condition. In fact, Diana could no longer deny that her grandmother was getting weaker by the hour. A somber mood hung over the house like a dark cloud, especially when they all sat down for Christmas Eve dinner. No one talked much, and although the food was excellent, as always, nobody felt hungry.

Early the next morning, Diana went to wish her grandmother a Happy Christmas. As soon as she entered the master bedroom, she knew something was terribly wrong. Her grandmother had the same serene smile on her face, but her hand was hanging limply over the side of the bed; there was no movement of breath and her hand was cold. Diana rushed to the phone, and the ambulance arrived a short while later, but the men only confirmed what she and her family already knew—Grandmother Eleanor was gone.

Vanessa called the notary, after voicing that she doubted he would be ready to leave his own family for a call of duty on Christmas morning, but he graciously came. He brought with him all the necessary documents to record Eleanor's death, including her last will and testament, and gathered the family to read out her last wishes and to collect their signatures. Many openly wept after hearing about the affectionate gifts the old lady had left to each and every one of them.

Diana watched her father pull himself together and help his wife as she went about the sad business of death. The funeral home was called and the burial ceremony arranged for Monday morning. Eleanor's body was placed in a casket in the large downstairs hall, and for three days, wreaths and bouquets of flowers came in from across Britain. Some were personally delivered by individuals from all walks of life who came to offer their respects and condolences. The family was not surprised by the outpouring of affection. During her long life, Eleanor Warwick had used her considerable wealth to discreetly help those in need, and she had many friends and admirers.

When she returned home after the funeral service, Diana went straight to get the small wooden box and the key from Grandmother's night table, wondering for the hundredth time why her grandmother had chosen *her* to solve this mystery, which no one else had been able to figure out.

Lying back on the sitting room couch, Diana pondered the situation late into the night. Soon, reasons for her grandmother's choice became obvious. First, she was goal-oriented. Second, she was very persistent when given tasks to accomplish. And finally, she had had a very close relationship with Eleanor. Now the mystery started to hound her; she had to find out the truth, and there was no other way but to dive straight into it.

It was early morning when she went online on her cell phone and made a plan. It was only a few hours journey from Leeds to Edinburgh. She could be at the Royal Bank of Scotland, Dunbar branch, on Wednesday morning, find out what the box contained, and then spend a few days relaxing at Rockforth before heading back to London.

Next morning, her mind made up, she walked briskly into the conservatory where her parents were sitting, warming up in the morning winter sun.

"Dad, Mom, I would love to stay with you for a few more days, but I think it's better if I go now." She checked the time on her watch.

"Where to?" asked her father with questioning eyes.

"I don't have that much time off from work, and I need to do something in Dunbar for Grandma, before going back to London." Diana tugged her ear.

Her parents looked at each other. "We surmised as much. Grandmother Eleanor often mentioned that she had a 'big secret', and you two were close." Her father squeezed her hand. "Take the Land Rover. I'll call the Godfreys and tell them you're coming."

"Thank you, Dad. I knew I could count on your support." Diana hugged her parents and hurried to her room to get her things.

* * * *

Diana arrived at Rockforth that evening. Seeing the grand castle rising in the distance over the hill just in front of the North Sea, she felt a rush in her body as she remembered time spent with her family in the castle, and especially with grandmother Eleanor. She drove up to the main gate and pressed the intercom button.

"Miss Diana?" inquired a voice.

Diana smiled at the familiar sound. The Godfreys had taken care of Rockforth ever since she could remember, but they had always been more like family. "Yes, Mr. Godfrey, it's me." She rubbed her hands on the steering wheel.

The automatic gate opened slowly and quietly. She drove up the hill to the main entrance, where she found the ever-smiling and ever-willing Godfreys waiting for her. They hurried over, hugged, and then helped her with her bag. For the second time that week, Diana felt like she had come home.

On Wednesday morning, she woke up early, dove out of bed and swung her arms, spinning loosely around her bedroom, with a happy-go-lucky feeling in her heart. Maybe it was due to the excellent dinner they had had the previous night. Maybe it was the rare, bright sunlight shining through the high windows of the castle. Or perhaps it was just the comfortable mattress and linen sheets on the antique four-poster bed. She felt something was about to begin, something important. She slipped into the dressing gown Mrs. Godfrey had hung over the chair, and as she was filling the tub with warm water and a handful of perfumed bath salts, a wonderful idea began to take shape in her mind.

By the time she headed downstairs to the kitchen, the idea was crystal clear. She could even smell the delicious breakfast's aroma permeating throughout the castle. "Mrs. Godfrey, thank you for being so kind to me. The dinner was excellent, and I slept like a baby. What do we have for breakfast? I cannot wait to eat; my stomach is rumbling with hunger." Diana licked her lips in a childlike manner, at the Godfreys' amused smile.

"Oh Miss Diana, we are so happy we could take care of you. We were so sorry about Mrs. Eleanor and we know how difficult it must be for you and your parents." Mrs. Godfrey's voice stammered; she was embarrassed and obviously struggling with her own anguish.

Diana's eyes filled with tears. She walked over to Mrs. Godfrey and hugged her tightly. "Yes, Mrs. Godfrey, we all miss her. But I am sure she's in a good place now, and she had a long and happy life."

The older woman covered her eyes with one hand. "Yes, yes, of course."

Diana, wanting to change the sad subject, guessed it was an opportune time to mention her idea to the couple.

"Mr. and Mrs. Godfrey, please listen carefully. Grandmother has left me the castle as my inheritance. I am thinking about bringing some more life to it."

"That is wonderful news, Miss Diana," replied Mrs. Godfrey, smiling.

"How about creating a luxury bed and breakfast?"

There was silence all around, as the Godfreys stared at each other, obviously taken off guard.

Diana quickly broke the silence. "After all, we have twenty bedrooms here, and they are in perfect condition. People would pay very handsomely to stay in this beautiful place, and they could enjoy the view, the beach, the woods and everything."

Mr. Godfrey began gently stroking his grey beard in contemplation.

"It could bring in a good income and your salaries would be much higher. We can also get a few helpers for you, to do the cleaning, get provisions and run errands. You and Mr. Godfrey could just take care of the management."

The older woman's eyes widened in surprise. "Why, Miss Diana, that sounds like a fantastic idea!" Her husband nodded in agreement.

"It's settled, then." Diana smiled, taking a sip of her coffee.

After breakfast, she figured she would go to the bank. She should be able to be done with her grandmother's business and head back to Leeds by Saturday morning.

* * * *

The Rover rolled down the road to Dunbar and turned onto High Street, where according to the mobile phone app, she would find the Royal Bank of Scotland's local branch office. She pulled to a stop in front of the four storey building and skillfully parked the car.

Diana elegantly walked through the revolving doors and into a large hall; there were counters where a few employees were attending to the customers. She easily found the manager's desk and was warmly greeted by a dignified and tastefully-dressed middle-aged man.

"Good morning, Madam," he said, gesturing to one of the chairs in front of him, "What can I do for you?"

Diana took the seat, carefully opened her purse and removed the key, which she put on the desk, together with her ID card and the notarized documents. The manager took the card and stared at it, then at Diana.

Her head held high, she said, "My name is Diana Warwick, and I have received from my grandmother, Mrs. Eleanor Warwick, the key to Safe Deposit Box No. 7 in your vault. She recently passed away and left me the contents. I would like to examine them, please."

At the mention of her grandmother's name, he stood and respectfully offered his hand, and his condolences, to Diana. The name of the Warwick family, owners of Rockforth Castle was sufficient to make an impression in this town. "I am honored to meet you, Miss Warwick. Yes, I am aware of Mrs. Warwick's passing, and I have been informed by the notary about the provisions of her will."

"This should be easy then," she said with a wide grin.

"Of course you can access your box. Please come this way. We'll take care of the paperwork afterward."

Thirty minutes later, she walked out of the bank, with a medium-sized bag in her hand.

As she drove back to Rockforth, Diana felt a slight flush, as her breath and pulse quickened, and a strange sensation enveloped her; the happy-go-lucky feeling recurring, suggesting something was about to happen very soon. She arrived at the castle safely, reassuring Mr. Godfrey she didn't need any help with the bag. She had some work to do in her room; she would take lunch there, and perhaps a nap. If Mr. Godfrey was surprised by her polite request, he did a very good job of hiding it, and Diana carried the bag upstairs. After a few minutes, Mrs. Godfrey quietly brought the lunch tray into the room. Upon seeing Diana busy, and with a tight-lipped smile on her face, she put the tray on the small table by the window, and went back downstairs.

* * * *

The Safe Deposit Box's contents were a wooden box—which contained some old letters—and another, smaller and more ornate box. Diana began to read the letters with great curiosity. The first, dated 21 September 1907, was signed by Edward and addressed to George, Diana's grandfather and Eleanor's husband.

My dear George,
I had hoped that your father Richard would be the one to solve the mystery of Grandfather Arthur's disappearance and clear his good name, but unfortunately, this no longer seems possible. My dear boy, I fully share your anguish. Losing one's parents at such a young age is a tragedy comparable to losing one's only son, as I have. Since your parents both perished in the bombing by the Nazis of our family home in London, I have become your legal guardian. I hope I have done a good job, although at times I feared I wouldn't be able to take care of you properly. But I have done my best, and we both have to be content with that. I leave the rest in God's hands.

For many years, I believed that it was my duty to protect my family and that the best way I could do so was by finding Grandfather Arthur's treasure and clearing his name. However, I have come to doubt this, as I now doubt so many things. Maybe what scares us is the only thing that can save us. It's difficult to say. But I have come to believe that there are good forces and bad forces around us, and we can take shelter in

23

either. What is good and what is bad, each man has to find out for himself. I know it's not much help, but at least it's an honest proposition, much better than trying to push others, in fully good faith, in a direction that might be disastrous for them.

When I die—and this may happen at any time now—all my properties will become yours, and so will my family obligations, moral and material. This includes the mission of clearing Grandfather Arthur's good name and finding the treasure. Some said he simply abandoned his family because he was an irresponsible man, but I do not believe that. Some said he was implicated in impious, illegal and dangerous dealings, and he deservedly died a violent and undignified death, and I don't believe that either.

As you will see from the letters I have enclosed, my grandfather was a very good person who embarked on a spiritual quest, searching for answers in faraway countries and cultures, and that during his wanderings he met with some accident or sudden sickness that prevented him from returning home with the treasure he might have found. The only possession he sent was the parcel that Auntie Elizabeth received in 1860.

It is also possible that someone else was interested in the treasure, people who had sworn allegiance to dark forces, and that

Grandfather was murdered. I suspect some of them may also have found our home, because we've had a few break-ins. I know there were no ordinary thieves, as no money or jewels were stolen. However, these suspicious events gave the servants and common folk the opportunity to think and speak ill of our family, and this has caused me great pain.

I beg you to heed my warnings when you are ready to investigate Arthur's disappearance, and please be very careful.

With all my affection and blessings,
Grandfather Edward

Diana re-read the letter a few times with great interest. She extended her hand into the box for another one.

The second letter, dated 21 June, 1865, had been sent by a Dr. Yuri Sakharov of Saint Petersburg and was addressed to: "The family of Arthur Warwick, Rockforth Castle, Scotland." Diana was surprised to know that a letter from Russia could even reach Scotland over a century ago.

Please accept my greetings. My name is Yuri Sakharov and I am a friend of your relative Arthur Warwick. He was my guest in Saint Petersburg when he visited Russia in 1855, after which we corresponded for some time. He also sent me some rare artifacts.

He asked me to write to you in the event he was unable to return to Russia in 1865, as he had planned. Since he has not arrived and I have had no further news concerning him, I believe he might have met with an accident or some other misfortune. Even as I write this, I pray it is not so, for Arthur is indeed a great man, a pillar of strength, and a courageous and virtuous friend.

Arthur wrote to me that he was living at the intersection of three holy rivers, and he wanted some of his relatives to go and find him, so that his descendants could find peace of mind and happiness of heart. He also said he had found clues to an incredible treasure, and was anxious to share it with his family. I do not know what sort of treasure he was talking about, as he did not explain further. It is possible such treasure may have brought the undue attention of envious people and the evil intention of dark forces upon him, so I recommend caution.

I would be happy and honoured to help any member of Arthur's family who come to visit me in Russia.

Yours faithfully,
Dr. Yuri Sakharov

Diana pulled out a third letter, addressed to Elizabeth Warwick. She carefully unfolded the old, yellowed pages, her eyes widening with wonder when she saw who had signed it.

21 March, 1865
Dear Bessie,
I hope you and Jonathan are well and happy. I am ever so grateful to you for your generous decision to take care of him. I will never forget it. I love him very much, but it would have been impossible for me to remain there in such a state of mental distress, without the opportunity to find the answers to my questions on life and destiny.
I would have been a terrible father, tormented and useless. My fits of depression would have brought me to drinking and destroying mine and Jonathan's lives, so my choice has been for the better, for all of us. I keep repeating this to myself every day, and I want Jonathan to know.
I cannot think of what might have happened to Jonathan and I after Joan and our baby died. Many times in those days I wanted to kill myself, but in my moments of lucidity I realized it would be a terrible stain on our family, a shame and a curse, and I could not let that happen to Jonathan and you, and our dear father and mother. Please believe I love you all, and the only reason I still have for living, is you. I hope I will be able to see you again someday, but for that day to come, I must find the answers, for they are the only chance for our salvation.

I have found something extremely valuable in my travels, and it is my greatest desire to share it with you. I know Jonathan is too young to travel and I don't want to put him in any danger, but if anyone in our family is willing to come, I would welcome their help in my quest. I am sending you something very valuable together with this letter. These are sacred things that belong to a saintly man. The talisman will protect you and anyone who may come searching for me. Also, remember the four sacred symbols engraved on the golden plate contained in this parcel are important keys to attain success on the quest. They all belong to the same traditional culture.

Please give my affection to our parents, and tell them I beseech their forgiveness for leaving them, but my quest is for the benefit of all.

Always keeping you all in my heart,
Arthur

Her hands trembled with excitement as she slowly refolded the letter and slipped it back into its envelope. The treasure was real! This letter proved its existence, and the fact Arthur had wanted his family to share it with him was amply clear. Was it too late to find? Probably. But it was worth trying, and she owed it to Grandmother Eleanor.

First, she needed to open the ornate box. But where could the key be? Had Arthur sent it with the box? She shook her head. That wouldn't make much sense. Why send a locked box together with its key? She shook the object gently. She could hear the soft rustle of the talisman within.

Wait a minute! Her mind froze for a moment in excitement, Arthur had not mentioned any box in his letter, and neither had Edward. Edward had only spoken of a parcel. She felt a sense of optimism. The key must have been hidden at Rockforth—that was the reason Grandmother had gifted the property to her! And, she deduced, if the ornate box was still in the bank, this meant Edward was not carrying the talisman when he traveled to Jerusalem. She was not superstitious—rather she often took a rational, even skeptical viewpoint on such things, but she could not help thinking Edward's accident might have been avoided, had he decided to carry the talisman with him as advised by Arthur.

Is there a great power in faith? Or maybe Edward didn't want that kind of protection after all. Where had Arthur procured it? If it was some ancient relic, found abroad under mysterious circumstances, Edward might have been afraid it was a pagan artifact with some ungodly power. After all, Edward's sister Rose had become a Catholic nun, and the Church— especially in those times—frowned upon that sort of thing. The sacred talisman would have to wait. Diana smiled in anticipation.

The last day of the year dawned bright and sunny, a very unusual occurrence, and Diana was grateful for the wonderful weather that seemed to be making her thoughts lighter and somehow, clearer. She also felt Grandmother's presence, comforting and encouraging, wrapped around her like a warm blanket. The Godfreys did not know anything about any special key; they had all the house keys neatly arranged on hooks, lined up on a wooden plank on the kitchen wall, but they were all ordinary keys— the bedroom doors, the main entrance, the storage rooms on top of the towers, the pantry, the garage, and the caretakers' own little cottage. There were also some smaller keys for cabinets and desk drawers, and she had used them all in her search. But Diana was not ready to give up; she was confident she would succeed.

The Godfreys prepared a special dinner for New Year's Eve, after which they left the castle to bring in the New Year with their friends, the Barclays. Initially they dragged their feet, hesitating to leave her alone on the holiday in the big castle. Diana, however, was convinced she would be fine spending a quiet evening by herself. She had been looking forward to it for a very long time and now was the opportunity.

As soon as the Godfreys' old car disappeared around the curve of the road, Diana locked the large main door and went to the dining room. Mrs. Godfrey had left a bottle of Dom Perignon chilling in the ice bucket. Well, it looked like she would have some celebration after all. She popped the cork, laughing to herself as it went flying across the room, and then poured herself a glass. After dinner, she browsed the collection of DVDs, finally settling on the trilogy of *The Da Vinci Code*, *Angels and Demons* and *Inferno*. She was ready for binge-watching on the big TV screen, next to the fireplace; being cozy in front of a crackling fire was hard to beat. At midnight, after the coming of the New Year, she made a few celebratory calls, and then slept satisfied.

On the first day of the year, Diana, who had never been alone in the castle before, savored the feeling—a strange kind of freedom, mixed with a sense of responsibility. She lazily got up and wrapped herself in her dressing gown. Passing through the great hall, she saw the fire was reduced to embers. She stirred them, adding a few small pieces of kindling, watched the flames flare up, and then walked into the dining room for something to eat.

Diana made some tea, taking time to choose her favorite mix, and helped herself to some of the excellent biscuits Mrs. Godfrey always had in the house.

She felt mischievous. Like a little girl, she filled the pockets of her dressing gown with cookies. She was planning a major castle exploration for the day ahead, and knew in order to find what she was looking for, she had to see the castle with new eyes; from a new perspective. She moved from room to room thoroughly inspecting each one.

After some time, as she wandered, something inspired her from within.

Could it be...? Suddenly, Grandmother Eleanor's last words flashed through her mind. Grandfather George's hobby was carving. It hadn't made much sense to Diana at the time, and she had thought her grandmother was remembering happier times before she died. But maybe there was more to it than that... What had she said exactly? "There is something else you need to know, my child. Your Grandfather George spent many summers at Rockforth, and he loved to carve wood. He personally made the desk in his room."

That was it!

All this while, Diana had been struggling to connect the dots, but now everything seemed to fall into place by sheer luck, or was it providence? She questioned herself. If Grandfather could carve wood, he could certainly make an ornate box. If he made the desk in his room, then the key must be there, in a place no one else had thought of. Then, he had entrusted the box and letters to the bank where he knew they would be safe. Realizing how smart he was, she placed her hands behind her head proudly.

Smiling, Diana hurried down the hall, her palms clammy. The moment she entered Grandfather George's room, she knew it was the right place. She sat at the desk Grandmother had mentioned, observing the fine craftsmanship. Grandfather George had certainly been a talented carpenter. She lovingly passed her hand over the inlaid woodwork, trying to envision an ancestor she had never known.

She opened each of the heavy drawers, sighing quietly when one after another they turned up empty. Then her eye was drawn to a device at the corner of the desk. It held a small, ancient, silver and glass ink bottle. The ink bottle had four sides and a square bottom, with four silver clips hinged to the desk—a brilliant system to avoid spilling the ink when moving papers and other small things about.

Diana flicked the clips open to remove the ink bottle and have a better look at it. She lifted the bottle and heard a distinct *click!* Startled, she watched as a very thin, hidden drawer sprang out from below the desk. A small silver key glimmered at her from inside. Diana stared blankly at it for a few moments, not quite able to believe her luck, but then quickly jumped up, grabbed the key and headed back to her bedroom.

A few minutes later, the secret of the ornate box was finally revealed. It contained two delicate necklaces of some kind of wooden beads, which were bound in silver filigree. One seemed to be made of carved wood; the other looked like the dried seeds of some exotic fruit. They resembled Catholic rosaries, but had too many beads and were all in a row without separations; besides, there was no crucifix attached to either of them.

Diana crinkled her nose as she carefully lifted them from the box. How old they must be! Yet they still were in fine condition. Instinctively, she decided to wear them. She couldn't say why she felt so strongly about it; she just knew, that's all.

The box also contained a small but thick silver medallion. It had irregular indentations on its back, but there were no engravings or symbols of any sort. Certainly this could not be the plate the letter was talking about. Diana bit her lip in concentration. The golden plate must have been lost sometime between Edward and George's times. Yes! Edward must have carried the golden plate with him to Jerusalem, trying to decipher the mystery, and that's when it was lost. How unfortunate! She didn't know what to do with the silver medallion. There seemed to be no use for it, except to keep it as a memory of her great-grandfather.

* * * *

The journey back to Leeds was uneventful. Andrew and Vanessa listened intently to Diana's account of what she had found at Rockforth, admired the beautiful design of the silver filigree necklaces, and read the letters carefully. Diana watched them eagerly, hoping for some suggestion as to where she should go from there.

Finally, her father stood and spoke, his hands clasped behind his back. "You have certainly done a great job, Diana, and you know your mother and I support you in whatever you do. But you have your studies and job to think about. Are you sure you want to devote so much time to something that just may turn out to be a piece of family folklore?"

Diana smiled, undeterred. She was not surprised by such words from her pragmatic father. Moving her hands in denial, she said, "I am sure, Dad. And I think we can agree from what I've found that there is more to this than just 'folklore'." She paused, smiling again. "In fact, I have a new business venture to attend to as well."

Diana excitedly hugged her parents, and began to tell them of her plans. They spent the better part of the afternoon discussing ideas for transforming the castle into a luxury bed and breakfast.

Chapter 2 - The Search Begins

Phew! Diana sat back in her chair and closed her aching eyes for a moment. The past few days at the FSA had been grueling—endless hours spent examining countless financial reports and stock market movements. Over the holiday, the World Bank had announced there were several suspicious operations requiring immediate investigations. The Financial Services Authority had managed to detect and stop a number of the operations the Bank had been concerned about, largely due to her diligence. Still, the family mission was never far from her thoughts.

Her flat-mate, Ana, had grown rather bored with Diana's "workaholic fanaticism", as she called it, and announced she was taking a week off to look for "adventures" on the other side of the Channel. "I'll try to come up to your standards. I'll just go and look for some work, and I will do it by going around and having fun!" Ana smiled, zipped-up her suitcase and slipped into her fashionable boots.

Diana threw back her head and laughed. "Don't worry, Ana, I'll have plenty of opportunities for adventures very soon. You know I'm leaving for Israel in a week."

Ana opened her mouth in shock. "Wow, the Holy Land?"

"Yep! I really must finish this office work before I go. Maybe we can take a trip together when I get back?"

"Oh, sweetie!" Delight showed in Ana's wide eyes. "That would be wonderful! We'll see so many beautiful places together and do a lot of shopping." Ana kissed Diana's cheek, said good bye, and left abruptly, saying she was late for an appointment.

Diana's thoughts returned to the funds she would need for her travel, and the remodeling of the Rockforth Castle. Although she was reasonably well-off and had some extra savings in the bank, she knew she would need more than that for what she was planning. She had considered taking out a bank loan, but that was a last resort, as she did not want to get into a debt trap at such a delicate time.

The solution came unexpectedly with the arrival of the mail. On Friday afternoon, she received a registered letter from the Warwicks' lawyer.

The letter was dated the 8th of January. It read:

I am delighted to inform you that the official property transfer has taken place and you have been identified and recognized as the sole owner of the Rockforth Castle, as requested by your Grandmother, Eleanor Warwick.
According to the request of Mrs. Warwick, I have also completed the clearance of the

Inheritance tax from the money your
Grandmother had assigned for it in her Will.
The remaining amount, after deducting my fees,
is 181,210 pounds. With this, the account is
settled, but if you have any further queries,
please feel free to contact me.
  Attached please find:
  1. The transfer document and record of the
change of ownership at the Land Registry Office
  2. Cheque for 181,210 pounds
  3. Details of the expenses
  4. Property value declaration
  Yours truly,
  Dawn Clark
  Solicitor
  Elite Law Firm

Diana instinctively put her hand on her mouth, amazed at the unexpected turn of events. She had not paid much attention during the reading of Grandmother's will, as she had been so distraught by her sudden loss, and then intrigued by the secret mission she had been given. Now, she felt a renewed pang of separation from her dear grandmother, and a deep gratitude for her kindness and foresight. The market value of Rockforth Castle had been estimated at 5 million pounds—which came tax-free, thanks to Grandmother's provisions. The remaining 181,210 pounds of the fund left to her would be more than sufficient to take care of the

Godfreys' salaries and the first expenditures of the renovation process. It would also see her through her travels until the castle was ready to be opened to the public. That evening she called Leeds to update her parents. Repeatedly pacing the length and breadth of her room, she spoke impatiently. "I'm planning to leave for Israel very soon," she paused, uncertain as to how to shape the question. "Dad, I would like to ask you something. I know that Great-Grandfather Edward died in Jerusalem, but I think I will need more information. Do you know anything about the circumstances of his death?" She held her breath in anticipation, hoping for an affirmative answer.

Now it was Andrew's turn to pause, and when he spoke, she could hear the clear anguish in his voice. "It was an accident. Edward's wife, Anne, received a message from Sir Nicholas O'Conor, the British Ambassador to the Ottoman Empire, saying Edward had been exploring some tomb when it collapsed. They were unable to recover his body, as the burial complex seemed to have been built within a system of underground caves. A local constable, named Yussuf El Kaukji, who had become Edward's assistant, was with him at the time of the accident, but was lucky enough to escape. He was standing near the entrance by a pillar that was part of the main support structure, while Edward was right in the middle of the room and deep inside. He was crushed when the floor caved in. El Kaukji sent a report about the events to the British Ambassador, who in turn wrote to Edward's family."

Upon hearing this, Diana bit her lower lip and remained silent. It took her some time to regain her composure. She rubbed her hands together in anticipation. "Did the letter contain any other information? Anything Edward might have left in his hotel room—diaries, documents, anything?"

Her father answered, "No, Diana, nothing came back. Edward's personal effects must have included some documents, or perhaps a diary with the address of his family here in Britain, otherwise the Ambassador would have been unable to contact Anne. However, I believe El Kaukji must have only sent some of the information and not the original documents to the Ambassador. Probably he wanted to continue searching for the treasure, alone."

Diana gasped when she heard her father's words. He knew all about the family search.

Andrew chuckled. "Yes, darling, I know about the treasure. I told you I knew your grandmother had a secret; she mentioned it when I was a young man. I suppose she was hoping I would try to find it, but I was never interested. But now that you are, my dear, I will do whatever I can to help you."

"Thanks Dad! That would be great."

"I will send the scanned copy of the Ambassador's letter to you; it will be handy. In the meantime, darling, try to enjoy your trip and please, be very careful."

Diana promised to call home whenever she could, told her parents she loved them, and slowly hung up the phone. For the first time, it was beginning to seem real to her, not only the trip to Israel, but the quest for the treasure.

On Monday morning she took a taxi to Heathrow airport. The security regulations were especially strict, more-so than she had ever experienced. When she finally settled into her seat on the plane, she was exhausted. Soon, she fell asleep, totally oblivious to the captain's periodic announcements. Once they landed, and after another intense check at immigration and customs, her passport was stamped and she walked into the bright sun of Tel Aviv. She had arrived in Israel, the Holy Land.

But her travels were not over yet. Diana was not interested in staying in Tel Aviv, and feeling refreshed from her in-flight nap, she was ready for the one hour bus trip to Jerusalem.

The bus dropped her at the King Hotel on David Street, next to the tomb of King David. At the reception desk, there was a pretty young woman of Diana's age. She checked Diana's Internet reservation papers, passport and credit card, while assigning her a room. She then called the bellhop to help her with the luggage. Smiling, she added, "Will you need anything this evening, miss? Room service, perhaps? Or would you like to dine at one of our restaurants?"

Returning the smile, Diana replied, "Some fruit and chilled beer, maybe, thank you very much. Then if you have a room service menu in the room, I'll go through it."

The desk clerk looked over the top of her glasses. "Yes, miss; have a pleasant stay."

It was a nice room, with a small TV and air conditioner. After a long, hot shower and a chilled beer, she made a brief call to her parents; she wanted to reassure her mother, who had been rather worried.

Diana woke up early and well-rested. Feeling in a good mood, she started quietly singing to herself one of her favorite tunes. She was ready to start the treasure hunt.

Within the hour, she had showered, dressed, and was out wandering through the meandering streets and back alleys of Jerusalem. It was like going back in time. The air itself seemed ancient and timeless; the streets seemed to be the center of life, with people buying and selling, eating and socializing, and many children playing around undisturbed.

Armed with directions from the hotel receptionist, and a map of the city, Diana reached the center of the town and found the General Register Office, where all the records of local births and deaths were kept. She walked into the building and approached an employee at the reception. Diana fixed her eyes intently on the clerk. "Good morning, sir. My name is Diana Warwick. I am a British citizen."

The employee gazed at her in silence, obviously wanting her to say more.

She continued. "I have come to find out about my Great-Grandfather Edward, who died in Jerusalem in 1908. The only information my family received, at that time, was a letter from the British Ambassador." She paused for a moment before continuing. "Could you see if there is anything in the official records?" Diana held the Ambassador's letter out to the officer. He just nodded his head, and taking the letter disappeared into an inner office for many minutes to talk to his supervisor, only to re-appear with a cup of coffee.

He smiled confidently; laugh lines formed near the corner of his eyes as he spoke. "I am willing to help you, miss, but unfortunately, we don't have records from that time. The British Mandate only started in 1920."

Diana dropped her chin, her mind in deep thought, then she looked up quickly with a smile and asked, "And before that?"

"This place was under Ottoman occupation from 1516 to 1917. Probably they maintained some sort of records, but I have no idea what might have happened to them."

Diana cast her eyes down in disappointment. First dead end, it seemed. She sighed, and asked for directions to the Archeological Department. Edward had been engaged in archeological research together with his local friend, so it was possible she could find some record of his work. She was hoping Plan B would pan out.

At the Israeli Antiquity Authority, Diana heard the same story. "Sorry, miss, our archives only have files from the days of the British Mandate." The staff member seemed rather sour and stiff, and Diana wondered why. Second dead end, for sure.

Diana pursed her lips in frustration and pleaded, "Could you please give me some suggestion on how to proceed from here?"

The clerk looked down, and then rubbed his forehead with his hand before answering. "Why don't you check the Institute of Archaeology at the Hebrew University of Jerusalem. I think you might get some help there. Sorry we can't do more for you here."

Diana felt a surge of disappointment rush through her. She barely managed a faint smile. "Thank you very much, I will."

The Senior Research Associate at the Archaeological Institute, Yitzhak Rosen, was cordial and relaxed, and seemed to understand the reason for the attitude of the Israeli Antiquity Authority staff.

He leaned back in his chair and folded his arms across his chest. "You see, Miss Warwick, here in Jerusalem, archeology presents a serious bone of contention for political and historical reasons. The Israeli Government wants to demonstrate that Jews were here before the Palestinians, and the Palestinians claim the original ownership of the city. Both sides are afraid that a new archeological discovery will give some credibility to the opponents, so the tendency is to let the sleeping dogs lie, or even to eliminate whatever doesn't fit with one's thesis; hardly the ideal background for archeological research."

Diana shook her head. "I see. But the University is free and independent, isn't it?"

Professor Rosen smiled. "May I call you Diana?" At her smiling nod, he continued. "Yes, we are free and independent, to a certain degree. Of course, Israel is a nation at war, whether it is openly declared or not, so we all need to be cautious." He paused. "But in your case, I don't think that you are representing some British Spy Agency, or some other politically motivated organization. I seriously believe you are just what you say you are—a great-grand-daughter who wants to solve a family mystery."

Diana stood up and reached across the desk to shake his hand. "Thank you so much for understanding, Professor. Do you think you can help me?"

"I'm not sure; we also have relatively recent records only, because during the Ottoman period there was no control over archeological research. Most researchers were treasure hunters, so they were not very keen on having the local authorities informed of their activities." Yitzhak smiled. "Oh, I'm not saying I disapprove of any of them. Treasure hunting and modern archeology are not very different in scope and motivation. On the other hand, many of those adventurers did a lot of damage to valuable artifacts and historical evidence, because they were only interested in gold and jewels, and they wanted to loot quickly and get away even faster. So, they were not so subtle in their methods."

Diana sat back and wrapped her arms around her body. Had Edward been ruthless in his search, damaging some ancient site in the process? After all, he was certainly not an expert archeologist and perhaps may not have recognized the historical value of buildings or some of the artifacts.

Professor Rosen seemed to read her mind. "Don't worry, Diana. I am sure your ancestor was a very good person, and in any case, as you said, he paid a very heavy price for his quest."

Diana sighed. "When my great-grandfather came to Jerusalem, he was following some clues based on four symbols. I am trying to find out more about them. If I learn something here, my journey will not be a total loss."

The professor placed his hand over his heart and offered a slight bow. "The study of ancient symbols just happens to be my area of expertise," he said earnestly, "so hopefully I can be of some help with the four symbols you are curious about."

He reached over and poured them both some tea then leaned back in his chair and began to tell her about the symbols. As he spoke, Diana felt like she was back in school. So detailed was his knowledge, she started taking notes.

He leaned forward and rested his elbows on the desk and folded his hands. "Symbols have always been the language of emotions, of subconscious connection, of spirituality and esoterism. They are still used in religious iconography. A lot of Christian iconography was derived from pre-Christian Pagan religions and cultures, but they are an essential factor to facilitate a psychological sense of belonging to a group or organization."

Diana slowly nodded.

He continued. "Take company logos, for example, the trademarks of popular brands, or the national flags of countries, or even family surnames."

Diana was startled. She had never thought of a company logo or her family surname, Warwick, in the perspective of a subconscious sense of belonging or loyalty, but it made perfect sense.

Professor Rosen correctly read her expression and smiled. "Yes, people develop an emotional, almost religious sense of loyalty toward a symbol, even without becoming aware of the sentiment because it remains on a subliminal level, especially if they are exposed to those symbols in association with deeply emotional experiences." He paused, giving Diana some time to digest the information. "The more subconscious it becomes, the more effective it will be. Because, in the deep levels of the psyche, we're not threatened by the intellect's logical and decision-making functions. This is the very foundation of the advertisement business. We unconsciously tend to choose a famous brand, even if the quality of the product is not objectively good or cost-effective." He paused, leaned forward slightly and dropped his voice. "But there is also a darker side to symbols, since not all emotions are positive. Some symbols are deliberately or naturally charged with negative emotions and carry fear, hatred, despair, or loathing, or they perpetuate prejudice."

Diana looked him squarely in the eye. She felt her heart beat faster. "So the four sacred symbols I am looking for might have been separated, modified and used for different purposes?"

He nodded. "Yes, Diana, that's certainly possible. I suggest you keep your mind very open to various possibilities regarding interpretation, time and space. You said four symbols, correct?"

"Yes."

"Ancient European culture considered the four elements of nature—Earth, Water, Fire, and Air—to be sacred, and they depicted them with symbols."

Diana leaned forward in anticipation. Four *sacred* symbols! "Please tell me more. Better yet, can you show or draw them for me?"

The Professor took a paper and drew four triangles, two with the base up and two with the base down. Two of each group had a line drawn parallel to the base. Smiling, he said, "These are Aristotle's symbols for the four basic elements of the universe." Then he drew two triangles, one on top of the other, forming a six-pointed star. "And this is another very ancient symbol representing the fifth element of nature, *ether*; that also came to be identified as sacred to Judaism as the Star of David."

Diana remembered reading in Dan Brown's book, *The Da Vinci Code*, about the two triangles pointing in opposite directions. They were explained as the representations of the

Chalice and the Blade, the ancient sacred pagan symbols for female and male. She looked up at Doctor Rosen, slightly embarrassed that she had learned about this from a novel. Then again, it didn't seem so farfetched in view of what he was telling her now. Shrugging off her self-consciousness, she asked, "This is one set of four symbols. Are there any other sets of four symbols belonging to one single religious or cultural group?"

"Not that I know of. I believe the only other ancient symbols that you will find in Jerusalem are those that were later appropriated by Jews, Christians and Muslims—the Star of David, the Cross and the Crescent, respectively. Jerusalem is considered sacred for all the 'peoples of the Book' who describe themselves as 'sons of Abraham'."

She nodded her head and felt herself becoming impatient. "But these are only three. What about the fourth?"

"I don't think there is a fourth, unless you want to accept Paganism as a legitimate religion. There are only three Abrahamic religions in Jerusalem; there has been nothing else for at least 2,000 years. What existed there before is not so easy to find. However, I am confident that Aristotle's four symbols might surely help you."

Diana sighed. This was proving much more difficult than she thought it would be. She thanked him for his time and the tea. After she left his office she continued on to the library and browsed through the titles in the religious symbols section, jotting down the names of books, and drawing symbols she thought might be of help.

She found that the Christian crusaders had come to Jerusalem to reclaim Christ's sepulcher, and had also excavated part of the ancient ruins of the Temple. It was said that the Templar Knights, a religious order of warrior monks, had found a mysterious and invaluable treasure that had been moved across Europe. *Could this be the treasure Arthur was after?*

The next day, the hotel receptionist got her a day pass for a tourist bus ride, and Diana decided she needed some time to unwind in the Holy Land. The first stop was the Western Wall, the last remaining structure of the ancient Temple built by Solomon. Also known as the Wailing Wall, it's where Jews from all over the world come to mourn the loss of the Temple and their sacred city, and to pray. Diana was not religious, but she felt deeply impressed by the sheer antiquity and historical importance of the place. Then the group visited the ancient Kotel Tunnels, the Science Museum and the Time Elevator—a great multimedia ride narrating 3,000 years of the history of Jerusalem.

Lunch was scheduled in a local restaurant at a busy intersection in the Western suburbs of the city, but Diana decided to temporarily separate from the group. She chose some street snacks instead, so she was not in the restaurant when the loud explosion and resulting shockwave ripped through the usual noises of the daily life of the street. The force reverberated through her bones. She instinctively ducked behind a stall for several moments. There was a deafening silence, and then she became aware of a loud ringing in her own ears. Slowly, screams and the sirens of ambulances and police cars converging on the location began to filter in through the chaos. She stood up and looked at the disaster, just in time to see people rushing in to look for survivors and retrieve any bodies. Suddenly, Diana's knees began to tremble. She felt weak all over and a bit nauseous; cold sweat glued her shirt to her skin. Her mind went blank for a moment; she did not dare to imagine what would have happened to her if she hadn't followed her desire for a more informal meal.

The police quickly searched the area for any remains of the explosive or other clues, and after checking Diana's passport, and taking her statement, advised her to return to her hotel immediately.

"What happened?" she asked, in a strangely high-pitched voice she could barely recognize as her own. The meal she had just eaten seemed unwilling to remain in her stomach.

Running his hands through his hair in obvious distress, the officer responded, "Miss, it was a suicide bomber. They often target public places in the Jewish quarter, sometimes buses, and sometimes restaurants; anything they think would cause mass causalities. Did you see anything suspicious?"

Shrugging in despair, she replied, "No, I was on the tour bus and I decided I didn't want a big meal in the restaurant, so I walked to this stall for something small and fancy. I don't know what made me think of it, but I am very glad I did. Or I would have been inside." Suddenly she was aware that she was grasping the sacred talisman hanging from her neck.

The policeman looked intently at her face, probably realizing that she was in a state of shock. He spoke kindly. "Miss, let me get you a taxi." He switched his mobile on, speaking into it in rapid Hebrew. Then he beckoned the food stall boy to bring something for Diana to sit on while she waited for her ride. She tried not to look at the devastating site of the explosion and the medics carrying the victims away, but her eyes kept falling on that lone shoe, that pool of blood, and the rubble of glass, cement and wood which had once been the restaurant's entrance.

After a couple of minutes that seemed to last hours, the policeman returned to help her to the taxi stationed outside the cordoned-off area; he seemed to know the driver well, and they spoke again in Hebrew. Still feeling numb, Diana was just lucid enough to direct the driver to the King Hotel; then she leaned back in her seat, trembling and suddenly feeling excruciatingly hot. Her mind was thinking fast. She had enough of the Holy Land which was turning into a *horror land* and now she desperately wanted to go back home to the comfort and safety of Leeds.

When she felt a little calmer, she called home, telling her worried parents about the bombing incident and reassuring them she was all right. She promised she would leave Jerusalem the very next day, as planned.

The return flight to London was due to disembark in the afternoon. Diana packed her things, got herself a massage at the hotel's fitness center, and had a delicious brunch from room service. At the airport, on the TV screens, news was being flashed that the suicide bomber had been identified as a seventeen-year-old girl and resident of East Jerusalem. ISIS immediately claimed responsibility for the attack on the Zionist state, promising more such attacks in the future. Standing in the queue to board the aircraft, Diana sent a thought to Great-Grandfather Edward, who had probably felt the same dejection at not achieving his goal for which he had come—or rather, much worse—

disappointment about his journey to the Holy Land which was a complete disaster. Even though she had not uncovered the mystery of the treasure, she felt deeply thankful for the fact that she was at least returning home alive and well.

* * * *

Over the weekend, Ana called, saying she was returning to London on Monday afternoon. She listened in horror as Diana recounted what had happened in Jerusalem. But when Diana told her she was planning a trip to Russia the following Thursday, her mouth fell open in shock. Diana hadn't travelled outside of England in years; now she was planning two trips, back to back? What was she up to?

"That's not all," Diana said slowly, but with a smile in her voice, "I wanted to ask if you would join me." After what happened in Israel, she said she just felt more comfortable taking a friend along. Besides, she said it would surely be more fun going with Ana who was from Russia and spoke Russian fluently.

Ana let out a little scream of excitement. "Oh really? Of course! It will be wonderful!"

"Great! So I am making flight reservations to Moscow for Thursday for the both of us, and booking a hotel."

Ana felt a surge of excitement rush through her at the thought of visiting her native land, especially in the company of her dear friend.

She immediately started to make a list of all the important places to visit.

* * * *

Diana stayed in Leeds longer than expected, returning to London on Wednesday, just one day before the departure for Moscow. She was on the train going home, when her mobile started to buzz. She was startled to see that Ana had sent her a message. *Call me now, please, something has come up.* She immediately called her friend.

"Ana, are you okay? Is anything wrong? Where are you?"

"Yes, I'm fine, and I'm in London already, but I wanted to tell you my agent has called me for an important fashion show that's scheduled on Friday; someone just dropped out and they need a replacement. Is it possible to postpone the reservation for a couple of days?"

"Uh, okay. I think I can do that, don't worry. And congratulations on the show! I'm on the train to London now, so I'll see you tonight."

"Thank you, my dear friend!"

Diana immediately pulled out her laptop and inserted her wireless Internet connection. Unfortunately, there was only one seat left on Saturday's flight to Moscow. She decided she would leave tomorrow as scheduled and change Ana's reservation to the next available flight. She then called Ana to give her the new details.

* * * *

Aeroflot SU-242 from Heathrow to Moscow's Sheremetyevo airport took off on time at 13:30 hours. Once the aircraft had established the correct course, the passengers were served lunch. The landing at 20:25 was smooth, and the captain announced a local temperature of -5 C, definitely mild for a Russian winter.

Diana collected her luggage, and then climbed into a taxi for the thirty-minute ride to the Gostiniy Dom, the three-star hotel on Vasiliy Petushkov Street that she booked on the Internet. She briefly called her parents to inform them she had reached Moscow safely, and then ended the day with a nice warm shower.

After a good night's sleep and a breakfast of pancakes, with sour cream, near the fireplace of the hotel's restaurant, Diana asked for some directions at the reception desk. The employee obliged by writing an address and a brief explanation in Russian on a piece of paper with the Hotel's logo, address and phone number.

She told the woman what she needed, and together they wrote down a number of phonetically-spelled Russian sentences she would likely find useful for her outing, including the names of the Metro Stations on the map. She also circled the station near Red Square, where Diana was hoping to find some restaurants while sightseeing.

Diana repeated the basic sentences to the receptionist to make sure she had the pronunciation correct. *"Ya angleechanka, ya mala gavaryoo pa-rooskee, prashoo vas pamoch mnye,"* she said haltingly. The meaning was rather obvious. "I am English, I don't speak much Russian, and can you help me please?" The other sentences, written in Cyrillic, were meant to tell the kind stranger what Diana wanted, so that she could get the help she needed.

The receptionist also suggested she leave her passport, tickets and excess cash in the hotel's safe, and carry only photocopies of her documents, and a small amount of money that she was likely to need for the day. With a combination of excitement and trepidation, Diana tendered the exact amount for the Metro ticket then followed the receptionist's directions. She even managed the two necessary train changes to reach her destination without allowing herself to be too distracted by the beautiful architecture of the stations. Eventually, she emerged to the surface and was delighted to find Red Square without too much difficulty. Enjoying her success, Diana walked freely among the crowd, with the easy reference of the Kremlin to return to, and the clearly visible entrance to the Metro rail. After many hours of sightseeing, on Nikolskaya Street, she found a large, self-service restaurant, the "Drova", where people had their choice of fifty-five different courses for a fixed price. Diana had a lot of fun choosing tiny quantities of all the plates she found interesting. She found a good bean stew, stuffed aubergines, and pirozhkis filled with cabbage and cottage cheese. For dessert, she ordered slices of three different cakes, all rather buttery. Local beer and a very good coffee concluded the satisfying meal. For a long while after she had finished her coffee, she stayed in the warm restaurant, watching people come and go. When she finally got up to leave, it was already dark.

What happened next was probably to be expected—a mixture of overconfidence after finding her way unassisted through the maze of the Moscow Metro rail, the good food and beer that had probably gone to her head a little, and the confusion of the rush hour, when commuters crowded the Metro to return home after a day's work. Whatever the cause, Diana had either gone out the wrong exit or simply didn't recognize the street where she had emerged, and now found herself suddenly lost. The street was relatively silent and dark, with very little traffic and not many lights. She could not tell if this was Shodnenskaya Street, and there was nobody around to ask. Her map wasn't much use, as the name of the Metro station from which she had emerged was written in Cyrillic characters, and in the dim street light she wouldn't have been able to read even English very well. But she couldn't just stand there either; she needed to walk, and maybe she would find someone to ask for directions. Her phone was of no use. Its battery was dead. She had probably taken way too many pictures and videos.

She started walking at a fast pace, following the main street, but after several minutes she was only more certain she had lost her way. A creeping fear made the cold weather seem even colder. Diana wrapped her scarf tighter and looked around, at a loss for what to do.

As if to echo her feelings, a sudden scream came from a side street. Diana whipped her head in the direction of the scream, only to see a young woman in a black coat running out. Clearly terrified, the woman turned her head left and right, apparently looking for a place to hide. Diana wasn't sure what she could do, but she instinctively approached the girl, trying to help. But the young woman waved her away, saying, "*Nyet, nyet!*" and then she dove into the shaded entrance of a tall building.

Diana heard running footsteps approaching from the side street, but before she had a chance to turn around, she was suddenly grabbed from behind by very strong arms. A piece of cloth with a very pungent smell was forced over her nose and mouth, and she felt the strength draining out of her. Then everything became black and she collapsed on the pavement.

Chapter 3 - Finding the Clues

Diana slowly regained consciousness, gingerly moving each limb to make sure nothing was broken. She didn't know quite what had happened, just that she had been grabbed from behind, and her head was pounding.

She opened her eyes to find several other young women staring back at her. They were a study in despair, fear and horror; disheveled and bruised, some even tied up. A sudden jolt threw them against each other, and that's when Diana realized they were squashed in the back of a moving van. The windowless vehicle sped up, and Diana heard the faint sound of a distant siren coming closer. The other girls heard it too, and they seemed to find a new hope. Those who were not tied started to bang on the van's walls. They began screaming at the tops of their lungs, *"Pamoch! Pamoch!"* Diana didn't need a dictionary to understand they were crying for help.

She joined in, screaming "Help!" in English, as loudly as she could. Ignoring the searing pain in her head, she hit the walls of the van wherever she could reach with her fists and feet. A tall, red-haired girl shouted something in Russian above the cacophony, and all the women grabbed onto each other until they were one mass of bodies. They started to throw themselves from one side of the van to the other. They were trying to tip it over, as it sped through the streets of Moscow! Diana joined in and the vehicle started to sway more and more violently. The sirens were getting closer, spurring the women to move even more frantically. Then the driver must have lost control, and the van toppled to one side at full speed. All the girls were sent screaming and kicking into a heap on what used to be the left side of the now skidding vehicle, as the shriek of the metal against asphalt drowned out their voices and all other sound.

It finally screeched to a halt, and the girls who could still stand banged on the doors, screaming and crying, "*Politsya! Politsya!*"

The sirens were now very near, and then they suddenly stopped; car doors opened and closed, and finally a male voice shouted something in Russian. All the girls tried to move away from the van doors, and Diana understood that their rescuer was going to somehow open the lock.

She heard two distinct pops, and then the door opened. Suddenly, she felt the cold air of the night, saw car headlights and the blue-grey uniforms of the Russian police.

The young women were helped out of the van, most of them crying and some hugging the policemen like long-lost brothers, and muttering, "*Spaseeba, spaseeba.*"

After they were checked and treated for injuries by the paramedics who had arrived in the ambulance, a conveyance was called to take them to the police station, and, in contrast, this other van seemed almost friendly. The girls sat inside, hugging one another, helping each other to fix their hair and clothes, clean their faces and wipe their tears, and talking softly. Diana caught the word "Mafia" and the full extent of the danger she had just narrowly escaped, hit her in all its horror. She had been kidnapped by the human trafficking arm of the Russian Mafia, and without this miraculous rescue, she and the other girls would have ended up as sex slaves in some brothel, or in the 'private establishment' of some big boss.

At the police station, she found one officer who could speak English—albeit with a very strong accent and very limited vocabulary—and gave her statement. Luckily, she still had her papers in the inside pocket of her black parka, as the kidnappers had not wasted any time to rob her, so she could quickly prove her identity and present residence.

"Miss Diana, you very lucky. One girl called us from Metro Station and tell sex racket van go northwest city near airport, so we come to save." He smiled kindly and handed her a warm cup of Russian tea. "Now you back hotel with taxi, yes?" Diana sent a silent word of thanks to the unknown girl who had bravely passed the message to the police.

Diana nodded and thanked the officer again and again, smiling at all the people around her. She had had another very close call, and this time, too, she had come out safe and sound, without losing documents, money, or other important possessions. She absentmindedly fingered the two ancient necklaces she was still wearing. She had always been a skeptic in matters of religion and faith. Almost agnostic or atheistic, she despised superstition as a serious social evil and considered human relationships as the most important thing in life. Now, she was starting to think that the love and affection of her family—even distant members like Arthur—could not only support and give her more self-confidence and joy, but could also protect and guide her steps. And perhaps that love and affection could even become concentrated into objects, giving them a sort of sacredness and special power. *This could be the actual meaning of a talisman*, she thought. Maybe it had nothing to do with magic formulas or strange rituals; maybe it was all just about love.

Still terrified and shaken up by her experience, Diana decided to stay in the hotel until Ana arrived. She took a long, warm soak in a bath with perfumed bath salts before going to bed. The next day, she remained inside, ordering room service and surfing the web to cheer herself up and take her mind off the night before. She looked up symbols and interesting things about St. Petersburg, managing to resist the temptation to search human sex-trafficking and the Russian Mafia. The television was kept to a music channel, on low volume.

Ana reached the hotel at 7:30 p.m. and they had dinner together in the hotel restaurant.

Back in their room, her friend sat aghast listening to Diana's ordeal of the previous evening, appearing more horrified by the minute. Finally, Ana moaned. "But sweetie, not even Moscow's citizens wander around half-deserted streets at night. You don't know what the Russian Mafia is capable of! Every year, thousands of girls are forced into prostitution— it's a multi-billion-dollar industry. It starts with the false promise of some good job, and then they cannot escape. If they try, they recapture them and then it's even worse.

Diana, a little dazed, replied. "I guess I know better now. I don't think the gangsters were planning to kidnap me, but they mistook me for the girl they were pursuing. I'm not going to tell this to my parents; it wouldn't do them any good. Besides that, everything turned out okay in the end."

"I think they were scared enough with the terrorist attack in Jerusalem, they don't need heart failure." Ana smiled weakly, patting Diana's arm.

"Listen, Ana. I have to ask you something else. I need you to help me find some information. It's about a Russian friend of one of my ancestors."

Ana emitted a shrill laugh. "Hey, I know I said I like adventures, but you're getting a bit too much for my taste. Do I have your promise you won't get us both into trouble?" Ana winked and shook her head. "At least, not too much trouble?"

"It's a deal." Diana raised her right hand and the two girls high-fived. Ana was the best companion she could find for her search in Russia. Besides, she knew she could trust her completely. "This man I am looking for was a professor in Saint Petersburg. His name was Yuri Sakharov. My Great-Grandfather, Arthur, visited him in 1855 and hopefully, left some personal possessions and maybe some ancient artifacts with him."

"Wow, that's a really long time ago!"

"I don't know much about History, or for that matter Archaeology, being a Finance student. My hunch is, since the professor was interested in ancient things, we might be able to find out something about him at the university here."

* * * *

On Monday morning, they got up early and arrived at the university, the Russian Academy of Sciences. In the library, they found a number of volumes containing Yuri Sakharov's writings in Russian; for some reason, his writing was not found in British Libraries. Ana wrote down a list of discoveries and theories, and then she looked up at Diana. "This book says that Professor Yuri Sakharov resided in Tsarskoye Selo and studied at the Imperial Lyceum. He also had a house in Saint Petersburg, where his family stayed."

The librarian was a great source of information and told them, "Tsarskoye Selo officially became the Tsar's village in 1724, and was the favorite summer residence of the Romanovs. After the Bolshevik Revolution, it was renamed Soldatskoye Selo—the soldiers' village—and then Detskoye Selo—the children's village. In 1937, it was renamed Pushkin to commemorate the centenary of the death of the Great Russian poet, Alexander Pushkin, who had studied in the Imperial Lyceum there." Diana and Ana exchanged wide smiles.

Diana wasted no time; she started checking the train schedule from Moscow to St. Petersburg. With Ana helping her translate the timetable, she found a train leaving that evening, and breathed a sigh of relief.

She was excited to see the beautiful city on the coast of the Baltic Sea. She had learned about St. Petersburg in school and dreamed of visiting it ever since. She had read it was established in 1703 by Tsar Peter the Great of the Romanov dynasty and was the cultural capital of Russia. During the Revolution, it had been renamed Leningrad by the Bolsheviks, and it was only after the fall of the Soviet regime that it reclaimed its original name.

The first class, two-berth sleeper was comforting. When the train moved away from the station, Diana filled in the gaps in the story she had begun telling Ana in the hotel; she told her about Arthur, Edward, and Grandmother Eleanor. She gave the details she knew, including what she had discovered in Jerusalem.

By the time she finished telling the story, Ana's eyes were twinkling in anticipation. "Ah, this is really cool!" She laughed. "And it's good to know that you're not just getting into trouble because you're bored, you are actually on a serious quest! And I'm proud of you."

Diana squeezed her friend's hand. "Thank you, Ana, for coming with me."

Ana smiled in return. "Its a pleasure, anything for a friend."

* * * *

They were awakened early the next morning by a train announcement saying they would be arriving in St. Petersburg in thirty minutes. They went to the bathroom in turns, making themselves presentable, and when the train pulled up to the platform, they were ready to depart. They rented a car, and Ana drove. Along the way, Diana watched in awe as Ana pointed out some sites of the magnificent city. Even if this quest didn't go anywhere, at least she had broadened her horizons. The town of Pushkin was only twenty-four kilometres from the centre of St. Petersburg. After about fifty minutes of busy morning traffic, they drove past an impressive and completely unexpected Egyptian Gate, covered with hieroglyphics. Diana smiled. This was certainly a place for archaeologists.

They continued on to the Imperial Palace—now State Museum—which had been the summer residence of Catherine the Great. The Museum was within the palace compound, surrounded by a 1400 acre park, complete with a lake, pavilions, fountains, innumerable statues, and even a grand cemetery for the Empress' dogs.

They finally arrived at the Yuri Sakharov Memorial which was an old, aristocratic house. It was the original house where the archeologist had once lived, and resembled the house of Shakespeare in Stratford-upon-Avon in the UK, but was, perhaps, not as famous. Everyone in Pushkin seemed to know this place and so it was easy to find. They were greeted by a middle-aged man, who introduced himself as Sergey Mikhailovich Sakharov, the curator of the Memorial House. Diana couldn't believe she was actually face to face with a descendent of

Professor Sakharov. She asked Ana to explain who she was, not at all sure the name Arthur Warwick would mean anything to him. But when Ana spoke, Sergey's eyes widened— although with recognition or merely interest, Diana didn't know. In any event, he immediately invited them both to the sitting room for tea, and then excused himself to make some phone calls. Soon, Diana and Ana were surrounded by the many members of the family, and a flurry of introductions began. There were Mikhail and his wife, and their two children, and Mikhail's brother, Nikolay and his sister, Olga, plus a few cousins. A little overwhelmed by the sudden crowd with all their names and relationships, Diana sat down on a sofa to clutch a steaming cup of tea, poured from a magnificent Samovar of ancient silver. Ana, smiling broadly, took care of the public relations.

When the situation had calmed down a little and everybody was seated, Diana asked Ana to translate for her. She then produced the letter Yuri Sakharov had sent to Arthur's family, together with the medallion and the other letters she had found in the box in the bank vault. The Sakharovs listened to Ana with rapt attention as they passed around the items. Unfortunately, the letters were all in English; but despite being unable to read them, they still seemed fascinated with this piece of their family history.

After a few minutes, Mikhail stood up, clearly wanting to say something important. When he had everyone's attention, he cleared his throat and began to speak in slow, halting English. Diana was moved by the gesture and listened with rapt attention as he related the story of Professor Yuri Alexovich Sakharov.

As Ana quietly translated for his family, Mikhail spoke of a prodigious intellectual, born in St. Petersburg in 1825, who had showed a great talent for learning since very early childhood.

In 1855, Yuri met Arthur Warwick, who was traveling around the world on a spiritual quest; the two men formed a close friendship, which they continued on through several letters exchanged after Warwick left Russia. Yuri had lived in his father's house in St. Petersburg, often visiting Tsarskoye Selo. After his father's death in 1871, he finally moved there with his brother's family so as to totally dedicate himself to study and research. Yuri died in 1895 at the age of seventy, without marrying or producing any children.

When he was finished speaking, Mikhail smiled sheepishly, as if hoping his English had been understood.

"So your family was able to save Yuri's possessions?" Diana asked breathlessly, well aware of the implications of an affirmative answer.

"Yes, certainly, most of them. Especially Yuri's books, which were published by the Academy of Sciences in Moscow. And his personal possessions, diaries and letters have been preserved in this Memorial Home. Half of the house was used as the memorial which housed the works of Yuri, and the remaining half housed the curator and his family."

Diana tried to keep her voice steady despite the thrill of anticipation running up her spine. "Could we purchase copies of his books and make photocopies of the diaries and letters?" She paused, and then continued. "They might shed some light on the secret that Arthur Warwick alluded to in his letters to Yuri: some information that might help me find the treasure."

Ana translated for the Sakharov family, as surprise crossed their faces in varying degrees. "*Treasure?*" their eyes seemed to say. Ana and Mikhail had explained that the two men were writing about a secret, but they hadn't mentioned a treasure. But their family reaction did not appear to be a negative one, so Diana pressed on. "I can leave you the original of Yuri's letter to Arthur." Again she waited for Ana to relay her message, before adding in a pleading tone, "Please. Please help me."

Ana spoke with them again, clearly using her own words this time. The Sakharovs were still perplexed, but some of them started to smile and whisper to each other. Mikhail listened carefully to their conversation, injecting his own thoughts now and again. Just when Diana felt she was about to burst, Mikhail turned to her and again started speaking in English.

"We have a *better* proposal for you. You can be our guests here in Pushkin, and we will help you go through all the documents in our possession until you find what you are looking for. We will, however, accept your kind offer of Yuri's letter for this Memorial Home. That way, your story will become part of the history of our family."

All of the Sakharovs were now smiling and nodding. Diana laughed along with the others and spoke. "Thank you so much, I am so grateful for your help." She looked at Ana and the two exchanged a smile before she continued. "We would be honored to accept your generous offer."

With a loud clap of his hands, as if to cement the agreement, Mikhail sprang to his feet and started barking orders like a general to a battalion. Even Ana had some difficulty keeping up, so she summarized for Diana. "My children know a little bit of English, so they will sort through the documents to see if there are any more letters from Arthur. In the meantime, Olga and Nikolay will procure copies of all Yuri's books still on the market and make photocopies of those which are out of print—that way you

73

can take them back home with you. Then everyone will go through the diaries and other Russian documents to look for any references to sacred symbols, spiritual quests, or places Arthur visited." Ana paused, breathless.

Diana was silent for a moment, overwhelmed by the family's generosity. When she was able to find her voice, she thanked the Sakharovs profusely. It finally seemed she was getting somewhere. By evening, Diana was exhausted and the small but cozy room the family had prepared for her and Ana looked like heaven. Decorated in the 1800s' style, the room had two, four-poster beds, each covered by a heavy canopy and sheltered by velvet curtains. On one side of the room, a simple but elegant desk and chair sat underneath a window of double glass panels; on the other side was an antique wardrobe. The walls were covered with carved, wooden panels, and there was a large wood-burning stove in the corner opposite Diana's bed. Diana eyed the room critically for a moment, wondering how similar décor would look in the refurbished Rockforth Castle.

* * * *

In the ensuing days, the house was a whirlwind of frantic research activity, which yielded some thrilling discoveries. On Saturday, the fifth of February, the second day of the search, Ana was doing a preliminary reading of Yuri's diaries from 1855—the year he met Arthur Warwick.

She called out to Diana, who, with the help of one of the family, was looking for the English letters. "Diana, come here! I've found something very interesting!"

Diana rushed into the dining room and sat next to her friend, rubbing her hands together in anticipation. Ana handled the book carefully, as if afraid the ancient pages might disintegrate at her touch.

"Here it says, 'Today…'—the date is April 15th, 1855— '…I met Arthur Neville, Earl of Warwick.'" Ana paused, wide-eyed, and looked up at Diana. "Did you know Arthur was the Earl of Warwick?"

"Well, I know my family has some aristocratic ancestry, but Jonathan, Arthur's son, dropped the title and started calling himself, simply, Jonathan Warwick. I don't really know why. I think he didn't identify with the values of the British aristocracy of the time."

Ana turned back to the diary. "'…Arthur Neville, Earl of Warwick, who came to the Lyceum'—it must be the Imperial Alexander in St. Petersburg—'to search for information about certain ancient artifacts from Israel, Egypt, and Mesopotamia. We had a very interesting conversation. He has traveled extensively—most recently to Jerusalem, Egypt, Greece and Constantinople—collecting an immense wealth of knowledge on early Christianity and the ancient religions of the Mediterranean. He says that many things have been forgotten over the centuries, and that Jesus was actually teaching and practising a doctrine that was very different from what we are taught today by the Churches. He says this is the reason why there are so many differences between the various churches, and that one would find even more differences if we had access to the ancient Christian traditions of the Gnostics, Cathars, and Aryans."'

Ana quickly flipped through the diary, stopping again at the note dated the 17th of April. "'Today, Arthur came to my father's house, and we have invited him to stay with us while he is working on his research in the various libraries and churches in St. Petersburg. He has shown me the material he collected during his stay in Moscow last month, and it is extremely interesting, to say the least. Many of the ancient icons contain a wealth of symbols which most people do not understand—or even notice anymore—and so no questions are asked."'

"He's talking about symbols," commented Diana with an easy grin. "I think we are on the right track here."

Ana, her eyes still glued to the page, nodded slowly, and continued. "'Arthur has discovered the Old Testament of the Bible was compiled from 167 BCE, to the time of Jesus, by the Scribes—a priestly class of scholars who wanted to recreate what they called the 'ancient glory of Israel', but with a much stronger male orientation and political control of the general people. From the large, ancient collection of texts which composed the Jewish tradition, the Scribes only chose the books which could reinforce the political authority of the male members of the priestly class; all the books of the Prophetesses were eliminated, as well as many books of esoteric knowledge that were attributed to Moses himself. The Scribes, therefore, put all their efforts into depicting a 'jealous God', whose first commandment was hostility against all other Gods, religions, cultures, civilizations and ethnic groups. Special emphasis, with severe punishment, was laid against idolatry, blasphemy and disobedience to political theocratic leaders, turning centuries-old pluralistic and tolerant, middle-eastern culture upside down."'

In the meantime, Mikhail's children had also joined them, and were eagerly craning their necks to look at the pages of the diary. They had probably gone through the volumes before, but it was evident Diana's presence was making everything even more real for them.

Ana continued. "'The Gospels lend credence to the fact that Jesus descended from a royal family of Israel, and they supply genealogies directly connecting him with King David. Also, the description of Jesus' father, Joseph, as a 'carpenter' may not simply refer to his profession. For centuries, the Freemasons have used symbols of carpentry to indicate their leaders, and symbols of a carpenter's tools to indicate their tradition.

"'Shortly after the birth of Jesus, his family fled to Egypt because of King Herod the Great's very public response to the news of the birth of 'one who will be King of the Jews'. That's from Matthew, Chapter two, verses thirteen to fifteen. The family remained in Egypt for anywhere from six months to six years. Magdala, the place from which Mary Magdalene came, is the name of a Jewish village on the border with Egypt.

"'Matthew's Gospel gives great importance to the genealogy of Jesus, indicating he descended from royal blood. According to the early Gnostic Christians, Mary of Magdala was no prostitute at all, but the wife of Jesus, and also of the highest royal blood.'"

Diana tried to take notes, but she didn't want Ana to stop or slow down. Their time was limited and there was much more to gather from Yuri's invaluable diaries.

Ana paused, rapidly running her finger over the words, apparently looking for more relevant information. "There are a few pages of family matters, and then on April twentieth, we have another bunch of pages speaking about Arthur."

Suddenly Mikhail's son, Sergei, sprang up and spoke. "Yuri wrote a book about the traditions of the Coptic Church in Egypt and their connection to the 'Mystic' knowledge of Isis and Osiris. Moses was supposed to have transmitted this knowledge to a small, elite group of initiated priests; the Emerald Tablet is said to have been guarded in the Temple of Jerusalem, but it seemed to have disappeared around the time of Jesus and before the diaspora of the Jews affected by the Roman Empire." He went over to a shelf, plucked a thick volume from it, and returned to the group. The book was in Russian but had several sketched illustrations.

Sergei translated. "'The Coptic Church is considered the oldest branch of Christianity, having roots in the early Jewish community of Alexandria, Egypt. When Alexander the Great conquered Egypt, his goal was to create a huge centre of syncretistic culture for the many scholars who traveled the ancient world in their search for knowledge. Of course, for many centuries before Alexander, Buddhist and Hindu monks had already been walking the earth to teach and preach, and an even greater number of western philosophers and seekers had traveled to India, especially to the great universities of Nalanda and Takshashila.'"

Diana suddenly remembered Professor Frawley's observation. *My goodness, even he was talking about these things and I didn't know it.*

Sergei was still speaking. "'Alexander established the famous library and his

Victor Cosmos

successors, the Ptolemaic Pharaohs, expanded it to such an extent that—according to the Roman historians Gellius and Ammiamus—it contained 700,000 volumes.'"

Ana continued. "This is from the 20th of April. 'Today I had a long discussion with Arthur about the Coptic Church of Egypt, the Gnostic Church, and some of the ancient symbols that have been preserved by those traditions.

'"He is especially intrigued by the appearance of the *swastika* symbol, as well as the cross at Lalibela, and he is more convinced than ever that the original teachings of Jesus, the real knowledge he passed on to a chosen group of his early disciples in Jerusalem, was actually very different from what the later Church put together and canonized as the official doctrine of Christianity under the direction of Emperor Constantine. In fact, they were much more in line with the teachings that were preserved in the ancient Library of Alexandria, among the Sanskrit and the Chaldean texts of the secret mysteries. He is consumed by the desire to find the roots of this mysterious knowledge, and he strongly believes he will find it in India.

'"Arthur has given me a large bundle of his notes and asked me to keep them for him while he travels, as he is planning to proceed to the Himalayan region of India before the winter sets in.'"

The reading was interrupted by Mikhail, who entered the dining room with an armful of old files. He said something in Russian and Ana translated, "He says he found the letters in English." Diana jumped to her feet and helped Mikhail spread the papers out on the table, moving aside the other documents. Ana inserted a bookmark in the diary and closed it.

Now everyone gathered around Diana, who began turning the pages, one after the other. "These are actually Arthur's notes," she said in a faint, incredulous voice. "And here is a page with four symbols!"

She removed a sheet that looked even older than the others. It didn't even look like paper, but seemed to be some kind of vegetal fiber. *Maybe papyrus?* She had never seen papyrus before, but had read that the ancient scrolls, on which the Egyptian priests used to write their sacred texts, were made from thin layers of the pith of the papyrus, an aquatic plant which grew abundantly on the banks of the Nile.

Her heart skipped a beat when she recognized the symbols that Yitzhak Rosen had shown her in Jerusalem, two of them matched: the Star of David ✡, and the Crescent ☾. The Swastika 卐 was the third symbol. Also, there was another strange one—no doubt the fourth as mentioned by Arthur in his letter. Although she couldn't place it, she had the strange feeling she had seen it somewhere before. It was something like a large number 3, but with two small appendages, one on the top and another on the right.

In silence, Ana gave her a new sheet of paper and a pen, and Diana copied the symbols very carefully, including the unidentified one: ॐ

The entire Sakharov family was thrilled to get such a fresh perspective on Yuri's cultural legacy and threw themselves into the work, accumulating photocopies and rough translations of the Russian texts. Mikhail's children, worked feverishly with Ana, who was by now capable of sorting out the information into levels of priority, according to relevance to their search.

Arthur's letters to Yuri, arranged by dates, showed he had indeed been traveling a lot. After leaving St. Petersburg in July of 1855, he journeyed through Khorasan, or present-day Afghanistan, where he found substantial settlements of Jews. He then journeyed through Gagh, Bokhara, Kokhant, Samarkand and Tibet.

In Lhasa, where he had been stuck during the coldest months of the winter, some documents still remained. They had been preserved by the Tibetan Buddhist Lamas there, who seemed to be extremely eager to protect all ancient manuscripts in their libraries.

The very next day, Diana eagerly unfolded another letter from Arthur written to Yuri, this one dated the 25th of April, 1856. She lovingly scanned the now familiar elegant and strong handwriting of her ancestor, and then began to read aloud.

"'Certainly, these discoveries are extraordinary. The records here in Lhasa say that Jesus traveled in these very places—as I had already heard in Levant, Constantinople and Khorasan—and on his way he visited the tomb of Sem, the son of Noah, at Ain ul Arus, and Mount Ararat in the present-day Ottoman empire. I was not able to find these places, though, because my guides were greedy and unruly, and I did not really trust them. I would like to return to these places later, probably in a few years. I have heard that in Kashmir there are the tombs of Jesus himself and his mother, Mary. They say that the place where Mary died is known as Murree.

"'I have also heard that Jesus visited many more places in India, and I am anxious to follow in his footsteps. It seems that this journey of Jesus to India was the final one but not the first, as he had visited this wonderful place when he was a young man on a spiritual quest, before starting his preaching in Israel.'"

The letter went on to describe pleasantries unrelated to the search, and Diana placed it back in the pile. The next was a long letter dated the

30th of July, 1858. Arthur described his travel in India, how he was intensely studying the ancient traditions and texts, as well as directly learning from *gurus* and *yogis* in various parts of the country. Arthur received the *sanyasi* renounced order initiation in the Shankara line, thus becoming a *yogi*. Settling in Allahabad, at the confluence of the three sacred rivers, he had started an *ashram* where many disciples had been drawn to listen to the "*White Sadhu*". Diana immediately recognized the clue and noted the place where Arthur finally settled.

The last letter, dated September 1861, announced his intention to return to the West in 1865, after collecting a treasure he had heard about, adding that it had an unparalleled value within the history of humanity. He also confided his most serious concerns to Yuri, saying there was a strong possibility he would be attacked again by dark forces trying to steal the treasure. Therefore, he said, he was sending Yuri all the clues he had gathered. He also requested Yuri contact his family and urge them to follow in his footsteps and help him recover the treasure.

From what happened after that, it appeared Arthur's foes finally succeeded in eliminating him.

Diana looked up from the clutter of papers; she realized she had learned all she could in Russia. The trip had certainly been fruitful, and the most important clue was Arthur had set up an ashram at the confluence of three holy rivers, in a place called Allahabad. And she was also able to uncover the four ancient symbols, which she desperately needed. It was to be Diana and Ana's last night in Russia.

Chapter 4 - The Tour of Duty

Major William Buford Johnson sat in a stiff folding chair at the field table, swatting away an especially persistent fly. The insect seemed determined to land in the glass of tepid water sweating on the corner of Bill's desk. He almost felt sorry for it. The desert air was filled with dust, and the temperature had hit an unbearable—but not uncommon—120 degrees Fahrenheit. He longed to take off his helmet, but quickly put the thought from his mind. The intermittent sniper fire made such a thing unthinkable; nothing less than suicide. The fly dive-bombed toward the glass again, and this time Bill let him, watching as the thin, black legs thrashed about in the clear liquid. When the insect had stopped moving, Bill tossed the contents of the glass onto the sand and refilled it with fresh water. Just another day in sunny Iraq.

The company under Bill's command was part of the United States Army, which had joined the multi-national effort overseeing operations in Iraq to stabilize it. Although the major fighting was over a decade ago, the present tour had not been an easy one for any of them. Now, as part of the residual force, they were helping to keep the peace by training the Iraqi army. And if push came to shove, they would be the front line boots on the ground against the Islamic State and other notable terrorists still active in the middle-east.

The killing of Osama bin Laden by the U.S. Navy Seals had taken much of the wind from Al Qaeda's sails and greatly reduced the chances of any significant attacks by them in the immediate future. However, all this did not stop attacks by the insurgents, backed by multiple hostile countries seeking regional dominance, and the sudden emergence of the more dangerous ISIS Islamic State terrorists. Just a few days back, one of his deputy commanders, Captain Robbins, had been seriously wounded—and two of his men killed along with ten Iraqi trainee soldiers—by a roadside bomb laid by ISIS. Bill was losing men regularly to tenacious and invisible enemies. And to make matters worse, replacements for injured and dead soldiers were hard to come by due to the decreasing number of new recruits. The insurgents, however, never seemed to have this problem; there were always more waiting to join the ranks from around the world, in their lusty pursuit of the seventy-two virgins in heaven, thanks to social media and tech-savvy terrorists. The terrorists created ingenious ways to keep their flock together by paying handsome salaries to the fighters, and to the war widows and their orphans. More than anything else, the biggest deterrent was deserters were beheaded with impunity to keep the order.

The major threw a disgusted look at the letter on the table. *Those geniuses at Headquarters, in their plush and secure offices, should come and have their vacations here for a change.* That would give them a taste of what his men were facing every day.

Then they would see about two hundred odd soldiers and officers in his Company who were already stretched to their limit. Frowning, he looked up from the letter to see his second-in-command, Captain Miguel Lopez, approaching. Captain Lopez snapped to attention and saluted; Bill returned the salute.

"At ease, Captain. How's Robbins?"

"Recovering, sir, but he won't be seeing any more combat. The surgeon is getting ready to operate on his legs in the next couple of days— see if he can save them."

The muscles around Bill's stomach gave a twist. He would never get used to news like that, no matter how many times he heard it. These fine men and women had joined the army with an ideal to defend the values of the American people, but this was not America. They were trying to bring freedom and democracy to ungodly places like this, and being maimed and killed for their noble efforts. How long could this go on? Each new president had a different plan, pushing his soldiers from one theater of operation to another. He used to think the pacifists back home were a bunch of idiots, but now, after many years in Iraq, he was starting to think they had a point. His deeply-held beliefs about his country's foreign policy were flagging under the weight of this harsh reality. He was sick and tired of the whole thing, and so were his men. He looked up at Lopez, who was still standing there, waiting for orders.

"Sit, Captain. Take a breather." He watched Lopez as he settled on the folding chair across from the desk. The Latino officer was definitely setting an example for the others; he kept himself together with sheer strength of will. "Captain, I have a letter here from Operation Headquarters. Colonel Henry Nickson has recommended our company be redeployed to the Helmand province in Afghanistan, once our tour of duty is over here next month."

Lopez merely blinked his eyes in response, but it was not difficult to imagine what was going on behind his resolute face.

"Colonel Nickson," Bill continued, his voice hardening as he said the colonel's name, "thinks the situation in Helmand requires an experienced battalion like ours. Those damned Taliban have been attacking the NATO forces with impunity and they need us to help them stabilize the situation. What do you think, Captain?" Bill's tone softened. "And please speak freely, Miguel."

Lopez seemed to allow himself a little sigh. "Thank you, sir. It won't be easy to get the men to digest this. They are exhausted and their morale is at an all-time low. Most of 'em would quit if it didn't mean a court martial and a loss of pension. They are homesick and worried about their families, and another deployment may just send some of them over the edge. Sir, these men need a break and a very long one— they need to go home, at least for a while, to rejuvenate."

"Thank you, Captain. I think I need to take a radical stance here. I'm going to the Operation Headquarters tomorrow to brief Colonel Nickson about the situation and ask him to reconsider. If things go wrong, you take care of the battalion." Bill winked, to Miguel's obvious surprise.

* * * *

The next day, Bill stood in the doorway of Colonel Nickson's office, stiffening in an impeccable salute as he waited for Nickson's assistant to announce him.

"Major William Buford Johnson to see you, sir," the young man barked, and then followed with a sharp salute.

Colonel Nickson looked up at Bill and gestured him in. "At ease, Major. Come in and take a seat."

The colonel dismissed his assistant and the young man left, closing the door behind him.

He appeared to be staring at Bill with piercing eyes, and waiting for him to sit down. The colonel spoke, "I heard you wanted to speak with me about the redeployment of our Battalion."

Bill took a deep breath, debating for the hundredth time how far he was willing to take this. "Permission to speak frankly, sir."

The colonel frowned. "Please, Major. Go ahead."

"Sir, I believe it's a mistake to send the men to Afghanistan. At least, not without a long leave back home first. They're exhausted and their morale is very low, and another deployment right now could result in human errors in action and unnecessary casualties."

"Nonsense, Major." Colonel Nickson gave him a sharp look and moved some papers on his desk. "This is not the sort of talk I was expecting from a highly-decorated officer and brilliant West Point graduate like yourself. We have a duty and we will do what is needed. The men will get some rest on the journey and a few days leave in Afghanistan."

Bill took another breath. This was a risk, but he had no choice. "Sir, with all due respect, I think this is a big mistake. Can't they send some other well-rested battalion to Helmand?"

Colonel Nickson's jaw muscles twitched. "And what will the enemy do while our boys are on vacation back home? They'll take a break,

91

too? I won't tolerate a defeatist attitude in my battalion. This discussion is over. We ship next month, and that's it. Your report has been duly noted. You're dismissed."

Bill looked down at the colonel's desk for a moment. He had expected this reaction. The colonel had great career ambitions, and was obviously ready to sacrifice good and loyal men to climb up the ladder. Bill knew there were other troops, fresh men fully rested who could be deployed with better results. On many occasions, his commanding officer behaved like a rogue general, giving him illegal commands, which he flatly refused to follow, and he knew, for that one reason alone, his company had been specifically targeted by refusing vacations for the troops, and putting them on long tours as a way of punishment. He felt his blood boil; he would not take this anymore. He braced himself for the dive of his life. He was going to stand against the chain of command.

"I'm sorry, sir, but I cannot follow this order. This goes against the spirit of the Army." His hands were sweating; it was not a normal conversation.

The colonel froze in his paper-shuffling and looked up at Bill, his eyes dangerously narrow. "What did you say?"

Bill tried to reason it out. "Sir, the men are not ready. It would be a disaster. The terrorists don't value their own lives and are ready to die, but we Americans value every life, and even more-so if they're soldiers."

The colonel jumped from his chair, red in the face. "This is insubordination! Do you realize what you're doing? I'll have your apologies!"

Bill stood too. He knew he would be shot dead by a firing squad if the colonel had his way. He had no choice, though, as it was about his men who loved and respected him, and he had to look out for them. "With all due respect, Colonel, I'm ready to bring the matter to higher levels of command." He didn't flinch at the ferocious look the colonel shot at him, and he stiffened in the military salute again. There was nothing else to say at this point.

The colonel crashed into his chair, with his hands on his forehead, obviously making an effort to control himself. "This means a court martial, Major. Get out now."

* * * *

One week later, Bill found himself in the courtroom, facing the Judge Advocate General. He tried to remain calm. The days leading up to the trial had been a blur, and he still couldn't quite believe this was happening.

"Major William Buford Johnson, you are hereby accused of insubordination to a superior officer. This court has also examined your grievance against Colonel Henry Nickson, as well as your request to change your reporting structure due to lack of trust in the colonel's command. I understand, if this request is denied, you ask to be immediately relieved from your duties. Explain yourself, Major," said Major General Ruth Feinstein.

Bill recounted his conversation with the colonel concisely, but with all the relevant details. He also informed the court that on multiple occasions, Colonel Nickson flouted the military rules of engagement and ordered them to perform unauthorized kidnappings, torture male suspects, and commit deliberate sexual assaults on women suspects and informants. When Bill turned down such illegitimate commands, his battalion was made to suffer by denying them leave and putting them on prolonged deployments. This was the latest attempt: the straw that broke the camel's back.

As he spoke, he could feel the heat of Nickson's disgusted glare from across the room. When he was done speaking, the Judge Advocate was silent for a long time.

She spoke, looking straight at Bill. "Major Johnson, we understand your concerns for your men, but insubordination is a serious charge. You should have submitted a written report, as per standard procedure, and limited yourself to suggestions. However, you refused to follow a direct order from a superior in the chain of command. Is that true?"

"Yes, ma'am. I believed it was my moral duty to bring the situation to the attention of higher authorities. I believe the honor of the U.S. Military is at stake. The values we stand for as Americans have been compromised. I had the best interest of my country at heart, ma'am."

"Very well," the judge said, rubbing her chin in thought. "You'll have our decision after a short recess."

As the members of the court filed out of the office, Bill saw Colonel Nickson stride confidently over to him. "Bill," he said, wearing a smile so forced it looked like a macabre mask, "it's become apparent to me that you are having some sort of reaction to the pressures of your command, and it seems unlikely you will change your mind." He attempted to place a hand on Bill's shoulder, but Bill shrugged it off. The smile faltered, but remained. "I'll tell you what, Major, I will support your discharge and drop the insubordination charge. But you must withdraw the grievance against me. And you must keep your mouth shut on what happened in Iraq under my command. Don't rock the *damned* boat, for God's sake! You will not interfere with any operation from now on, even from the outside. If I find out that you're lobbying stateside, you'll be very sorry."

He knows the grievance is a death blow to his career. Bill stared at the senior officer in front of him. Suddenly, he saw just a scared old man, afraid of losing his position of power and feeling threatened. Nickson had obviously hoped he would be intimidated by the court martial and give in, but it hadn't worked. Raising a grievance against him and asking to change his battalion's reporting structure due to lack of trust, revealing the dirty secrets of the colonel's command, and staking his own career in the process, had been a very bold move indeed, but Bill was just now beginning to realize its deepest implications. However, Nickson could not afford a public clash with a black officer who had a remarkable history of bravery and valor; a brilliant graduate from West Point whose family was known for their important political contacts. All this, Bill could read in the Colonel's eyes.

"No, sir. I will not create any problems for you, or for the Army, sir."

The Colonel's smile relaxed, becoming almost sincere. "All right then, son. After all, you have completed many years of active duty in the field, and with great success. Your country could not ask for more. I'll recommend your discharge on health grounds, as you seem to suffer from incapacitating Post Traumatic Stress Disorder. You'll need to report to a military health facility for some time; maybe get some medication. I'll talk with the Medical Officer here in Baghdad." He leaned in toward Bill and lowered his voice. "Just stay out of the way and you'll even be able to keep your medals."

Bill felt a wave a rage inside him, and once again had to fight hard to remain in control as he answered. "Thank you, sir. I appreciate that." He even managed a deferential tone.

Later on, when the verdict came, Bill was not surprised. The charges of insubordination and the grievance had been dropped. The colonel lost the command of his battalion and was sent on administrative leave, pending his own possible discharge from the Army. Bill was escorted to the Army Hospital, admitted to a private room, and put on suicide watch.

Sometime later, William Buford Johnson left Baghdad, still under strict surveillance "for medical reasons", and with a maintenance dose of pills that he threw into the airplane toilet as soon as they were in the air. He was not sure he wanted to numb himself and forget. He was angry, frustrated, and bitter. He requested a pillow and a blanket, closed his eyes, and pretended to sleep until they arrived in New York.

* * * *

The stress of the past few months seemed to evaporate when Bill walked into the McGuire Air Force Base and found his family waiting for him, just like many other military families waited for their loved ones arriving from the battlefield, some of whom were his fellow passengers. His mother and sister were waving frantically and were laughing and crying at the same time. Father hugged him then concealed his emotions by helping him with his duffel bag and hurrying ahead to get the car. The chilly weather enhanced a wonderful homecoming and he loved every bit of it.

Bill stared at his little sister, Shirley, with an incredulous smile. When he left, she had been an awkward and lanky teen with braces on her teeth, and wearing weird clothes while searching for her own 'personal style'. Now, she was a gorgeous young woman. She had always been intelligent and mature beyond her years, but now she also exuded a self-confidence that only added to her beauty.

"Hey, Pumpkin! How are you doing?" he asked, grabbing her in a tight hug.

Shirley smiled at the nickname and patted him on the back. "We're so happy you're home, big bro." She stopped speaking as her eyes filled with tears. It was obvious his many years in Iraq had been very hard on his family, as well as himself.

His parents, Vivian and Desmond, were prominent members of New York City's African American community, known for their political activism, the pro-bono legal counseling they offered to the less fortunate, and the great lengths they had gone through to uncover their roots in Ghana, discovering their forefathers had been sold to European colonizers by Arab slave traders in the 1700s.

The Treasure of the Pandavas

The drive to their home in the Bronx was like a dream, or—even better—it was like waking up after the bad dream had ended. Here he was, back with his family, as if no time had passed since the day he'd left for Iraq. He knew returning to civilian life wouldn't be easy, that there would be difficult days ahead when he would have to come to terms with what had happened, with the memories of his men, and the years of fighting and horrors. But right now, he just wanted to bask in the love of his family and not think of anything else.

In the weeks that followed, Bill settled back into his old room and into a new routine as a regular citizen. His family allowed him his space, but as time went on, they worried about his state of mind. When they finally heard the circumstances under which he had returned home, they'd expected some kind of crisis or outburst, but Bill's silence was worse.

His days were spent hiding in his room, nibbling snacks of junk food and sipping beer, usually at room temperature, as he didn't want to go to the kitchen too often, as he might run into someone. He even kept a few bottles on his bedside table.

The nights were worse. He was restless and often angry, but didn't want to disturb his family by moving around the house. He'd stare blankly at the TV deep into the night, half-dozing during foolish programs or old movies.

In these moments, he'd kick himself for throwing away the pills, but as each dawn broke on another day, his good sense would return. He would, once again, decide to do this on his own. The Army had been a mixed bag, with some good, bad, ugly, and then beautiful experiences, but he would eventually recover if he just kept going. Time was the ultimate healer.

During his short encounters with his family he was nice and polite, and he always left his room for dinner with them, doing his best to look relaxed.

One evening, everything seemed the same, but there was a palpable tension in the air. Mother had red eyes, but smiled at him brightly, and Shirley looked uncertain about what to say. As usual, Bill concentrated on the excellent food, now and then smiling reassuringly at his family.

Finally his father cleared his throat, a sign he was about to say something important. "Bill, I hate to bring up the subject, but I really think you should try to get out sometimes. You know, the only failure is when you stop trying." Bill just nodded, and nothing more was said on the subject.

After dinner, he decided to go out for a walk, trying to remember how it all was before he joined the army. He wandered aimlessly, ending up in a bar on the corner of Bassford and Third Avenue, his favorite hangout in the old days. It was a sport's bar with pool tables, dancing and meeting lounges, and of course, huge televisions on every wall. The vibrating music system seemed to climb a few decibels after 9:00 p.m. Bill chose a seat directly in front of the TV, at the far end of the bar.

Marty, the club owner, recognized him and greeted him warmly. "Hey, my man Bill! It's great to have you back! Have a drink on me! Veterans are most welcome!" He gently nudged Bill's fist with his own. The waitress returned with a cold beer and fries. Bill smiled at Marty, lifted the bottle in a toast to his friend, and returned to stare at the TV, where the New York baseball team was playing Chicago.

Suddenly his attention was distracted by loud, angry voices. A brawl seemed to be developing between two groups of teenagers at the other end of the bar. He watched as the bouncers quickly controlled the situation before it got out of hand.

He finished his beer and got up just as Marty walked past him again. "Hey, Marty, everything okay?"

"Sure, dude. Everything's normal. The kids get loaded and sometimes they play the fool a bit. They just need help to snap out of it sometimes."

As Bill walked out the door and onto the street, he realized that war was going on at home, too.

* * * *

The next morning, Vivian Johnson came home from the market to find her son sitting at the breakfast table with a mug of coffee. He seemed willing to talk, so she sat down with him. Bill told her about the club scene, which had somehow broken the dam of his unanswerable questions, repressed frustration, and despair. They sat for hours, with Vivian listening intently, often pressing her son's hand lying on the table, and sometimes wiping her eyes. They talked of lost hopes, of the purpose of life, and of non-violence and human rights. They spoke of Martin Luther King and Mahatma Gandhi, Bayard Rustin and Rosa Parks; about Jesus, religion and patriotism; about Iraq, Syria, Afghanistan, Vietnam and Korea; about the old days of the Civil Rights Movement and the problems of the present—teenage pregnancy, gang violence and people on drugs. Finally, they talked about the age-old quest for peace of mind. Vivian knew her son was lost, and was terribly worried about him. For a moment, she was tempted to encourage him to find a good girl and settle down, but she knew that in his frame of mind, entering a relationship would be a mistake. Although she was not a particularly religious person, she and Desmond had done civil rights work with the local Baptist congregation. They had even gone to services back before Bill had gone to Iraq. She suggested they visit the church and talk to the pastor. He would certainly be competent to answer all of Bill's existential, moral and spiritual questions. Of this, Vivian was certain.

That afternoon, Vivian and Bill walked to the church and found sixty-year-old Reverend Clive Gray sitting alone in his office. Vivian took a chair and sat to the side, while Bill sat next to the Pastor, who smiled brightly and shook his hand.

"Will you look at this? Isn't this young William Johnson? I'd heard you went to Iraq— welcome home!"

"Thanks, Reverend, it's good to be back."

The pastor smiled again and looked at Vivian. "I can only imagine how happy your family is to have you back safe." She nodded solemnly. "Now what can I do for you folks today? Dare I hope you have come to join the congregation?"

Bill gave Reverend Gray a sheepish smile. "Actually, Reverend, I came here for guidance. Since I've been home, I...." his voice trailed off. He didn't know what else to say.

The pastor clapped his hand enthusiastically. "Hallelujah! Jesus certainly has a place for you in his house, and there is so much work to do. Our dear brothers and sisters will be happy to see you attend our worship services. We even have a Patriotic Service in the park. We are all called to his missionary work. Jesus said, 'I must work the works of Him that sent me, while it is day; the night cometh, when no man can work.' Have you accepted Jesus Christ as your personal Savior, and are you ready to become a vessel for his grace and ministry, to reach others who may not know him?"

Bill drew back, startled. "Actually, Reverend, I came here today because since I came home, I have felt lost, like I don't know where I belong." Bill sighed, struggling for the right words. "I have some questions about.... I am having a hard time reconciling my beliefs with what I saw over there."

The reverend nodded, his smile still in place, and grasped Bill's shoulder. "Is *that* all?" When Bill didn't laugh at his attempt at a joke, the reverend continued in a more serious tone. "You have come to the right place, son. We have all the answers here."

Two hours later, Bill and his mother emerged from the church, exhausted. Bill felt more confused and frustrated than ever. He had gone to the church for answers, answers as to why there was so much killing and war in the world, much of which was done by people who called themselves Born Again Christians, Jihadi Muslims, left-wing guerrillas and right-wing death squads." But instead of answering his questions, the reverend had served up the same routine answers Bill had heard his whole life, that the killing was the work of Satan, and the only way to salvation was to accept Jesus as his personal savior. Those who didn't, the reverend said, had a one-way ticket to hell.

The worst part was whenever Bill challenged any of this, the minister's mouth would twitch in annoyance. Then he would paste the same beatific smile on his face and spew more repetitious rhetoric. All Bill needed to do, apparently, was to ask forgiveness for his sins.

"I'm sorry, honey," Vivian said, pulling Bill back to the present, "I really thought he would bring you some peace."

"It's not your fault, Mom, I just don't believe that God would be so judgmental, or that you have to believe one way or the other in order to have a happy and meaningful life."

Vivian remained quiet until they reached their home. Then she hugged Bill, and kissed his cheek. "Bill, I want you to know that we will always support you, no matter what you decide to do with your life. We love you very much, and I'm sure God is greater than churches and religions, so I'll pray for Him to help you find your path."

Bill smiled and hugged her. "I know, Mom. Thank you so much. I love you, too."

That night, Bill remained awake as usual, but this time he had a new feeling of hope. He'd been wrong to expect that one visit to a church would bring him all the answers. He would have to find out what he believed on his own. And his mother was right—God was greater than all the religions of the world. He just had to find the right path, the one which suited him best.

* * * *

Bill smiled to himself as he recalled the recent events, took his seat on the plane and fastened his seatbelt. The look on his father's face when his parents dropped him off at JFK was one of concern. His mother smiled and hugged him, but there was worry around her eyes. He knew his parents were afraid he was making an impulsive decision, but it was what he needed to do.

Bill had taken his mother's words to heart. After that meeting at the church, he began researching different religions and even non-religions. He didn't tell anyone at first, but began to spend his sleepless nights researching different religious schools of thought on the internet. He started reading about Islam, which did not come out much different than Christianity; it was very similar. He tried New Age thought, but it didn't entice him. He wanted something original and authentic. When he finally tried Buddhism, and then *yoga* mantra meditation to attain inner peace, it helped him the most, and he instantly knew this was what he had been looking for. It wasn't long before he joined a few online discussion rooms and met fellow seekers from all over the world. Many of them, he learned, had survived worse traumas than him and were now thriving. One day, an online buddy suggested he take a trip to India. It had been referred to as the Motherland of Mankind and of all spirituality. At first, Bill thought the idea was crazy, but as he pondered and talked it over with his contacts, he realized he was excited by the idea. It was always better to try and find things out for oneself, instead of judging from the outside.

When he broke the news to his family over dinner one night, they thought he had finally gone crazy, "You're going where and for what?" his parents had exclaimed, almost simultaneously. Shirley had just lowered her eyes toward her plate of chicken and potatoes. But Bill had held his ground. He explained that even Martin Luther King Jr. went to India in 1959 to learn the Gandhian ways of nonviolence before he embarked on his own journey and style. It was true. This fact convinced them he was serious and had given his decision a lot of thought. In the end, he was a grown man and there was nothing they could do to stop him. They also voiced that they hadn't heard him sound this alive in, well, in years.

The hard part was going to be dealing with the sixteen-hour flight to New Delhi. He struck up a conversation with the woman in the seat next to him, a pretty Indian girl whose name, as he soon discovered, was Priti. She laughed when he explained the odd linguistic coincidence.

"In Sanskrit language, Priti means 'pleasure'. My full name is Priti Gosvami." She extended her hand and gave him a warm hand shake. "Nice meeting you."

Bill said, "The pleasure is all mine." They both had a hearty laugh.

Now that the ice was broken, Bill was ready with questions, since he *was* on a quest.

"If I may ask, what does that signify?" Bill boldly inquired, pointing to the strange white, U-shaped mark on Priti's forehead. She was not offended, but simply smiled and replied instantly, "My family is originally from Vrindavana, and the mark, called a *tilak,* indicates that we are the traditional devotees of Lord Krishna. Do you know about Krishna?"

No, he did not know about Krishna, and Bill thought it seemed to be the right thing to say, because Priti gave him a big smile and began telling him about her favorite God.

She smiled and lifted her head. "Krishna taught the wonderful knowledge of *Bhagavad-gita* to his friend Arjuna. They had a discussion on the purpose of life and its meaning on the battlefield of Kurukshetra. The *Gita* is the most important text in Hindu spirituality, or simply, it is the Hindu Bible."

"Ah, I read an article about the *Gita* online. There were some quotes; very interesting," said

Bill, returning the smile. "I was looking for information about *yoga*, and it seems that the text contains a wealth of instructions about the various forms."

"Certainly," Priti said, leaning forward enthusiastically. She seemed pleased to have such a willing student. "The *Gita* is extremely valuable for its instructions on *yoga*, but devotion to Krishna, Himself, is also very popular in India, and is called *Bhakti Yoga*. You see, Krishna is the sweetest and most intimate form of the One God or *Bhagavan*, as we usually call Him. He is especially famous for His loving relationships, when He played the role of a young cowherd boy with His foster parents and friends in Vrindavana, where He appeared about 5,000 years ago."

Bill nodded appreciatively, stunned to know that Krishna existed some 3000 years before Jesus.

She continued. "Once, Einstein mentioned—regarding the *Bhagavad-gita,* 'When I read the *Bhagavad-gita* and reflect about how God created this universe, everything else seems so superfluous.'"

"Ah...so he was something like an Indian...err...I mean, Hindu prophet?" asked Bill curiously.

"Not really," said Priti, who swayed her head sideways a couple of times. "Krishna is directly God, who descended personally on this earth to manifest His transcendental activities and also to deliver religious teachings. He came for all humankind, not just for Indians or Hindus. Whenever God descends, meaning 'takes *Avatar*', it is for the benefit of everyone, and He chooses a particular form that is most suitable for the mission He wants to accomplish at that point in time."

Bill looked at her blankly for a moment. The only "*avatar*" he knew of was the movie he had seen on movie night at the army base. "Do you mean to say that according to Hindus there is only one God, but that He has many different forms, or *avatars*, as you say?"

"Precisely. God has unlimited forms, and in Hinduism—which is correctly called *Sanatana Dharma*, meaning the eternal, natural way of life—everyone is free to choose the form they like best and cultivate their devotion to that particular form. That is called *ista-devata*. However, there is nothing wrong if one who is devoted to a particular form of God shows respect and devotion to other forms worshiped by other people. Actually, it is recommended, so that our narrow-mindedness goes away and we become broad-minded and appreciate more and more the greatness of God. Exclusive devotion to a particular form of God should never imply demeaning or demonizing other forms, or trying to destroy or stop their worship, or trying to negate their existence. That would be offensive.

Bhagavan is certainly not limited by sectarian considerations and can manifest in many different ways, according to the particular time, place and circumstance, to better bless a devotee. God has a unique relationship with every individual, therefore for as many individuals there are, there are as many relations,"

Bill was wonderstruck. He had never heard such a simple and deep explanation. This had nothing to do with the picture of ignorant superstition that was usually presented as "pagan polytheism" in school textbooks. He suddenly saw Priti as more than just an attractive girl to pass the time with. She was an excellent teacher. "Thanks for letting me know all this. I feel like I'm getting a crash course in a boot camp." He winked at her innocently. She smiled.

Bill changed the subject. "What about you, Priti? Do you live in India or are you just visiting?"

She told Bill she had gone to the States to get her Masters in Communications & Journalism. She was returning to India to marry her fiancé, Dhiraj Jain.

After Bill congratulated her on her recent graduation and upcoming wedding, Priti asked, "Is this your first journey to India?"

"Yeah! I'm very excited. I'm planning to visit several *yoga ashrams* and holy places." He smiled. "I'm a seeker on a quest, you know." They both laughed.

When the flight attendant asked if she wanted the vegetarian or non-vegetarian option, Priti promptly chose the vegetarian meal. Bill decided to go for it, too. After all, he didn't really know what any of the food was anyway, so he might as well get off on the right foot. Bill asked Priti about the food, and she kindly obliged by taking him through a detailed explanation of *puri chola* and *basmati chawal*. It was actually rather good, and the friendly company made it taste even better. They also were served a subji, roti, yogurt and a dessert.

When the flight attendant came to collect the empty trays, Bill was ready with more questions for Priti. "There's so much I'd like to know. You're a good teacher. What is your understanding of *karma*? I've heard this word so many times, but it seems to me it means something like 'destiny' or 'fate' or 'fatalism'?"

Bill was afraid he was pestering her, but Priti told him she was used to answering questions like those, and actually enjoyed doing so; moreover, her recently acquired degree helped her in effective communications. "*Karma* means 'action'," she said, "but it also means 'reaction to an action', and it also indicates the connection between the two. *Karma* constantly develops with each action we perform, so we are building our own destiny every day. But, we can also counteract the reactions to our old actions. In financial terms, *karma* can be a credit or debit in one's 'destiny account'."

Bill listened eagerly. These explanations were much easier than what he had found in books or on websites. The Indian native religions, he was learning, seemed extremely tolerant and accommodating, allowing full freedom to individuals and groups in regard to a vast range of beliefs and practices; provided such beliefs and practices were in accordance with what Priti called "the universal and eternal principles of religion." Bill was starting to understand that these universal principles—truthfulness and honesty, compassion and non-violence, cleanliness and purity of mind, and self-discipline—were also the foundations of all ethical and moral philosophical systems, irrespective of the personal beliefs of the people involved.

Bill had found out through study, and now by listening to Priti, that freedom, was paramount to a Hindu, a basic value—the freedom to think, speak and act according to one's conscience; taking full responsibility for one's choices and respecting the choices of others. This "live and let live" approach was not based on indifference, but on genuine consideration, and even love for all human beings, supported by honest and deep personal introspection, as well as the selfless dedication to one's own duty to set the best possible example for others.

"Wait a minute, let me see if I understand this," interjected Bill. "You are saying that according to the Indian religions, even if someone doesn't specifically believe in or worship God, it's sufficient to practise these basic ethical principles to be considered a good person?"

"Precisely," Priti replied, nodding her head up and down vigorously.

The rest of the journey was equally interesting. After lunch, while the other passengers snoozed or read magazines, Priti quietly explained reincarnation, saying that after death and before birth, the soul gradually builds itself a new body according to the possibilities afforded by the positive and negative consequences of the previous life's actions, habits and desires. The purpose of reincarnation was to better understand, through experience, the results of specific actions—especially violent and cruel ones.

"The human life offers the extraordinary opportunity to become liberated from the cycle of birth and death, and to attain spiritual perfection and total happiness."

"And *yoga* is supposed to help you get to that, right?" interjected Bill.

Priti laughed. "You are a very quick learner, Bill Johnson."

"One last question," he pleaded. "To be a Hindu, does one have to be 'born' into it or 'baptized'?"

"Of course one can be born into it, *or* baptized, er...I mean initiated into it. There is, however, a much better way. Just practise the universal principles on your own wherever you are, without any intermediaries or approvers, you being in full control of the relationship with the Divine, which is empowering and enriching. Also, whenever you want, you can leave Hinduism, without anyone trying to hurt you. Hope I was of some help to you?" Priti smiled.

"A big thanks to you. You have no idea what your kind words of wisdom have done to my mind and heart. I relished every word of it and it makes me feel on top of the world. I will always remember you as my first teacher, or *guru* as you would say, for giving me this basic knowledge." Bill put his hand on his heart.

"You are most welcome," acknowledged Priti. "Just one more thing. One needs to walk the talk to derive the true benefits. I am trying my best." She smiled.

"Yep." Bill nodded.

Several hours later, they were interrupted by the captain's voice with instructions regarding the flight's descent and eventual landing in Delhi.

"What is your plan when we arrive in Delhi?" she asked, "Are you going to visit some particular *yoga ashram* straight away? Do you have some address already?"

Bill smiled and replied, "I'm planning to visit the Himalayan region. At Dharmasala, I'm going to stay for a few days with the Lamas and if I'm lucky, meet the Dalai Lama. Then I'll go to Rishikesh, to the Shivananda Ashram. Then...I don't know. I'll see from there."

"Cool. I am staying in Delhi for some time. The marriage will be celebrated there, because almost all my relatives from Father's side live there or can come there easily. Will you be able to attend, if that is not too much to ask?"

Bill was initially surprised, but soon he understood her generosity and smiled. "Sure! I'll be happy to come. I've never seen an Indian marriage, and I have a feeling that this one will be very special." He pulled out a piece of paper and a pen from his carry-on bag and wrote down his email address for Priti.

"Okay, I will send you the details. You must come; you will have a good time. Also, if you need any help in Delhi, let my uncle know." She handed him a hotel business card bearing the name of her uncle. He took the card, amazed by Priti's kindness and active support. His journey to India had certainly begun under the most encouraging and auspicious circumstances. Bill decided to try the hotel Priti's uncle worked for.

* * * *

The Treasure of the Pandavas

The taxi ride from the airport was Bill's first impression of India, and it absorbed all his attention. When he reached the hotel, he found Priti's uncle, waiting for him. Her uncle said he had been alerted by a text message from Priti. Again, Bill was touched and surprised by her prompt behaviour. They went into the reception lounge, and a waiter brought over cups of Indian tea. They had a very pleasant talk, and Bill felt like he'd known the man for years, instead of only an hour. As Bill sipped the sweet, milky liquid, he learned that Delhi's ancient name was Indraprastha and that it was ruled over by the famous Pandavas of the Kuru dynasty.

Priti's uncle explained that after the Kurukshetra War, some 5000 years earlier, the victorious and legendary Pandava kings had reorganized the capital and the entire kingdom, ensuring its prosperity for many centuries to come. Then, around 1200 CE, the region had fallen under the control of the invading Muslim hordes and become a Sultanate for 500 years, then a colony of the Imperial British Empire for about 200 years. Finally, Delhi became the capital of the new nation when India obtained its independence on the 15th of August, 1947.

He also told Bill there was much to see in Delhi, including the famous Red Fort, the Mahatma Gandhi Samadhi, or tomb, the Parliament house, the India Gate and the Presidential palace. Regarding religion and spirituality, there were a few famous temples and mosques, but no notable *yoga ashrams* as they were generally located in the quiet countryside.

Bill remembered that Priti had mentioned Mathura and Vrindavana, and said he might need assistance to visit them. Her uncle smiled and explained they were a relatively short taxi ride from Delhi.

"Great, I'd be very interested in visiting both those places; they're on the top of my list. I need to say hello to Krishna." He smiled.

The uncle talked to the hotel travel desk and arranged the tour. While saying goodbye, he assured Bill he was available for any other help Bill might need.

The next morning, upon reaching Vrindavana, Bill visited many places of interest as outlined in the guide map. At the end of the tour, when he went to a sacred lake called Kusuma Sarovara, on its banks he met a Caucasian man, clad in a *dhoti* and *kurta*—the traditional Indian male dress of a wrapped cloth from the waist down and a tunic-like upper shirt—who was collecting some water. The middle-aged man of Greek origin introduced himself as Radhapati, or Rasmus Papandreou, and said he had been worshiping Krishna in Vrindavana for many years. Radhapati was his Sanskrit name. This triggered an unsual level of interest in Bill's mind.

Radhapati greeted him with *"Har-ee Krishna!"* instead of the usual *"Nom-a-stay"* which generally accompanied the folded-hands movement. Bill replied, *"Nom-a-stay!"*—spelled *"Namaste"*—the greeting he had learned from his online buddies.

"Very interesting!" Bill exclaimed. "I want to know more about your life, and how you came in contact with Krishna, and Hinduism. What does all this mean for you? Can you tell me everything?" Bill pleaded in earnestness.

Radhapati's face lit up in a big smile and he nodded in agreement.

Bill spent the next two weeks in Vrindavana. He was amazed at how much he learned during his full-immersion experience and was astounded when Radhapati said that around 113 BCE, Heliodorus, the Greek Ambassador for India, along with his followers, publically accepted Vaishnavism, a spiritual path within Hinduism, and erected the Heliodorus pillar in current day Bihar State as proof of their commitment to Hindu *Dharma* and the path of *yoga*.

They also visited the small dungeon in Mathura, where Lord Krishna was said to have appeared 5,000 years earlier. Bill learned the beautiful temple that once stood around it had been destroyed by invading Muslims, who had converted it into the mosque that still stands on the site; it reminded him of the Hagia Sophia church in Constantinople and the Temple Mount in Jerusalem. Both were similarly converted into mosques. Bill returned to the hotel that night, exhausted, but happier than he had been in many years. He was learning history, culture and religion all in one go.

He decided to proceed to his original schedule and explore the *yoga* and Buddhist traditions. Radhapati helped him get a train to Dharmasala, and Bill promised he would keep in touch and return to visit him whenever possible.

* * * *

Bill stepped up into the long distance train. It had air-conditoned compartments, where people could sit and sleep as needed. It was full of people with some little kids running around. The air inside was fresh and fragrant. He checked for his seat number only to discover three foreigners, like himself, already there in the compartment. The relative silence within the train was almost a relief from the cacophony outside on the station platform. A tall, attractive, dark-haired woman, who was maybe in her late twenties, stood and offered him a somewhat calloused hand.

"Hi, I'm Laura."

He noticed she was wearing loose-fitting, white cotton, draw-string pants that he had seen others wear in *yoga* classes, sturdy boots, and a T shirt with an Ohm sign on it in rainbow colours. Her even taller and very muscular, similarly-dressed friends introduced themselves as Nick and Bruce. At that point, Bill took a chance and asked, "Are you guys heading to Dharmasala?"

"Good guess, we're going to there for a vacation at the Tushita Meditation Centre, where we'll be taking a course on Buddhism and Tibetan culture." Laura smiled.

"Great! It's a real blessing to meet you guys. You don't mind if we travel together, do you, this is my first time here?"

"You're certainly most welcome," Nick answered.

During the discussion that ensued, he learned they were members of the Australian Rugby team, spending their vacation to discover the world of *yoga*. Bill was beginning to feel like he'd come home after being lost for many years.

Chapter 5 - The Dharma Warrior

He was hiding in the bushes. It was night and he was afraid. He heard voices, angry voices, of people he didn't know. They were wicked people, and he was very frightened. He didn't dare to cry out, or even move, because they were certainly looking for him with an evil intent. *Mother!* He silently cried out. *Father! Where are you?* He was afraid to know. He couldn't hear their beloved voices. They were gone. He was alone and in danger.

Time seemed to stretch into an infinite stillness. *I am dreaming*, he told himself. *No,* the little voice inside him whined, *this is no dream. They hate you. They want to hurt you.*

Then, as if triggered by these semi-conscious thoughts, the scene started to move again. The voices came nearer, and he saw the lights of the torches oscillating in the trees and on the ground of the forest. *I can't just stand here, I need to run away!* He immediately found himself sprinting through the low vegetation, away from his pursuers. But they heard the leaves rustle under his small feet—*yes,* he thought, surprised, *my feet are indeed very small*—and the voices started to shout, one on top of the other, echoing into the night. He could hear them running after him. Crying desperately, he tried to run faster, as fast as possible, faster than possible.... Then two strong arms caught him.

Jai Bharat woke up with a start, his heart racing, his body slick with cold sweat, his mind still active within the fading dream.

It took him a few seconds to realize where he was, to feel the firmness of his bed beneath his body and hear the heavy breathing of the other boys sleeping in the room. He found the dimly lit florescent digital clock in the far corner. It was 2:00 a.m.

He breathed a deep sigh of relief. It was only a nightmare; one of his recurring bad dreams.

With another deep breath, he lay back down, grateful for the softness of the mattress. He shivered as the sweat began to dry on his body, and pulled the blanket up, wrapping himself tightly, as if in a cocoon.

The terror of the dream had vanished, but as always, the pain remained. Jai hardly remembered his real parents, but he was haunted by his anguished dream of the night he lost them. The conscious memories of his childhood were rather confused. His most vivid ones were tied to this place, where he now slept, the house of Nanda and Yashoda Agarwal. The people of Pune, where the house was located, often called it the Jijabai Orphanage, as it was a registered charity, but to Jai it had always seemed more like the home of a big family; a place of happiness, affection and nurturing. He had come here at the age of seven, growing up with a small group of other boys and girls of various ages. Despite the fact these children came from vastly different parts of the country, they shared a common bond, rooted in terror and tragedy.

Nanda Agarwal originally hailed from the state of Rajasthan and was from a wealthy family who owned real estate properties, rental apartments and small houses in various areas of Mumbai. Within two years of an otherwise happy marriage, Nanda and his wife, Yashoda, learned they could not have children. After a brief period of depression, the Agarwals decided to welcome orphaned children and foundlings, and turn their misfortune into a greater good.

Now, as Jai's eyes slowly grew accustomed to the dim light, he forced out the dream from his mind by looking around the room at the indistinct shapes of his sleeping brothers.

Lying only a few feet from him, lay his friend Avinash, covered in a blanket from head to foot. Jai still remembered how, when he had arrived at the Agarwals' house, lost and scared, Avinash would stay with him, sitting on his bed until he fell asleep. By that time, handsome Avinash Kapoor, had already been living with the Agarwals for four years. He had quickly become the self-appointed welcoming party of the house, providing support and affection to the new children; there was no dearth of warmth in him.

On the mattress next to Avinash lay Tejinder Singh Walia of Delhi, who had joined the Agarwal's household the same year as Avinash. Tej slept silently and still, but Jai knew he could instantly wake up and jump to his feet, at the slightest unusual sound or movement. Quiet and extremely proud, even as a small child, Tej was known for his bravery.

Jai's reminiscing was interrupted by a sudden loud snore from across the room. He smiled. In their early days as cadets, nobody in the dormitory had wanted to sleep next to Ganesh Rao Ambedkar; he had been known for his loud snoring ever since he had come to the Agarwals' from Mumbai. But Ganesh didn't care. He would laugh and tell the others they should work harder during the daytime, so that at night they would be too tired, and sleep too deeply, to hear any noise. He was famous for speaking the truth without any reservations.

Jai chuckled softly, as from another mattress Vikram moaned in his sleep. Intelligent Vikram Goud was from the state of Andhra Pradesh. A tactful soft-spoken boy, with a dark complexion and beady, black eyes that never missed a detail, he had joined the Agarwal clan at the age of five. He was the most intelligent of all.

Next to Vikram slept Ranil Bandaranaike, from from Galle, Sri Lanka. The two had often been mistaken for real brothers—even twins— because of their dark complexions and identical body types. They also wore similar clothes when they were not required to wear the cadet uniform at school or at the Military academy. Ranil was magnanimous in whatever he did.

In the far corner of the hall slept two other closest friends, Satish Nair and Lachit Phukan. Originally from Assam, Lachit had been the first child welcomed by the Agarwals, when he was only eleven months old. Near Satish and Lachit slept Mahendra Thapa, the youngest of their group. He was from Katmandu, Nepal. Satish was from the state of Kerala and known for his renounced attitude toward life. Lachit was known for nimbler skills with gadgets and Mahendra for humor. Each had a dominant trait, which made life fun for the brothers.

There were also two girls, Nila Razdan and Lilavati Mondal, sleeping in an adjacent room. Nila and Lilavati had also been chosen to be members of the Vajra Team; they all trained together. Jai had heard their stories. They had certainly suffered a lot, even more than the boys, although the boys certainly had their share of trouble. The two girls had thrived at the Agarwals', but it had taken a lot of time, patience and care. Nila was from Kashmir and known for her environmental consciousness and living a healthy lifestyle, whereas Lilavati, who was from Bangladesh, was known for her intelligence and analytical power.

Jai yawned, feeling more relaxed now, as if the dream had never happened. He was no longer that terrified child, running through the forest from those who had tried to kill him. He was part of the Vajra—a special action team defending his country. He felt a surge of positive pride, a deep thrill that made him feel invigorated, and a sense of purpose for his life. All the boys and girls had been given a four-week break; that's why they were all together again in this big and wonderful house. He smiled in the dark. But things hadn't always been so easy. When he had first gone to a nearby private school to learn and study, he did very well in sports and academics and most times stood first in class. Some of the other boys, probably out of jealousy, would taunt him, so as to demoralize him, by saying he was an orphan and didn't know who his mother and father were, as if that was a sin. This really hurt Jai.

* * * *

One day, Mother Yashoda found him crying. When he told her what was wrong, she took him aside and recounted a story he would never forget.

His tears forgotten, little Jai had listened with wide eyes as Mother Yashoda described Satyavati Jatav, a beautiful little Dalit girl who had to walk with crutches after contracting polio. The doctors failed to immunize the Dalit

127

population in time, despite full government support. Satyavati was born in the village of Rampur. She lived there with her widowed mother, Dayavati, after her father, a police constable, was killed fighting left-wing extremists in the thick jungles of Chhattisgarh state.

Mother Yashoda continued her tale. "Satyavati had received the nickname Choti Jhansi, or "little Jhansi," because of her passion for defending truth and justice. Her mother had often told her the story of Jhansi Rani, the brave queen who fought against the Imperial British to protect her homeland. Jhansi knew much about struggles from her personal fight against polio, to her own birth in the low caste of sweepers, which taught her a lot about the difficulties of the Dalits—the 'downtrodden' people. Since early childhood, she always tried to help the disadvantaged fight for basic human rights, without avoiding their responsibilities and duties.

"From childhood, religion was an important part of little Jhansi's life. Her mother used to volunteer her for menial service at the temple as an act of devotion, and Jhansi loved to sing *bhajans* there; she found great inspiration in Meera Bai, the legendary Rajput princess devoted to Lord Krishna. Jhansi's beautiful voice and contagious devotion won over the villagers, who welcomed her, above the protests

The Treasure of the Pandavas

of a few casteists who strongly opposed the Dalits' right to be admitted into temples.

"It was in the village temple that Jhansi met young Ramakanth Sharma, also called Bhola, or 'innocent', because of his simple nature. Bhola treated everyone with equal kindness and respect, despite the fact that his father was the main priest and held in great regard and well respected by the villagers. When people reminded him of his high social stature, he only laughed and repeated the relevant verses of the *Bhagavad gita, Bhagavatam,* and other scriptures he had heard from his father, which spoke about equality of all human beings without any birth prejudice. His classical refutation of the caste system incensed the few casteists, those who considered themselves superior due to their so-called birthright. The casteists clearly knew that no Hindu scripture promoted discrimination of any kind; the verses spoke for themselves, teaching the lofty principles of life. Since they could not change the words, they decided to twist the original meanings to suit their nefarious plans, namely, to control the villagers through perverted practices and information. This way, they could maximize material gains and enjoy life without breaking into a sweat.

"Old Raghunath Sharma had been thrilled when his wife, Mandakini, a woman of relatively advanced years, blessed him with a son after a long struggle. Young Bhola was his father's life and soul. The boy had always been vivacious, sincere and affectionate. Some people said he was not very intelligent and had low self-esteem, but his father knew Bhola was just straight forward and had a very deep faith in both the letter and spirit of the scriptures. Bhola was also deeply interested in the worship of the Deities of Sita Rama, Lakshman and Hanuman; in fact, his name Ramkanth was derived from the presiding Deity of the temple, Lord Rama.

"During temple festivals, Bhola loved to dance in the temple room, for the pleasure of the Deities, his parents, and the other devotees in attendance. And although he had no formal training, he become an expert in his own version of Indian classical dance, and was able to express and mimic the sacred stories of Rama, Krishna and other *avatars*, moving gracefully in tune with the popular folk songs that described them. It was a God-given talent which no one else in their community possessed.

"Bhola was much beloved, so everyone had been horrified when, at age twelve, while running in the village, he slipped on a mossy stone and hit his head, hard. He lost consciousness for several hours, and when he finally awoke, had problems seeing clearly. He had become partially blind in both eyes. To his shock, he entered a new, hazy world. The doctors told his parents the optic nerve had been seriously damaged by the trauma, reducing his sight by sixty percent and there was nothing that could be done to rectify it. In spite of this tragedy, Bhola remained peaceful and brave, often consoling his parents, and patiently navigating his way around this new, partially-dark world, performing his chores so naturally, people rarely noticed his handicap unless they watched him very closely. Bhola even continued to dance in the temple, skillfully and intelligently measuring his steps within the space enclosed by the pillars which supported the roof. He was an extraordinary person.

"Jhansi, who also struggled with a serious handicap, without ever giving up hope and hard work, had watched the amazingly brave, graceful and intelligent Brahmin boy with growing admiration. When she realized that despite the difference in their caste, he was quite willing to socialize with her, they became fast friends. Of course, this caused a great scandal among the few casteists in the village, but the opposition of their bigoted and insensitive neighbors only succeeded in bringing them closer together, as they both believed behavior, personal qualities, knowledge and wisdom are the real measure of a person's nobility and not caste, race, color or class. They clearly saw the casteists as very ignorant and degraded people who were totally devoid of spiritual knowledge and consciousness.

"Old Raghunath, Bhola's father, loved watching the two youngsters sitting and talking together about the *Bhagavad gita* and *Bhagavata Purana*, but his heart was also full of pain, because he knew that ignorance and prejudice, rather than wisdom and compassion, often have a greater appeal to the emotions of un-evolved people. Those two beautiful souls were destined to suffer a very harsh awakening to a brutal and cruel reality.

"But Bhola and Jhansi only grew closer as time went on, and Raghunath was not surprised when the friendship between the two young artists blossomed into a pure and radiant love. When the time had come, he and his son went to the home of Jhansi's mother for private talks, and a few days later, a simple, secret ceremony was performed at a dilapidated temple in the dense jungle of Madhav National Park. Jhansi and Bhola built themselves a modest hut and lived there, collecting fruits, roots and leaves. Their parents visited often, bringing gifts of food and other supplies.

"A year later, their happiness was blessed with a healthy and strong son, who was born in the forest hermitage, just like the famous Emperor Bharata. Thus, his ecstatic parents named him Jai Bharat. The baby was adored by his parents and grandparents, who kept their visits a secret from the villagers back home.

"When Jai was four years old, the issue of Bhola and Jhansi's mysterious disappearance came up for discussion in the village council. An old lady who had no sons—and therefore no daughters-in-law to harass—pointed out that in spite of the general belief that Bhola and Jhansi had been killed in the forest by a bloodthirsty tiger, their parents did not seem to be sufficiently aggrieved; rather, whenever the topic came up, Bhola's mother was given to smiling, as if she were actually happy about something.

"Besides that, the nosey old woman had observed a scandalously close friendship between Bhola's parents and Jhansi's widowed mother, who seemed to be on very good terms with each other, in spite of the fact that the Sharmas were from the Brahmin high caste community, while the Jatavs were of the low caste Dalit community. The woman had also received information that Raghunath visited the old dilapidated temple in the forest very often. Thus, she suspected the two youngsters had not died at all, but had eloped together with the permission of their families, in defiance of the established social norms and the judgment of the village council. The old woman's husband, an arrogant casteist who had many times tried to stop Jhansi from attending the temple functions, reported his wife's clever deductions and openly accused Raghunath of having betrayed his caste.

Bhola's father, suitably offended, denied any wrongdoing and immediately left the assembly. In truth, he was very worried about his son's young family, and anxious to save them from the self-righteous and cruel mob who would soon be hunting them. He was sure the old lady had investigated the matter further and may have already guessed Bhola and his wife were living in the forest. She may even have known about Jai's birth. Raghunath knew there was no time to waste.

"After leaving the meeting, the old man hurried to his own house. He made sure nobody was around and quickly disguised himself in a large shawl and set out for the woods to alert his son. But it was already late in the day, and getting dark. As he was walking in the jungle, he heard other people shouting and marching; what's worse, he saw the lights of the torches, and his fears worsened.

"When he reached the small wooden hut, Bhola's father found only Jhansi inside; Bhola had gone out with the child to fetch water from the nearby pond. She immediately grabbed her crutches and hobbled out with Raghunath toward the pond, but the mob was too fast for them. Raghunath told her to hide, but the girl looked at him with desperate yet resolute eyes; they both knew very well she had no hope of escaping in time. Raghunath's eyes filled with tears, but he turned his back to the young woman—as his priority was to save the child, Jai—well-aware that his daughter-in-law was in imminent danger of being tortured or even killed. They had all heard the stories of casteist violence in nearby villages, and knew what was coming. She prayed that Jai would be saved by her father-in-law, and knew he had come, for that reason alone, at this late hour.

"Bhola was at the pond when he heard the noise of the mob approaching. He heard his father's hurried steps and immediately recognized him through his hazy vision. He hid the small boy inside a thicket of bushes and walked toward his father. 'Where is Jhansi?' he asked.

"His father's eyes were filled with tears. 'She is on her way,' he choked, his throat constricted. 'She cannot run nor does she want to hide, knowing you and Jai are in danger.'

"Bhola paused only long enough to hug his father. 'Take care of little Bharat,' he said, then quickly walked away, back toward his hut to be with his beloved wife. He found her before the mob arrived, but only because the bloodthirsty villagers had wasted time torching the small cottage and destroying the fenced kitchen garden. 'Oh my beloved husband!' she called out, not surprised to see him.

"'My dear love,' said Bhola, lifting his wife from the ground and carrying her toward another area along the bank of the pond, far from the place where he had left his father and young son. 'Jaya Sri Ram!' he shouted glorifying Lord Rama's name, before entering the pond with his wife in his arms. The mob heard him and many shouted in their bloodlust, rushing after him on the old forest path. The pond was deep and cool, and his wife's body became lighter to carry once in the water, but she was still clinging to his neck as he held her close to his heart. Deeper and deeper, Bhola waded into the cold, dark waters, but he needed no light beyond the radiant love that was in his heart. When his feet lost contact with the bottom of the pond, he and Jhansi kissed one last time; then, embracing one another, they sank beneath the surface, holding each other down until all memories and consciousness faded away."

Jai recalled what had happened next. The strong arms which lifted the child had been his grandfather's. Raghunath Sharma had found him and calmed him down, keeping him quiet. At that point, they were protected by the darkness of night, and nobody was looking for him or his grandfather. And, luckily by God's grace, his birth had not been discovered yet.

Mother Yashoda continued. "Raghunath watched his son from a distance, in the light of the torches carried by the furious casteists, and prayed for those two beautiful souls to find happiness and peace in the next life. He waited for the villagers to vent their anger by throwing stones into the pond, as no one among them was interested in risking their own life to recover two dead bodies. An eerie silence descended upon the forest. Back in their home, his wife was terrified by several villagers who stormed it to ask where he was. Somehow she convinced them that Raghunath Sharma was feeling very offended and angry when he had returned home. He said he was leaving the village for few days and had walked out without saying where he was going. When they told her the two youngsters had not died but eloped, she had the good sense to say that if they had, then her son really was dead to her, as he had disgraced his family and ancestors.

"Then someone remembered Jhansi's mother, Dayavati, and the small group left the house. Mandakini sat on the floor of her modest home, shaking and crying. She covered her ears when she heard the mob's shouting and Dayavati's wails of terror. Finally, silence fell on the village once again. A strong smell of smoke wafted in from the open door, and she saw the red glow from Dayavati's torched house. Paralyzed with fear and exhaustion, she could only lie on the floor and cry herself to sleep. Meanwhile, Raghunath Sharma took the boy to Gwalior which was more than a hundred kilometres north of his village.

"The horrible night had passed. Raghunath returned a few days later, very tired but peaceful. He told his wife he had hidden their grandson Jai Bharat in the town of Gwalior. The matter was laid to rest.

"Bhola's parents increasingly dissociated themselves from the rest of the village, and the local people stopped supporting his temple. One winter night, they both quietly died in their sleep."

* * * *

Jai had filled in the gaps in the story of his childhood, when on his sixteenth birthday, he traveled along with Colonel Kartikeyan Vanniyar, or Karry, as Jai called him, his mentor at Vajra, an elite counter-terrorism squad, to the small hamlet of Rampur and the abandoned temple of Sita Rama, Lakshmana and Hanuman, where his paternal grandfather had once lived and worshiped. They also visited the thick jungle nearby where his parents shared their brief but profound happiness together. Facing all these facts stirred anger in Jai, and he desired revenge on the culprits. It was human nature. Karry, understanding the situation, calmed him down and suggested that he convert his anger to love, through *yoga* meditation, and serve the country, perhaps helping to create a future where no one else would have to face situations like Jai. That would be the best tribute he could give to his parents and a thumbs down to the casteists. Finally Jai relented and promised himself to change society for the better.

The few people who still remained in the small village stared suspiciously at the two men. Yet the villagers had not insisted on questioning the two, upon hearing the young man was a student doing research in the rural villages around Gwalior, on the subject of forest cultivation. As time passes, people change; old prejudices reduce or die down. The village had surely changed. Jai returned to Pune with a heavy heart, but with a strange sense of peace, as well. After the trip, he concentrated even harder on his studies and training, favorably impressing all his teachers, especially Karry.

* * * *

Colonel Karry met Jai Bharat face to face, in a dramatic way, when he was fourteen years old.

On that Sunday, Karry was visiting his wife's relatives in Pune. In the late afternoon, beyond the vast stretches of the green rice fields, and the sparse rural homes dotting the fertile landscape, Karry and Manpreet, his wife, had spotted some commotion near a small village. A large crowd had gathered in which at least two or three people seemed to be very agitated. Karry stopped the car and went to see what was happening, while Manpreet, who was in her early months of pregnancy, preferred to stay put inside the vehicle. A five-year-old child had fallen into an old, open-bore well while playing, and his father and some other villagers were frantically trying to get him out. A young woman, apparently the child's mother, was sobbing in the arms of a sympathetic neighbor.

The child's father was pushing a long cloth into the well and shouting to his son to grab it, as some other villagers came running with a bundle of ropes.

Unfortunately, when the rope was tied together and lowered into the well, the child was too terrified and confused to understand what he was supposed to do with it. Yelling in frustration and anxiety, the father tried to push the rope further down, but the child just kept crying. Edging nearer to the well, Karry looked inside. The hole was not even two feet wide, but seemed to go rather deep, probably about fifty feet. The child was stuck at around thirty feet down, too far to be reached by the anxious hands of his father. Karry saw the child had bent his legs and that position had kept him from falling deeper into the well, but probably not for long. At any moment, he could lose his weak grip on the mossy lining of the walls and slip down to his death into the dark water below him, or the soil could cave in and bury him.

At the same time, Jai Bharat had been jogging among the rice fields on the outskirts of town when he, too, noticed the lone, stationary vehicle and gathering of people.

The teenager came closer and assessing the situation, took action immediately. Leaning over the opening, he reached out for the rope that was hopelessly dangling into the well. He then pulled it up and tied it tightly around his own waist, all the while quickly explaining his idea to the villagers in the Marathi language. With renewed hope, the child's father and friends moved a few feet away and grabbed a good length of rope at the other end, while the teenager slipped into the well, head first. His slim body was sweaty from his long run, and slid into the small opening with relative ease. After a very long, anxious time of carefully inching down the tube, Jai grabbed the child around the middle and shouted to the people outside to pull them out. Many more hands grabbed the rope, and in a matter of seconds the crying child was out in the open, covered in dirt and slime, terrified and shocked, but safe and sound and ready for his mother's comforting arms.

Karry watched the teenager extract himself from the rope and clean up a bit—helped by the villagers who brought him water to wash. He heard Jai explaining to the villagers to keep the tube well-covered at all times, to prevent any similar events in the future.

Karry wanted to know more about this brave and intelligent young man, who displayed great leadership and heroism.

"Very good job there, my boy," he started, "I am Colonel Kartikeyan Vanniyar, originally from Chidambaram now living in Mumbai."

Jai had greeted Karry respectfully with folded hands. "My name is Jai Bharat, sir. I live in Pune, with the family of Mother Yashoda and Father Nanda Agarwal, in Shivaji Chowk."

"Yes, I thought I recognized you, but you have grown tall since last I saw you. You may remember I've visited there a few times. I've been their friend for quite a few years. You're doing very well, young man."

Jai seemed extremely pleased. "Thank you, sir."

"If you don't mind, can I drive you back to Pune? I'm on my way there and would be happy to visit the Agarwals along with you."

"Certainly, sir, it will be my honor," said Jai with a slight bow.

Shivaji Chowk was a roundabout square in the Vitalvadi neighborhood, and the Agarwals' house was on a corner by a side road. The sign near the gate read "Jijabai House," without any mention of it being an orphanage or children's shelter.

When they got out of the car and walked along the access path, Karry clearly heard the sound of sacred mantras coming from a large house on the other side of a neatly kept, open park filled with swings, slides and other playground structures. There were few large trees, but many smaller plants and flower beds, as well as a sizeable kitchen garden on one side and a small cow shed near the boundary wall. Karry recalled the last time he had visited the place, several years earlier, when he had come to check on how young Tej was doing. Tej was related to his wife's family. Walking into the large entrance hall, Karry removed his shoes and looked around, noting the seriousness and dignity of the boys and girls of various ages. They were sitting in rows, chanting mantras together loudly, under the expert guidance of Mother Yashoda.

Jai bowed down to the small altar on the opposite wall. Karry and Manpreet also offered their homage. Karry noticed that the shrine and large library hadn't been there the last time he visited, and he was rather pleased with the progress of the Agarwals' dedicated work.

He looked around the nice hall and happily observed pictures of the various forms of God and the portraits of Indian national heroes from different historical periods.

After the evening recitation of mantras and the religious worship ritual of *arati,* performed by Nanda, the guests sat with the Agarwals and the children. Jai Bharat had seemed a little embarrassed, but very happy, listening to the high words of praise the Colonel spoke about him as he recounted Jai's heroic rescue of the child and his leadership qualities. As he spoke,

Yashoda and Nanda nodded, their eyes brimming with tears of pride.

Nanda said, "Our lives have become successful because we have been able to raise such amazing children. We have been practising what our parents and Guru taught us, and I feel we have this duty to the future of our country and to the entire human race."

Upon inquiring, Karry was pleasantly surprised to learn the Agarwals were also disciples of Gokarnath Swami, his own beloved Guru, and this discovery opened even more avenues for discussion of spiritual topics and the extraordinary qualities and teachings of the Swami.

Inspired, the next day Karry returned for breakfast, and after the meal had a long talk with Nanda and Yashoda. From that day on, he kept a closer eye on all the children of the orphanage, especially Jai, sending as much financial aid as he could contribute personally and also collecting more from among his relatives, colleagues and friends.

When he spoke about the Agarwals, his heart felt warm. To those who asked him if it was an orphanage, Karry would reply, "Many people have mixed feelings about ordinary orphanages, because they're usually run for the sake of making money. But the Agarwals are totally different. They treat the children exactly as their own, so no one thinks they're not their real parents. In fact, they're a great example to be followed by everyone in the education and training of children, because they don't merely feed, house and clothe the kids, they constantly shower them with love, affection, attention, support and encouragement, inspiring them with excellent values and the true spirit of *Dharma*."

He started to spend more and more of his vacations and even weekends in Pune—as it was a relatively short distance away from Mumbai—grooming Jai and the other Agarwal children, even after Manpreet gave birth to their own twins; such was his dedication. He actively helped the boys to be admitted into the prestigious National Defense Academy in Khadakwasala, with its grueling, four-year military course, which most Indian Military officers take, and then into the Indian Military College, in Dehradun.

Karry regularly kept in touch with them through email, sending links to interesting websites and introducing the boys and girls to a totally new world. Karry had always been there to help them put things into the proper perspective, always in a proactive and progressive way, and inquiring about their results at school and the other aspects of their lives. He truly became their mentor.

He also continued to visit Pune, and their meetings became more and more meaningful. They discussed politics, history, religion, morality and duty, and many of the things they talked about challenged the notions they had learned in school, but in an intelligent and positive way. There was always a convincing answer to all questions.

Jai Bharat was the most inquisitive and inspired among them, and as the years passed, the other Agarwal boys came to consider him as their leader. He was serious, responsible and reflective, and he always looked out for his 'brothers'.

* * * *

On an important festival day, Colonel Karry explained how their Motherland needed brave, intelligent and strong young people like themselves. He directly asked if they were willing to work with him full time in the future, explaining his plan and requesting it be kept secret. Everyone agreed enthusiastically, clapping and cheering, and then remained with rapt attention and in perfect silence while their mentor detailed the strategy for their further training.

"Now that you have completed the four years of the NDA successfully, it's time to get immediately enrolled at IMA, the Indian Military Academy; but you will not complete the course, and you will not become commissioned officers," Colonel Karry said categorically. He paused for a moment to let the strange idea sink in. In fact, everyone seemed confused.

"Your first few months at the IMA will be crucial for your training and education, and will also give you a chance to observe the dynamics of the army and the people involved in it. You are all very intelligent and so it shouldn't take a long time." He smiled. "IMA also has a Special Forces course, and I want you to get all you can from it."

"I know for sure the IMA has to relieve you as they cannot force students to be commissioned and sent into war unwillingly. However, we need to pay them money for the training you will go through, plus the penalty amount, which I will cover from my own funds; also I have contacts in the defense ministry who will ease the process without anyone knowing. Once commissioned, you will not be able to leave the military easily. All this is fair, as you will still be engaged in the security of the nation, but in an indirect fashion." Karry had inside information and knew very well, that there were very few legitimate grounds by which one could leave the military, without any hassle. Every year, a few cadets did leave and it was not entirely unknown to the authorities.

Karry gave them sufficient time to absorb the idea. Some looked very excited. Some looked like they were deeply reflecting the implications of the plan. He knew they all had faith in him and would do exactly what he wanted them to, because he was their mentor and teacher. The plan also had the Agarwals' full support.

Karry leaned back on the cushion by the wall and smiled.

For the rest of that memorable day, he remained with them, 'the grown up kids', on the large, sheltered terrace, atop the Agarwals' house, and replied to their many queries. He informed them about the 'Valley', a super-secret facility near Raigad in the Sahyadri Hills range, in Maharashtra state. He had been developing a program to train a special counter-terrorism team to defend the security of the nation. The Valley was fully self-sufficient and a beautiful place to live, tucked away between steep hills and protected by a thick cover of forests. They would most likely be required to travel around the world, and be reasonably paid for their missions, as any other government employees would be; they simply would not be part of the formal government structure. Basically, they would be non-state heroes of India, taking on non-state villains of enemy countries.

* * * *

Jai drifted back to the present. *Now our training is complete and it will soon be time for the real action.* In the meantime, he wanted to spend some quality time with his big family. After a while, he drifted off into a contented sleep.

Chapter 6 - The Eggs of The Scorpion

A pleasant breeze blew in from the sea. It was 6:00 a.m., Tuesday morning, the first day of March. People were walking and jogging; all enjoying the cool, early morning breeze. And among them, Colonel Karry was halfway through his morning run along Marine Drive. After a good five kilometers, at Nariman Point, he slowed down and finally sat on the roadside bench provided by the local municipality. He gradually quieted his breathing and slowly relaxed, listening to the chirping of birds flying overhead.

The beach width was narrow, but went for a long stretch. Passersby of all sorts strolled along—elderly and young alike; couples, hand in hand. In the distance, Karry could see various ships anchored out to sea, waiting to be harbored in the port. As India's financial hub, Mumbai was a center for trade, most of which passed through these shipping lanes. His normal twenty-minute break was coming to an end; soon he would be running back to his house on Siri Road near Chowpatty. With a sigh, Karry stood up, stretched his arms over his head, and began jogging back along the same track.

149

A half hour later, he entered his top floor penthouse. The building—called the Gopinath Complex, and named after the nearby and famous Sri Sri Radha Gopinath temple—was new, but it already felt like home. As soon as he opened the door, he smiled at the sound of his wife, Manpreet, in the kitchen, talking to their two young sons as she prepared their breakfast and got them ready for school. The twins, Aditya and Bhaskar, were very intelligent and disciplined, and they had a very clear understanding of the boundaries in which they could act up, be a little naughty, and have their childish fun. They also knew not to disturb their father during his own morning ritual. If things worked out, both of them would be part of the Vajra team sometime in the future.

After a quick shower, Karry sat down in his favorite armchair to read the newspaper, the *Mumbai Real Times*. As part of his daily drill he first opened to page eighteen, the ad section. His eye was caught by a small advertisement: "Sanskrit coaching classes. Last few seats available. Call Garuda as soon as possible at the Taradeo Institute for Sanskrit studies in Mumbai."

It gave a phone number, which Karry dismissed as irrelevant window-dressing to make the ad look authentic. For there was no Taradeo Institute for Sanskrit studies in Mumbai; the "Institute" was the Indian Federal

The Treasure of the Pandavas

Agency, the country's first integrated central intelligence agency, and "Garuda" was the code name for its head, Balaram Singh Yadav, and Sanskrit was Karry's code name. The IFA dealt with both internal and external espionage, with a special focus on countering contemporary terrorism. Karry had worked with the IFA for some time, but eventually left in disappointment. Excessive bureaucracy and political interference had seriously hindered its effectiveness. On several occasions, missions had been compromised, leading to the loss of lives, agents, resources and objectives. IFA was full of moles placed by hostile foreign agencies, as well as domestic enemies.

Balaram and Karry had become close friends over the years Balaram certainly understood Karry's frustration, so when Karry talked of leaving, Balaram suggested the creation of a private agency, Security of the Nation, which they affectionately called "SON." Such an agency could engage good and capable officers like Karry with greater chances of safety and success for the benefit of the Nation. Terrorists waged asymmetrical warfare, so they were India's asymmetrical warriors targeting the terrorists and neutralizing them.

The more patient and less rebellious of the two, Balaram had remained with the official agency, always very careful to tow the government line. He made the necessary adjustments and kept his mouth shut. He was optimistic, knowing that soon there would be better and safer methods to take care of things, especially for those difficult and tricky tasks. Karry was presently in hibernation without an assignment and enjoying a restful interlude. Being old-school boys, this was the standard, agreed upon method of contact.

Karry re-read the message carefully. It meant that in the "last few" days something important had come up and he needed to "call immediately." He looked at his watch, relieved that it was only 8:30; there was still plenty of time. He stood up from the chair, folded the newspaper and tucked it under his arm. It was a primitive way to contact him, but it was the safest and most reliable.

Manpreet Singh Bedi was a beautiful woman in her early forties. The daughter of an eminent military general, she was accustomed to the rewards and sacrifices of military life. When she was young, she met a handsome young officer under her father's command. The meeting led to romance, and she and Karry were married two years later. She supported her husband throughout his career, when he was a major with the Special Forces attached to her father's elite Strike Corps, later when he was with the Defense Intelligence Agency, then the Research & Analysis Wing, and eventually, the IFA and now the SON. She understood the dangers involved, but never interfered with his professional activities. She had profound faith in his ability and judgment. These days, Karry worked officially as a journalist and writer. He was a published author with several articles and a couple of books to his credit, all of which were carefully engineered to promote information and ideas supporting the interests of India, both at home and abroad. Karry's frequent journeys were presented as research trips and Manpreet had become used to them, adjusting her life accordingly. Before Aditya and Bhaskar were born, she often travelled with her husband, but now she spent most of her time and energy taking care of them. She often took them to visit her cousin, who was married to a naval officer who commanded the Indian Navy's prestigious nuclear submarine group. They lived nearby with their young son and daughter.

The newspaper still tucked under his arm, Karry entered the kitchen and sat down at the breakfast table with the boys. He couldn't help but laugh as they started chattering to him all at once. No matter how busy he was, when he was home, he made a point to have a least one meal and say one prayer a day with them. His motto was "the family who prays together, and eats together, always stays together." As soon as the youngsters had grabbed their lunch boxes and schoolbags and headed out to catch the school bus, Karry turned to Manpreet with a look she had come to know all too well. "I am going to be in my den for a while," he said, smiling reassuringly to let her know there was nothing to worry about. Please keep a lookout as usual."

"Yes, my dear." She nodded and kissed his cheek before he left the room.

The penthouse was one of four on top of the fourteen-storey building. On the terrace, he had installed a large, photovoltaic cell—or solar panel—which rested on the enormous water storage tank positioned directly above the room he used as a private study, so that it could capture the constant sunshine of Mumbai, keeping the water hot throughout the day and providing power for some of his electronic gadgets.

Karry entered his room, locking the door from inside. He then pressed a switch, and a trap door—dissimulated in the ceiling decoration— unlocked and slid down, opening a small, foldable ladder. He climbed up into the small den he had built inside the extra-large water tank serving his apartment. This perfectly insulated hideout, with its thick water layer and thin vacuum layer, guaranteed that no one could easily pick up his conversations while he was talking inside, especially when the double-insulation trap door was closed. Air circulation was supplied by a pipe connected to the flat's air conditioning system, and a small monitor

received the images from the tiny camera
hidden just outside the room below. In this way,
he could see if anyone was coming to call on
him. His sons knew that when Daddy was
locked inside his den, he was not to be
disturbed, but a good agent always has
contingencies.
The tiny den only had space for one person,
but it was comfortably outfitted with a small
table and folding chair. Its walls were lined with
shelves housing all types of electronic
equipment and firearms. The transmitter and
receiver of the tiny 120 GHz microwave radio
ran on the solar energy stored in the battery just
outside the room, using an almost invisible
network of small microwave dish antennas that
could radiate the signal to a distance of up to
two kilometers. This was sufficient for Karry to
hook up his radio to the 100 meter tower that
powered naval communications for India's
western naval command HQ in Mumbai. In
addition, the tower's small microwave dish
system pointed toward the official residence of
the Governor of the State of Maharastra, and the
seat of power for the State legislative assembly.
Karry had only to turn his antenna net toward
the naval tower and 'borrow' a
communication's channel according to
Balaram's instructions. Since he only
occasionally used this system, his operations
were hardly visible to the State Government—

something like temporarily hooking a small electrical wire to the power lines. Calls were set at four minutes in duration, from 10:01 a.m. to 10:05 a.m., sufficient enough to make contact without being traced. The time of day was perfect, too, given the morning rush; the communication would be buried under the heavy call volume flowing in and out of the State Legislative Assembly. Even if it was noticed, Balaram knew how to take care of it.

* * * *

Karry looked at his precision watch. At exactly 10:00 a.m., he switched the computer and radio on, steering the microwave antennas electronically toward the naval tower; then he scanned his fingerprints. The biometric recognition code identified Karry and gave him access to the radio. He punched in Balaram's sixteen-digit secure phone number, which the radio picked up, digitized, scrambled, modulated and mixed with a code, before sending it through the radio waves over a secure communication's line.

On the other side of the connection, Karry imagined that his friend was sitting in his office in a secret bunker in Delhi, the nation's capital, eagerly awaiting Karry's call.

Balaram would straighten in his chair when he finally saw the stream of data displayed on the radio screen, indicating the successful reception of the signal and messages. Once the connection was established, he would smile as Karry's image appeared on his computer screen.

"Good to see you," Karry said, smiling in return. "How are you doing? It's been a long time."

"Yes, I'm good, my friend; hope you are doing fine too. Something has come up—something urgent—and I need your help immediately." Balaram looked around furtively.

"At your service." Karry bowed his head in a show of respect and his colleague returned the gesture.

"We've learned from reliable sources that a very disturbing consignment has been dispatched, one that will wreak havoc greater than ever seen."

Karry took a sharp intake of breath, remembering the horrors of the 26/11 attack in Mumbai and the 9/11 attack in New York City. Greater devastation was hard to imagine, even for a seasoned agent. Balaram's information concerned six, low-intensity nuclear bombs that had been smuggled out of a North Korean underground nuclear facility and carried aboard a small fishing trawler, to be sold to Pakistan's rogue military generals for a handsome price. On the 17th of February—twelve days earlier—the trawler made contact with Pakistan's only nuclear submarine about fifty kilometers from the town of Nampo. The sub, a very large modern vessel of Chinese origin, had been very recently acquired and was proceeding from the Chinese port of Dalian to the Pakistani port of Karachi, through the Yellow Sea bordering China and Korea. Commander Zia surfaced the sub at a designated location and took the consignment of six low-intensity nuclear bombs from the trawler on to the sub, and within no time several big suitcases were passed from the submarine to the trawler, before the vessel disappeared into the deep waters. The trawler quickly returned to shore, with a payment of hundreds of millions of dollars in cash, gold and diamonds to be handed over to the communist regime, who were in desperate need after the recent economic block by the international community.

As a standard practice, the North Korean regime tried to assassinate the sailors who were the only witnesses to the transaction, but the plan backfired when one of the sailors miraculously escaped the ambush and defected to South Korea.

"On the morning of the 22nd," Balaram continued, "a stressed-looking man showed up at the door of the Indian Consulate in Seoul, South Korea, and demanded to see the Consul, saying he had important information concerning national security for the Indian Government. And he's not a fraud," he said. "He spilled the beans on a number of previous operations to convince us. I have spoken with him, too, and he seems to be genuine. Also, the Mongoose has confirmed his story of the six small nuclear devices, code name "Eggs of the Scorpion," smuggled out of North Korea by Pakistani ISI agents. We've already given him an Indian passport with a new name, together with a plane ticket to Kolkata.

"Where is the sub now?" Karry enquired.

"It has positioned itself off the Maldives where it made contact with a luxury yacht. Our air reconnaissance reported seeing six waterproof containers tied together, which were released from the submerged vessel and collected by the yacht crew. We have every reason to believe they contain the Eggs of the Scorpion, especially since the yacht belongs to Ibrahim Jr." Balaram paused, biting his lips. "I don't have to tell you the implications of that."

Karry grunted in affirmation. Ibrahim's resume was well-known. Upon learning the Indian authorities had issued a warrant for his arrest, Ibrahim Jr. fled to Somalia. He frequently travels to Karachi to see Ibrahim Sr., who heads the notorious Mumbai Mafia.

"Karry, I want you to get on this as soon as possible."

"I shall prepare my team straightaway." The timer only had a few seconds left before the conversation would be terminated automatically.

"Thank you, my friend. I will keep you posted as I get more information."

"Good."

"Thanks again, Karry. Over and out."

The radio connection fell automatically; the timer had expired.

Karry waited for a few more minutes, and then scanned his fingerprints and the biometric recognition code to the radio once again. This time, he punched in a different secure telephone number. The process of modulating and encoding the system began; the timer started, and Karry heard ringing at the other end, then the voice of the Valley Warden. "Upendra, here."

"I'm coming to the Valley; get ready," said Karry.

"Yes sir, we will!" he replied, obviously recognizing the urgency in Karry's voice.

After the brief message, Karry switched off the radio, computer, and other related equipment; then he unplugged the wires and climbed back down the ladder into the study. Another switch electronically withdrew the ladder into the ceiling before he locked the trap door.

Karry left the den, locked the door behind him and began preparing for the mission. When Manpreet returned from the local market an hour later, she saw the suitcase near the door and understood.

"I guess you'll be travelling again." She smiled.

"Yes, dear. I probably won't be back until after Shivaratri."

Manpreet seemed unperturbed. "You love adventure and I love you. I will keep the children busy and spend the festivity with friends." As Karry smiled, she walked over and put her arms around him. "Take care, dear." He returned her hug, awestruck once again by his good fortune to have such a wonderful wife who made things so easy for him, so he in turn could make the country safe. He looked into her eyes with passion and they made love like never before.

* * * *

Karry placed his luggage in the trunk of his HSUV, a hybrid model running on gas and electricity then pulled into the heavy traffic of central Mumbai. Finally, he crossed the Vashi Bridge connecting Mumbai to Navi Mumbai, and then picked up Highway 66. To the east, he could see the steep and imposing Sahyadri hills, also called the Western Ghats. Running from north to south on the Western edge of the Indian Peninsula, they separate the region from the coastal plain along the Arabian Sea. The area is long, 1600 kilometers, with an average elevation of about 3600 feet. The hills cover 60,000 square kilometers, and are a perfect catchment area for forty percent of India's rivers. It also

161

has the greatest biodiversity hotspots, with thousands of species of flowering plants, over a hundred types of mammals, several hundred species of birds, and almost two hundred kinds of amphibians.

After a few hours, he reached Mangoan, where the difficult part of the drive began.

About twenty kilometers from Mangoan, where tourists take the wide Raigad Road to Pachad, Karry avoided the turn and instead continued forward toward Birwadi, taking the narrow, less-traveled secondary road toward Raigad Fort. The drive became arduous as the elevation of the road climbed toward the imposing Raigad Fort Hill, and Karry passed only an occasional bus or car. About six kilometers before the Fort, he turned onto a small, unpaved road. He continued for another two kilometers through a thick forest, finally reaching an unnamed, unmanned gate. He stopped the truck, got out to open the combination lock, and then drove onto the 3000 acre property. This was the only accessible side, as the small plateau was surrounded on all the other sides by steep ravines over 150 meters deep.

He slowly continued down the narrow dirt road for a few minutes, until he came to a guard post that served as the camp's checkpoint. The guards, immediately recognizing him, opened the inner gate and saluted as he passed through;

he returned the salute. Karry continued for another 200 meters, finally bringing the vehicle to rest in front of a solitary, three-story building that seemed to be leaning against the hill behind it. It appeared empty and abandoned, but Karry was unperturbed. He grabbed his luggage and walked through a yard of overgrown weeds up to the front door, which he unlocked with a large key he pulled from his pocket. He carefully entered the building and climbed the creaking staircase to the third floor; it was deliberately designed to discourage any potential intruders. There he unlocked another nondescript door and pushed it open to reveal a surprisingly large space. On one side of the room was an electronically operated hatch. Karry knew it lead into a sixty meter tunnel that stretched through the hillside, emptying out into the beautiful small valley at the heart of the property. Legally registered to the Raigad Horticultural Society, the property actually housed a secret training center. Karry took great pride, as well, in the fact that his staff had indeed developed a very good cultivation and forest gardening program.

He leaned forward, let the machine scan his retina, and then entered the tunnel. After moving through it, he marveled, as always, at the gentle slope to the flat bowl of land in the center, a beautiful natural park with a great variety of trees and plants, constantly watered by small creeks. He walked across to the hillside and into the mouth of a small cave. About four meters inside the natural cave, he passed through the concealed door and was greeted by Upendra Dogra, chief warden and one of the custodians of the Valley.

"*Namaste* sir, welcome home," Upendra said, holding both his palms together. "It is so nice to see you, once again." Karry returned the greeting. "*Namaste*, thanks a lot; nice to see you as well."

The main cave was large, about the size of four tennis courts. It was also well-ventilated and nicely lit, thanks to several miniature wind mills, camouflaged with green paint and strategically positioned around the property, slightly above the tree canopy. The large hall received natural illumination from skylights set into the rocky slope of the hill outside, which also acted as solar energy producers. These were set at an angle, so that they would not be spotted from above. There, a staff member was conducting classes on interpersonal relationships to her very attentive audience. The eleven members of the Vajra Team, nine young men and two young women, had all been carefully selected by Karry. They were the bravest and the brightest, but the best among them was their leader, Jai Bharat. In Sanskrit, Vajra means both thunderbolt and diamond. The thunderbolt is the celestial weapon carried by

Indra, the Lord of Heaven. As a material device, it has the symbolic nature of a diamond (it can cut any substance), as well as that of the thunderbolt (irresistible force). The Vajra represents strength of spirit and spiritual power.

The Valley's facilities had the capacity to train fifteen students at a time, plus accommodate ten faculty members and twenty support staff, for a total of forty-five to fifty people. The students were trained in ancient and modern martial arts, combat and strategy, as well as special and intelligence operations, thus gathering the best from both worlds. The men and women had also undergone formal military training before they joined the Vajra team. Each trainee was taught to be self-sufficient, but they usually worked in small teams. They spoke many languages and often communicated in Sanskrit, the ancient, Mother-tongue of India.

Upendra and Karry walked through another door to the Command and Communications Center, called the Cube. This was the place from which all operations were conducted: a high-tech facility discretely funded by the IFA.

Karry did a quick check on the printouts and ledgers, nodded his approval and walked out with Upendra. "How are the trainees doing?" he asked with an easy grin.

Upendra walked briskly next to him. "Very well, sir. Their course is complete and they've all gone through the four levels with very good marks. Their physical form is also very good."

"We need to put them on an assignment. It is time to perform the oath-taking ceremony, and then we will celebrate the festival of Shiva Ratri. Please make the necessary arrangements."

"Yes, sir." Upendra acknowledged.

"Tomorrow, early morning, they will come to the Raigad Fort. I want to see for myself how they manage under stress."

"Yes, sir."

After taking his leave, Karry went to his quarters, unpacked his suitcase, took a shower, and exchanged his modern, western-style clothes for the traditional warrior-style Salwar suit that everybody used in the Valley. It was a powerful, symbolic statement that Karry knew created an almost religious and mystic feeling of dedication and concentration among the members of the group.

* * * *

The Valley also had a small temple, manned by a trusted celibate priest, or *pujari,* who permanently lived on the grounds. The temple had three altars. On one was seated the Deities of Sri Sita Rama, Lakshman and Hanuman. The second had the Deities of Radha and Krishna, and the third, an impressive Deity of Mother Durga. She was in her ten-armed form, depicted as slaying the buffalo demon. Next to her, a

Shiva Lingam was decorated with flowers and bilva leaves.

Karry reached the temple just in time for the evening *arati* ceremony. The *pujari* blew the conchshell three times to announce the start of the worship and prepared the *arati* plate. Suddenly Karry saw a familiar figure clad in flowing saffron clothes walking toward the temple. He sprang to his feet and rushed to greet the elderly but still robust man, who wore his rather long, grey hair tied neatly in a bun. Gokarnath Swami was Karry's spiritual advisor, and he reverently bowed at the old man's feet. The swami, smiling, opened his arm to affectionately lift Karry up to a standing position. .

Swami Gokarnath was a truly remarkable person. The extent of his knowledge and wisdom was unfathomable. He even appeared to be extraordinarily well-informed about the latest national and international events. He seemed to be able to answer any question and find the solution to any spiritual or material problem presented to him. No one really knew where he lived. When someone asked him, he simply replied, "In a small hut in the forest." He usually travelled on foot and had the uncanny ability to appear exactly at the proper time on important occasions. Some believed he had perfected magical powers or *siddhis*, like some gurus have. He staunchly upheld the fundamental principles of religion and the basic tenets of knowledge. He loved and cared for those around him and always had time for everyone. His approach was very simple and informal, but highly educative and motivational; but the thing that most impressed the people who met him was his humility and modesty. No one knew any of his background, except that he was an exceptional guru.

The swami immediately went to pay his respects to the Deities, and then exchanged some friendly words with the priest. In the meantime, other members of the valley arrived for the worship ceremony and offered their respects to the Deities and to the venerable swami. They also bowed to Karry, for he was their mentor.

The ceremony started and everyone participated eagerly, some by playing the large drum, small gongs and cymbals, or ringing the suspended bell in front of the altars. In the end, the consecrated flames of the *ghee* lamp were passed around for the customary blessing of the congregation, and everyone settled down for the evening spiritual discourse.

After the program was over, people left and the area quieted.

Taking the opportunity to chat, Swami Gokarnath turned to Karry, smiling. "How are you, my son? Is everything going well? Are you happily engaged in your duties?"

Karry smiled back and bowed his head, offering his homage with folded hands. "Yes, Gurudeva. For your blessings and the blessings of the Lord, I am happily performing my duty to the best of my ability."

"Very good, son, nice to hear"

Sitting in the modest guest room reserved for the swami, Karry relaxed and opened his heart to his guru, informing him of the new threat that had been discovered.

Rolling his eyes, he said, "Baba, we are fighting a very difficult battle. We have enemies, even among those who are supposed to be on our side, and therefore our progress is slow and we need to proceed with great secrecy. How much easier it would be if we had more cooperation!"

The swami smiled, his shoulders bowed. "Unfortunately, this is not a new problem, my son. As you already know, Chatrapathi Shivaji faced a similar situation. He needed allies to fight against the oppressive Moghul invaders, but many kings refused to cooperate with him, so he had to do it alone. He succeeded by sheer determination and the generous blessing of Mother Goddess Bhavani."

Karry nodded in agreement, as it was a fact.

The swami continued. "India was weakened and she succumbed more due to the betrayal of her own sons—blinded by material greed and illusion—than to the superior power of her enemies. However, the bright side is India always overcame its enemies, for eventually truth wins. So long as we are on the side of truth, India will not lose.

Karry nodded; he knew the story well. The colonial British and the Muslim invaders would have never been able to conquer India without the active help of many Indians who were happy to be employed by their armies and governments. They clearly lacked any sense of patriotism; instead, their loyalty was for sale to the highest bidder. At the same time, it was due to the joint efforts of Mahatma Gandhi, Subhash Chandra Bose and many more, which got India its freedom.

"Also," continued the swami, "you need to understand that *Dharma* has priorities. When you become free from all material attachments and identifications, you become a more suitable instrument for the Lord to carry out his missions." He looked Karry straight in the eye.

Karry listened intently.

"We always need to remember what *Dharma* is. We must always be ready to sacrifice ourselves for the greater good, as has been demonstrated by the examples of the illustrious kings of the past; kings like Sibi, Harischandra, and Sri Rama himself."

Karry knew very well he must never hesitate to do what was required for *Dharma*, even if it might destroy a person's name, fame, family, wealth or life. In the *Gita,* Lord Krishna clearly stated that one should perform one's *dharmic* duty faithfully, without being confused by the possibility of victory or defeat, gain or loss, fame or infamy, joy or suffering.

The swami continued. "Very dangerous weeds must be completely uprooted, without pity, just as farmers do to save their crops. Not just cut them down, mind you, for if merely pruned, they come back, and these same weeds will become more poisonous and spread even more, thus destroying the crop."

As the swami spoke, Karry thoughtfully gazed down at his own hands. Should he uproot hardened and resolute enemies, without any consideration of material compassion or self-righteousness? When the time comes for the final clash, would his natural compassion be an impediment? *Never.* He must engage in his *Dharma* with dedication. Certainly that seemed to be Krishna's instruction to Arjuna, on the battlefield of Kurukshetra, where the *Bhagavad-gita* was spoken.

"Swami-ji," Karry said with concentration, "where can we find help? The Pandavas found many allies for their war. We also need allies for our own battle of Kurukshetra."

The swami smiled sagaciously. "Yes. A *kshatriya* needs allies, wisdom, weapons and wealth to fight his battles, and win his wars. I have been meditating on this, and I tell you that allies will come from the most unexpected places. Allies and treasures." He paused, his face illuminated by internal inspiration. As if in a trance, he spoke again. "Yudhisthira asked his brother, Arjuna, to collect wealth to support their kingdom and prepare for the war, and Arjuna obliged. It is said that north of Kailash, near the Mainaka Mountain, there is the Golden Peak, the Hiranya-shringa, a mountain filled with treasures. Just imagine the tremendous impact the discovery of this fabulous treasure of the Pandavas would have upon not only India, but the entire world!"

Karry smiled, skeptically rubbing his eyes. "How likely is it to find such priceless treasures these days?"

"More likely than you think, my son. In fact, I believe that something momentous is going to happen soon, and I am sure you will have an important part to play in it."

Karry was about to ask another question, but stopped himself. He had learned long ago not to question the swami's predictions, for they often proved amazingly correct.

"I understand, Swami-ji. I will follow your advice and remain alert for any such opportunity."

His Holiness remained silent for some time, and then added, "Follow your heart, your intuition. You are a sincere soul, and *paramatma*—the voice of God within your heart—will guide you in the right direction. Carry on with your duty without undue attachment, and remember that our *highest* duty is to serve the mission of the Lord."

He looked intensely at his disciple. Karry felt there was something more, but clearly the swami was not going to tell him. He would have to figure this out for himself.

* * * *

The Raigad Fort, or King Among Forts, had been Chatrapati Shivaji's capital for twenty-six years, but it had been famous as a military garrison for at least two thousand years before that. It was in a line of famous forts, including Kondana, Purandar, and Torna. At about 820 meters above sea level, the Fort Hill was very difficult to climb; it had three, layered fortifications and a base of forty square kilometers on top of a hill that was already 320 meters high. The final test for the trainees was to reach the top of the Fort without using any roads and in the semi-dark hour before dawn, using their bare hands on the natural features of the terrain, such as rock corners and shrubs growing on the face of the hill. They had night-vision goggles, wore comfortable Salwar suits, with the shirt or *kurta* tucked inside their belt, and carried light cloth backpacks.

In spite of his age, Karry was still in splendid shape, thanks to the constant conditioning his life in the military had required. Even now that he was technically a civilian, Karry not only jogged every morning along the beach, but also spent several hours a day exercising and practising *yoga* and martial arts in his home. He even went swimming at the neighborhood health club.

The next day, the Vajra team began their morning by climbing down from the valley's plateau into the vast gorge below, and jogging toward the fort. When all the trainees had caught up, Karry gestured to the fifteen-meter-high fort walls and led the team to scale them, after which the team silently ran up the fifteen-hundred steps to the top.

The early dawn light began engulfing the sky, slowly, and majestically. The moon and stars were still visible. The Vajra Team stood in a circle around the Bhagavad Dhwaja, the saffron flag on which the ancient Kings swore to protect their *Dharma*, lands & people. This was the same flag which was atop the chariot of Arjuna during the Kurukshetra war, leading him to victory some 5000 years ago. A similar flag had been erected in this very same place by Chatrapathi Shivaji Maharaj in the 17th century.

Karry addressed them in a low, soft voice. "Now the time has come to prove yourselves. In this place, Chatrapati Shivaji tasted victory after victory against the oppressive Moghul rule. He liberated the Hindu people of Bharat and raised this flag as a symbol for all Hindus to unite and defend *Dharma*. Shivaji was in turn inspired by Krishna's potent message to Arjuna within the *Bhagavad-gita*, a message that shook him out of his confused inaction into a state of righteous action."

Karry approached them with the *arati lamp*.

"Today, like Shivaji did before us, we are taking the solemn vow to serve our Motherland and the greater world with our bodies, minds and souls. We take the solemn oath to defend *Dharma* in all its dimensions from enemies both within and without, a *dharmic* way of life, based on compassion, protection, truthfulness and cleanliness, that which considers the people of the world as God's family. We call upon the moon, the stars and the sun as our witness. We call upon the day and the night, the earth, the sky and the waters as our witnesses. We call upon the sacred fire and the sacred flag of *Dharma* as our witnesses. We call upon all humanity and the gods and our forefathers to bear witness. May we never break our oath, and may we always be ever ready to sacrifice absolutely everything we possess in this sacred mission, for the benefit of one and all."

Standing in a circle, the Vajra team repeated the oath word for word, as they all respectfully placed their right hand over the burning flame of the *ghee* lamp. They were India's best bet, the world's hope and they knew it in their hearts.

That night, on a secure telephone line, Karry called his friend, Balaram, and in their simplest code informed him that the "chess team was ready to leave for the tournament." Balaram smiled and wished them good luck.

* * * *

National Security Advisor, Dr. Mohandas Patel, was already present at the Joint Intelligence Committee, the JIC, briefing, together with the members of the other agencies. The meeting was also attended by a few politicians, who acted as observers. Dr. Patel advised the Prime Minister on all important matters pertaining to both internal and external security.

Lieutenant General Patnaik of the Defence Intelligence Agency began. He presented information on how Pakistan was once again attempting to smuggle in Jihadi terror groups across the international border into the Jammu & Kashmir regions of India. He stated that the jihadis were recruited from multiple countries; these recruits were trained in Pakistan, and then sent into India to create a disturbance so as to provoke the Indian security agencies. Not a single day in India went by without some cruel acts of terrorism. The jihadis' ultimate dream was to capture the entire region of Kashmir by increasing the number of separatist Muslims there, demand 'independence' from India to join Pakistan, and then, bit by bit, swallow the entire Indian sub-continent to create a huge Muslim

Nation under the rule of sharia law, as was being attempted by ISIS in the Middle East. After Patnaik finished, the representatives of other specialized agencies gave their reports and analyses. Finally, it was Balaram's turn—as director of the coordinating agency—to sum up the meeting. He decided to speak a bit about his own investigation into the latest problem. "Thank you all for your valuable input. My office is currently keeping track of a new Pakistani nuclear submarine. It has not been commissioned, as of yet, into the Pakistani Navy. However, it seems to have been engaged in some unannounced mission.

"It was last spotted near the Maldives. It almost goes without saying that this mission is clearly a threat to our national security. We are investigating this matter and will have a more detailed update at the next meeting."

Chapter 7 - At the Confluence of Three Sacred Rivers

Heathrow to Delhi. Diana fastened her seatbelt before pulling out the travel guide for India she had purchased at the airport. She briefly skimmed through the pages on Delhi, where she only planned on staying a few days, and then move on to the city of Prayagraj. Originally called Prayag, and then Allahabad, this ancient city was a famous pilgrimage center situated at the confluence of the three most sacred rivers—the Ganges, Yamuna and Sarasvati. But Diana was not going there for its history; she was going because it was where her great-grandfather Arthur had lived while in India.

Suddenly Diana felt as if someone was looking at her. When she turned, she saw the passenger next to her, a lanky man of Indian origin, watching her intently. She took a shot at polite conversation and offered a friendly smile. "Hi, I'm Diana."

The man smiled back, offering her a hand. "Hi, my name's Sam Randy. I'm a U.S. citizen, but originally from India, and now living in Arkansas. I'm traveling to Hyderabad via London." His smile widened. "Soon I'll be running for the U.S. Congress. I plan on becoming a full time politician," he added a bit boastfully.

Oh, thought Diana, surprised by his mannerism and name. "Right." She decided to change the subject.

"Have you ever been to Prayagraj?" she asked politely, hoping to get some advice. "I will be spending part of my trip there."

The man seemed to be uncomfortable with something. He paused for a moment with arms crossed, his face reflecting an internal debate, and then finally said, "I prefer calling it Allahabad. It's been renamed as Prayagraj in 2018, just to appease the Hindus."

Diana's curiosity was aroused. "But isn't it a *Hindu* holy place?"

"Holy place, my foot?" scoffed the man. "It's all superstitious pagan B.S.; a myth propagated by Hindu Priests to attract gullible people like you, and make money off of them in the name of pilgrimage." He quickly returned to a seemingly fake smile.

Diana drew back, surprised by his harsh words. But she felt the need to press on for more information. "But what about the historical and religious value of the three sacred rivers that meet there? I have read that there is a large religious festival—Kumbha Mela—in Prayagraj, at the confluence of these three rivers." She quickly searched through the book she'd been reading. "Here!" She pointed at the paragraph with her finger. "It says that the Triveni Sangam, the confluence of the three holy rivers, the Ganga, Yamuna and Sarasvati, is the holiest place for the one billion Hindus worldwide." She looked at him, smiling for validation. "That is about one-eighth of the world's population, so it must be really important, right?" Sam only smirked in response, and she turned back to the book. "Each January, a religious Magh Mela is held, and once every twelve years during the famous Kumbha Mela, millions of people go there to purify themselves from their bad *karma*."

She looked up from her travel guide again, annoyed to find that Sam's smirk was still in place. Although she had never been particularly religious herself, she was uncomfortable when others' beliefs were ridiculed.

Sam chuckled, as if he were enjoying a private joke, but this time Diana could read a touch of coldness and spite on his face. "No," he insisted, "There are only two rivers, sorry to burst your bubble, but it's all these Hindu superstitions that keep India down. Sacred Rivers? Really."

Diana frowned. This conversation was becoming awkward. Sam continued, seemingly unaware of her feelings. "You know, this is why I've become a Christian. Since moving to America, I've freed myself from all these idiocies, and now I attend the Baptist church of

Arkansas." The smirk returned. "My parents still cling to the old backward superstitions of pagan Hinduism, but one day I'll put an end to that, and the sooner the better. I'm surprised you western people fall for these fake things; don't you have anything better to do? You need to return to Jesus. He's the only way,"

Diana had had enough of this unpleasant man. She managed a smile and a feeble, "Good for you!" before turning her attention back to her book.

To her utter shock, Sam pulled out a famous white supremacist magazine from his backpack and started reading it with gusto, as if he was enjoying and agreeing with every word. As she was wondering how to get rid of him, the flight attendants appeared with the dinner cart. It was curry and rice—one of her favorite dishes to order in London's many Indian restaurants—and Diana was pleased to find it surprisingly good. She ate with relish, glad to have something to concentrate on besides Sam's disturbing remarks and his lusty gaze.

He seemed to sense his fellow passenger was in no mood to continue a conversation, so he devoured his chicken in silence. When the air hostess came to collect the trays, he ordered a whisky, drank it, and then promptly dozed off. Shortly after dinner the cabin lights were dimmed and the passengers settled in for the night. Diana spotted two empty seats on the centre aisle and took the opportunity to change her seat so she could stretch out a little more comfortably. It also ensured there would be no more chats with her obnoxious neighbor.

After many more hours, the captain announced they would soon be landing in Delhi. Diana felt genuinely relieved. It seemed her journey to India had not started on a very good note. Her encounter with Sam had unnerved her, but when she remembered Arthur's mission, it gave her some hope and put a smile back on her face.

* * * *

As soon as the immigration officer stamped her passport, Diana collected her luggage, and then finally emerged into the hot, noon sunshine of India. A moment later, she found herself surrounded by a gaggle of taxi drivers, each of them apparently anxious to give her a ride.

She picked one and followed him to his car, showing him the address of the Golden Palms hotel she had booked online. He nodded, smiling, and slid the taxi into the flow of traffic. During the ride, Diana took the opportunity to call her parents and let them know she had arrived safely. After having her meal in the hotel restaurant, she slept soundly in the room in an attempt to overcome her brief jet lag.

The first place Diana planned to visit was the Indian Council of Historical Research in Delhi. So, early the next morning, she walked to their office on Feroze Shah Road, which was a short distance from her hotel. The building looked like a large library, and for a place that had just opened for a day's work, it didn't appear very busy. After asking several people, she was finally directed to the office of Mrs. Ormila Naukar, the Library and Information manager.

At Diana's knock on the glass door, Mrs. Naukar looked up from a stack of papers on her desk and told Diana to come in.

"Good morning, Mrs. Naukar. My name is Diana Warwick, and I'm searching for information about my great-great grandfather, Arthur Warwick. He came to India in 1856 on an archeological research project." She extended her hand, a warm smile on her face.

Mrs. Naukar's expression immediately hardened at hearing the name Warwick. "May I ask what are your academic credentials, Miss Warwick?" The woman appeared to deliberately ignore the handshake.

Diana was startled by her rude behavior. "I am completing my Master's degree at the London School of Economics. I'm sorry, but how is that relevant to any information about Arthur Warwick?"

The smile on Mrs. Naukar's lips was unmistakably cold. "If you are not a qualified historian or archeologist, miss, you cannot access the information of our Institute. Do you have a sponsorship letter from a recognized institution of our country?"

"Why would I need a sponsorship letter?" Now Diana was not only perplexed, but irritated. Her unpleasant encounter with Sam, compounded by the change of time zone, climate and temperature had already strained her patience. She was in no mood to deal with this woman's attitude. "I am perfectly capable of taking care of myself without any sponsorship."

"Oh, are you now?" Mrs. Naukar's smile broadened, but her eyes remained open and as cold as a viper's. "May I ask what type of visa you have, Miss Warwick?"

"A regular tourist visa. Why?"

"For your information, miss, a tourist visa is not sufficient to conduct any investigation, including the sort you are attempting. You will need to report to the Central Police Station in Delhi and get the appropriate permits from the Superintendent there, as well as from the Foreign Registration Office. Until then, we cannot, and will not, help you in any way." She waved a dismissive hand in contempt.

By this time, understandably, Diana was fuming, but she realized that getting into a fight with this bitchy woman was not going to help her quest. She summoned all the strength and patience she could, and managed a passable smile. "Thank you, Mrs. Naukar. You have been very helpful. I'll follow your advice and try to get the required permits."

Mrs. Naukar looked like she had bitten into a lemon; it was as if she had hoped Diana would lose her temper so she could call security and have the English woman manhandled and unceremoniously thrown out. Instead, she hid her intentions with a, "Very well, miss. Good day to you."

In spite of her mounting anger, Diana tried to keep her face expressionless and the stride in her walk as normal as possible as she left the office. Upon leaving the building, she climbed into a waiting taxi, and headed back to her hotel.

* * * *

Ormila Naukar's cold smile returned as soon as Diana had left. She picked up her cell phone, browsed through her contact numbers until she found the one she was looking for and pressed 'send'. She heard three rings on the other end of the line, and then a man's voice answered.

"Professor Jawahar."

"Good morning, professor. This is Ormila Naukar, from the ICHR, Delhi."

"Ah, good morning, Madam. Are you calling with any new information"?

"Yes, sir." Ormila repeated the conversation she'd had with Diana, and then added, "She has a tourist visa, sir, so it should not be difficult to get her into trouble with the police."

"Arthur Warwick? Thank you, Mrs. Naukar. Please keep me informed if you learn anything more about this."

"I certainly will, sir," she nodded enthusiastically.

* * * *

Professor Jawahar Katju hung up the phone and sat back in his favorite leather armchair, lost in thought. The telephone call from Mrs. Naukar had thoroughly shaken him up and filled him with a vague feeling of alarm. Who was this Arthur Warwick? He was sure he had heard that name before.

Suddenly, it came flooding back to him. Yes, it was that crazy British man who had made an idiot of himself by embracing and supporting the foolish superstitions of native pagan Hindus. He had been a real troublemaker in the 1850s, a major embarrassment for the Imperial British and their English education policies.

Warwick! Britishers were one thing, but nothing disturbed Jawahar more than these do-gooder foreigners. *Damn them!* When they start going native, it completely counters any efforts to expose the superstitions of the pagan Hindus. And now they had another Warwick to deal with, and a woman, to boot! Hopefully, she was an old hag and not one of those stunners who instantly attract support and attention to her cause. In any event, she was here in India, nosing around where she did not belong. *Ahh!*

But the girl's nose can be easily crushed, thought Jawahar confidently.

Jawahar glanced around the drawing room of his luxurious on-campus apartment; a symbol of his status at the University. Ormila Naukar was a bright lady, but below-average looking; she had surrendered to his carnal desires on repeated occasions. She had also instantly understood the importance of this matter and reported to him without hesitation; such loyalty deserved some reward. He would have to introduce her to some people, a new and higher level of officer or politician who she could network with. This would facilitate her social climbing and maintain a dependable ally where it was needed. But first, he must alert the president of the Society for the Eradication of Pagan Superstitions and get his advice and permission. Jawahar stood up and went to his bar to pour himself a glass of whisky, then returned to his desk and dialed the number he memorized long ago, when he first became a member of the Society.

Lord Dyer answered on the very first ring, as if he were expecting the call.

"Yes, Jawahar. What's the emergency? I'm having lunch." he responded gruffly.

"Good morning, sir. Sorry to disturb you. Yes, I know that it's not the usual time for routine updates, but something came up," he replied in a timid voice.

"All right, go on."

Jawahar cleared his throat before continuing. "Sir, today a Diana Warwick visited the Indian Council of Historical Research here in Delhi. She was searching for information about her great-great-grandfather, Arthur Warwick."

There was a momentary silence. "*The* Arthur Warwick? How is it possible, after all this time?"

"I'm not entirely sure, sir. We only know she is British and just arrived in India with a tourist visa."

"If she is who she claims to be, that means only two things: she might be just curious to find out more about her great-grandfather's stay in India, or, she might have some clues as to the whereabouts of his treasure. I bet it's the second one. All right, I'll find out all I can about the family here in Britain, and see how much they know about Warwick's activities. This could be a real breakthrough for us. Something that has eluded us all these years."

"You do the same on your end. Find out when she entered India, where she is staying, and where she is going next. Keep a tail on her."

"I was already planning to, sir," Jawahar replied, irritated. He did not like to take orders, but neither did he want to jeopardize his position in the SEPS—an organization founded in 1836 by Macaulay himself. But like it or not, Lord Dyer was the Society's highest ranking member, the president, and to cross him was unthinkable.

Lord Dyer was able to read the silence correctly, and Jawahar knew it. "Very well, sir," he quickly added. "I will keep you updated with any news." The call ended.

In addition to his duties as Director of SEPS operations in India, Professor Jawahar was also the head of the History Department at the prestigious Nehru University in the heart of Delhi. The university provided free education through scholarships and was supposed to groom the brightest students of India for the best government positions, to take the country progressively forward. Unfortunately, on too many occasions, it has turned out to be a sanctuary for anti-Indian, anti-Hindu, and anti-democratic elements, who are out to destroy anything that does not conform to their narrow world view. Jawahar was the fountainhead of their product and they took great pride in him. In his fifties, he was highly reputed in academic circles, feared equally by his students and his peers. Known for his savvy, he was often referred to as "the Fox," although many in his milieu actually called him "the Jackal"—mostly at a safe distance from the ears of his minions. In truth, Jawahar Katju was basically just a cunning fellow, without any real talent for teaching or research. He had quickly risen to the top of his profession, not only by carefully cultivating his family's political contacts, but also with further networking of his own. He regularly attended seminars and conferences, and had even published some papers and books. These, however, were phony accomplishments that he had paid—or pressured—colleagues to write in his name. His wife had died ten years earlier, and his two sons were studying at the prestigious Dehradun's Doon boarding school, so he practically lived alone. However, Jawahar did not like to sleep alone. He had always flirted with his female colleagues, and sometimes even with female students. After his wife's death, he found himself free to pursue these flirtations more openly. At times, he had been reprimanded for his lewd behaviour, but he usually succeeded in getting what he wanted, often because the women were too intimidated to protest.

When women did refuse him, Jawahar exacted revenge in one way or another. He had become a trusted confidant of the Vice Chancellor of the University and it was not difficult for him to get female lecturers sacked for 'incompetence' or even 'immorality' if they refused to go to bed with him. His power at the university had even helped him assemble a group of rather ruthless students who supported him to the hilt and were more than happy to harass female students in exchange for protection and favors.

Professor Katju also had another ally, the wife of the Vice Chancellor of the University. She was known as something of a nymphomaniac and very dissatisfied with her much older husband, so Jawahar used all his charisma to manipulate her into helping him with his schemes. She cleverly spun gossip among the teachers and even resorted to complaints about personal offenses she had supposedly suffered from this or that person, thereby ensuring Katju's opponents would be removed from the campus.

However, all this power was nothing compared to what he could have if this Diana Warwick turned out to have information about her ancestor. Imagine if he were able to find the famous and mysterious treasure! He was overwhelmed with excitement at the very thought. He briskly walked up to the bar again and poured himself a second glass of whisky. He would have everything he had ever dreamed of…and more.

* * * *

Diana paced her hotel room, trying to figure out her next move. It was still early—only 11:45 a.m. Normally, she would have gone sightseeing around Delhi, but she had been so frustrated by her visit to the Indian Council of Historical Research that she wasn't in the mood. Finally she decided she wasn't going to waste

one more minute of her trip and would move on.
.

Diana logged in and checked for the next available flight; there was one in a few hours' time. She made an online reservation, and after quickly checking out of the hotel, took the taxi to the airport.

After a short flight, the aircraft landed at Prayagraj airport. Diana heaved a sigh, picked up her bag and made her way to the exit, hoping she would have more luck this time in the holiest city.

The next day, she awoke with the sun and went to the barred window of her hotel room to look outside. The streets of Prayagraj were very narrow and packed with busy people going about their daily routine; it reminded her of Jerusalem.

She took a quick shower, chose a conservative dress—as advised by the travel guide—and with renewed hope and energy, packed her handbag with her research papers. Then she went to the reception desk and asked for directions to the Triveni Sangam, the place where the three rivers merged, as mentioned by Arthur in his diaries.

The banks of the river were not far from where she was. She walked off the main road and soon reached the *ghats*. Here she saw the large stone stairs, which were built for the pilgrims who came there for bathing, descending into the river. The Sangam's view was amazing; a treat to the eyes; calm and peaceful in the morning under the shining sun. The two broad rivers were distinctly joined as if in a fond embrace—the muddy, pale yellow waters of the Ganga which was just four feet deep, and the blue waters of the Yamuna, which was forty feet deep. But there was no third river to be seen. Had Sam been right after all? *No, it can't be. Why would Arthur have lied? Maybe the confluence with the third river is a little further and I can't see it from here.*

She stood on the stone step to take a good look around. Several people were sitting on the bank, some meditating, some doing *yoga* exercises. She decided to rest there for a while. As she sat soaking up the gentle sun, and contemplating the slow current, her thoughts turned to Arthur. He had lived here for many years, watching these same rivers and maybe praying for his family. He must have found something in this place which brought him peace and enlightenment. As she closed her eyes and listened to the murmur of the water and the faint echoes of temple bells and sacred chants, she sincerely hoped she could find it, too. When she opened her eyes again, Diana saw an elderly gentleman in his mid-seventies, sitting a few feet away. The man smiled kindly and Diana returned the gesture.

After a few moments, the man turned his gaze to the rivers and spoke. "This is a very sacred place. I have been living here all my life, and my fathers before me. I am very fortunate. I believe you are also appreciating the beauty and peace of this place."

Diana nodded in silence.

"There are fourteen Prayagas," the man continued as if talking to himself, but loudly and clearly, "or places of ritual sacrifices, along the sacred river Ganga, and this Prayaga Raja is the greatest. Here, in this holiest of places, called Tirtha Raja or Kaushambi, the adult Ganga finally meets the Yamuna and the Sarasvati to form the Triveni Sangam."

Diana could not restrain her enthusiasm. "It is true, then! There are three rivers meeting here! Where is the third one?"

The man smiled. "Mother Sarasvati, the mighty river described in ancient Vedic texts, is now flowing underground, and her waters mix with the other rivers away from our mortal eyes."

Diana was not entirely convinced. "Someone told me it's not true; that it's just a bunch of lies invented by the Hindu priests to make money from the pilgrims. Is that correct?"

The man turned to watch her, seemingly amused by her question. "I have not introduced myself yet. Please forgive me. My name is Madhava Gupta; I am named after the famous

Vishnu Deity here in Prayagraj. I was the chief librarian at the Public Library near Alfred Park, but after my retirement I started the Prayagaraja Sankalana Samiti, a non-profit organization for the restoration of the ancient glory of Prayag. I am very passionate about river Sarasvati, I come here every morning to pay my respects to her, and I have always been inspired to read and research this subject.

"In Vedic Hindu scriptures Sarasvati is not only a river, she is the Goddess of learning, music and flowing words. She is worshiped not only by Hindus, but by Buddhists and Jains, as well. We consider her the 'power of knowledge' that enables us to overcome illusion and ignorance, and to attain liberation through wisdom. She is similar to Sophia of Greek legend, or Khokhmah of the Jews.

"In ancient times, when people lived in greater harmony with nature, rivers were the lifeblood of civilization. Cities were built near rivers where people could easily get water for drinking, cooking, bathing, washing their clothes and utensils, cleansing their houses, quenching the thirst of their animals, and even enjoying a healthy swim. A river is vital for agriculture and the production of food, not only because plants need water to survive and grow, but because the current of a river carries different minerals from the various areas it flows through. Rivers provide a smooth, safe and easy road for traveling and transporting goods, thus helping to spread culture and prosperity into a larger area.

"It is not entirely surprising that rivers have been considered sacred Mothers to these peoples. Can you imagine a day without water? Every drop of water is sacred because we cannot live without it, so then what to speak of a river, which has trillions of water drops, or even yet, a place where three mighty rivers meet?!"

Diana listened intently. There was something here she had never found before, a feeling of deep connection with nature and the really important things in life—perhaps this was what religion meant for these people.

"Interestingly, the existence of the ancient Sarasvati River has recently been confirmed by archeology. My nephew, who is a computer buff," Madhava continued with a smile, "tells me that NASA, the American Space Agency, has published satellite photographs of the ancient basin of the Sarasvati River, even though it is now dry. After originating from the Himalayas, the Sarasvati divided into two forks, one going to the Arabian Sea near Rann, in the Kutch region of Gujarat state, and the other running through the Triveni Sangam here, to the Bay of Bengal. However, an earthquake changed its course and eventually the entire river disappeared underground."

"This actually makes sense to me," said Diana. "You know, our projections for global economy clearly show that one day water will be more valued than oil, and it will probably be the main cause for the wars of the future."

Madhava sighed. "Let's hope and pray that war will not be necessary. This beautiful world has all the abundance we can possibly wish for; it can perfectly satisfy man's needs, but man's greed is unlimited and if it is not checked, it can spoil everything."

This is all very nice but how will it help me to find Arthur's last location?

Seeing the elderly man seemed ready to leave, Diana decided to seize the opportunity to ask him for information. "Sir, if I may ask your help... You seem to be so knowledgeable about the history of the city. I have come to Prayagraj to search for the last resting place of Arthur Warwick. He came to this holy city in 1859. Have you, by any chance, ever heard of him?"

Madhava stared at her in surprise. "Arthur Warwick? You mean the 'Gora Baba'?"

Diana's heart gave a mighty skip in anticipation.

"Yes," nodded the elderly man. "Gora Baba was a great man. He was in Allahabad, or Prayag as it was known long ago, just when the British government was fully bent on implementing Macaulay's plan for the total destruction of native Hindu cultural heritage and thus India's identity. This was during the British repression after India's first failed freedom uprising. He gave much inspiration and encouragement to the native people, for he embraced the Vedic path even though he was born into the heart of the Christian colonial nation which spread its brutal power throughout India."

Diana's face lit up with excitement. "I know he must have passed away in Allahabad, but his family never came to know his final resting place. I was hoping to find it. I am his descendent."

"It must be the Gora Baba Ashram. It is about ten kilometers from the Sangam; you can find it by following the course of the Ganga toward the east, in the direction of Chandi." Madhava looked amazed, perhaps struck by the realization that it was a momentous event to have met the descendent of the famous Gora Baba. "I will be honored to offer this service to such a great soul. If you are willing to wait a couple of days—as I have to take care of a few important things—I can take you there on Sunday."

"That would be fantastic!" Diana exclaimed, moved by his kindness, "Thank you so much." She pulled out a pen and paper and began writing. "This is the address of my hotel here in Prayagraj. Please come and pick me up at your convenience."

Madhava smiled and arose. Diana also got to her feet, uncertain as to how to show her gratefulness, but his kind smile told her that no thanks were necessary. "Namaste," he said with folded hands.

"Namaste," she responded.

She was happy that her venture into this holy land was now beginning to move in the right direction.

* * * *

Diana found she really liked spending time on the bank of the river. While she was walking along the *ghat* shore the next morning, she was approached by a gypsy man dressed in red robes, with an impressive heap of matted hair piled atop his head. He insisted on reading her palm, and began to talk about "the Goddess Mother" and "not happy, no money." Diana was very doubtful about his meaning, but told herself, half-jokingly, that she had been getting some good clues in the most serendipitous ways, so what the heck, this might be one, as well.

Diana went to sit on a dry step of the *ghat* and the man crouched on his heels, apparently quite comfortable in that position. He reached out and took both her hands in his, examining them very studiously, before he started to explain, "Madam, you have very good hands. You inherit very valuable property from your family. You interested in economics and charity and how to give benefit to people." He looked up shrewdly. "You searching for something hidden, like a treasure, and you will find it with the help of three friends. One of them, a black man, you will meet very soon; the other two, your heart and mind will recognize. You need to ask help from *Sani*, Saturn, to find this man. Tomorrow is *Sanivara*, Saturday; you go to temple of Hanuman or Shiva. *Sani* likes Shiva and Hanuman. Okay?"

Totally thunderstruck, Diana nodded. The man looked satisfied. He stared at the necklace Diana was wearing, the one Arthur had sent to his family. The man pointed to it, then his own large necklace of reddish-brown beads. Diana noticed the beads were almost identical, only hers were smaller and mounted on ancient silver.

"This Bhagavan—God—blessing. You protected," said the man in broken English. "Enemies try to harm, but you always protected." He smiled reassuringly, and then he rummaged in his ancient shoulder bag of red cotton cloth, extracting a small picture of a deity—a half-naked woman with many arms, garlanded with a necklace of skulls but wearing a kind and peaceful smile. The man touched the photo to his forehead, and then showed it to Diana by delicately holding it within his two hands. "This my mother," he said with unblinking eyes, showing immense pride and love. "She says she guards the hidden treasure.

Keep photo, please. Today Friday; her sacred day, she gives blessings."

With great trepidation, Diana extended her left hand to receive the gift. The man shook his head. "Wrong hand, use right hand."

"Sorry," stammered Diana, as she received the image in her right hand. Then she took out the file folder she always carried in her bag and carefully laid the image inside it. The man seemed to approve. He stood up, apparently ready to depart.

Diana extracted her purse and offered the man a two thousand rupee note. He did not seem excited, only pleased. He took the money with both hands, and touched it to his forehead. "This also Mother. Maha Lakshmi, Maha Sarasvati, Maha Kali. Blessing! Blessing!" Then he rolled up the money carefully and put it in his bag, lifted his right hand showing his pinkish palm, and walked off without looking back.

That night, it took Diana hours to fall asleep. Her usual skepticism was being shaken to its very roots. How could that man know she was looking for a hidden treasure just by looking at her hands? She could have been a very normal tourist visiting the famous Sangam, without any plan except for some restful and entertaining days in contact with an exotic and colorful culture. *Did Arthur's necklace really protect me from the bomb blast in Israel and the kidnapping attempt in Moscow? Yes, it seems so. And who is this Mother Goddess adoring skulls?* Everything seemed odd, and yet natural. Things were happening as if by design and not by her own effort. Why was this strange feeling enveloping her? What was happening to her?

She opened her file and took a peek at the Mother Goddess. It gave her a feeling of peace, and so, like a child, she slept with the photo on her chest.

* * * *

The next morning, Saturday, Diana woke up very early and, with a feeling of excitement in her stomach, prepared to leave, She skipped breakfast and rushed to the street to catch a rickshaw. A few moments later, she was standing in front of the famous Hanuman temple, a bright orange building with a stream of people coming and going. For several moments she watched the women, children and men in their traditional Indian clothing, many entering the temple with baskets or small trays loaded with flowers, fruits, desserts and incense, and all leaving with a bright orange-red mark on their forehead and a blissful expression on their faces. While she was contemplating the idea of joining the crowd of pilgrims, Diana noticed a tall, powerfully built man who looked much more African than Indian, exiting the temple. Also clad in a white cotton Indian suit, he had the orange mark on his forehead and a blue flower in his hand.

Her heart racing madly, Diana debated whether or not she should speak to him. Could this be the person the palm reader had spoken of? Of course, if he wasn't, he would think she was a crazy woman. Just when she was about to turn away, the man walked over and greeted her with a friendly smile. "Excuse me, miss," he said, with an American accent, "but you look lost. Can I help you find your way?"

Diana's doubts evaporated. The palmist had been right. "Hi, I'm Diana Warwick," she said, flashing him a smile. "I'm visiting from England and someone suggested I go to the temple of Hanuman today to be blessed with success in my...uh...quest." Diana made it sound funny, as if she didn't really take the notion seriously.

"It's a pleasure to meet you, Diana," he said, smiling. Instinctively, Diana felt she could trust this man. He radiated integrity and an inner strength. He seemed at peace with himself, yet open to the world.

"I saw you just visited the temple. Do you think I can get inside, too?"

"Sure. Today, many people visit the temple to pay respects to Hanuman, as Saturday is his special day. Have you ever been in a temple before?"

"No, never. And I've never really attended church either; I think only a few times when I was really young, but I don't remember much.

My family has always been rather agnostic, more interested in knowledge than faith. They tended to take inspiration from Darwin and Hawking," she added, almost apologetically.

The man looked slightly amused, as if he'd also experienced the same things in the past. "So I guess you'd like a chaperone for your first visit?"

Diana smiled, grateful and relieved. "Yes, please. That would be marvelous."

"Okay, let's go! Oh, by the way, I'm Bill. William Buford Johnson is my full name, American, and...also on a quest." He gave Diana another friendly smile, and her heart skipped a beat. *I wonder what his quest is? Is this the man who will help me find Arthur's treasure? It certainly seems like it could be.*

When the ceremony was finished, Diana and Bill left the temple and walked toward the river bank.

"I really enjoyed the ceremony," she said. "I've never seen anything like that before. Thanks for being my guide."

"I'm glad you liked it, Diana."

She nodded eagerly, and suddenly she realized she liked Bill, as well.

"I'm eager to know more about you, if you don't mind," she added with a big smile. She hoped to find out if he was the man the gypsy had described.

Bill looked at her as if making a decision. "All right," he said. "The short or long version? If you want the long story, you'll also have to tell me yours, and this means we need to get some breakfast because I'm hungry. Just to let you know, whenever I visit a temple, I tend to have food after the *darshan*—meaning after seeing and greeting the Lord; make sense?"

Diana laughed. "Sure, I understand. Somehow I missed my breakfast, too! There's a café at my hotel, not far from here. Breakfast is on me."

"Cool!" Bill laughed. "I'm getting a date and the lady is buying me a meal to top it off?"

Diana blushed. "I proposed my hotel only because I don't know any other decent restaurants in town. I just arrived yesterday. You can certainly choose any other place if you like."

"No sweat," said Bill. "I was only joking."

Diana blushed even more, and to hide her embarrassment, stood up and looked around for a rickshaw.

"Allow me," said Bill. He whistled loudly at an approaching rickshaw, and raised his hand high, just like he would hail a cab in New York City. Diana laughed as the rickshaw pulled over next to them.

"Where to, Milady?" asked Bill. He winked at her playfully.

"Valentines Hotel, 7/3/2B, Clive Road."

Diana suddenly realized the oddity of the name, even before Bill offered the inevitable amused comment, "Oh my, my.... This seems to be a real omen..."

They both laughed, and Diana felt relaxed for the first time in many days.

* * * *

Bill ended up liking Diana so much that after they exchanged their own personal stories, he decided to take a room in the same hotel. Diana told him she was planning to visit the Gora Baba Ashram the next day, and Bill enthusiastically offered to accompany her. He was very interested in learning more about Arthur, so early the next morning the two met in the hotel lobby to wait for Madhava Gupta. He arrived at 8:00 a.m. and seemed surprised to see Bill. After introducing the two men, Diana asked if Bill could come along. There was no problem.

They traveled several kilometers east on Highway 76 toward Chandi, before the auto rickshaw finally reached a ferry *ghat* on the bank on the Ganga. Madhava gestured for them to get down, and they walked to the ferry that would take them to the small island in the river. This was where the Gora Baba Ashram stood. Madhava paid the ferryman, who proceeded to push the boat toward the middle of the river and into the fast current.

Soon the small island came closer and when they reached a landing site, the three travelers disembarked. The older man led the way toward the ashram with a confidence that showed he had been to this five-acre island more than once. He passed through the gate and greeted one of the young monks who was walking by with a big basket of garlands. "*Hari Om! Pranams*, Eeshan Baba."

The young monk, clad in flowing saffron clothes, smiled and called back, "*Hari Om!* Madhava Babuji. *Namaste!* Welcome. Are you staying for lunch?"

"We'll be happy to, Eeshan. I have come to introduce Miss Diana Warwick—a direct descendent of Swami Shivananda—to Swamiji. Is he here?"

The young *brahmachari* was so startled he almost dropped his basket. "Most certainly! What a great honor! Let me go and inform him at once." The young man slightly bowed his head and ran off with the basket toward the main building, followed briskly by the guests.

After being introduced, the three visitors sat cross-legged on mats on the floor and the swami, who was sitting on a raised platform, addressed them with a surprisingly strong voice.

"*Hari Om!* My name is Shukananda Sarasvati. Welcome to our *ashram*. The full name of our founder is Pujya Shivananda Sarasvati Swami, a name he received with his initiation into the Shankaracharya spiritual lineage; but everybody called him Gora Baba because he was white in complexion. I am told that this lady is the direct descendent of our founder. It is certainly a great surprise for us, and a great happiness, if this is true."

Diana looked into the swami's intense eyes. She could easily understand that he might still be unconvinced, probably because in the past, some impostors, or even Arthur's enemies, might have presented themselves as his descendants with the intention of discovering his secrets.

She spoke up, respectfully. "My name is Diana Warwick, and I have received the letters written by Arthur and Yuri, as well as the medallion that Arthur sent to his family. And these two sacred necklaces," she added, showing the necklaces she was wearing.

"Those are the *Tulasi mala* and *rudraksha mala*. Very sacred. *Tulsi* is used for *Bhagavan Krishna's* worship, and rudraksha for *Bhagavan Shiva's* worship," he said quietly.

Diana nodded in acknowledgement at the new piece of information which enriched her understanding of the native Hindu culture.

"Can we see the medallion?" requested the Swami.

Diana opened her bag and spread her valuables on the floor—the letters and notes contained within her file folder, and the medallion. When she opened the folder, the picture of the Mother Goddess, which she had received from the gypsy, came into full view.

"Can I see this picture, too?" he asked.

Bill picked up the medallion and picture and respectfully handed them to the swami, who seemed genuinely impressed.

Diana added, apologetically, "The golden plate with the symbols might have been lost when Arthur's descendent Edward died in Jerusalem trying to follow his route."

The swami suddenly looked up to her, and for the first time there was a trace of trepidation in his voice when he asked, "What will you do with Arthur's possessions?

Diana was surprised. She had never really thought about it. Until now she had simply focused on *finding* the treasure, not planning on what to do with it. "I don't know," she said sincerely. "I have only been tasked to find the treasure. I guess I will do whatever Arthur would want me to do with it. I am ready to follow the advice of the people who have learned from him and who certainly understand his mission," she concluded, stammering a little bit, embarrassed.

The swami exclaimed, "*Jaya! Wonderful!*" He was obviously very pleased.

"My child," he said, "where did you get this?" He held the picture of the Mother

Goddess up high, showing it to Diana and the others in the room.

"It's very strange." Diana explained what happened. The swami, Eeshan, Bill and Madhava looked amazed.

The swami got to his feet with surprising agility. "Come with me and you will see for yourself." He smiled.

Diana collected her papers, and the guests walked to the temple room behind the teacher. Once inside, he turned to Eeshan. "When we have entered the temple room, close the doors and do not allow anyone to come in until we have finished."

The young Brahmachari seemed surprised, but he nodded without hesitation.

The swami gestured to Diana, Bill and Madhava to enter the temple, and then the doors were closed. He explained a quick purification ritual and instructed them to hold a little water inside the palm of their hand, while he chanted some sacred mantras and sprinkled them with water from a small and brightly polished copper container. Then he silently gestured to them to come closer to the inner sanctuary of the temple, where he pulled aside a silken curtain, embroidered with marigold designs and woven to perfection, giving an aura of sacredness to the area. The smell of incense engulfed Diana's nostrils, sending a quiet thrill through her body.

She could tell, after a quick glance at Bill, that he was feeling the same.

While the swami and Madhava offered their respects to the deities, Diana and Bill remained breathless. In front of them, standing on an ornate pedestal, was the same deity of the picture Diana had received from the mysterious gypsy.

The swami explained, "This is Mother Maha Kali, with many arms, a garland of skulls, and a sweet and peaceful smile on her beautiful face. Next to her, two other forms of the Mother Goddess sit on similar pedestals—Maha Lakshmi, with four arms holding two lotus flowers and offering blessings and protection, and Maha Sarasvati, with four arms playing the *vina* and holding a scroll and a *japa mala*."

Just in front of the deity of Kali, a large Shiva Lingam was sitting, embedded with a mysterious head decorated with a large *rudraksha* bead necklace, identical to the necklace that the gypsy and Diana were wearing.

The swami smiled at their surprise. "These are the personal deities worshiped by Gora Baba, who prayed to the Mother until his very last days. It seems that the Mother Goddess and Bhagavan Shiva, have been watching out for you, too, Diana."

He motioned to Diana to come closer. "Now watch." He held the medallion up with a meaningful look, stepped closer to the deity of Maha Kali and placed the medallion onto the pedestal, on an ornate design that was exactly of the same size and shape. He pressed the medallion into the pedestal and smiled at Diana and Bill's amazement when the medallion clicked *into* the pedestal, now apparently becoming one with the structure. If they did not know better, they would have thought the medallion was simply a relief decoration of the pedestal itself.

The swami explained: "The medallion is a key which opens a secret passage that has been closed now for over a century. We had received word the secret would be revealed during these years, and we were eagerly waiting for that to occur, and now it is happening as we speak."

They bowed to the deity, and then the swami motioned to Diana and Bill to follow him toward another part of the main temple room. They stared in wonder at the old portraits hanging on the walls, the intricate lattice windows which allowed the cool river breeze to blow through, the grey stone flooring, and the painted pillars. At the side of the large room opposite the inner temple room, was a raised seat made of carved wood. The swami walked over to it.

"Please help me," he said, "I am not young anymore and the *asana* is heavy."

Diana and Bill understood and helped him move the heavy carved seat aside. Under it, a small portion of the weighty stone floor had slid off, revealing a dark passage with a steep flight of stairs. Diana and Bill looked at the guru.

"See," he said, "this is the passage that leads to the secret chamber under the Baba's *samadhi* temple. Only the *acharya* of the ashram is told about this from the previous *acharya* on the day he is appointed to succeed him; it's a secret that has been preserved a long time."

Bill looked around for some light, and the guru directed him to a cabinet on the opposite wall, where he found two flashlights. "We do not have electricity here, so we keep these for emergencies." He smiled. "Now you two people climb down the stairs and go find your secret. Madhava and I will be here waiting for you. It is said that Gora Baba was actually cremated in secret, so when his *samadhi* tomb was built, the extra place that was intended to preserve his entire body was used to hide his possessions. In this way, his enemies never found out about them. They believed that inside his *samadhi* there was only space for his dead body, as it is usually done for *sadhus* who are not cremated. Generally Hindus cremate their dead, but *sannyasis* and spiritual leaders are considered to have spiritualized their bodies through their *yogic* realizations, so there is no need to burn the body. However, Gora Baba specifically requested his body to be cremated, without anyone knowing, because it was part of his plan."

The stairs only went about six feet deep, then a narrow passage with smooth, earth flooring led to a small room. "We won't both fit inside there," said Bill. "You go ahead; you are relatively smaller than me and you can move around better. I don't think there is any danger here."

Diana walked in hesitantly, her knees a little weak. She stood breathless, minutes away from her first direct contact with her long lost relative. What answers would she find, if any? *Perhaps the mystery will only deepen.* Putting aside all doubts, Diana stepped forward.

The flashlight revealed a brass urn with a tight lid, most likely containing the ashes of Gora Baba, and a large wooden box. She lifted the lid of the box. It was unlocked and contained several bundles of papers and some small objects wrapped in a cloth. Diana collected these and the papers, which she tied inside another piece of cloth, and walked out of the tiny room. Then, she returned to the stairs and back up to the temple room.

"Have you found something?" asked the swami, raising an eyebrow, as Madhava and Bill looked on inquisitively. Diana lifted up the two bundles to show them, and gave him a big smile. "If you don't mind," she said, "I would appreciate your help in understanding the value of what I've found."

The swami's face burst into a huge smile. He gestured for Diana and Bill to help him push the *asana* back into its original place. He then went to retrieve the medallion from the pedestal of the deity. He pushed the temple doors open, and happily walked back to his room, followed by Diana, Bill and Madhava. Eeshan, who had been waiting outside, folded his hands and bowed slightly as they all passed by.

Chapter 8 - Four Mystic Symbols

After Diana and Bill came back up to the main room of the temple, they, along with Madhava, made themselves comfortable at the feet of the swami. Diana spread the papers out on the floor and opened the cloth bundle to reveal three different silver-colored symbols, each the size of a fist.

"Hey! I know these already!" she said excitedly. "They are the Jewish Star of David ✡, the Islamic Crescent moon ☾, and the Swastika 卐." She looked at each one carefully, adding, "If these were the symbols on the golden plate, I can understand why Edward thought he needed to go to Jerusalem to find the treasure."

The swami smiled. "Actually, these are all Hindu Vedic *Dharma* symbols, and they have very different meanings from what you have grown up with. What you call the Star of David, in India is known as a Sri Yantra, a sacred diagram we associate with the worship of the Universal Mother Goddess."

"Are you saying that the Jews appropriated this symbol from the Hindus?" she asked, tilting her head and narrowing her eyes as she looked at the swami.

Confidently, the swami replied, "Certainly Hinduism is much more ancient than Judaism, so it is possible the Jews learned of it. However, it is also possible both cultures used it independently, as both cultures may have had the same roots in Mother Goddess worship."

Diana frowned and contemplated the possibility; one which was opening up an entire horizon of new ideas. "All right, what about the Islamic Crescent?"

"Have you ever seen a picture of Lord Shiva?" he asked, leaning forward. He gestured at Madhava, who got to his feet and grabbed a book off the shelf. He opened it to a beautiful picture of Lord Shiva. His head was adorned by the crescent moon as he sat in a pose of meditative bliss. He showed it to Diana, whose eyes widened in surprise. Madhava went to get another book. This time it was one featuring various pictures of the great Kumbha Mela festival. Madhava pointed out one picture in which several Hindu banners bore the Crescent.

"Are you also saying that the Muslims appropriated this symbol from the Hindus?" she asked, her brows furrowed.

"The Hindus were the people who lived in Arabia before the advent of Islam, and so, one must come to their own conclusion," the swami responded

Diana looked shocked.

"The Swastika is probably the most misunderstood symbol of all," he continued. "In the Hindu, Jain and Buddhist traditions, it is an auspicious symbol of prosperity. In fact, its very name means 'blessing'."

Diana sat mesmerized and anxious to learn more of this mysterious history.

"The fact that the Nazis misappropriated it as the dreaded insignia of their a-dharmic evil regime cannot contaminate nor discredit it. For the sun can never be touched, even by the darkest clouds that may temporarily cover the sky," he added sadly.

"One more thing, the Nazi's, for their symbol of Nazism—I assume in trying to be fashionable—twisted the original Vedic Swastika one-eighth turn clockways making it sit on one of its points."

There was a momentary silence as the listeners appeared to contemplate his words. "What about the fourth symbol?" Diana asked, bringing the conversation back on track.

"Look at the cloth,"

Diana picked up the fabric in which the three symbols had been wrapped, and her eyes went wide as she opened it. Embroidered in red on the light saffron material was another symbol, repeated three times.

Smiling at her excitement, the swami explained, "This is a Sanskrit syllable, the famous ॐ OM or *Omkara*, the primordial sound of the universe, chanted daily by millions of people in their *yoga* practice and meditation throughout the world."

"Yes, the *yoga* symbol OM; I am aware of it, but what is this 'primordial sound'?"

"According to the Hindu scriptural narrative, the universe was created with the expanding sound of OM, and it will be withdrawn with the contracting sound of OM." He elaborated. "We can say that when Bhagavan, or God, utters the *Omkara* mantra, the sacred OM, while exhaling, the universe is manifested within that single breath, and when Bhagavan—in the form of Vishnu—inhales, the universe again collapses back and is withdrawn into His universal body. With each *Omkara* breath, a new universe is created and destroyed, like bubbles on the seashore. Here we are talking about trillions of human years to be equal to a mere second in God's timeline."

Bill quickly spoke. "Carl Sagan wrote that the Hindus counted the universal time scale in billions and trillions of years, whereas we in the west do it in thousands of years. The Native Americans, too, speak of a cycle of creation, preservation and destruction, unlike the Christian and Judaic idea of a singular and linear creation."

"The Hindu scriptures say that Bhagavan manifests Himself as Lord Brahma to help in the creation, Vishnu to help in the preservation, and

Shiva to help in the destruction of the universe; they are referred to as the Trimurti or Trinity," interjected Madhava, looking over the top of his glasses.

"So the fourth symbol we were looking for is the OM," observed Diana.

"Correct. And I think that it is also important to notice that the OM symbol is repeated three times on the cloth. It was done on purpose, so whatever way you apply the symbols, it seems that the OM should be repeated three times, for any endeavor to succeed." replied the swami smiling.

"Why three times; why not two or four?" inquired Diana

"When you pronounce anything three times, it completes the ritual," replied Bill, smiling.

"Thanks Bill. Now this takes us back to the search for the treasure, I guess," said Diana.

"Let's see the letters," Bill suggested.

Diana picked up the first one, dated March 1859, and began reading aloud for everyone to hear.

"My Dear Descendent,

Congratulations! If you are reading this, it means you have already followed the clues to my Ashram in Allahabad. This proves you are the Chosen One, for you have been helped by the Hand of the Divine Mother, and my blessings are with you always.

220

"The treasure you are searching for was first found by the very powerful Emperor Vikramaditya, who ruled Bharata Varsha, as India was called in ancient times. He defeated many enemies, including the powerful Shaka invaders. Under his protection and care, Dharmic civilization flourished, not only in India but throughout Asia. His influence was felt far and wide. His reign even impacted the civilizations of the Mediterranean. Vikramaditya was such a powerful and righteous ruler that every mother wanted a son just like him and every king, thereafter, tried to emulate him.

"During his reign, he discovered a great treasure which had originally belonged to the Pandavas, the saintly kings of the epic "Mahabharata," who had once ruled over India for hundreds of years. They kept the treasure in a secret place in the Himalayan Mountains, knowing the impending dangers of the advent of the Kali Yuga. This is the age we are in now, also called the Iron Age, (an age of degradation, where hypocrisy and quarrel would be its hallmark) that started with the disappearance of Bhagavan Krishna over 5000 years ago.

"Before leaving this mortal world, Emperor Vikramaditya hid the treasure, as he could not find any worthy person to safeguard it. However, he made sure to leave enough leads to

enable the worthy to retrieve it one day. Over a period of time, the treasure retreated into legend and most people began to doubt its very existence. Yet, by mere accident (or by God's grace), I have discovered these leads. I am writing to tell you that it is real, and you can find it using the information I have collected over the years, which is there to assist you.

"As you must already know, I am a good friend of Yuri Shakharov, the Russian archeologist and historian. We both share the conviction that Hindu philosophy and culture are profound and more suitable for the peaceful co-existence of all humanity than any other philosophy and culture, because that is the way God has designed the original Dharmic civilization.

"During these last years, I have dedicated all my energies to the study and practise of the teachings of the Vedic scriptures and saints. Many people have been attracted by my efforts. Now they come and listen to me, and in turn I have learned much from them, as well. I have seen the injustice of our Colonial Christian rule. I have defended and supported the Indian people's right to freedom and self-determination. I strongly support their spiritual practices and their wonderful wealth of knowledge, and the dynamics of their religion.

"Not unexpectedly, this has brought the wrath of the Imperial British Government and

the Christian missionaries down upon me. They have resorted to all possible means, including the foulest, to try to destroy this beautiful culture and knowledge. In their eyes, I have become a traitor and an apostate.

"I discovered that Jesus actually came to India to learn the divine knowledge of the Vedic seers before starting his public preaching. I also found out that much of Jesus' original teachings had been distorted by the Churches for materialistic and political purposes. As soon as I started sharing this vital information, I was called a heretic and a great danger to the 'God-given authority' of the White Man to rule over India.

"But the fact is, Jesus never ordered his followers to enslave people. He never supported the exploitation and destruction of the property of others. He did not ask his followers to demean and persecute anyone's legitimate beliefs and traditions which focused upon an authentic relationship with God. I actively spoke these truths loudly, boldly and publicly. I was asked to quiet down and desist from my 'trouble-making', as they called it. I replied that no matter what they say or do to me, they will never force me into silence, nor get me to renounce my conscience and knowledge. This has enraged my opponents even more.

"They have actually tried to kill me several times, but by the protection of the Mother

Goddess, I have always escaped unscathed. However, I remain worried about the safety of my family.

"I did send them a letter with two necklaces composed of sacred rudraksha and Tulasi beads, as well as a golden plate engraved with sacred symbols, and the medallion which opens the secret chamber. I am hoping they will preserve them as valuable heirlooms, even if they don't understand the deeper meaning. I hope they have preserved them until you, the Chosen One among my descendants, appear to complete my mission."

Diana's voice faltered for a moment, she was so overcome with emotion. It was as if Arthur was reaching out to her over the years…

"There is a dark secret organization…" Diana sat bolt upright before continuing to read from the pages in front of her, *"…that calls itself the Society for the Eradication of Pagan Superstitions, or SEPS. It was founded by Macaulay in 1836. He wanted to establish the major center of his organization in Allahabad, and he arranged an alliance between the various denominations and affiliations of Christian missionaries. In 1845, the Apostolic Vicariate of Patna was established here in the sacred Hindu city of the Triveni Sangam.*

"When I first came here in 1856, I saw the disaster the Colonial regime was causing to this beautiful and sacred land, persecuting or

pressuring saints and destroying or distorting their sacred scriptures. I expressed my thoughts to the educated Indians here, and I think I gave them some inspiration and hope to reclaim their own dignity as a people and a culture. Unfortunately, the Governor came to know of my efforts. I had to escape from Allahabad, yet my friends and supporters had to endure an even more strenuous persecution at the hands of the British Administration at the behest of the churches."

As she paused, Madhava interjected, "So Gora Baba was one of those who inspired India's uprising of 1857? How amazing! What happened next?" he said, smiling broadly.

Diana returned his smile, fully understanding his excitement, and continuing to read.

"I fled, first, to Calcutta, where I found a very difficult situation, and then, hiding within a caravan of Bengali Hindu pilgrims, I reached the famous holy place of Purushottama Kshetra, Jagannatha Puri. It was here that Jesus is said to have lived for some time.

"It is a beautiful little town on the ocean shore, with a little more than 2,000 residents, but it is visited by a great number of pilgrims yearly, and during the Ratha Yatra or Car Festival, I have seen about 20,000 attending. It has been a wonderful place for me to hide from both the British government and the Christian proselytizers." Diana remembered once seeing a

Rathayatra in downtown London, in Trafalgar square, where they distributed free food.

"In Puri, I found shelter in the wonderful doctrine of Sri Adi Shankara and remained there studying and practising with full dedication. It was there that I met my Venerable Guru, Ugra Narasimha Bharati, and the great and saintly Acharya of the Sarada Matha.

"I followed him in his travels around India, and in his kindness he accepted me as his disciple. I was soon awarded the sacred order of sannyasa with the name of Shivananda Sarasvati. My guru also ordered me to establish my Ashram in Allahabadj and preach boldly and without fear. My Most Venerable Guru Maharaja also kindly visits me in Allahabad every time he comes to the city.

"In accordance with his orders, I have been living and serving the Divine Mother here at the sacred Triveni Sangam. I am ready to die at any time as a testimony to my faith. Leaving this material body is only a natural passage everyone must face, and the constant awareness of the danger to my life has actually helped me to quicken my realization that I am, indeed atman, an immortal soul, and transcendental, eternally liberated from the conditionings of matter. I am pure spirit made of consciousness, eternity and bliss.

"I plan to return to Europe, soon, to present this transcendental knowledge to the most

educated and powerful class in Britain. They must understand the damage they are inflicting upon India. If possible, they will also become interested in studying these transcendental truths for their own benefit and the benefit of their people."

Everyone in the room seemed enthralled by Gora Baba's powerful words. Diana felt awed by her ancestor's dedication and determination. She contemplated, for a moment, what kind of life Arthur had embraced and how happy he must have been. He gave up everything and never hesitated, even when faced with extreme danger and death.

While Diana was reading, Bill shuffled through the other documents. Now he held up a thicker sheet of paper for Diana to see. It was the portrait of a rather imposing man in his late thirties, with extremely short hair and a beard; he also had several sets of three horizontal white marks traced across his forehead and upper body. He was dressed in the traditional robes of a renunciate, and wearing a *rudraksha* bead necklace. While sitting cross-legged on a decorated seat, he was holding a staff which appeared to be wrapped in cloth. The man's expression was peaceful and content, and exuded confidence. Diana's emotions welled up as she studied the image of her ancestor, Gora Baba, a famous Hindu saint and hero.

Bill allowed Diana a few moments to deal with her emotions before urging her to continue. "What about the treasure? Does Gora Baba say anything about it or how we can find it?"

Diana answered, lifting her head, "That's all I have."

Bill handed her the next page, and Diana continued to read.

"Although real treasure lies not in material possessions, it is still a fact that worldly wealth is necessary to establish a prosperous and progressive society, even when it is based upon the universal principles of religion. This is why Arjuna, the dearest friend of Bhagavan Krishna, was entrusted by his elder brother, Yudhisthira, with the important task of collecting riches for the treasury of the kingdom. The value of the tributes collected by Arjuna, who thus earned the name Dhananjaya or 'Winner of Wealth', is immeasurable. Now this vast treasure must once again be used for those same Dharmic purposes of Emperor Yudhisthira and Maharaja Vikramaditya....

"During my journeys, I visited Srinagar, the capital of that ancient epicenter of Hindu civilization known as Kashmir and named after the great sage Kashyapa. I was invited for an audience with the venerated Hindu king, who sought my blessings and counsel. There, in the palace of Maharaja Gulab Singh, of the Northern Kashmir Kingdom, I was shown an

ancient manuscript with some strange verses. He claimed it as the signs left by Emperor Vikramaditya for his future successors, to unearth the lost treasure of the Pandavas. He graciously shared the clues with me. The good-natured king also informed me that the other three signs were with the Eastern Manipur Kingdom, the Southern Travancore Kingdom and the Western Kutch Kingdom. I met with the three noble kings and they generously shared their respective information, knowing me to be a spiritual person having everyone's interest at heart. I soon realized that Emperor Vikramaditya had made sure the clues were spread out in the four directions of Bharat; Allahabad being the center.

"Here are the translations:

"The first verse reads: 'The great archer, during his exile, mistakenly fights with his own son and loses consciousness. He is awakened with the help of a magic jewel, dear to the Naga or serpent people. The jewel needs to be returned; the Nagas are awaiting its return since a long time.'

"The second verse reads: 'The apes in their apparent curiosity removed the celestial fiery Crystals of Light from the magical healing mountain, and later on, they placed them beneath the bridge, bathing in their light throughout the time of night.'

"The third verse reads: 'Three sacred symbols adorned the abode of the Lord. Yet this abode sank into the Sea during the Great Flood.'

"The fourth verse reads: 'The entrance to the treasure begins at the meditation place of the first Preceptor in Kashyapa Mira. This will lead you to the chosen destiny.'

"One last piece of advice, before you can begin using this knowledge to find the treasure, I would request you start in the East, it being a very auspicious direction. Go to any one of the fifty-two Mother Goddess Shakti pilgrimage sites to seek her blessings and ask for her active help. After the treasure has been found, it is my wish that you, my worthy descendent, dispose of the ashes of my cremation in the waters at the Triveni Sangam, the place where I have lived so happily. Only then will my soul be happy and able to move on along its journey."

Diana stopped, with tears in her eyes, overwhelmed by thoughts of Arthur.

Madhava remarked, "It looks like the first lead refers to an episode in the *Mahabharat*. Perhaps following it will lead you to the jewel. I think the second refers to an episode in the *Ramayana*, the third to the ancient city of Dvaraka, and the fourth—to Kashmir. The leads, themselves, do not seem sufficient. You may need the help of an expert who can research and discover more information to help you find the treasure. I would suggest you meet with my friend, Professor Vivek Cariappa, to discuss this further; he is an expert in this subject matter. If anyone can help you, I believe it is he."

"Yes," said the swami, "I agree."

"I think we can leave all these things in the secret chamber for a later time," said Bill holding the papers in his hands. "Let's take a picture of the information about the four clues and take that with us."

Diana nodded in agreement and took out her cell phone. "I'll also leave the medallion and the other letters here with you, if you don't mind." She looked directly at the swami and added, "If there are hostile people who want to lay their own hands on the treasure or harm us in any way, we won't hesitate to destroy our photos, knowing the originals are safe."

The swami nodded his head. "You are very intelligent, my child. You deserve to find the treasure. Whatever blessings I can give, they are yours."

Diana felt a sudden surge of affection and gratitude for the old man. She felt an impulse to bow down on the floor and touch it with her forehead as she had seen in the other temples. Bill and Madhava followed suit, and the swami blessed them all.

Madhava got to his feet, visibly moved, and said, "Swamiji, I will go to alert the ferryman.

He will take us by boat back to the auto rickshaw stop and we can return to town before dark."

After eating *prasadam*, or sanctified food, the swami and the other residents of the Ashram went to see their guests off at the ferry *ghat*. Their separation was as emotional as the parting of old friends.

The three companions remained silent all the way back to the hotel then Madhava respectfully saluted them. "It has been a great honor to meet and know you, my friends. Please come to see me when you return to Prayagraj." He fished a small piece of paper and an old pen from the pocket of his *kurta,* and wrote down both his and Vivek Cariappa's address and phone number. "Please also make sure you stay at a safe distance from SEPS."

Diana nodded gravely.

The next day, she and Bill resumed their trip back to Delhi from where they could catch the flight to Bengaluru to meet Professor Cariappa.

* * * *

Professor Jawahar Katju was also feeling confident, and answered his ringing mobile with the arrogance of one used to getting what they want. His mood quickly changed, however, when he heard Lord Dyer's voice on the other end.

"Good evening, sir. Thank you for calling me," Katju promptly said in the servile tone of a sycophant. "Is there any news?"

"Yes," replied Dyer in his usual commanding tone. "We found out that Eleanor Warwick, a descendent of Arthur's, died recently, and left a substantial amount of her fortune to her granddaughter, Diana. It is confirmed Diana left Britain for India on the 7th of March, after brief trips to Israel and Russia." Dyer paused for a moment, possibly waiting for Jawahar to digest the info, before quietly adding, "To this, we add your information that a Diana Warwick has been in India inquiring about Arthur. It appears that, contrary to what we had all believed, the secret of the treasure may very well have been handed down to Arthur's descendants.

"This, as you well know, could be either very good for us, or very bad, depending on who finds this treasure first," Dyer added sarcastically.

"Yes, sir, I agree."

"You seem rather unconcerned by this information, Jawahar."

Jawahar could almost see the frown on Dyer's face. He immediately stiffened like a chastised child. "Not at all, sir, how can I risk such an indulgence."

Dyer continued. "It's very likely Miss Warwick has gone to Allahabad. If you have not already set up a tail, I suggest you send some of your men to the old place on the river island, and find out where she's staying, and track all her movements from now on."

"Yes, sir. I will do it tonight." Jawahar could feel actual palpable fear course through his body.

"Very well, you will be rewarded for your good service. But remember to keep me updated!" The conversation ended abruptly.

Jawahar switched off his phone, as an overwhelming fatigue overtook his body. He took a deep breath and summoned a sense of determination to take its place. *This big British pig thinks I am working for him. So, let him. I will get his money and use his contacts, and in the end I will keep the loot for myself. I am sure I can disappear in some Arabian country and spend the rest of my life in luxury. Ah, the life! A large harem full of young girls and whatever other pleasures I can think of, just like those wealthy Arab Sheiks. Living 'large and in charge', as the Americans say.* He laughed aloud, alone in the comfort of his room. *I am sly like a fox, indeed, and I'm just getting started.*

He made a few phone calls to get things in motion.

* * * *

Within the hour, Jawahar's three favorite students, Nalayak, Jacky and Habib, had boarded the night train to Allahabad. They had been provided with a good stock of cash and a message showing Diana's passport photo, obtained from the hotel where she had stayed on her first day in India. The next day, they checked the three decent hotels in town and soon found out she had stayed at Valentines. For a few thousand rupees, the hotel receptionist supplied all the information he had. She'd met two men, a foreigner and an Indian, and gone out with them.

"She left yesterday with the foreign black man," volunteered the hotel employee.

"Where too?" enquired Habib.

"They mentioned the Taj Mahal."

"Okay," said Jacky.

The three boys hired an auto rickshaw and took the ferry to the island where the Gora Baba Ashram was, but they only found a young monk. The monk said that yes, three guests had come to visit the Ashram recently, and were interested in the story of the Gora Baba. "We showed them around and then they went away," said the young monk politely. "Why? Do you need to contact them?"

"You are very smart, eh, saffron asshole?" snarled Nalayak aggressively in Hindi, as he pointed a finger at him. "Where is your old man?"

"Our Swamiji?" The young monk seemed unperturbed by the offense. "He is not here. He has been traveling, and we expect him to return by next week."

235

"Oh, really?" leered Habib. "What if we have a look around, eh?"

The young monk did not seem pleased. "Well, I suppose if you do not believe my words, you will probably give little consideration to my objections."

Without any warning, Jacky violently slapped the monk. "You have such a smart mouth, filthy Hindu, don't you? It's time you people were put in your proper place."

The monk stepped back, still appearing unruffled by their behavior. The three hooligans left him on the verandah and stormed the Ashram, banging all the doors open and barging through them easily, except for the main temple doors, which were securely locked and very heavy. After a few minutes of useless effort trying to break them down, they went around the temple building and had a try at the latticed stone windows, again without success. So they peered through to see if anyone was hiding inside the temple room, but saw no one. Finally deciding their job was over, they stormed off, but not before knocking down a few potted plants and throwing around the kitchen pots, as well as the contents of the food storage-room.

* * * *

From a safe distance, Eeshan wiped the blood from his cut lip and watched the young thugs get on the ferry, and then reach the river bank where the auto rickshaw was waiting for them.

The vehicle sped off, after which the brahmachari, with a small silent laugh, went to the temple to call his Godbrothers and Swami, who were ready to defend the deities with their lives, if need be. The Ashram had been attacked many times in the past and the monks had a precise plan for such events. Today, they were especially well prepared, for they had been expecting hostile visitors. The altar had a safe inner room right behind the deities, where the swami hid along with the others. The young among them had long sticks called *lathis*, which can be used as weapons. In most Indian villages, people are trained in this type of martial art as part of their daily routine. Lucikly, they hadn't had to use them, today.

* * * *

Professor Jawahar Katju was not a happy camper. "You bloody idiots!" he blurted out. "Do you really think Diana Warwick is going around innocently, like a simple tourist visiting the Taj Mahal? Do I have to do all the work myself!? Good for nothing scumbags!" he yelled, before slamming down the phone in Jacky's ear.

After his fourth double whiskey, Jawahar began to feel a bit more optimistic; he would come up with a solution. He was smart. He'd fix this.

* * * *

Wisely, they took the pilgrim route after visiting Varanasi, Ayodhya and then Mathura. Bill and Diana later left for Delhi, without actually visiting the Taj Mahal. It was a clever deception they created for the hotel receptionist, after deciding they might not be able to trust him.

After a good night's sleep in the Golden Palms, the same hotel Diana first checked into upon her arrival in India, Diana and Bill awoke early Tuesday morning, prepared to play the role of ordinary tourists, visiting the museums and parks, while they planned their next move to reach Bengaluru at an opportune time. The day went very well.

It was 11:00 p.m. before Diana and Bill returned to the hotel and went to the reception desk to pick up the keys to their respective rooms. The receptionist handed them over, and then said, "Miss Warwick, you have two guests waiting for you in the lobby. They've been here for about two hours."

Surprised, Diana threw a look in that direction. "Really? I'm not expecting anyone at this late hour. Are you sure they want to see *me*?" She narrowed her eyes in suspicion.

"Yes, Miss. They specifically asked for you, and they knew when you had checked in."

Diana and Bill looked at each other. Bill shrugged, and they both walked to the lobby area. Diana stopped right in her tracks when she saw Mrs. Ormila Naukar, wearing a sharp suit and a fake smile, getting on her feet to welcome her. She was accompanied by a short man in a costly suit. He had short dark hair and was clean shaven.

With great effort, Diana forced herself toward the awful woman and her companion. Diana introduced Bill, and then looked questioningly at the man next to Ormila.

When they had all taken their seats, Mrs. Naukar began the conversation in a rather friendly tone. "Miss Warwick, this is Professor Jawahar Katju, from the JNU, in Delhi. Yesterday, he and I were speaking, and I happened to mention your search for information about your ancestor." She paused, perhaps looking for acknowledgement from her audience. When none came, she continued. "He has graciously offered to help you, albeit in a non-official way. So...I decided to come personally to give you the good news."

Diana observed that the woman seemed very ill at ease, which, to her, felt like a clear indication she was lying. Professor Katju was also wearing a smile that seemed unnaturally large, especially for his thin lips. Diana noticed his eyes were blood-shot, as if he had drunk one too many shots, and she smelled strong cologne which didn't seem to be coming from Mrs. Naukar.

"Yes, Miss Warwick," Katju cooed, "you will be glad to know I have also been investigating Arthur Warwick for several years; a fascinating character, indeed."

Diana eyed him warily. She felt an instant dislike for this man, and it wasn't just because he'd come in the company of Mrs. Naukar. There was something slimy about him; something almost physically repulsive. Diana instinctively knew she had to choose her words carefully. "I know Arthur Warwick lived in Allahabad for some time, so I went to pay my respects. I found an Ashram where it was believed he had stayed, and where he died." She added, "The monks tried to explain to me some of their mythology on reincarnation and vegetarianism, but I didn't really understand it all. It seemed like a lot of Hindu mumbo-jumbo to me." Diana turned toward Bill and placed a hand over his. "Wasn't it, William, dear?" she said, meeting his eyes. "So fascinating, so colorful, and so folkloristic, but totally impossible to understand."

Bill easily followed her lead. "Yes, honey. I would even say it was childish. But hey, you gotta love India and all its fascinating superstitions, right?" He rolled his eyes.

Diana nodded and offered Katju a winning smile.

* * * *

The professor watched Diana, taking in her bright eyes and amused expression. Was she telling the truth about her disdain for Hindu

240

superstitions? *Not likely*, his long experience told him. But if she was lying, this woman was certainly a formidable opponent. He gave her an appraising look, keeping in the habit of his special way of dealing with women. Great legs, good breasts, beautiful face. Could she be that clever, too? *Watch out*, he told himself. *This situation could be tricky. Let's see how she takes this.*

"You have probably heard about the story of the treasure Arthur Warwick was looking for," he announced, in a cordial tone.

Diana and Bill reacted in seeming surprise. "A treasure, you say? How fascinating! We don't know about that. What kind of treasure?" Diana had placed one hand on her heart.

The ball was in Jawahar's court. His heart raced—his adrenaline pumping; the excitement of the chase was taking over. "Oh, it's a legend in these parts," he added dismissively. "I thought you might have heard about it, as you *are* a descendent of the man."

"Not really," insisted Diana, looking very innocent. "My grandmother, Eleanor, asked me to come to India to find Arthur's tomb and say a prayer for him, because my family feared that he had lost his good Christian faith in his last years." She sniffed.

"My grandmother was a very religious lady, but I don't personally care much for religion. The good thing is she paid for my vacation to

India, so I'm having a great time going around and seeing various places, and best of all, I don't have to spend even a penny from my own pocket!" Diana smiled quite cheerfully.

Professor Katju looked on stiffly, uncertain about the label he could stick on these two foreigners. *People without decency*, is what Mrs. Naukar will think. She would believe things like that should never be said aloud, in front of strangers. He knew her oh so well. He, on the other hand, was all stirred up, like a hound dog sniffing the scent of its prey.

"Ah, that is wonderful, Miss Warwick!" he exclaimed, nodding his head quickly as his impatience rose to the surface. "May I ask which places you have visited already, and which ones you are planning to visit?"

Diana responded, a placid smile still on her lips. "Oh, we have already been to Allahabad and Agra. After Delhi, we might head south. Which places would you recommend?" She stared back at him.

She is good, he thought. "Well, Miss Warwick, it depends on your visa. It's good for three months, am I correct?"

Diana nodded.

Jawahar continued. "Our spring season has just begun, so you can enjoy any location you like. Here in India, we still have large tribal areas, too," he added, with a half-smile. *She could easily get herself in trouble and disappear into some dangerous place among the heathen uncivilized tribes.*

"Oh, how very interesting!" said Diana, leaning forward slightly. "But tell me more about this treasure you were talking about. I find it a very fascinating topic; very exciting, actually. What is the legend that surrounds it?"

Jawahar chuckled to himself. "Of course it's just a legend, but it is very fascinating, indeed. Legend says a great treasure was hidden in an ancient temple in the jungle, guarded by thousands of poisonous snakes. Many fools have wandered in those jungles, but only a few have come back alive," he concluded. *At least the story of the snakes sounds realistic.*

Diana and Bill looked horrified. "Gross!" said Bill. "I'm not sure I want to see that place. I don't have an appetite for those kinds of things. I'm no Indiana Jones."

"Me, neither!" added Diana.

"So you'd better forget about treasure hunting altogether," said Katju; he tried to suppress his slightly threatening tone, but was afraid he may have failed. "Then you can visit our beautiful cities instead. Enjoy the markets, the monuments, the parks, and all the tasty food we have in India! I am sure you will have a great time. Here," he added, extracting a glossy card with the JNU logo, "please do not hesitate to call me if you need anything. I will be more than happy to assist you." He ran his hand through his hair, unsure of what to do next.

"Thank you so much. We'll certainly keep that in mind," Diana took his card and stowed it in her purse. "Now if you'll excuse us, we're tired and need to sleep." She stood before stifling a yawn.

Jawahar pressed his lips together in annoyance. These two were not going to be easy to trick. He sighed in frustration.

* * * *

Diana and Bill walked out of the lobby toward the elevator which would carry them to their floor. It wasn't until they were sitting in Diana's room, sure that no one could overhear, that they relaxed and exchanged comments about the strange meeting.

"You know, Diana," Bill said, very seriously, "you got brains, girl. I think these people may have underestimated you." He put his arm around Diana's shoulders affectionately.

Diana giggled. "Well, I really had a good time with those characters. That sleazy fellow was really comical, making a huge effort *not* to show how interested he was in the treasure, and how anxious he was to find out what we knew and believed."

"You got that right!" Bill threw back his head and laughed loudly.

"We need to be very careful from here on in. Especially since they know where we're staying. That makes me uncomfortable, because it means we're being watched all the time. My gut feeling is they're part of SEPS. What do you think?"

Bill agreed. "They're SEPS alright; no one else would have known about the treasure. We need a plan to outwit them, but...before that, we need some sleep." He stood up, and then stooped and kissed her goodnight on the cheek, before heading to his own room.

* * * *

The next day was pretty much similar to the previous one, only Bill and Diana made a point to visit the Red Fort and Mahatma Gandhi's Mausoleum in Delhi. They went for ice cream at the India Gate and visited the War Memorial inside the hexagonal garden, moving around among the crowd of Indian families and running children.

They talked less than usual, and just enjoyed each other's company.

Diana got online on her cell to book two seats on the early morning flight to Bengaluru.

"Here it is," she whispered to Bill, who was sitting next to her eating an ice-cream. "Air India flight, departure 06:15 and arrival 08:45. I bet the crooks hounding us don't get out of bed before nine o'clock, so we'll be able to outrun them easily. When they eventually find out we've left, they won't know where to look." She turned to him, a sly smile on her face. "Two can play this game..." She winked at him, playfully.

Bill grinned. "Good thinking! I'm enjoying this game of cat and mouse."

That night they ordered room service and watched an old movie in Diana's room, feeling more and more content in each other's company.

* * * *

In stark contrast to Diana and Bill, Professor Katju was *not* enjoying himself.

"All right, Jawahar," Lord Dyer demanded, "what did you find out?"

"She went to Prayagraj, sir, and she was at the old place on the river island." He wriggled in his seat.

"Well, this much we knew already, didn't we?" Dyer responded in that crisp tone of British superiority that Jawahar had loathed all his life. He silently cursed. What was he supposed to say?

"Find out what she's up to," said Dyer, obviously annoyed.

"She said she does not believe in Hindu fairy tales and treasures," Jawahar said sourly. "I tried to scare her off, but if she keeps saying she does not believe in the existence of the treasure. Well, it's like beating a dead horse." He began rocking himself, back and forth, in distress.

"Can you throw her some bait? Maybe she can work for us."

The Treasure of the Pandavas

"I doubt it," replied Jawahar, momentarily displaying a rare confidence. "But I will try all the tricks in my book."

"Alright, keep me posted." The line went dead.

Professor Katju had to down half a bottle of whiskey before going to sleep. Also, nobody had found him a girl yet. All in all, it was not a good night.

* * * *

By 4:00 a.m. on Friday morning, Diana and Bill stood at the reception desk, their luggage in hand. The night shift employee sleepily checked their room bills and received their payment, before calling a taxi to take them to the airport. Before 5:00 a.m., they arrived at their gate. Everything went smoothly, and they boarded the flight without any problem.

* * * *

By the time the dayshift receptionist was able to speak with Jawahar's henchmen, it was already six o'clock. A very groggy but frightened Habib gathered all his courage to call the professor on the phone.

Jawahar, suffering a hangover from the previous night's heavy drinking, was beside himself with anger when he was awakened by the ringing cell.

"*Who the hell is this?!* Is this a decent time to call me?" he snarled.

"Sir...it's Habib. I am very sorry to disturb you, sir, but it is urgent. Please don't be angry, sir. We are your loyal boys, sir. The hotel receptionist just called to say the American man and the English woman checked out very early this morning without our knowledge. They were headed for the airport. Sir—"

Poor Habib was not able to finish his sentence. His next words were drowned out by an explosion of rage, in which insults were mixed with sounds which could hardly be defined as human. By the time Jawahar was able to express himself coherently, Habib had had the opportunity to think of something to sweeten the blow.

"But we know where they went, sir. The driver was very attentive to their conversation, as we had already ensured his cooperation two days ago."

"Where did they go?" Jawahar snarled.

"They were talking about Kolkata, so we just need to put someone at Kolkata's airport this morning from 8:00 a.m. to noon, and we should be able to catch up with them. Sorry for the messup, sir."

Jawahar remained silent for a minute; Habib could almost hear his boss's thoughts buzzing inside his head.

"*Tikh hai*," said Jawahar in Hindi at the end, still in a bad mood. "Okay. I guess we can still catch them fairly easily. Just be more careful next time."

"Very well, sir," Habib replied meekly. "We will not disappoint you again."

* * * *

After hanging up the phone, Katju got his address book and searched under Kolkata. It took him a few minutes to explain the situation to the SEPS local contact there. Two agents belonging to the Indian Communist Party reached the Netaji Subhash Chandra Bose airport before 8:00 a.m. and sat in the Domestic Arrivals lounge, armed with the photos of Diana Warwick and William Buford Johnson forwarded to them by Habib. They waited for a long time.

* * * *

At 9:00 a.m., from a public telephone inside the Bangalore airport lounge, Diana called the residence of Professor Cariappa.

A female voice answered the phone speaking Kannada language.

"Hello. My name is Diana Warwick, and I would like to speak with Professor Cariappa, please," she responded.

"Oh, good morning, Madam. My husband is having breakfast. Please wait a moment; I will call him to the phone."

Bill was standing guard near the public phone, watching to see if any suspicious characters were hanging around. So far, it didn't appear as if anyone was tailing them. After a minute, Professor Cariappa spoke. "Good morning. Professor Cariappa speaking. How can I help you?"

"Good morning. Please forgive me for disturbing your breakfast," said Diana. "My name is Diana Warwick; I have come to India for important research."

"Yes?"

"I got your phone number from Madhava Gupta in Prayagraj: he wanted me to meet you."

"Ah, Madhava! He is a good friend of mine. How is he doing?"

"Very well, Professor. He sends his regards, and he has recommended that I visit you to discuss some important and *urgent* matters."

"Very well. You may come to see me. Where are you?"

Relieved, Diana replied, "I am at the airport, sir. I would like to come immediately, if it is not too much trouble for you."

"What did you say your name was, Madam?"

"Diana Warwick. I am the blood descendent of Arthur Warwick, the Gora Baba of Allahabad. I have come to India to search for more information about him." Diana leaned forward against the phone booth.

Cariappa remained silent for at least one full minute. Diana thought the connection had been lost, but then she heard the background noise of his home. "I will call you back from another number," he finally replied, in almost a whisper. Diana was a little surprised. A moment later, the payphone rang.

When he spoke again, he sounded worried. "In this case, Miss Warwick, I would strongly advise you not to advertise your identity in the presence of strangers." There was a pause. "I also think it is better not to show my home address to anyone. Rather, write down this other address. I will come personally to meet you there and take you to my house; I hope this is clear to you."

"I understand, and I thank you very much." Diana wrote down the second address—a vegetarian restaurant not far from the airport— the professor's physical description, and his car's licence plate.

Diana and Bill arrived at the restaurant with plenty of time to spare before the professor was to meet them, so they decided to order some breakfast. When they had finished their food, at the appointed time, they picked up their luggage like ordinary tourists and headed outside.

Only a few steps down the street, they saw a blue sedan with a man sitting behind the wheel. The car's licence plate matched. Diana peered in the window, recognized the professor from his description, and climbed into the seat next to him. Cariappa asked for their passports to make sure their identities were accurate. Apparently satisfied, he seemed to relax.

Bill quickly loaded the luggage into the trunk, and then settled himself in the back seat. Cariappa had already started the engine and the car rolled away smoothly, at a normal speed.

The professor shot a cautious look at Diana while driving along in the heavy morning traffic. "You don't seem very surprised at my request for extra safety in our meeting. Does this mean you've already encountered complications during your journey?"

Diana smiled. "Yes, you could say that, although nothing bad has happened to us yet. We have actually been rather successful in our mission, except for some not-so-pleasant encounters with a Jawahar Katju of the JNU in Delhi, and his friend Ormila Naukar of the Indian Council of Historical Research."

"Ah!" Cariappa didn't seem surprised. "You started in the most difficult place, I see. And how did you get in touch with Katju, if I may ask?"

"Well, on my first day in India, I thought that the best place to start my search for information about my ancestor was the Indian Council of Historical Research in Delhi. So I went there and met Mrs. Naukar, but she wasn't very friendly."

The professor chuckled. "I am not surprised," he commented. "Please carry on."

Diana continued, explaining how the pair was waiting for her in the hotel lobby when she and Bill returned from Prayagraj. "I also wondered how they found out which hotel I was staying in, on the very day I arrived."

"My dear friend," said Cariappa, frowning, "as a first step in your search for your ancestor in India, you have walked right into the arms— if I may express myself in this way—of the Society for the Eradication of Pagan Superstitions, the same super-secret criminal organization that persecuted, and was responsible for the death of your beloved ancestor. This group has systematically tried to destroy Hinduism and the other native religious systems of India for the last 175 years, at least. They are certainly capable of tracking your movements in India in a flicker."

Diana's eyes widened. "Oh," was all she could say. Now all the pieces were falling into place. Of course, if there were some historical records to be suppressed, someone who wanted to prevent the truth from being discovered would first of all try to control the archives, the academic Departments of History, and the like. *How stupid I've been!*

"Do they know you came to Bengaluru to meet me? Do you think you might have been followed?" asked Cariappa, his voice sounding concerned, while the car was waiting for the green light at a road crossing.

Suddenly, and in spite of their difficult and dangerous situation, Diana and Bill both laughed at the same time. "We think not. We left very early, and we almost as good as told the hotel car driver that we were going to Kolkata."

Professor Cariappa turned to gaze at Diana and Bill in obvious relief. "Very well done. I am sure there will be some very embarrassed people in Kolkata, this afternoon." They all had a hearty laugh.

* * * *

And how right they were.

At 2:00 p.m., a fuming Jawahar was informed by his contact in Kolkata that Diana Warwick and her friend never arrived.

"They could be anywhere by now," said the student on the phone.

What Professor Katju said could not be easily understood or repeated, but the student didn't even think about being offended. That raging *'shithead'* at the other end of the phone line was the all-India Supremo of SEPS, next only to Lord Dyer, himself. One simply could not and did not want to confront nor complain about such an horrendous man.

The student quietly hung up the phone, grateful to be in far-off Kolkota.

Chapter 9 - Lost Knowledge

Professor Cariappa seemed to visibly relax as their car entered Koormangala, an exclusive neighborhood of Bengaluru, known for its population of highly educated residents. Bengaluru is the 'silicon valley' of India.

He asked how their trip had been so far, listening as Diana spoke of the many sites they had visited. "How did you like Prayagraj and the Sangam?" He glanced at Diana curiously.

"Oh, they were wonderful!" she said in excitement. "The confluence of the rivers was amazingly beautiful and so serene; I went there every morning to soak in the peace, as well as the sunlight. That's where I met Madhava Gupta."

"Spoken like a true descendent of Gora Baba," said Cariappa. He kind of casually looked into the rearview mirror at Bill, as he clutched the steering wheel firmly. "And you, my friend, are you a *yogi* too?"

"Well...er..." Bill stammered, seeming a little embarrassed. "Not really. I've visited Vrindavana and studied the Vedas and Puranas with an expert, especially the *Bhakti Yoga* tradition. I have also been in Dharmasala and met a Buddhist Lama, an extraordinary man who gave me many hours of his valuable time, opening my mind to an immense world of *yoga* spirituality."

"As I said," smiled Cariappa, "another *yogi*."

Cariappa pulled to a stop in front of a medium-sized two-storey villa, and then got out of the car to open the wrought-iron gate, before driving into the yard. Two house servants came out to help with the luggage, and Cariappa led the way up the stairs to the second floor. An elegant, middle-aged lady, draped in a traditional *sari,* was waiting at the door, and she smilingly offered her greetings in the usual Indian way with her palms pressed together.

Diana and Bill greeted her in the same way, saying *"Namaste"* with folded hands.

"This is my *ardhangani*, my good wife, Jayanti," said Cariappa with an affectionate smile. "In Sanskrit, *ardhangani* means 'the other half of my body'. Vedic knowledge, the knowledge of *yoga*, teaches that male and female are only halves of the 'reality'; the actual realization comes with the integration of the male and female energies that transcend the material body." He smiled again at their expressions of curiosity. "A rather advanced concept, isn't it?" he teased.

After entering the spacious drawing room, Cariappa directed his guests toward a sofa and armchairs made of dark, beautifully carved wood and cloth.

"I know you've had your breakfast already so I will just offer you a cup of tea for the moment. In the meantime, Jayanti will prepare our lunch."

Mrs. Cariappa nodded, and then disappeared through the wide-arched passage. She returned a few minutes later with cups of hot and dense *chai*.

"Let's talk about your ancestor now," Cariappa began, looking at Diana and leaning forward attentively. "My extensive research allows me to confidently say that during the time of the British Raj in India there were many who opposed it, and not only just the Indians, but some of the British as well. Chief among them was Arthur Warwick."

Bill jumped in. "We came to know from Arthur Warwick's letters, which we found in the Gora Baba Ashram, that the British Raj considered him a thorn in their side for encouraging Indians to stand up for their civilization, culture and religion, against all odds. This is what I like most about him."

"You are absolutely right," commented the Professor, as he looked at Bill and then back at Diana.

"I have read his letters and some of his papers which were scattered across Britain, Russia and Allahabad," added Diana, "and much of what he wrote concerned the attempt of the British to eliminate or, at best, undermine

Indian culture through the deliberate distortion of History and Religion."

Cariappa nodded appreciatively. "Arthur Warwick's writings are an important discovery; credit goes to the two of you. I am glad you have not only found the writings but understood the salient points. The consensus among scholars, so far, has been that they were all destroyed. He was too much of an embarrassment and a loose cannon for the British Administration, besides being a sworn adversary of Macaulay."

"Who is this Macaulay?" questioned Diana.

"He is the main piece of the puzzle; knowing him will let you know what Arthur had to undergo." Cariappa smiled. "Macaulay chose the exact epicenter of ancient Vedic thought, Prayagraj or Allahabad, as the HQ for SEPS, a group diametrically opposed to anything Vedic. He was positioned in India by the Colonial British Raj to undermine India's history and religion, and open the way for Christianity. The aim of the system was to keep the colonies under control ideologically. In this way, the few could control the many. Power was established in such a way that very rarely would they have to use actual police or a military force to keep the native people subjugated. A developed and sustained sense of apathy was much more effective. To destroy the sense of worth, two main weapons were used: one was racial prejudice, and the other, religious persecution, which was administered through the English language. The British had a thousand-year plan to rule over their colonies, and India was its crown jewel, and they would do anything to secure it for generations to come. In the end, they would successfully rule for two hundred years."

Diana and Bill nodded, appearing to understand the Imperial British plan.

"I would like to know more about this Macaulay character, if you are willing to share; it'd be of great help," urged Bill.

"Yes, it would be my pleasure," the Professor replied.

"He leaned back, comfortably settling into his armchair. "Thomas Macaulay was a British historian, who was born in 1800 and died in 1859. He is best known for introducing the English education system to India. Though he wasn't a missionary, he believed Christianity held the key to the problem of eliminating what he called 'India's ignorance'. Although he confessed to having no knowledge of Sanskrit, he did not hesitate to belittle the Hindu scriptures which were written in that language. He abolished the Sanskrit college in Calcutta."

Bill interjected, "From what you say, it seems like most Colonial conquerors had a similar mindset and used the same tactics.

Native Americans and Native Africans have also had to pay a heavy price."

"Agreed." Diana nodded.

The professor spoke. "Macaulay wrote to his father that if his education plan succeeded, there would not be a single idolater among the respectable classes in India. He promised to do it without any efforts to proselytize, or without the smallest interference with religious liberty, but by natural operation of knowledge and reflection, meaning distorting Indian religion and historical texts in a way to colonize the Indian mind, which they eventually did very successfully."

Cariappa paused, took a sip of water and continued. "Macaulay planned to create a class of Christian–English educated Indians and use them to uproot their own traditions. He called them, 'Indian in blood and color, but English in taste, opinion, morals, and intellect.' Thus he proceeded to create a class of 'brown clerks' with a mentality that is comparable to what you have seen in Professor Jawahar Katju, who calls himself a true secular Indian."

Cariappa continued. "The British used the English language and mannerisms to enslave India, but what an irony that the same language was used by Mahatma Gandhi and other freedom fighters to free the country. But it wasn't about language, really, but natural resources and their ultimate control."

Bill looked very shocked and Diana buried her face in her hands, as she seemed to realize what her countrymen had done to India and Hindus in particular.

Bill asked, "Is Macaulay the only villain, or are there others?"

The professor shot back. "There were others, yes, but Max Mueller, he is as important as Macaulay. They were two mutually destructive forces who focussed their evil eyes on India and its native peoples. Max Mueller was a German who met Macaulay in London and was commissioned by the East India Company to translate the *Rig Veda* into English. His *magnum opus* was his series *The Sacred Books of the East*, a fifty volume work which he began editing in 1875. His sole intention was to deliberately undermine Hindu culture by casting it in a poor light, so that the world, and especially Indians, would start hating it for generations to come, thus making way for Christianity to triumph. For this to happen, he urged everyone he knew to pitch in with money and power, and he promised his life to make it a success.

"Max Mueller, in his own words, said, 'India has been conquered once, but India must be conquered again, and that second conquest should be a conquest by education... the ancient native religion of India is doomed, and if

Christianity does not step in, whose fault will it be?'"

Diana and Bill asked many more questions and Professor Cariappa answered them showing sufficient proof from his research to convince them of his points. Two hours passed and finally when he had finished, Diana leaned back in her chair. Bill looked simply astounded.

Cariappa noticed his guests appeared weary, and glanced at his wife. "Time for lunch," he announced cheerily. Smiling with obvious relief, Diana admitted she was famished.

Cariappa led the way to the dining area, where his wife, along with her house-helper, was bringing in a variety of dishes.

"Wow! This looks great!" exclaimed Bill. "This is all vegetarian, right? Since coming to India, I've decided to no longer eat meat, fish or eggs since they are a hindrance to my new *yogic* way of life."

"Yes," Mrs. Cariappa assured him, smiling, "this is all pure vegetarian food. We do not even use onion and garlic in our cooking, as they are not good for meditation and *yoga*."

Everyone sat at the dining table and had their lunch.

"The food tastes even better than it looks," Bill remarked. "Thanks to the 'lady of the house'." He jovially gestured toward her with hands folded in *Namaste*.

Jayanti smiled. Finally, Professor Cariappa suggested, "Please take rest for a while. Let's meet back in the drawing room around 3:00 p.m."

Bill and Diana nodded.

The professor led them to two beautifully decorated guest rooms and left them to their leisure. The wooden furniture was classical and arranged neatly. Through the windows could be heard the background noise of traffic and the sound of airplanes, from the nearby airport, flyng overhead.

* * * *

After a short nap, Diana felt refreshed. She took her papers from the bag, called Bill, and went to the drawing room to wait for the others to join her. Professor Cariappa was alerted by the housemaid and arrived almost immediately, ready to resume their conversation. Diana spread the papers neatly on the low, wide, coffee table.

"What do we have here?" Cariappa asked as he sat in his armchair.

Diana quickly replied, "These are the clues we found within Arthur's letters which will, hopefully, lead us to the treasure everyone is talking about."

"That's fantastic." The professor leaned forward to examine the documents.

Mrs. Cariappa came into the room with a platter of savories and sweets, followed by her housemaid with a tray of coffee. They set everything on the table, and then left as quietly as they had come.

"Arthur writes about the treasure of the Pandavas found by Emperor Vikramaditya and about the four passages containing the information we need to retrieve it." Diana looked at her notes. "The first piece speaks of a 'Magic Jewel' and says, 'The great archer, during his exile, mistakenly fights with his own son and loses consciousness. He is brought back to consciousness with the help of a magic jewel, dear to the Naga serpent people. The jewel needs to be returned, the Nagas are awaiting its return since a long time.'"

Professor Cariappa asked her to repeat some of the information, and Diana obliged.

As soon as she had finished, Professor Cariappa, looking momentarily pensive, began, "Hmm, this reference seems to be from *Mahabharat* times. The story goes like this...Arjuna, who was the great archer, while on exile in the eastern part of India, in error confronts one of his own sons. During the fight, he passes out and goes into a coma. Upon realizing Arjuna is his father, the young man, along with his mother, seeks the help of his step-mother, one of Arjuna's other wives, who happens to be the Naga princess. The princess immediately brings the Magic Jewel, 'Nagamani', up from the underworld—where

264

her shape-shifting serpent clan dwell—to cure her husband, Arjuna. Seems like the Pandavas kept the jewel with them since then, and now it needs to be retrieved and returned."

"How can we do this? We don't even know where the jewel is." Diana could sense her frustration levels beginning to rise.

"Professor, what do you think?" asked Bill.

"Well, my research shows the jewel was handed down through many generations of Manipuri Kings and it stayed at the Kangla Fort, located in the heart of present day Imphal. However, during one occasion, the Manipuris almost lost their kingdom during an invasion, and at that time, they may have shifted their treasures to a more friendly location. My guess is the Nagadevata Temple inside the Kaziranga National Park, in the state of Assam, because it was constructed by the Manipur King just after the invasion."

"Do you have a map to this temple?" asked Diana.

Cariappa smiled. "I know where the national park is, but I'm not sure where the temple might be exactly. Once you reach the park, I'm sure the guides there can help."

Bill looked up from his cell phone. "I checked it out. It says the park is pretty big, like 430 square kilometres, and full of rhinos, tigers and elephants. It could be quite an adventure!"

"Alright, we have no other option but to go and see if we can find it," Diana stated matter-of-factly. There was a momentary silence.

"What does the second lead say?" inquired Cariappa.

"The second paragraph speaks of a 'fiery crystal' and says, 'The apes in their apparent curiosity removed the celestial fiery crystals of light from the magical healing mountain and later on, they placed one beneath the bridge, bathing in its light throughout the time of night.'"

Professor Cariappa listened thoughtfully for a moment, closing his eyes in seeming meditation before he spoke. This seems to refer to an episode in the *Ramayana* where the army of ape warriors helped Lord Rama build a bridge across the sea to Lanka. This bridge, called *Rama Setu* or 'Rama's bridge' still exists today—although partially submerged—and it connects India to Sri Lanka."

"That is what Madhava said, too!" exclaimed Diana, with excitement.

Bill looked perplexed. "I've never heard of any bridge between India and Sri Lanka."

Cariappa stood up and went to his large library to retrieve a book. He showed Bill and Diana some satellite photos, clearly revealing the bridge line stretching across the Indian Ocean. He even showed them the latest internet video from NASA, suggesting the rocks had been placed to form the bridge. Bill and Diana looked at each other, eyes wide in surprise.

"The *Ramayana*, the story of Lord Rama, says that the evil *rakshasa* King of Lanka, Ravana, kidnapped Sita, the wife of Rama, and took her to his capital city with the intention of marrying her. So Rama secured the help of the ape people and built a bridge of floating stones from India to Sri Lanka." Cariappa smiled. "Yes, this is more than a hundred-thousand-year-old history; the apes were not ordinary monkeys like many people believe. They wore clothing, built palaces and lived in cities, and were also expert in the use of weaponry, engineering, and in medical science, as well. After crossing the bridge, the ape army engaged in a terrible battle against the *rakshasa* army. Rama's brother, Lakshmana, was seriously injured and left unconscious by poisonous arrows shot by Ravana's son, so the physician sent Hanuman to fetch a special medicinal herb from the Himalayas. As time was short, Hanuman did not want to spend hours searching for the herb, so he lifted the entire hillock and jumped back to the battlefield in Lanka. Lakshmana was revived and finally Rama killed the evil Ravana and rescued his wife, Sita."

"That's an amazing story. How does the crystal fit in?" asked Diana.

"I believe the crystal was some kind of highly fluorescent mineral found on the hilltop, and some of the crystals fell off and attracted the attention of the apes. A fluorescent substance absorbs sunlight and radiates it back in the dark, so if several of these crystals were stuck between the stones of the bridge, they would radiate light in the night. It would be easy for a night crossing to get supplies. Vikramaditya could have found the crystals and used them to find the treasure in a dark cavern; in this case their fluorescence must have been extraordinary."

"Do you think the crystals are still embedded in the bridge, after all this time?" asked Diana.

"Quite possibly? It's very likely that in the course of time, the crystals have become encrusted and covered with coral or mollusks, as usually happens with submerged rocks and even to the surface of sunken ships. In this case, their fluorescence could be totally covered up and nobody would be able to tell them from any other rock."

Diana interjected. "If we can find this fiery crystal that would be the best option, but how can we know if it's a rock or an actual crystal? If we can't find it, can we just use powerful flashlights instead? It seems to me that they are only to be used for illumination purposes?"

"That, my friend, is up to *your* good luck, and to God's help. The fiery crystal might be of more use than we know. Maybe it's part of the puzzle. We cannot afford to miss any links mentioned in the clues." Cariappa stood up.

Diana nodded her head. "Understood."

"The third paragraph." Bill pointed to a spot on a page and handed the paper to Diana.

"Yes," she said. "Here it reads: 'Three sacred symbols adorned the abode of the Lord. Yet this abode sank into the sea during the Great Flood.'"

The professor immediately answered. "I am quite sure that refers to Dvaraka, the ancient city built by Lord Krishna upon an artificial island on the north-west coast of Gujarat. According to tradition and history, it was submerged by the ocean about 5,000 years ago. Today, there is still a small town called Dwarka, on the seashore in front of the area where the original Dvaraka stood."

"How did the city get submerged? Do we have information about that?" Diana put the piece of paper she had been reading on her knee.

"We certainly have," replied Cariappa. "After the great war described in the *Mahabharat,* there were several signs of the imminent arrival of the Kali Yuga or Iron Age as the West calls it, and Krishna and his brother, Balarama, left the city, warning the inhabitants to take precautionary measures before the impending disaster."

Bill spoke up. "Krishna, in Hinduism, is an avatar of Vishnu, like Rama, right?"

"Correct," said Professor Cariappa.

"Then certainly Krishna must have known what would happen in the future," said Bill. "Being God, it only makes sense that His knowledge and compassion would have been limitless."

"Of course." Cariappa nodded.

Diana interjected. "Has anyone actually seen it beneath the water?"

"Yes, it was found in the latter part of the 20th century by a marine archaeologist from the National Institute of Oceanography," said the professor. "It's on the ocean floor, not far from the western coast."

"Great, that helps." Diana smiled. Diana spread out the paper with the four symbols in front of her. "The swami in Gora Baba's Ashram explained the meanings of the symbols to us, but what is their connection with the submerged city?

"That is very difficult to say, and the verse is not helping much. I think when you get to Dwarka, the connection should become apparent. In any case, I believe they should not be hidden to the point of being unrecognizable." Cariappa smiled confidently. "I am sure if you go scuba diving near the site, you should be able to get to it without much difficulty."

"Very good," said Diana. "Then we'll see when we get there. And what about the fourth and final clue—the route map?"

Bill promptly handed over the fourth clue.
Diana read the lead again. "The entrance to the treasure begins at the meditation place of the first preceptor in Kashyapa Mira; this will lead you to the chosen destiny."

Professor Cariappa sat with his eyes closed for some time before speaking. "Kashyapa Mira is known today as Kashmir. The name 'Kashmir' is derived from the illustrious Kashyapa Rishi who was the first preceptor of *Dharma* in the Kashmir valley. It was once a vast lake that geologists have dated back to 50,000 years ago, but it was drained by the *yogic* power of Kashyapa Rishi, himself, who wanted a safe and secluded place for *yogis*, and thus the Kashmir Valley was created. Since time immemorial, Kashmir has been the home of *rishis*, who are mendicants in search of truth, just as monks living in a monastery.

"There is also a connection with the Pandavas here. It is said that the Pandavas walked through this valley—perhaps while they were on their way to heaven—by climbing the Swargarohini Mountain. I see there might be a connection with the Pandavas' Treasure. If that is so, your hunt is of enormous proportions.

"I believe the first preceptor mentioned here is Kashyapa Muni himself. Of course, much later there was Adi Shankara who was also globally known as the first preceptor, so the clue seems rather clear. We know that both

Kashyapa Muni and Adi Shankara remained for some time at a small hermitage on what is now known as Shankaracharya Hill near Srinagar, Kashmir."

Diana spoke. "I heard that Gora Baba was initiated into the Shankara line."

"Indeed he was, my friend," confirmed Cariappa. "As you have seen, the four leads have been quite simple to decipher. Which means the goal is simple, but the path itself may be very arduous."

"Yes, I get it, Professor." Diana sighed.

* * * *

When they were done for the day, Cariappa insisted Diana and Bill stay the night and they happily accepted. While they waited for dinner to be served, Bill got an email with a wedding invitation from Priti, the woman he had met on the flight over. He found her phone number and gave her a call. Priti was delighted to hear Diana would be attending the ceremony as well.

After he hung up, he looked at the others and confessed he had no idea what to get Priti as a wedding gift. Professor Cariappa suggested an auspicious item, such as cloth used in decorating an altar, or perfume, or a traditional Indian sari for the bride.

"Tomorrow morning, before you return to Delhi, we can go shopping along with my wife. She knows all the good places."

"I'd love that, actually," Diana said smiling. "It seems like forever since I've done something as ordinary as shopping. I relish the idea."

When Jayanti arrived to oversee the dinner, her husband explained the situation. She seemed more than happy to oblige, and immediately started recommending different saris and scarves. She also suggested they consider sandalwood oils from Mysore and perhaps a variety of scented incense sticks, as well.

The dinner was as wonderful as the lunch had been. This time the conversation was focused on their personal lives and experiences, and family traditions. They spoke for hours before finally bidding each other good night.

The next day, after shopping, it was time to say goodbye to their new friends.

"Come and visit us again! We certainly enjoyed your company," the older couple repeated, as they dropped Diana and Bill at the airport.

There was a flurry of 'thank-yous' and 'we wills' before the guests finally left for Delhi to attend Priti's marriage.

Chapter 10 – On the Trail of the Scorpion

Commander Zia walked into the room of a nondescript apartment building in uptown Karachi. Though dressed in civilian clothes, he was in fact the commander of the Ghaznavi, the only nuclear submarine of the Pakistani navy. Seeing the other people already seated at the large table, he saluted, then took his place in the empty chair. He looked around at each of them, perceiving them as brothers-in-arms.

Lt. General Aurangzeb, the Director of Pakistan's Inter Service Intelligence Agency, or ISI, met his glance. He was in plain clothes as well.

Three more men were sitting at the table whom Commander Zia had never seen before. Two of them were dressed in relatively modern—although rather conservative—Western attire; the other was more fashionable, in casual yet costly clothing.

Commander Zia had every reason to feel confident. He had completed his mission successfully and was ready to brief his superiors, official and non-official, state and non-state.

The general introduced him. "Brothers in the service of Allah, this is the Commander who has taken delivery of the six nuclear devices—code named Scorpion Eggs—and forwarded them to their specific destinations. We are waiting for the six explosions to take place on the designated day." He smiled in delight, then turned to Zia, lifted his chin in superiority and ordered, "Give your report, Commander."

The briefing inspired their zeal. With smiling faces, the members of the meeting congratulated one another with enthusiasm.

In the end, the general boasted, "So you see, brothers, our plan is proceeding well. The six devices will go off one after the other. This will create much confusion among our many enemies around the world, including those in Pakistan who act as obstacles to the establishment of a pure Islamic government based on Sharia law." He paused to light his cigar and taking a few puffs. "As long as the civilian government in our country is supported by anti-Islamic forces and Western devils with their bloody dollars, we can never establish a Sharia state."

Everyone nodded in quick succession.

"Once Pakistan lives up to its name as the 'Land of the Pure', then and only then will it take its rightful place as the rallying point for all the Islamic peoples of the world. We can do much better than ISIS, as we have the Islamic nuclear bomb. We must continue this struggle, for Pakistan is at the core of the future Dar al-

Islam, the global Islamic Nation. By strengthening Pakistan and making it pure, our battle in the Dar al-Harb, the Field of War in the very lands of the infidels, will achieve infinite success. The duty of Jihad will thus be facilitated and will be carried forth in the most favorable conditions. We will never stop until the entire world is either converted to the one true faith or is firmly subjugated under our divinely inspired Islamic Khilafah rule."

The audience seemed mesmerized by the general's talk, as they gazed into his eyes in obvious delight and listened to his prophecies.

"The Western countries are in a state of profound decadence. By Allah's grace, within the last several decades large communities of Muslim migrant and refugee populations have been established in their midst. Our Jihadi cells have taken advantage of the golden opportunity and been working relentlessly and diligently. We have succeeded in even converting many whites, blacks and Hispanics of the effeminate and weak members of their inferior and immoral Western civilization.

"In the meantime, the laws, media, academia, financial and political systems, and even the welfare system and human rights bodies of their present governments are offering us great opportunities to 'release the beast' from within."

As the general continued, the men sitting around the table imperceptibly nodded. "This preparatory stage is almost complete; the opportunity to implement the purpose for which our very nation of Pakistan, the 'Nation of the Perfect Believers', exists. This is why the success of this mission is so imperative. Now," he jeered, baring his nicotine-stained teeth, "it's Pakistan's turn." Then he smiled at Zia. "As agreed, Commander, you will soon be promoted to a full member of our inner circle. Congratulations."

After many more minutes of talking, the meeting was adjourned.

* * * *

Ibrahim Jr. was careful to follow the protocol. Immediately after the collection of the six cases wrapped in large waterproof bags, from the submerged Ghaznavi submarine, he called his elder brother in Karachi to confirm he had picked up the cargo. All was going as planned.

The next day he met with a team of Maldivian fishermen, to whom he passed the cargo earmarked for India via Malappuram in Kerala. His local contact in Malappuram, one Hakim Kutty, would receive it. The fishermen had been paid well, and they had thoroughly camouflaged the luggage. Once prepared, Ibrahim Jr. proceeded leisurely through the Arabian Sea—destination Somalia. There he would deliver the other five cases to the ISIS affiliated cells, known by different names to confuse the civilized world.

* * * *

The Indian cargo reached Malappuram and was now in the safe custody of their agent. Hakim was a thirty-five-year-old leader of the Islamic Students' Movement affiliated with ISIS in his native town. It was a beautiful town, but ironically, it was this very beauty itself that fueled his extremism. Beautiful Malappuram was a great tourist attraction, surrounded by lush green forests and the dreamy Nilgiris, the Blue Mountains, with their scenic landscape and fertile riverbeds. However, Hakim strongly believed that the best things on this planet were destined for the enjoyment of the Muslim faithful alone. Such beauty should be controlled by the faithful for the glory of Allah and his blessed prophet. He actively participated in ISIS online propaganda and sent foot soldiers from Kerala to the Middle East.

Only a small number of Hakim's most loyal followers, however, knew about the nondescript hut located in his father's mango orchard. And even fewer knew about the mysterious case that had been delivered there on the 27th of February. Six of the most dedicated students of his Islamic Students' Movement were taking turns keeping vigil around the hut. Their families had been told they were going to an intensive study on the Koran in preparation for a new Madrassa, or Islamic school, that Hakim wanted to open in town.

The Treasure of the Pandavas

On the morning of Saturday, March 12, Hakim received a phone call from his contact in Hyderabad. The news was not good. Indian Intelligence had tracked the shipment of the "Scorpion Eggs" to the Maldives, and now the single remaining one on to Malappuram. Hakim was instructed to take all necessary steps to avoid detection and move the mission forward.

* * * *

The Air India flight out of Thiruvananthapuram was soaring smoothly through a clear sky. From his seat near the window, Jai Bharat looked down at the wide collection of small islands, beautiful jewels scattered in the Indian Ocean. A long time ago, they had been part of historical India, but now they were an independent country.

Avinash and Satish of the Vajra team, both dressed in casual clothing, were dozing quietly in their seats. The three men were going to spend a few days in the Maldives as tourists, following the trail of the nukes.

The Valley had supplied them with Indian passports bearing Muslim names to help them smoothly pass into the Islamic country without suspicion. The Valley's Upendra Dogra was a master of forgery; the best of his kind.

Jai looked at his two companions. They appeared peaceful, as if resting before the battle. *Let them sleep while they can.* He picked up the in-flight magazine. Absent-mindedly browsing through the pages, Jai thought of the other members of the team, who had also left the training facility for their specific missions. It was their first; Jai could feel the tension and prayed they wouldn't botch it up.

Tej and Ranil had traveled to a tribal area of Mizoram. There the Korean fisherman informant had been secretly relocated by the IFA. With a new identity, he could easily pass as a member of the many north-eastern tribes of India. This part of the country is dominated by a population with Mongoloid features; the man would blend in with them and live a safe life. There they had a long and detailed discussion with him, giving the team members precise descriptions of the cargo delivered to the Ghaznavi submarine.

Based upon this intelligence and combined with Karry's valuable support, Vajra Team members Lachit and Mahendra now dedicated their attention to the search for any scientists who could support their mission. The other two members of the team, Vikram and Ganesh, had remained at the Valley to coordinate the mission in the background.

The aircraft touched down smoothly at the international airport in Male, Maldive's island capital. The members of the Vajra team retrieved their overhead luggage and filed out of the aircraft, chatting about their next meal like ordinary tourists.

Their first move was to stay at the same hotel where, according to their local informant, Ibrahim Jr. had stayed. It was one of the largest, a skyscraper with thirty floors. They had already made reservations in advance, as required, in order to obtain a visa. The airport and city were on different islands.

It took less than thirty minutes of driving and ferrying to reach the hotel. They settled in a spacious suite on the twentieth floor, overlooking the ocean. The view was spectacular; the clear blue skies and crystal clear waters, enchanting.

"Let's do the typical tourist thing," said Jai, smiling. "Let's go have a swim and a drink, then a good dinner, before we get into any other action. What do you think guys?"

Satish and Avinash smiled, took their swimming trunks out of their luggage, and then changed and headed to the beach.

As they walked out, Jai stopped for a moment to speak with the receptionist about their plans during the stay.

The following morning, with the assistance of the travel desk, they hired a yacht for a "live-aboard" experience of a few days, to sail on a tour of the most beautiful places in the archipelago. It was a cover; the main reason was to go to the one particular island where Ghaznavi dropped the Scorpion Eggs and find the trail.

Being originally from Kerala, Satish was better able to understand Dhivehi, the local Maldivian language which was close to his own, Malayalam, so he was the one who came forward to speak with the locals and win their trust. After a bit of discreet investigation on some of the no-go islands, they found that the Maldivian fishermen had moved the cargo from Ibrahim's yacht to Malappuram in Kerala. Maldives is a tourist destination and lives off its tourist trade; however, to protect the culture, they have set aside several islands, where non-locals are not allowed. With the help of a substantial amount of money and a meeting without intermediaries, the team challenged the fishermen's memory power and obtained a detailed description of the cargo, including its size, weight and whatever else the men were able to recall, plus 'Hakim Kutty', the recipient's name. Basically it was just a single nuclear bomb that was shipped to India. This was real progress, a major success, which more than justified the trip. They had gathered whatever intelligence was available and necessary. It was time to move on, as they were alerted by their local contact that the police had started to investigate their illegal landings on a few of the forbidden islands.

Back in Thiruvananthapuram, the three members of the Vajra team split up, and chose different methods of transport to continue their journey and avoid being tailed. On the way, at a nearby safe house, they disposed of their trendy suitcases, forged passports, and the clothes they had used to play wealthy tourists on vacation. They only kept one set of ordinary clothing in a small bag and each purchased a set of Indian clothes, *dhoti* and *kurta*, to visit temples, as if pilgrims.

On the 14th of March, they met again in Guruvayur, briefly visited the famous ancient shrine there to offer their homage to the deity of Bala Narayana called Guruvayurappan, and then proceeded together to Malappuram. Because they were trained as warrior monks, and also because it was part of their cultural upbringing instilled by the Agarwals, prayer was part of their DNA. They often visited famous temples to seek blessings in the activities they performed, so they were always on the path of *Dharma*.

On the next day, Tuesday, they were joined by Vikram, who had specifically come to replace Jai.

As soon as they were alone in a quiet place, Vikram gave them a message. "Jai, Karry wants you to get to Mumbai as soon as possible to work with Lachit and Mahendra and the nuclear scientist they've found. He's ready to help us better understand the device in question. Combined with the info you obtained in the Maldives, and that which Tej and Ranil have discerned, hopefully we can figure out how to handle this mess."

Jai nodded. "Okay, I'll leave it to you guys to find this 'Hakim Kutty' and the device. Satish, you're in charge of the team for now."

"Okay," confirmed Satish.

"Thanks. We'll meet soon. God bless you and the mission."

* * * *

The next morning, Vikram, Avinash and Satish woke up to the dawn, *namaz,* call from a nearby mosque, followed by a few other muezzins summoning the faithful from the more distant ones, drowning the city in loud prayer. It seemed as if there was a competition going on for the ears of the faithful. It was easy to notice that Malappuram was a Muslim-dominated district.

After a good breakfast, the three friends dressed for the occasion and left the hotel for their tour of the local mosques, each separately, discreetly searching for Hakim Kutty. They didn't need to search for long, he was well known and they soon located his house, and the place of worship he regularly attended, and were able to obtain his phone number.

After a week of following him closely for leads, the three left Malappuram, unable to find any other clues. It was time to move forward with the mission.

Ganesh, back at the Valley, monitoring the communications, had not found any unusual talk on Hakim's phone. Unfortunately for the team, Hakim had already delivered the device to his Hyderabad contact and now was lying low and maintaining radio silence.

* * * *

Jai reached Mumbai on March 16th and immediately went to meet Professor Nathuram Sarabhai at the Baba Atomic Research Centre, or BARC. He was greeted by Lachit and Mahendra, who introduced him to the illustrious scientist; the professor had been instrumental in developing India's own range of nuclear weapons. He had studied at Cambridge University, worked with the late, renowned Dr. Abdul Kalam—the former President of India—and lectured in premier institutes around the country. He was an elderly, good-natured gentleman dressed in very modest clothing, with thinning hair and a gentle smile. Although he had retired earlier, the staff at the BARC still treated him as an important member of the Center, and the Director came personally and offered him office space where he could sit and meet with his guests.

Tej and Ranil joined them soon afterward, just as the discussion was beginning. "Professor," Jai said softly, with respect, "as Lachit and Mahendra have already mentioned, we are a team of young researchers working with the IFA, and our present assignment is focused on how to protect our country from nuclear terrorism."

The professor nodded attentively, looking over the top of his glasses. "Yes, this is a very real and present danger. I understand your concern and am more than happy to help your team in any way that I am able."

"Thank you very much, Professor. As we all know, today, even a non-professional with relatively simple equipment can build a portable nuclear weapon. A well-equipped laboratory could prepare sophisticated devices of very small dimensions. We would like to learn more about these types of bombs, how to recognize them, how to neutralize them, and any other relevant information to facilitate the recent government directives on anti-terrorism," said Jai passionately.

Professor Sarabhai looked very serious and wrinkled his forehead. "It is indeed possible for almost anyone to make a portable nuclear device. Today, there are two forms of nuclear bombs, both generating the required power for an atomic chain reaction. The more primitive model consists of two rather large chunks of fissile material that are propelled together to obtain the trigger effect. As you know, fissile material is a radioactive substance capable of sustaining a nuclear chain reaction. The other model is a more advanced implosion device, in which very precisely shaped explosives simultaneously compress a perfect sphere of fissionable material. Unfortunately, all of these can be obtained on the black market by any determined terrorist group."

Lachit spoke up, looking concerned. "Professor, how do we neutralize a device like that? I think the weak part is the trigger—the pulse device, the microwave generator, or whatever is used in the particular bomb. Can the trigger be disconnected or disabled?"

"Certainly it can be done, but you should understand that it is an extremely delicate and dangerous operation. I would not recommend a non-professional to attempt it, as it could have disastrous consequences."

"But if an anti-terrorism unit," Jai pressed, smiling, "found one such device and wanted to neutralize it, what should they do?"

The professor frowned. "This is not just a theoretical question, is it? You are talking seriously?" Everyone remained silent.

The professor studied his hands for a brief interval. When he spoke again, his voice was subdued. "We scientists are certainly largely responsible for what is happening today, so we have an obligation to help, as this is a universal problem. It's about righting wrongs." He looked up. "I am ready to help you. I *will* help you. My family will understand. Whenever you need my assistance, I will personally come to do whatever is required."

"Thank you, Professor. We thought as much. But please keep this matter strictly confidential," said Jai, The professor nodded in agreement. He was probably used to such protocols.

Lachit looked around and motioned imperceptibly to Jai before turning toward the professor. "Sir," he said, "would it be possible for you to give me some personal training on the practical aspects we have discussed? I am very interested in the topic."

"Of course, Son."

* * * *

Meanwhile, Ganesh, who had remained at the Valley to coordinate the mission and use the powerful computers in the command center, finally struck gold. As luck would have it, the Hyderabad contact innocently confirmed, via cell phone to Hakim, the receipt of the device. It was more than enough for the Vajra Team to restart the chess game. It was decided that Tej and Ranil would immediately leave for Hyderabad to investigate Hakim Kutty's contact there.

Ganesh had succeeded in connecting the Valley's computers to that city's police database; this was how they had tracked Kutty's contact.

However, they had a problem.

The cell phone of the contact was registered in the name of one Fatima Osaivi. A database search of the city's electoral rolls gave a residential address where several other Osaivis were also registered.

Finding this Fatima would lead them to the person who was really using the phone, so they needed to tail this lady—and tailing a Muslim lady was no job for a man. At this point, they needed Nila and Lilavati.

* * * *

The next morning, Karry and his team traveled to the Valley from Mumbai to meet the two women.

"Good morning, sir," they said as they walked briskly into Karry's office and offered a *pranam* with folded hands in respect.

"Good morning, ladies. Please sit down." Karry smiled from behind his desk. Nila and Lilavati were each dressed in a traditional *shalwar kameez*—a long tunic and trousers— draped with a *dupatta* or light scarf. They quietly sat and looked at him.

"Your trainer and teachers tell me that you are doing very well and you're eager to start going on real missions." Karry eyed their faces for any sign of emotion. They nodded, and then waited for him to continue.

"The time has come. You have the opportunity to leave for your first mission tomorrow." He continued to study their reactions. The two were clearly pleased, but didn't say anything.

"Are you ready?" Karry asked.

"We are, sir," Lilavati replied.

Nila agreed. "We certainly are."

"Very well." Karry leaned back in his chair and began briefing the two agents on the information that had been gathered up to then. The two listened attentively until he finished.

Lilavati spoke up. "So we need to contact this Fatima in Hyderabad, find out what she knows, who is using her cell phone, and then track that person down?"

"Precisely. It should be a relatively safe job because you just need to listen and won't be required to take any other action, except in case of an emergency. You will of course have back-up—Tej and Ranil will play your husbands. They have precise instructions to come to look for you if you miss any pre-arranged meetings."

The two nodded slowly.

"Very well, then. Get your things ready. Tomorrow you will leave together with Tej and Ranil." Karry smiled as he stood up.

"Thank you for this great opportunity, sir. We will not disappoint you." Lilavati lifted her head confidently and looked Karry in the eye.

Later in the day, Karry called another meeting; this time, besides Nila and Lilavati, there was also Tej, Ranil and Jai.

When everyone was comfortably seated in his office, Karry summarized the task assigned and the guidelines they must follow.

* * * *

Later, Karry and Jai left the Valley and headed to Mumbai. Karry called his wife to let her know that he and Jai were coming home for dinner. After the meal, the family spent some time playing various board games; it was one of those happy evenings that make life worthwhile.

At 9:00 p.m., Manpreet put the children to bed and sat in their room reading a story. That gave Karry an opportunity to use the secure channel in his hidden chamber to ask Balaram for any news from 'Mongoose', the informant who had given them the first warning about the nuclear sub and its destructive cargo.

Balaram lived in Delhi with his Farsi wife, Tanaaz Nariman, and daughter, Shanti, in a four-room government flat. His daughter was now twenty-five, a university graduate and actively searching for a suitable husband. Many of her friends were already married and she was often invited to social functions and parties which she attended accompanied by her mother, to whom she was much attached.

This allowed Balaram sufficient freedom to dedicate himself fully to his job, not only during office hours, but whenever the circumstances required.

291

The Indian Federal Agency Headquarters were in a discreet underground facility—quite literally—and covered several thousand square feet and many levels under the famous Buddha Jayanti Park near the Presidential Palace, in the southern part of Delhi's forest ridge.

That Friday morning, as per usual, Balaram walked the relatively short distance between his apartment and the non-descript side-entrance of the IFA headquarters, near the railway crossing on Sardar Patel Road. It was a pleasant walk alongside the South Campus of Delhi University. The bit of exercise gave him the opportunity to keep in relatively good shape.

The other entrance to the underground facility was from the Presidential Palace itself, about three kilometers away, and was used by most of the IFA staff, whose movements in and out of the building merged with that of the staff of the President.

The entrance on Sardar Patel Road had a back door leading officially to the Director's office, and stairs going underground which started right behind Balaram's desk. A large portion of the tiled floor could slide back under the surface, revealing a four-foot-wide flight of steps into an illuminated tunnel. The entire facility was heavily guarded and powered by huge generators that were on the same underground level of the main computer rooms, although at the opposite end. The generators worked on geo-thermal energy which meant they didn't need exhaust vents, nor did they consume fossil fuels, *and* they never stopped working.

After about 300 meters of tunnel, deep inside the area of the Buddha Jayanti Park, Balaram entered the real operation center of IFA after going through the standard security check.

Balaram entered his office and sat at his desk. He switched on the connection, and the computer screen lit up. Somewhere, hundreds of kilometers away, a silent alarm went off.

The 'Mongoose' would feel the vibration of the alarm and switch the device, which looked like a mobile phone, into the 'waiting' mode. On Balaram's computer monitor a window opened, with the heading *'waiting for connection'*.

After a few minutes, a chat window popped up. Balaram typed: "The egg was real. Thank you for your help."

A few seconds later, in the right column of the window, Barry read the response, "I am glad to be of assistance."

He smiled to himself. 'Mongoose', the codename of their agent in Pakistan, was a civilian who had contacted them and offered information, saying he wanted to prevent terrorist attacks, and never asking for money or any other reward. No one knew if 'Mongoose' had another reason for assisting them. A few months earlier, one of his valuable tips had enabled the IFA to bust a terror cell planning to contaminate, with a deadly microbial culture, the water tanks of Le Meridian Hotel, not far from the Presidential palace. A small team of three had infiltrated the kitchen staff, but it was Balaram's special anti-terror squad who apprehended the terrorists.

The cursor had automatically returned to the left column. Balaram typed. "We know the package is on its way to Hyderabad, but we haven't been able to locate it yet."

There was a longer pause. Then the cursor jumped to the right column and wrote, "It will not be easy. There is a rabbit in your garden, and if I put the cat out too far, my lid may easily be blown off."

Balaram pondered the danger before replying. "This is important. We don't want to lose a good friend, but we really need to find the package."

The next pause was still longer. Then, slowly, the letters appeared in the right column. "All right. I will look for the route map. Wait for the Nightly News at 2."

Balaram sighed. The 'Mongoose' was saying that it could take at least two days to get the information they needed, and that it was too risky to transmit it on a direct line. The message would be sent in the night and on the next morning Balaram would be able to access it through his coded password.

"Thank you, my friend; we owe a lot to you," he typed.

The Mongoose responded with a smiling emoji.

"Over and out."

Balaram closed the chat window and called Karry's mobile through the secure line.

Karry answered immediately.

"Probably not less than two days till we know," Balaram said, his voice flat.

"If that's the best our friend can do, it means the place is really hot," Karry commented.

"It is. We'll meet here tomorrow."

"Yes. See you soon."

* * * *

In Hyderabad, Pakistan intelligence agent, Major Babur, in civilian clothes, was enjoying a quiet morning. He had finished his early morning *namaz* at the mosque and was officially on vacation in the Maldives. He had quietly landed at the beach in Malpe, India, a tiny fishing village near Udupi. One week later, still incognito, he reached Hyderabad railway station coming from Bengaluru. The host family had been honored to have him stay as long as he liked, and were careful not to pressure him socially.

Babur needed quiet so he could think.

He rubbed his chin, thoughtfully. Three so-called businessmen had been going around in the Maldives asking questions about Ibrahim's yacht and its cargo. On the 12th of March, Babur was still in the Maldives, and a yacht owner came to see him with some very serious concerns. Unfortunately, by the next day the three visitors had left, so there had been no time to run a verification of their identities. The ones he got from the hotel were dubious at best, and didn't give him anything of substance; most likely they were Indian Intelligence officers.

He had directly reported the situation to General Aurangzeb, the Director of the ISI, and told him Ibrahim's name had never been mentioned in any of the ISI meetings, and beside himself, only three other persons, at the highest level of power and above all suspicions, knew of Ibrahim Jr. and the route the Scorpion Eggs would take.

The information leak must have concerned the Ghaznavi. Many more people knew about the new nuclear sub and the delivery in the Maldives. But who was the traitor?

Absent-mindedly, Babur reached out for his chilled sherbet, and sipped it slowly.

I'm sure the Big Boss is going to set a trap. Most likely, he'll purposefully leak a false route for the device and probably announce the planning of the final event for a later date than the actual one.

My work here is finished. The training camp is proceeding very well. I have organized everything for the actual route of the bomb, and from now on, I can leave the rest in the hands of the Islamic Students Movement.

Babur suddenly got up from his comfy armchair in the enclosed garden. Walking into the house, he unexpectedly announced to his hosts that he would be leaving on the very next day.

Back into the battle. His vacation was over.

Chapter 11 - The Marriage Party

Priti Goswami was more excited than she had ever been in her entire life, for tomorrow she would marry her childhood friend, the handsome and fun-loving Dhiraj Jain.

The Jain family had traditionally been in the jewelry business, for their religion frowned upon all occupations that could involve any degree of violence. They were very strict vegetarians and observed all the festivals and rituals of their faith.

Dhiraj, however, had higher aspirations. The jewelry business had been rather weakened by the new trends where modernity and imitation of Western fashion seemed to be more desirable than traditional ornaments and clothing.

Listening to his keen business instinct, he decided to use the marriage event as a test launch for the new cable television station called Welcome India Network or WIN TV.

Dhiraj worked as talent scout and Public Relations director, as well as serving as the Editor-in-Chief of the News Service, and being in charge of the program schedule. Priti took care of the advertising department, the production of feature documentaries, and filled in for anything that came up which was beyond the capabilities of the local staff.

The upcoming marriage had the blessing of both families, for the bride and groom's fathers, Giridhari Goswami and Dharmendra Jain, had been friends since their school days. In fact, they had decided to jointly host the marriage and reception, moving away from the tradition of just the bride's side footing the bill; it was innovative and a welcome surprise. The Goswamis were from a lower middle class family of priests, whereas the Jains were from a very rich family of jewelry merchants.

The event was to be held at the Tivoli Garden Resort, one of Delhi's largest and most luxurious hotels. The families had booked the entire place, all the rooms and suites, and sent out invitations to many friends and family, including foreign guests.

* * * *

Diana and Bill's flight landed in Delhi on schedule. They collected their bags and took a taxi to the Tivoli. At the reception desk, they were startled to learn they had been assigned the same room. The manager was extremely sorry but had somehow imagined Diana and Bill as a married couple. They didn't complain. After all, Diana had sagely observed, if all the other rooms were taken, they would simply have to adjust. Bill noticed she didn't sound too disappointed or irritated by the situation, and he could hardly hide his own happiness. The two young people had grown increasingly attached

299

to each other, and suddenly the idea of sleeping in the same room didn't seem that strange to Bill.

* * * *

The next morning, Sunday, the 20th of March, was a beautiful day. At promptly 10:55 a.m., the flight from Mumbai touched down at Indira Gandhi International Airport.

Karry and Jai, dressed like Western businessmen, in elegant suits, and carrying costly briefcases, collected their luggage and walked out of the terminal toward an awaiting vehicle.

When they reached the safe house, Jai quickly changed into a chauffeur's uniform. They set out again at around 3:00 p.m., this time in an official-looking luxury car.

Balaram was expected to reach the meeting from his own home in Delhi.

At the entrance to the Tivoli Garden Resort, Karry showed his wedding invitation and credentials. The security guard cross-checked the guest name against the manifest, and satisfied, waved the car through. Jai parked in the already crowded lot, next to a couple of cars with license plates which obviously belonged to diplomatic staff. Karry walked toward the main entrance of the hotel, while Jai joined the group of chauffeurs who had assembled near the refreshment table set up outside for them at the rear of the building. When he walked into the

foyer, Karry was greeted by members of the
bride's family, along with a small group of
elegant young ladies dressed in matching, bright
pink saris. They were the welcoming party,
whose job was to offer small bouquets to the
lady guests. They directed him to the Grand
Ballroom where the ceremony was going to take
place.

The hall was starting to fill up. In the center,
a large, traditional, wedding pavilion was
lavishly decorated with a great number of
flower garlands; around it were placed many
rows of chairs.

Karry walked to the side of the huge hall and
got himself a cup of tea and a small plate of hors
d'oeuvres then took a seat in one of the back
rows and carefully regarded the scene. After
about twenty minutes, Jai, now wearing an
immaculate waiter's uniform, appeared at a
back door and walked through to the
refreshment table to attend to the guests. At
exactly 3:50 p.m., Karry spotted Balaram
entering the hall and calmly got to his feet.
Balaram saw him, too, and headed toward the
refreshment table, which Karry approached,
presumably for more snacks. They casually
moved along the table, looking at the various
serving dishes without giving the impression of
knowing each other. After a moment or two, Jai
walked over to assist them.

* * * *

"What would you like, sir?" he inquired politely. Balaram appeared to recognize him from the photo Karry had sent through the secure phone line.

"*Jaljeera* and some *paneer ka tikka*, thanks," he said smiling.

"Tomato soup and *papad*, Son," added Karry happily.

Jai smiled back, looked around; nobody was near them. He prepared two trays with small bowls and plates, cutlery and cloth napkins. Inside the napkins he had hidden two identical slips of paper which read, "@7:30 pm, Room 721." He handed a tray to each man.

He watched as they carried their trays to separate side tables, each keeping his back to the hall as he ate. Balaram left a little drink in his glass, Karry a little soup in his bowl, and their paper slips ended up there after being torn into pieces. The special paper soon dissolved into the liquids.

At that very moment, another couple, a young woman with a tall, black man, walked into the hall and headed toward the refreshment table. When Jai asked them what they would like to have, they took some orange juice and a couple of *samosas and masala vadas* each. The woman appeared to be British and the man, American, by the way they spoke. Then they, too, walked off to one of the tables to eat.

Jai was about to exit the refreshment stand, as his job was done, when Professor Jawahar Katju walked over unceremoniously.

"Hey you, waiter, get me something to drink. I'm thirsty," snarled Katju.

Jai turned around and was startled for a moment...*the jackal from Nehru university*...but he quickly recovered. "Certainly, sir. We have tea, coffee, *jaljeera*, orange juice, sweet or salty *lassi*, lemonade, fizzy apple juice, fizzy grape juice, mango juice, iced green tea, and green coconut water." He smiled, maintaining his decorum.

"Get me something with *alcohol* in it!" Jawahar scowled.

"I am sorry, sir, but the bride and groom have given precise instructions not to serve alcoholic drinks. It's because of their religious tradition. There are no alcoholic beverages tonight." Jai smiled calmly at the obviously irritated man.

He watched Jawahar look around, his blood-shot eyes would see there was no booze on the buffet tables, only pitchers of children's drinks and a few bottled beverages of the 'healthier' type.

"What about food?" Jawahar snarled.

Jai repressed a little smile and tried to maintain a professional appearance. He looked at the steam-heated containers lined up along the refreshment table and recited, "Tomato soup, *sambar, idli, wada, samosas, pakoras, papadam, puri, kachori, paneer tikki, alu tikki, bhajya, chana masala, dhokla*, and a variety of sweets, sir."

"What about chicken? Mutton? Fish? Egg curry?" demanded Jawahar, running his hands through his hair in distress.

"I am sorry, sir," repeated Jai, firmly. *This buffoon seems to be at the wrong party.*

Jawahar finally snapped. "Are you a waiter, or what? Go to the kitchen and get me something decent, you idiot! And I want whiskey now! Go tell the host."

"Very well, sir," Jai replied calmly. "I will inquire in the kitchen." *I guess it's time to stop playing waiter.* He turned and walked away.

Jai had temporarily taken the place of a hotel staff person who suddenly remembered another urgent task after Jai offered him a handsome amount of money to borrow his uniform. Jai told the boy he was a student of Hotel Management and really wanted to have firsthand experience at the Tivoli Gardens.

* * * *

Bill, hearing the commotion, looked over at the refreshment table and grimaced when he saw who it was. "Hey, Wile E. Coyote is here; check your eleven o'clock."

Diana's eyes went wide. "What, that old slime ball? You're joking!"

"Nope, no joke could be this bad," Bill said sourly. "Don't turn around. Let's see where he goes, and we'll just head in the opposite direction."

Bill watched him intently. Jawahar took out a small flask from his pocket and downed something. Suddenly he looked around and spotted Bill—it was not very difficult, considering he was over six feet tall with rather large shoulders. Bill watched Jawahar choke on his drink.

"Uh oh," he said. "Here we go. He's seen us. Let's pretend we didn't see him."

Diana chuckled.

* * * *

Jawahar couldn't believe his eyes. *Here they are; the two bloody, hopping rabbits. Sure, jump, jump, and jump. You'll always end up in my trap. You're not so clever, after all. I'll corner you soon enough and I'll skewer you both!* He moved away from the refreshment table and took a seat where he could watch the two of them. He tried to remain inconspicuous as he feverishly chiseled out a plan in his mind.

He extracted his cell phone and hit the speed dial. "Nalayak," he said quietly, "I need you, Jacky and Habib here, now! No dilly-dallying. Tivoli Gardens Resort. The two *damn* rabbits are here, I saw them. Find out if they are staying in this hotel, and in which room."

"Yes, sir, I'm on my way. Will bring Jacky and Habib," said Nalayak. The line went dead.

* * * *

At five o'clock, the bride and groom entered the hall, accompanied by their families and a group of priests who chanted *Sanskrit* mantras and sprinkled the couple with rice, grains, rose water, and other auspicious substances.

Diana and Bill walked to the front row of chairs to greet them. Priti appeared to recognize Bill immediately, but encumbered as she was with an incredible amount of jewelry and a very heavy sari, just gave him a small nod of her head in greeting. Bill turned to Diana. "It looks like these Indian marriages are really serious stuff." He smiled back at Priti.

Priti's family must have noticed the exchange as Bill was soon surrounded by a gaggle of Indian relatives. A stout man in his fifties offered his hand. "You must be Bill. Priti told me about you, and that you would be traveling with a friend."

"Yes, I am," replied Bill, smiling. "This is Diana."

Diana broke into a large grin.

"I am Giridhari Goswami, Priti's father. I am very happy to meet you both."

Bill and Diana delighted all the assembled relatives by returning the greetings with folded hands and saying, "*Namaste*."

* * * *

In his chair, several rows behind them, Jawahar heard the soft beep of his cell phone and checked the messages. It said, "*Room 115.*" He quickly wrote back, "*Get their luggage!*" before erasing the messages. He sat quietly, watching Diana and Bill engaged in conversation with the two young Indians in the third row of chairs. He had to make sure they did not return to their room, just yet.

The marriage ceremony continued for hours with soft, sacred music playing in the background. The bride and groom went through various activities, at one point exchanging garlands, and walking seven times together around the sacred fire.

The guests moved freely throughout the day, heading in groups to the banquet hall. It had been organized as a buffet, which the guests would enjoy before coming back to watch the proceedings.

At 7:00 p.m., the marriage ceremony was complete, and the bride and groom walked around the large ballroom greeting relatives, guests and visitors before taking a seat on two beautifully decorated chairs set on a raised platform. The line of guests meeting and greeting, while offering gifts to the newlyweds, smoothly moved along before they scattered outside on the lawn, where a large dais had been built for the main entertainment. Diana and Bill, too, went to congratulate the couple and present their gifts before returning to their seats.

* * * *

At the appointed time, Jai walked the corridor and reached Room 721. He pulled out the electronic key card and touched the lock pad. It opened and he entered quietly.

At 7:30 p.m., Karry and Balaram discretely slipped away from the crowd and also went looking for Room 721.

Jai turned on the TV which was playing a musical program. All the curtains were closed. He heard the patterned repeated knocks on the door—a code—and recognizing it was Karry, opened the door and let he and Balaram in. They locked the door and quickly checked for any listening devices. When it was deemed clear, they settled to talk near the television, whose blaring sound could act as a shield.

Karry spoke first. "Balaram, this is Jai, the leader of the Vajra team. Jai, this is Balaram, the Director General of IFA."

Balaram extended his hand. "Nice to finally meet you, Jai."

"It's an honor to meet you, sir," Jai answered.

Balaram smiled at him. "I'm very proud of the Vajra team. I've been watching you all closely and find everyone to be dedicated and professional. We expect you to be an example for the new and future generations, teaching them to protect our Motherland with its unique and ancient, dharmic culture. This is the time when we all need to come together and combine our efforts, for our Motherland is today in very grave danger." Balaram hesitated before continuing, his face grave. "We have lost track of the nuclear bomb."

The three men regarded each other for a moment with wide eyes.

"The Vajra Team now needs to come to the forefront, albeit discreetly. There is no more time for intelligence gathering. We must respond with action and be ready for anything and everything." Balaram paused briefly before continuing. "You understand that the Government will not be able to support the team in any way, or even acknowledge its activities. Of course, that's the exact purpose of the team—to function freely without red tape, bureaucratic and political complications, and without any moles or traitors. This is precisely why we cannot rely on any official government agencies, including the IFA."

Karry looked at him.

"We are well aware of this, sir," Jai said, nodding at both men.

"You will not be able to call for any outside help," Balaram continued, gravely, "Not from the government, police, or any other official branch."

"We understand, sir. We do not work for the government. We do not exist. We have to get the task done using our own strengths and resources," he reassured them.

"Correct. And so, all our hopes are in your hands. However at any time, if we feel the Vajra team is unable to deliver, we will then involve IFA agents directly," said Balaram, leaning forward in earnest.

"Two of our young men and two of our young ladies have already reached Hyderabad," Karry said, "I am sure they will do an excellent job of tracing the Scorpion Egg."

"Keep me posted, will you?" said Balaram.

"Of course," Karry replied, before his face burst into a wide grin. "All right, now let's go and join the party. Are you going to dance, Jai?" he winked in a playful manner.

Jai said nothing.

Karry looked over at his friend. "Watching Jai dance is a treat, you know."

"I will talk to my daughter, Shanti, straightaway." Balaram smiled and threw his head back in amusement.

Jai regarded Balaram with a quizzical look.

"She's Priti's best friend, and is sitting on the main dais with the bride and groom right now. I am sure they can slide you into the program."

Jai's smile suddenly faded and he looked down at his clothes. "But, sir, I have no dance costume, just the waiter and chauffeur uniforms."

"Then we will arrange for one. Go to Rangela, the show manager, and tell him you are Shanti's family friend," assured Barry.

"Thank you, sir," said Jai, deeply moved. "Now, let's get out of here, but not all together. I will go first." Balaram opened the door, looked up and down the corridor, and then quickly turned back to Karry before walking out. "Karry, when the party is over, meet me in the parking lot. I'll give you a ride home."

Jai watched the man disappear around the corner, then he saw Karry go in a different direction. Jai waited a moment, and then walked out in his waiter's uniform, heading straight for the Oakwood lawns to speak with Rangela.

* * * *

In the meantime, Priti and her new husband, Dhiraj, had changed into more comfortable outfits before joining their guests in the main entertainment area in Oakland Lawns; the newlyweds took their seats in front of the main dais. Two cameramen recorded the proceedings as a long-haired young man, dressed in a shiny, red outfit that resembled one of Michael Jackson's, climbed onto the performers' stage with microphone in hand.

"Welcome, ladies and gentlemen. I am Rangela, your host, and tonight I will keep you happy and entertained with a number of specials. We have an incredible line-up!" As he spoke, a group of elegant young women in Bollywood dance costumes came up and took their positions.

"Now, without further ado, I introduce: 'The Bollywood Apsaras'!" He punched the air in true rock star fashion before leaving.

The crowd clapped and roared their approval. When the performance was over, the women graciously bowed to the extensive applause and exited the stage elegantly. Rangela returned to the podium.

"We have now a very special surprise for you. Our main artist tonight is not from India, nor is she from the West. Aha! I see you pondering this mystery. Well, Folks, you are in for a real treat." Rangela flashed pearly-white teeth to the crowd.

"Tonight our exotic and charming Chinese Butterfly, Masako Chi Wang, will present a series of exquisite dance styles. Her first piece is a traditional Chinese dance. In the past it was presented solely by Chinese princesses of the court and for the exclusive pleasure of the Emperor. Ladies and gentlemen, please welcome our special guest, Masako Chi Wang!"

A slender, and beautiful petite lady, with black hair and eyes, and Asian features, appeared on the stage behind Rangela. She was wearing a feather-light gown of pale green. It had very long, wide sleeves and a tight, richly embroidered bodice. She carried a number of brightly-colored scarves, as light and narrow as ribbons. She had no visible makeup, and her long hair, flowing like black silk, was tied loosely in a bun at the nape of her neck.

Masako bowed to the audience, and then began moving gracefully to the sound of slow, sweet, high-pitched music. The huge sleeves of her gown flowed like a butterfly's wings, and the thin scarves around her neck waved in the evening breeze. The music quickened, became merrier, and the dance followed in a whirlwind of colors and elegance. At times, she was waving and spinning as if suspended in air; other times she bent backward, then forward, as if she were flying.

The audience watched, completely enthralled. When the music ended and the "butterfly" touched the ground again, it seemed as if a magical spell had suddenly been broken. The audience was quiet for a moment as the faint echo of beauty and grace hung in the air, then they began applauding wildly. Masako bowed again, and then silently departed the stage.

Karry and Balaram sat watching the show some distance from each other in the second row of chairs. Next to them, Diana and Bill were talking with Shanti.

In the meantime, Jawahar's henchmen, Nalayak, Jacky and Habib, carefully scanned the hallway before walking out of Diana and Bill's room with two suitcases and two bags. With Jacky leading the way, they slipped into a stairwell, went down the stairs, and out a back door used by the hotel staff. Once outside, they disappeared past the hedges of the hotel park; then, aided by two other men with a ladder, climbed over the boundary wall and disappeared into the dark night.

Patiently sitting in one of the last rows of the main entertainment area, Jawahar stifled a yawn as Rangela introduced the next dance of the evening. Jawahar was starting to doze off when his mobile began vibrating. He answered, grunted, and then said something in a low, commanding voice before snapping the phone shut. Then he left the venue for good.

Masako returned to the stage, this time wearing a beautifully ornamented costume of the finest silk as she danced in the classical Indian Bharat Natyam style, enthralling all.

Next, Rangela announced an instant Bollywood dance contest in which young men and women each performed a brief solo to a musical medley. Jai, who had been entered at the request of Shanti, delighted the audience by combining classical moves with new, brilliant ones never before seen.

At the end of their performances, Rangela announced the top male and top female winners of the contest. They were none other than Jai and Masako. They stepped forward and Priti and Dhiraj presented them with a special cash prize and an invitation to perform for WIN TV.

* * * *

After the brief ceremony, Jai and Masako went backstage to change their clothes. As luck would have it, they came out of their respective dressing rooms at exactly the same time, almost bumping into each other.

They laughed, awkwardly, and then stood frozen, Jai observing Masako's sparkling black eyes fixed on him, as if she was assessing him.

Jai broke the silence and stretched out his hand. "Hi Masako. I'm Jai Bharat. You are a fabulous dancer; I liked your numbers."

Masako, smiling shyly, placed her slim soft hand into his and replied, "Thank you so much. You're a great dancer, too."

Their hands lingered together, as if under a magic spell. It seemed that many unspoken words were being exchanged as their eyes locked.

Suddenly, the spell was broken and they let go. Jai heard DJ Rangela's loud announcement, "Ladies and gentlemen, it's time to roll onto the floor." And the music began to blare.

Smiling, they both walked to the front to see many of the guests had joined Rangela, and were happily swaying to the music.

Jai turned to his left. Masako was next to him. He swallowed, cleared his throat and slowly extended his left hand. "Masako, would you like to dance?"

She giggled. "Yes...yes...sure, Jai." Jai felt her hand smoothly slide into his own. He walked her to an empty spot on the floor, took her hand in his own and slowly eased them into the rhythm of the music.

* * * *

It was now late at night, and Diana was sitting with the bride and groom, when Bill returned. The two winning dancers were also nearby, locked in conversation. Bill had gone to their room, briefly, to charge his cell phone. He looked furious. "Our luggage is gone!" he said, his face flushed.

Diana felt resigned. "It's as we expected though, Bill."

Luckily most of the guests had already left, including Jawahar, but the small clusters of those remaining who were within hearing distance, stopped in their tracks and looked on, surprise and horror registering on their faces.

"Did someone steal your luggage from your room?" Dhiraj exclaimed.

Priti looked petrified. "The hotel manager will have to answer for this!"

"Ma'am?" The young man, who had waited on them at the refreshment stand and had won the men's dance contest, and was now sitting at the next table talking to the beautiful Asian entertainer, interjected, "Excuse me. I'm sorry, my name is Jai Bharat. If you don't mind, what did you mean when you said you were expecting this?"

Diana decided to tell the truth. The young man had a very honest-looking face. She was sure he wasn't one of the professor's men. "Okay, I'll try to explain this as briefly as I can. We are being watched by this strange group of people called the Society for the Eradication of Pagan Superstitions. They are after some documents I am carrying with me. Luckily," she said, with a wink, we didn't leave them in our room. It's a long story; difficult to explain."

At the mention of SEPS, Diana noticed that Jai and the two older-looking distinguished gentlemen sitting near him, who had moved their chairs closer when they heard Bill's comments, exchanged rather sly glances.

"Ma'am," Jai spoke again, very politely and quietly, "this SEPS is an extremely ruthless organization. Because you are our guests in India, it is our duty, as Indian citizens, to offer you complete assistance and protection. My family's house isn't far from here. We have a car just outside in the parking lot." He shot a quick look at the taller of the two older men, and Diana detected an almost imperceptible nod from one of them.

"We appreciate your kind offer, however we don't want to get you or your family mixed up in this," stated Bill.

"No trouble at all; it would be our pleasure," Jai responded with a small smile. "Our house is very well protected."

The other older man nodded, and then spoke to Priti's dad. "Giridhari ji, I really think your guests should go to Jai's house, at least for the night. He is a very responsible young man; he and his family have been acquainted with mine for a long time. I can guarantee his ability to protect our guests and take care of them." At that point, the older man stood up and introduced himself as Balaram Singh Yadav.

Priti's father turned to Diana and Bill. "We do feel responsible for your safety and wellbeing; please go with Jai for a short time and decide afterward what you wish to do. Balaram and I will keep in touch."

It seemed their fate had been decided. Diana looked up at Bill, who didn't appear to object, and then nodded in agreement.

"I'll talk to the hotel manager immediately. We need an explanation," said Dhiraj, pulling out his cell phone. "Please check your room and see what was left behind by the thieves." He dialed a number, moved a few feet away and proceeded to have a very animated conversation on the phone.

Accompanied by Jai, Diana and Bill went to their room to assess the damage.

It was a mess. The pillows and sheets had been stripped off the beds and were lying all over the floor with the dresser drawers upside down beside them. Diana and Bill collected their remaining personal belongings and followed Jai back to the reception area. Dhiraj and Priti were now talking to Masako, the dancer, and standing together with their respective fathers, all apparently appalled and worried—although the embarrassment and concern on their faces was nothing compared to the sheer horror on the face of the hotel manager.

"The door to the room wasn't damaged," said Jai, confidently. "This means that whoever it was, had an electronic key and was probably wearing a staff uniform as well."

Diana noted a slight change in Jai's demeanor at the presence of the young Asian dancer. He seemed suddenly to be more aware of his posture and even his voice deepened and sounded more serious than it had before. Could there be something going on there?

The manager, however, seemed on the verge of fainting.

Diana quickly came to the poor man's rescue before things got out of hand. "We don't blame the hotel management or staff," she interjected quickly, "and we don't intend to lodge any police complaint whatsoever."

Bill nodded his agreement.

"The personal effects that were stolen," Diana continued, "were not very valuable and certainly not worth the effort to retrieve them, or the time we'd have to waste with pointless police investigations."

"Thank you very much, Miss Warwick," the manager said, raising his hands. He was obviously relieved that she wouldn't be pursuing the matter. Diana did not want the manager to lose his job.

"However, we'll be checking out immediately," Bill said. "I'm sure you understand."

"Of course, of course." The man reached out and grabbed Bill's hand in a double-handed grip. "Do not worry, sir. I will do all the paperwork personally, and as a goodwill gesture, you both will have one week of free accommodation on your next visit; it's a promise."

"Thank you very much," concluded Diana.

Diana grabbed Bill's arm and turned to bid goodbye to their hosts, but stopped when she caught sight of Jai locked in conversation with Masako. They were smiling and laughing at each other. It was obvious there *was* an attraction. She looked up at Bill in time to see a mischievous smile on his face as he glanced in the same direction.

"It's time to go," she whispered in his ear, before turning to kiss Priti on the cheek, offering a *namaste* to Dhiraj and the two elders, and turning around to wait for Jai so they could head to the parking lot.

"Can I come with you guys?" asked Masako. She and Jai had stopped talking and she was pointing toward the parking lot. "My car is there, too," she added.

Jai spoke in the affirmative before anyone else could answer. Diana nodded her head, and then turned to look at Bill, only to find him already smiling and quietly laughing.

* * * *

It was now midnight. The walk to reach the parking lot was a bit of a distance and it appeared nearly deserted. A group of men sitting on a low iron fence swiftly stood as they saw the four people approaching. Jai observed Masako wave her hand at a man in uniform, probably her driver, but he turned and ran away when the other men suddenly pulled long knives from their jackets.

When Jai and his companions were within a few yards of the men, they yelled, "Your handbags, if you please!" One of them thrust the long blade he was carrying into the air.

As Jai stepped forward, he heard Diana gasp in fear and saw Bill throw his small bundle of remaining possessions toward her before he moved in the direction of the advancing men. Then, to Jai's surprise, Masako threw her small suitcase in Diana's direction before joining them as they faced their would-be attackers. He saw

Diana, out of the corner of his eye, quickly push the luggage together, place herself in a determined stance over the bags, unzip her purse, bring out a can of pepper spray and hold it up into firing position.

Jai and Bill rolled up their sleeves as Masako struck a menacing martial arts stance.

The ruffians howled with laughter at the scene, probably sensing what they thought would be a quick victory. The stout man who seemed to be the leader, signaled to his team. Three men moved forward, coming closer to each of their targets.

One of them, wearing a brown leather jacket, swung his knife parallel to the ground at Masako's legs, but she expertly jumped into the air, and while coming down kicked him hard in the solar plexus, knocking the wind out of him, and leaving him rolling around on the ground in agony.

A taller attacker jabbed at Bill's face with his long knife, but Bill moved sideways in the nick of the time and landed a sharp uppercut to the man's jaw, sending him crashing to the ground. Meanwhile, Jai caught hold of his attacker's hand, before he could even swing, and then wrestled the knife from his opponent, using it to slash him across his forehead. Blinded by the blood running into his eyes, the man stumbled around in a panic, crying in pain. The leader of the thugs seemed to have realized his mistake of underestimating his opponents. He screamed at the remaining six. "All of you, get back there! Get them and their stuff!"

As the six attackers kept Bill, Jai and Masako busy, the leader of the pack approached Diana from behind. But he was soon screaming in pain as the burning pepper spray temporarily blinded him.

In less than five minutes, the six attackers were incapacitated, some tasting their own blood, some with broken bones, one struggling to maintain consciousness, and their leader screaming at all of his defeated gang to help him get away.

After a moment or two of uncertainty, those who could still walk grabbed their semi-conscious and injured friends, and their now-moaning leader, and made their way as quickly as possible out of the parking lot,

Jai looked up as Masako yelled, "That was a great fight!"

He smiled in return, as he took assessment of his own injuries. Except for a few scrapes, and bruises which would show up soon enough, he felt pretty good.

"You're like a Samurai warrior!" Masako yelled out, losing some of her carefully crafted English accent.

Jai blushed in embarrassment.

Suddenly, Diana burst out laughing, an obvious nervous release after their incredibly harrowing experience. She hugged Masako. "Perhaps our Masako is more than just a beautiful and graceful 'Dancing Butterfly'?" She looked inquisitively into Masako's eyes.

The Asian dancer leaned forward excitedly and said, "Dance and martial arts have always gone hand in hand for me. As soon as I was old enough to stand on my feet, I began to learn martial arts from my mother." She made a small bow to her new friends.

Bill looked confused. "Are you Japanese or Chinese?"

Masako smiled. "My mother is Japanese and my father, Chinese,"

"So, where are we going now?" interjected Diana, as she began to hand them back their bags.

"We should take Masako home," Jai interrupted, "since her driver is probably still running." They all laughed at the image. "Then the three of us can go to my place. Tomorrow we'll decide what to do."

He scanned the parking lot and was not surprised to see Karry quickly approaching them. He figured Karry had been watching the fight from a distance and would have stepped in had things gotten out of their control.

"Very well done, Jai and team," Karry said giving him a high five, before turning to speak to Diana. "Clearly the people who attacked you were the same crooks who stole your luggage, Miss Warwick."

"Do you know them?" asked Diana, staring at Karry.

"I think so. Was a Professor Katju involved?"

Diana and Bill looked at each other, startled.

"Yes," she said.

"Then we are fighting on the same side, and against the same enemies. I work for a quasi-government agency specializing in investigation and security. We have already found many dark secrets about SEPS. Anything that interests them needs to be watched carefully." He turned to Jai. "Stay with them and take care of whatever they may need; I will see you all tomorrow morning."

Jai bowed his head slightly, and then watched as Karry walked toward Balaram's car, which was parked in a dark corner away from the light.

The four climbed into the luxury car Jai had originally arrived in. Jai announced they would first stop at Masako's place, and then go south. Diana nodded in agreement as Bill yawned.

Jai saw Masako chuckle and he returned the smile. He pressed the accelerator and the car zoomed ahead into the night streets of Delhi.

* * * *

Professor Katju was waiting in his sitting room. It was one-thirty in the morning by the time Nalayak, Jacky and Habib entered, carrying the bags and suitcases they had stolen from the hotel. Nalayak seemed to be limping a little.

"What happened to you?" demanded Jawahar.

"I slipped off the ladder while carrying the suitcase from the hotel."

"Get that stuff over here." Jawahar scowled at them before he proceeded to rip open the suitcases and begin searching them.

When he saw the contents, he was not a happy man—a miniature replica of the Taj Mahal, a bunch of tourist brochures, some Buddhist and Hindu books, some clothing, and two pairs of shoes. This was certainly not what he had hoped for. The two small bags were just as disappointing—a few personal hygiene items, a tiny flashlight, a battery charger, two small wallets with very little money, some tourist maps, and some blank paper and pens.

"Where are the *fucking* papers?" exploded Jawahar. "*You bloody idiots!* You did not even manage to get their passports and credit cards! Not even their *god-damned* phones! What use are you? *What the fuck* am I supposed to do with these clothes and crappy books? Masturbate? Ah!"

The three students kept their eyes on the ground. There was dead silence.

"We sent our best boys after them, sir," said Jacky, mustering up some courage. "But Warwick and Johnson had help. They all got into it in the parking lot outside the hotel, and our boys got trashed."

Jawahar was beside himself with fury. "What do you mean, they had help? How many others were there?"

"Two of them," Habib said. "A Chinese woman and an Indian fellow, and both were extremely well-trained in fighting." He rubbed his jaw for effect, and then whined, "It's not our fault. How could we know?"

Jawahar didn't answer him. *Something is wrong here. They were expecting us, and they obviously have contacts we know nothing about.*

"*Teekh hai,*" he said at last, walking briskly across the apartment floor. "We need to find out who these other people are…and where those two bloody foreigners have gone. I want to know what their plans are—then we can figure out how to catch them."

* * * *

They dropped Masako at Chanakyapuri, the diplomatic enclave in the heart of Delhi. Jai walked her to the door and exchanged phone numbers before saying goodbye. He continued driving toward Gurugram, finally stopping in front of the tall iron gate that opened onto a rather large estate. He pressed some numbers on his mobile, and a few seconds later the gate clicked, opening automatically. The car rolled into an elegant laneway flanked by tall trees, then down into a wide drive that went deep under the house. They stopped in a subterranean parking lot next to an elevator.

With Jai leading the way, the three of them got in and rode up to the main floor of the house. There, they were greeted by a polite young man whom Jai introduced as Uttam Chaudhary. Uttam directed them down a corridor. "These will be your rooms," he said, with a welcoming smile, as he opened the door to a clean, brightly-lit suite.

"Inside, you will find some basic necessities, including night clothes and duffel bags in which to keep your personal belongings. If you need anything else, just press that purple button near the light switch; I'll be here in a flash." He beamed.

Jai added, "Don't hesitate to call us if you need anything. Tomorrow morning we'll make our plans." He smiled reassuringly. "You're perfectly safe here."

* * * *

Diana and Bill thanked Jai and Uttam, and then walked the corridor to one of the assigned rooms. It was large and comfortable. Both sat on the sofa, relaxing from the long eventful day.

Diana went first. "From what I see, this is not Jai's family home. It looks like some sort of a hideout. Should we be concerned?"

Bill shook his head. "Not at all. I think this is a safe house. And I trust Priti and her family. They wouldn't have thrown us to the wolves."

Diana nodded her head slowly. "Yes, you're probably right. But all this is freaking me out. Are you sure these people are not connected to SEPS? Maybe they're just conning us."

Bill looked straight at Diana. "My gut feeling is, by the grace of God, we're in safe hands, and we shouldn't worry. I think we both need a cup of coffee. That should do the trick." Bill walked over to the coffee maker on the dresser.

Finally they turned in for the night, still rather perplexed at this new turn of events, but grateful they had found a safe haven and someone able to protect them from Jawahar and his cohorts. One thing they were sure of, they probably hadn't seen the last of him, or SEPS.

As she lay in the comfortable bed, Diana recalled the psychic reader in Prayagraj telling her that three friends would help her. There had been Bill, of course, and now Jai, and also Masako. She smiled, thinking about Masako's obvious attraction to Jai, and her own growing feelings for Bill. Then she closed her eyes and drifted off.

* * * *

Jawahar didn't sleep well that night. He'd had a few too many drinks while sitting up contemplating the mystery Diana Warwick had turned out to be. It seemed he had greatly underestimated her, and now he'd have to invent something to tell Lord Dyer. *I need to be ready before he calls.* He started to scribble notes in his diary, planning his moves for the next few days.

First on his list was to find out the identity of these new people helping the two foreigners. He wrote down a note with the name of a famous Delhi politician and the letters "IB".

After two more shots of whiskey, he decided the only solution was to call a general meeting. *Yes, this is what I need to tell Dyer. Scare him. Get all the guns out, and pool our resources.*

"In other words, pass the *bucket of shit* to someone else," he said loudly to the empty room, before laughing drunkenly.

* * * *

The next morning, Diana woke up feeling rested and strangely peaceful. The morning sun was beaming through the thick, glass panels of the curtained window. Diana felt light at heart as she stretched luxuriously. After taking a warm shower, she found a comfortable, albeit oversized, tunic and trousers and quickly dressed, before slipping into the hallway.

She found Bill and Jai in a sitting room down the corridor, leisurely enjoying a breakfast consisting of bagels with cream cheese and steaming mugs of tea. With them was one of the older men whom they had briefly met the previous night. He introduced himself as

Kartikeyan Vanniyar. "My friends call me Karry," he said with a captivating smile. Diana smiled in return and took a seat in an armchair near a side table. Jai filled two more cups with tea and handed them to her and Karry. "How are you feeling this morning?" Bill asked her. "I'm all right. In fact, I slept very well. What is this place?" "This is where the good guys hang out," Bill said, smiling. "I've already told them about my journey—how I came to be in India—and I found that we have a lot in common. Now that you're up, I think we can safely discuss Arthur and the treasure."

Diana relaxed into her chair, sipping her tea. Starting with her grandmother's death, she recounted the past few months. She told them the story of Arthur's life and work, including the information they'd gathered in Prayagraj, and from Professor Cariappa in Bangalore. Jai and Karry listened very carefully, nodding from time to time, and not showing much surprise, as if they had somehow already been privy to many of the details.

"We've heard about Arthur Warwick," said Karry, "and we're very happy and honored to have met his direct descendent. Your mission definitely falls within the scope of our work, for our team's job is to protect people from the threat of terrorist acts. We also investigate groups whose ideologies oppose peace, freedom and the universal principles of *Dharma*. We take action to stop them whenever and wherever possible." He paused for a moment, taking a sip of tea. "SEPS is definitely one such organization. It's run by a dedicated core group with connections and support at the highest levels. We've never found any concrete evidence of a crime we can arrest them for. They're pros at covering their tracks; but now we may just have a chance to expose and destroy their network once and for all."

Diana listened intently, but said nothing. All this information thoroughly rattled her, and now they had been plunged right into the middle of it. She felt heat radiating from her dizzy head as she thought more and more about SEPS and their heinous acts against Arthur. Her heart began to race and her palms oozed sweat, as she now fully understood the implications and dangers of her treasure hunt.

She was SEPS next target.

Chapter 12 – Temple of the Celestial Snake

All of a sudden, lights started flashing on and off in the safe house, the security alarm beeped after every few seconds. Everyone was stunned for a moment.

Jai yelled, "Might be a break-in. Quick, move inside the secure room and lock yourselves in! Let me look out front!" He pulled out a Beretta 92FS 9mm from the rear waistband of his jeans and walked quickly toward the entrance to the house.

Karry took out his own gun. "Jai, I'm going to check the backyard."

"Okay!"

Diana and Bill quickly headed into the secure room which Jai pointed them toward, where they locked the door from the inside. They waited a long, almost breathless ten minutes before Jai and Karry returned and tapped twice, paused, and then three more times on the door.

"Bill, it's me Jai; it's all clear."

Bill opened the door. Jai and Karry stepped inside and closed it behind them.

Without saying a word, Jai went straight to the surveillance recorder located in the room. He ran the tape for few minutes, and then stopped at one picture. A black cat tripped one of the sensors. Everyone laughed in relief.

Karry talked with them for a while then announced that he had business to attend to elsewhere. He bid them goodbye, but not before cautioning Bill and Diana not to share the safehouse location or any of the other information about people or events with anyone, as that could endanger all of them. He was almost to the door when he turned back to Jai, smiled, and reminded him that he and their guests should wear very casual clothes when they went out that day.

Jai nodded before turning to Diana and Bill, and smiling at their puzzled expressions. "Today is the main day of the Holi festival, or Festival of Colors. It's customary for people to roam the streets, throwing colored dye on each other."

Diana smiled. "I'd love to go out and see it. Sounds like fun."

Bill winked at Diana before adding, "Me, too."

Then Jai, nonchalantly added that Masako had called him earlier and asked if they would like to have lunch.

Diana and Bill exchanged brief smiles and knowing looks before saying that it sounded great.

On the way to the restaurant, small groups of boys and girls roamed the streets, grinning happily and laughing. There was a feeling of celebration in the air, as men, women and children threw colored powders on one another and squirted colored water from all kinds of contraptions. Some of the kids offered Diana, Bill and Jai some powder as well, and soon the three friends were involved in a fun exchange. By the time they arrived at the restaurant to meet Masako, they had even managed to overcome the initial embarrassment over their appearance. Still, when she hurried over to them, shouting, "Happy Holi!" they managed to throw even more powder on her and each other.

As pleased as they were to see their new friend, Jai couldn't take any chances with their safety and security. After receiving Masako's invitation to lunch, he'd immediately texted Karry to, "Run profile check on butterfly." He experienced a fleeting sense of guilt at spying on her, but knew it was necessary; not only was Masako's father a member of the Chinese Consulate in Delhi, but she had shown a great deal of interest in Diana and Bill's impressions of India and the places they'd visited.

Masako seemed to be asking Jai many questions as well, but this may have been for another reason. He sensed she was attracted to him, and felt a bit embarrassed by it. For the past several years, his life had been focused almost exclusively on work. It was difficult to maintain relationships with women when he couldn't tell them about his job or his sudden unexplained absences. In response to Masako's questions, he'd told her that his work required him to travel a lot.

Masako launched into her own story, talking about family, her house, her passion for dance and the martial arts, and the schools she'd attended. She was born in Shanghai, but at the age of fifteen, her family moved to Hong Kong where her father was stationed doing cultural and public relations. For about three years, Masako remained in Shanghai, in the house of her uncle and had visited her family only during school vacations. After completing secondary school, where she had continued to study music, fine arts and languages, she'd moved to Tsinghua for higher education, and then joined her family, who had since relocated to Delhi, India.

She finally obtained a degree in foreign languages and one in art history. During her summer vacations in Hong Kong, she'd developed an interest in Bollywood dance and Indian culture; it totally fascinated her. Her father encouraged that passion as he had studied Indian culture himself. He used to say India greatly influenced China for more than 2,000 years, with its spirituality, culture and knowledge, without ever sending a single soldier across its borders. "None of them came to fight in war, but only to share in wisdom."

"I remember that statement," Jai said, smiling. "It was said by Hu Shih, the Chinese Ambassador to the U.S. from 1938 to 1942."

Masako smiled, nodding. "Yes. Many Chinese people have a great appreciation for Indian history and culture, especially due to Lord Buddha, and I am one of the most enthusiastic among them. I like India's freedom and family-centric lifestyle; I feel very much at home here."

Masako appeared to simply be a kind, intelligent woman with many interests, but until he heard from Karry, Jai had to be careful. As the four of them ate their lunch, he did most of the talking, spinning a cover story for himself that resembled reality as closely as possible and leaving out any information which could endanger his missions, team members, Karry, or the Agarwals. Masako seemed satisfied to hear about his musical preferences, his favorite foods, the places he had visited, and small endearing bits of trivia about his adopted parents. She looked particularly pleased to hear that Jai did not have a girlfriend.

When he felt he had exhausted all the legitimate topics of conversation, Jai moved the spotlight onto Diana and Bill, who spoke of their personal lives, and described the places they'd seen in India; they said nothing, however, of their quest for the treasure. The buffet was in a large open area. Most customers' clothes were drenched in color, as they moved past the tables and made their choices. As the friends proceeded along the buffet line, Jai explained the significance of Holi, and how it had come into being. It was the celebration of the coming of spring when nature blossoms into all types of colors. It was also to commemorate the legendary play of colors between Lord Krishna and his eternal consort, Radharani. After lunch, Masako explained she had some errands to complete, and took a cab and left. The others headed back to the safe house.

* * * *

That evening, Diana, Bill and Jai were joined by Karry on video phone.

"I have good news," he said smiling, "we've run all possible searches on Masako, and both she and her family appear to be clean. Her father is a cultural attaché without any political connections. Of course, it's always possible the Chinese Embassy and Secret Services are keeping an eye on her and might become interested in running a similar search on her friends, but I don't think she's going to press you for any secret information."

"I think we should tell her about our hunt and bring her onboard; I clearly remember the prediction of the psychic and I'm starting to understand the greater connections," said Diana.

"Yeah," agreed Bill, "she's certainly a great fighter, and I think she's also trustworthy. Not many would help strangers in a fight like that." He winked at Jai playfully, adding, "Plus, wherever we go next, she just might be willing to come with us...especially if Jai's on the team."

Jai blushed.

"You know, guys," Bill said, looking slightly worried, "there's one thing we haven't thought of—Masako's safety. In the eyes of the SEPS, she's one of us. From now on, I think Masako should be here."

Karry nodded. "Yes, I think you're right. Katju will probably find out where she lives and she could be attacked again, or even kidnapped. Then they'll try to find out what she knows. And you know what that could mean."

Diana's eyes went wide, and Jai inhaled a sharp breath at the ominous possibilities.

"With your permission, sir..." interjected Jai.

"Yes, Jai," Karry confirmed, "get on it immediately."

* * * *

Jai sent a short text requesting Masako to call him at the earliest possible time. No sooner had he sent the message, the phone vibrated in his hand. It was Masako.

"Hi, how are you doing today?" he greeted her.

"Great! What's up? Is everything okay?"

"There's something you need to know. We have a hunch the goons we encountered the other day at the parking lot, might be looking for revenge. So, we *all* need to be careful *all* the time."

"Is it that serious?"

"Yes, it might be, but we don't want *you* to get hurt, or any of us, for that matter."

"Alright, what do you want me to do?"

"If you can spare a few days, come join us; that would probably be the best."

"Yep, that I can do, for sure. I'll join you guys tomorrow."

"Wonderful."

They talked for a few more minutes about lunch, and Holi, and getting the dye out of their clothes. After a few more minutes of casual conversation, they hung up.

* * * *

The next day Masako left her home, to be discretely escorted to the safehouse. Unknown to Jai and the others, a young man with thick, black hair, dressed casually in a light blue polo shirt and wearing sunglasses, was watching from a black sedan parked across the street. He pulled out his phone and sent a text: *"Butterfly flew the coop w/2 unknown."* Just as he was about to start the engine, a police patrol approached him. The officer questioned him about his parking in the 'no parking' area in the prohibited diplomatic enclave. The young man, instead of giving a polite response, got agitated and mouthed-off at the officer, who frowned and proceeded to pull out his ticket pad and start issuing a violation. Seeing he was about to get a ticket and sensing he was losing valuable time to follow Masako, the young man threw the name of Katju into the conversation. This time the officer got really mad and arrested him for trying to influence him.

Needless to say, Katju was extremely pissed off when he received a phone call asking him to send someone to bail the fellow out of jail.

* * * *

After a strategic discussion, the four friends decided to confuse Katju's henchmen by unexpectedly flying from Delhi to Gawahati; they would then continue their travel by road in a large SUV.

Also, since Katju's men were likely looking for four people, Jai and Masako took a separate flight. They agreed to meet around 9:30 a.m. at a safe location inside the airport.

The next day, they landed at Bordoloi International airport, and after determining they hadn't been followed, continued on to the safehouse on GS Road. After quickly refreshing themselves, Diana and Bill decided it was time to brief Masako about their quest and Jai agreed.

As Masako listened to the incredible story of Arthur, and of Diana's travels during the past few months, her eyes widened with excitement.

341

"That's extraordinary!" she gasped. "And you say there are also dangerous people tracking you to get hold of whatever you find? So this was why we were attacked at the Tivoli hotel in Delhi at Priti's wedding?!"

The new and unexpectedly adventurous twist to the expedition only seemed to increase Masako's interest.

"Of course, of course!" smiled Masako. "I will be very happy to help. It's an honor."

When Diana disclosed the prediction of the palmist, about three friends from different races who would help her, Masako was flabbergasted.

Jai reminded the team that Professor Cariappa had wanted them to visit a Mother Goddess temple before embarking on their pursuit of the treasure inspired by the first clue. The most famous of the Mother Goddess temples in Eastern India was none other than Kamakhya Temple in the heart of Guwahati city. Diana agreed to the plan as she remembered the photo given by the psychic, and Arthur's personal deity, plus Bill and Masako said it was fine with them. The next day, early in the morning, the four friends visited the famous temple and offered their prayers to the Mother Goddess, asking for the success of the mission.

There were three vehicles at the safehouse, and, luckily for them, an SUV which would suit them the best. After thanking the custodian, they drove the 200 kilometre drive on the AH1 highway. It took them about five hours, including occasional breaks. They passed through Nellie, Kampur and Nagaon cities, before reaching their destination, the Professor's suggestion, Kaziranga National Park, a World Heritage Site, and host to the great one-horned rhinos. It also contained a tiger reserve, and was home to many elephants, water buffalo, swamp deer, and a bird sanctuary. With four rivers passing through it, the place was extremely conducive to wildlife.

Since the day ends much earlier in the east, they booked their rooms in the National Park as soon as possible. The site's officials arranged the four's stay in a hotel near the entrance to the park. The restaurant served a wonderful meal with an eastern Indian touch. The tour would begin in the morning. The officials briefed them about the park's importance and the dos and don'ts. The friends came up with a strategy as to how to approach the search without alerting anyone. During the night, the sounds of the many wild animals echoed all around them, making it very difficult to sleep.

* * * *

Soon after breakfast, the elephant safari began. They walked up an elevated ramp; elephants were standing in different bays below. On their tour guide's cue, they glided on top of their designated elephant, two persons per animal,

343

with the *mahout* sitting in the front. They straddled themselves on the raised saddles so as not to fall. The height gave them a good view, far above the surrounding tall, thick grasses.

The animals moved slowly along a known trail, before passing through a herd of wild water buffalo. Thirty minutes later, they were able to see a herd of elephants in the distance. Jai started a friendly conversation with the tour guide, gaining his confidence as time passed. Bill mapped the route, looking for clues as they went along. Diana and Masako were left to simply enjoy the site of Mother Nature as they passed through the park.

As time progressed, there was a slight commotion in one area along the path. They could hear a few of the tourists yelling. The *mahouts* immediately slowed the six elephants down. As everyone looked in the direction of the commotion, they soon saw a huge one-horned male rhinoceros. Most tourists brought out their cameras and began taking picture and selfies. It was a very stimulating sight.

Diana spoke. "I always thought rhinos were only found in Africa; what a pleasant surprise seeing them here."

"These are one-horned; the African have two; two different races of rhinos. Isn't it fabulous?" Bill said.

As the safari moved on, they could see a crash of rhinos grazing. They noticed the elephants and rhinos allowed each other a certain amount of space.

When the *mahouts* announced it was time to return to the base camp, Jai inquired about a visit to the tiger reserve. The *mahout* said it had been closed, temporarily, after a fatal tiger attack. They arrived back at camp in the late afternoon, and after a meal and a good rest, the four friends gathered together to plan their next move.

Jai spoke first. "As per the *mahout*, the tiger reserve is deep in the jungle on a separate route. Now that it's temporarily closed, we won't be able to go deep enough."

Diana said, "We need to find an alternate way in. Did he know anything about the Naga snake temple?"

"He's new to the job, so I didn't ask him. However, he recommended a camping safari for a few nights, where we stay deep in the jungle in a log house, to experience the *real* jungle. He said the senior guard out there is about to retire and knows the area inside and out. I guess we could take our chances out there. What do you think?"

Bill was staring at the map intensely while listening to the conversation.

Diana turned to him and said, "Bill, what do *you* think?"

Bill looked up before pointing to the map spread out before him on the coffee table. "See this green shaded area—it represents the park. However, if you look at the computer and the online map, that area looks double in size, and the bottom section is grayed out. Any chance there's a military base there?"

Jai checked both maps. "Yeah, you're right, there is a difference. Maybe it's a military base; let me find out from the front office." He quickly got up and left.

He returned with a big smile on his face. "You were right, Bill, that southern region hosts the Indian Army's elite jungle-warfare school. It's a 'no go' for us." He paused. "However, this is interesting." He pointed to an area between the park and school, which was about nine square kilometres.

"What about it?" Diana asked.

"This stretch of land acts as a buffer zone between the park and the school. My hunch is this could be the place where the temple might be. Tomorrow, let's take the camping safari which goes closest to the tiger reserve, that way we'll end up close to that strip of no-man's land. We can take our chances and camp as close as possible."

* * * *

Next day, the tour guide was a senior forest guard, and the driver, his young assistant. They were friendly and professional. The tour went down a dirt road and skirted along a different route from the previous day. They saw wild buffalo, elephants and rhinos all over again, stopped at lakes and rivers and viewed a variety of flora, fauna, fish, reptiles, birds and even crocodiles.

Finally, late in the evening, they arrived at a small rise in the land, on which stood a log house. It doubled as an animal control center, and so there were several communication towers attached to the building. The base of the rise was surrounded by a thick, strong fence to ward off any wild animals. Once on top, the view of the forest was fantastic. When they checked the map, they realized just how close they were to the tiger reserve. But, as the park rules stated, they weren't supposed to go outside the fenced area, so they would need to spend the night in this secluded place and figure out what to do the next day.

They grabbed a quick meal of sandwiches and soup, and then the guests assembled in one of the rooms to chat and play some games. The assistant locked all the doors and bid them good evening.

Throughout the night, they could hear the sounds of many different animals from the smallest insect, to the largest elephant. It was an eerie experience.

In the morning, just as they were about to resume their journey, there was the sudden loud sound of an elephant trumpeting in distress. It was confirmed by the junior guard. The senior guard, swearing and mumbling under his breath about poachers, pulled a rifle out of one of the vehicles and checked to see if it was loaded. He yelled at the guests to stay inside before ordering his assistant to call the rangers to come to their aid. He then jumped into one of the park's land rovers and took off in the direction of the commotion.

For a moment, the four friends weren't sure what they should do. Then Masako said, "Let's go and check; he might need our help."

Diana tried to see in the direction of the guard's vehicle. "It doesn't seem too far. We can't just stay here. We've got to go."

Bill agreed. "Six are better than one." He turned toward Jai, who ordered the junior guard to bring the other vehicle and follow his boss, as he knew the topography. The distressed assistant took a while before he agreed and let them jump in the rover.

As they closed in on the location, Jai signaled the assistant to slow down and stop. They got out and approached carefully, so as not to alert any poachers.

Some large bushy trees and shrubbery provided enough cover for them to be able to assess the situation. They could see an enormous elephant, trapped inside a huge thick net, being pulled from a deep pit by giant pulleys operated by heavy machinery; the poor thing was halfway out of the pit and responding very slowly, as if drugged. They realized that once it was out in the open, the poachers could easily cut off the ivory tusks, without much resistance from the animal. They were shocked to see the senior ranger tied up and being held by two armed poachers. The third one, the apparent leader, was brandishing a gun and barking orders at his dozen or so unarmed helpers to pull the animal out and quickly cut off its tusks, before the park reinforcements could appear.

Jai realized time was running out, and he needed to take charge of the situation; the junior guard was new to the job and didn't have much experience in dealing with such happenings. He gathered everyone together and whispered his plan. They all agreed. Bill took the assistant's gun and positioned himself on the western flank along with Diana. Jai moved to the northern flank with Masako.

As per the plan, the junior guard moved to the south, grabbed the megaphone and made a loud announcement in the Assamese language, informing the poachers they were surrounded on all sides by park rangers, and they needed to surrender.

The lead poacher immediately fired two rounds in the southern direction, the bullets passing within a few yards of the junior guard. The man was brave; he didn't flinch and proceeded to give them one last warning, asking for their surrender and for them to give up their weapons.

The poachers jeered and one among them started moving menacingly toward the guard. That was enough for Jai. He threw his combat knife, piercing the poacher's right shoulder blade. The poacher dropped his gun and screamed in pain as he tried to stop the bleeding with his other hand. His cohorts froze in their tracks, leaving the elephant in the open, but still trapped in the nets. The remaining two poachers started firing indiscriminately in the direction where the knife had come from, as Jai and Masako took cover.

Bill, taking advantage of the situation, aimed his rifle and got off a clear shot. He fired twice, wounding one of the gunmen in the hand, and hitting the stock of the other's rifle, rendering it almost impossible to use. Before the confused poachers could escape, the junior guard moved into the open, ordering them to get down and raise their hands, otherwise he warned the next bullets would go through their heads.

The frightened poachers obeyed him instantly and dropped to their knees on the ground with their hands raised. Once the senior guard was released, they tied up the poachers, took them into custody and put them into one of the vehicles, to be transported to the nearest police station, outside the Kaziranga National Park.

The guards were able to determine that the unarmed locals had been forced by the poachers to do the dirty work, fearing for the safety of their families. They were dismissed by the senior guard, and told never to return if they valued their lives. The four friends remained hidden to protect their identity and let the guards handle everything.

The senior ranger and his assistant were incredibly grateful and asked if they could help the four in any way. Jai realized this was the perfect opportunity for him to ask for the location of the Nagadevata temple.

The older ranger looked intensely into Jai's eyes for a moment, before marking the exact location onto the map that Jai was carrying; it was within the same buffer zone that Jai had initially guessed. The guard explained that no one goes there, and the place is practically abandoned. He said the temple belonged to the Manipur Royal Family and confessed he had never been there himself, but his late grandfather, who was also a forest ranger, had gone a long time ago.

The four thanked the man profusely, saying they needed to visit the place for spiritual reasons and promised to return by nightfall, so no one in the park would notice their absence. The man agreed, but not before warning them that some people who had gone there had never returned, and they should be exceedingly careful.

The six carefully approached the distressed elephant and freed her from the net. Masako and Diana gently stroked the animal to soothe her. They would have to leave her there till she regained full consiouness, but by then the other rangers would have arrived and would look after her. Masako observed the letter "G" inscribed on the elephant's collar. She was told by the junior guard that most elephants had names, and this one was called Gajendra, hence the "G". The guard explained that Gajendra was unique, it being the largest, tallest and oldest elephant in the park. It was also very special. Having served the park for years, it was retired honorably and seemed to live a solitary life, being called a *yogi*-elephant by many.

After bidding the elephant and the two rangers goodbye, they borrowed one of the range rovers and headed out on the dirt road. The two guards planned to escort the three poachers to the nearest police station to press charges.

With Diana driving and Bill navigating, Jai and Masako kept watch out for tigers. After a kilometre or so, they saw a metal mesh fence with a sign, on which was written: Tiger Reserve: Closed to Visitors. Masako got out and opened the lock with a key given to them by the park ranger, while Jai kept a close watch. Once inside the reserve, they closed and locked the gate, and re-boarded the vehicle. The area was large and it would take them several more kilometres before they would enter the no-man's land where the snake temple was supposed to be located.

* * * *

During conversation with the junior ranger, they discovered there had been a recent tiger attack. An armed *mahout* had accidentally fallen off an elephant, which had been rushed by a single male tiger. He fell right in front of the cat, but his rifle dropped into the tall grass and was lost. The man was unable to recover his weapon and the angry tiger had killed him. By the time the rangers and other *mahouts* came to his rescue, the tiger had dragged the man's body into the tall elephant grass. So far, the park rangers were unable to trace the man-eater, so in the meantime, the tiger reserve was closed to tourists.

Masako had inhaled a sharp breath while looking at Jai. "I hope we don't have to confront any tigers."

"Me neither," said Jai, "especially a man-killer." He kept his eyes focused on the tall grass on either side of the dirt road in case any big cats were hiding in the foliage, hoping for some prey. Diana continued to drive while Bill navigated.

After some time, Jai spotted something on the road far ahead; it was small and had black stripes. He looked through the binoculars. It was unmistakably a tiger cub.

Jai quickly called out, "Diana, there's a tiger cub at our 12 o'clock; stay calm and keep driving, slowly, but *do not stop.*"

Diana's body stiffened. "Okay."

Bill turned to her. "If the mother is around and comes at us, use the horn to shoo her away. Hopefully that'll work."

Diana nodded. There was nothing much to say; only action was needed. Their fear was palpable.

As they approached the cub, Diana slowed down to see if it would give way to them; unfortunately, it didn't.

Bill said, "See if you can go around her."

The path was narrow. Diana tried to go around the cub by aiming one of the front tires into the thick grass. In seconds, they were stuck.

Masako grabbed Jai's arm and pointed behind them. As he turned, he saw a huge tiger emerging from the high grass, very much within striking distance.

Jai whispered, "The mother tiger is right behind us."

"The wheel is stuck. What should I do?" Diana whispered.

Bill answered. "Put the vehicle in reverse." The cruiser moved backward sharply. To make matters worse, the cub started making noises. The mother tiger, upon hearing the cub's distress call, started to run toward them.

Diana honked the horn, trying to scare the baby off the road so they wouldn't run over it. The mother was closing in quickly. Finally, after repeated honks, the cub moved. Diana had just enough time to accelerate the vehicle before the tiger, who was within a few feet, reached them.

Jai had readied a few tranquilizer darts and loaded the rifle, just in case. Thankfully, he didn't have to use them. The metal mesh over the vehicle was quite sturdy; it would have taken more than one cat attacking simultaneously before it would give way. The furious mother tiger snarled as she ran behind them for a considerable distance, before becoming disinterested and leaving the chase to go back to her baby.

Their hearts were still pounding as Diana bravely navigated the vehicle to safety, continuing down the road.

Bill was the first to break the silence. "Bravo, Diana!"

"That was mighty scary; I can now write a book about it." Diana smiled.

Masako laughed. "Phew! What an experience! I can certainly appreciate the park rangers' job, now."

"We'll need to keep a close watch on our return journey." Jai laid the rifle and darts back down on the seat beside him. Everyone let out a deep breath, but they all knew the danger wasn't over yet.

After some time, the dirt road started turning east, and they could see a high fence to one side. They realized they were coming to the end of the tiger reserve as well as the park, and beyond it was the no-man's land they were seeking. They would have to leave their vehicle behind, unless they could find a way through. The question was: how would they climb over the high sturdy fence, as well as mark the location so they could find the cruiser when they were done.

Jai had the solution. He stepped out of the vehicle while the others prayed for his safety. He quickly climbed the tallest tree whose trunk was on one side of the fence and had several of its branches leaning across. He pulled himself up on top of one of the sturdiest limbs, securely tied a long rope to the branch, and then let it drop to the ground. When done, he called them to come up the tree one at a time, with the help of the rope. Bill was the last; he made sure the vehicle was camouflaged with grass and foliage. One by one they maneuvered along the large branch and over the fence, until finally descending from the tree and dropping down into the 'no-man's land'. Jai was the last. He marked the location with the help of the compass, noting the readings and sharing them with the team.

Jai cautioned, "We don't have to worry about tigers anymore, but there could be other dangers we don't know about." He remembered the senior ranger's words that many had gone in but only a few had returned. Reality started to sink in as they began their trek through the jungle, moving toward the location on the map. Bill led the way with everyone keeping a strict watch on their surroundings.

* * * *

Suddenly, Bill stopped and checked the map closely. "We're about two kilometres from ground zero. Follow me." He gestured with his hand, and made a turn, adjusting their course.

Jai spoke from behind. "Just be careful, and watch your step. We don't know what's waiting for us." Diana and Masako walked between the two men.

The part of the jungle they moved through had much thicker growth; it was doubtful any humans had come that way in a very long time. Naturally there were no trails for easy passage. Bill and Jai had to cut through the growth with machetes they found in the Land Rover. The going was slow and arduous. After some time, they observed intense bird activity high up in one of the trees and stopped in their tracks.

Masako whispered, "It looks like a snake is trying to steal the eggs from the bird's nest."

Jai took the binoculars from her. "You're right, it's a snake attack, and the birds are trying to ward him off. It seems like an ominous sign."

"It could also mean we're very near the temple."

They kept moving, but after a few moments, Bill, who was up front, signaled for everyone to stop. He knelt down. Taking a cue, the rest did the same and inched closer to him for a better view.

What they saw astonished them. In the dense forest, there was a huge clearing right ahead, with a large stone structure right in the middle of it, and huge abandoned termite mounds all around. In India, it is well known that snakes sometimes use abandoned termite mounds as their temporary dwellings. The trees along the periphery had enormous branches, forming a canopy almost completely blocking the sky, but just leaving enough space in the center for a trickle of light to come through.

Bill pointed to the map where a circle had been drawn by the senior park ranger. "This is it; this is the place we're looking for."

Masako sighed in relief. "Now what?"

They all looked at each other.

Bill spoke up. "Let me go in first. I'm the oldest and a military veteran; you guys cover me."

Diana looked at him, her face a mask of concern. "You take care."

Bill just smiled to cheer them up, even though his heart started to race, both in fear and anticipation.

Jai readied the small crossbow which he carried in his backpack. Diana had the lone rifle in her hands; Bill stood up and carefully worked his way through the tall shrubbery, stepping into the forest clearing. Nothing moved in the surrounding area; there was calm all around. He cautiously walked forward a few steps. Nothing happened. Feeling more confident, he moved more rapidly toward the centre, where the big stone structure was. He signaled the rest to follow, which they did.

As they approached, they saw the smile on Bill's face, and soon realized the central stone edifice was nothing but a dilapidated temple, covered with a lot of overgrowth.

Jai whispered, "Let's clear this path; I can see some steps." He pointed the machete toward a particular spot on the ground. They started hacking away at the foliage in earnest and soon made sufficient progress to easily pass through. The opening revealed two huge stone serpents standing guard and looking as if they were very much alive.

Diana reached out and patted Jai on the shoulder. "This should be the temple entrance; if we're correct, the Nagamani Jewel should be inside the inner sanctum."

They all nodded in agreement and walked slowly and quietly so as not to disturb the surrounding reverent atmosphere. More and more serpent statues of different kinds, shapes and sizes appeared as they proceeded inward, until finally they came face to face with the biggest of all in the center, its five raised hoods and ten eyes staring down at them from ten feet above. Its fangs were positioned in such a way as to suggest its tongue was actively darting in and out through its open mouth. If it had been real, it would have given anyone a heart attack. Nagaraj seemed like a blend between a snake and human, the face and hands said it all.

Jai stood at attention, folded his hands and paid obeisances to the Nagaraj deity, the King of the serpents. It represented the celestial snake of Lord Shiva. The others followed suit. Then Diana signaled them to start searching for the jewel. The search seemed futile, with nothing found except insects and dirt. Jai came up with an idea and suggested someone attempt to stand on another's shoulders, so as to look on top of the serpent's hood for the jewel. With Jai and Masako's help, Diana climbed onto Bill's shoulders. She could clearly see over the top of the statue's hood. Nothing was there, except the scales on its hood and the furious eyes looking at her; it was an eerie moment.

Finally, Jai checked the time. It was getting quite late and in a couple of hours was going to be dark. They needed to go.

The return journey went surprisingly smooth, but the mood was somber and no one spoke.

They arrived at the log house just before dark; there was no sign of the forest rangers. They prepared a meal, and then relaxed in the living room. It was time to take stock of the situation.

Diana spoke first. "We were so close."

Jai nodded in agreement. "We're missing something; I'm sure the jewel is right there in the temple, but why can't we find it?"

"It's possible someone might have taken it already, after all these years," said Bill

"That's a possibility, but I hate to even think about it." Diana sighed.

Masako finally spoke up. "I'm sure we'll find it. Why don't we ask your Professor Cariappa; you said he knows everything about it. Maybe he can give us some more ideas as to where exactly to search."

Jai looked up. "That's it; we need to get the professor involved again."

Jai took out his satellite phone and dialed the number Diana handed to him, waited until the professor answered before quickly passing the phone to Diana.

"Professor, it's Diana Warwick, with Bill and two other friends. I'm putting you on speaker phone."

"Hello, how are you? And how can I help you?" replied the professor eagerly.

Diana briefly narrated the events of the unsuccessful expedition. Everyone held their breath in anticipation.

After many moments of silence, the professor said, "It seems like you have been lucky to find the Nagadevata temple. I think that is a good omen. I doubt if anyone has been there in the last one hundred years." He paused. "No normal person would be able to take the jewel, as it's part of a puzzle—that means it should be right there, but you probably cannot see it."

Diana spoke up. "We checked every corner and even on top of the hood."

"Wait just a moment; let me check the calendar. I will be back in a minute." Footsteps could be heard in the background as the professor walked away from the phone and then returned.

"Today is the seventh day of the waxing moon. The serpents become more active on the full moon night, especially at midnight. I am sure you will find the jewel somewhere near the Nagaraj deity during that time. Don't forget to repeat the *Omkara mantra* in endeavors of this kind; it will calm your mind and ensure you will uncover the mystery. That is all I can say," he advised.

Diana took a deep breath. "Thank you, Professor, we shall keep that in mind."

"Before we end this call, let's pray to Ganesha to remove all obstacles in your pursuit to unearth the treasure," suggested Cariappa. "Please stand in a circle and hold hands. Repeat the mantra along with me, with full attention, respect and trust." He paused, giving them time to form the circle. He recited the Sanskrit mantra. "*Vakra-Tunndda Maha-Kaaya Suurya-Kotti Samaprabha, Nirvighnam Kuru Me Deva Sarva-Kaaryessu Sarvadaa.*"

The four friends repeated the mantra word for word. The call ended with them feeling a new found confidence, determination and hope.

"We have seven more days to go; what shall we do till then?" Masako finally broke the silence after a few minutes.

"Let explore India's north-eastern states. They're known as the 'Seven Sisters'." Jai's face broke into a smile.

Everyone agreed. Almost immediately, they heard the approach of a vehicle. It was the junior ranger. They had a pleasant talk and he informed them his boss had to stay back at the police station to make sure the poachers were properly prosecuted for their crimes. The next morning, they left the park to visit the seven states, starting with Nagaland and Manipur.

* * * *

One day before the full moon, they took the same overnight camping tour, reached the same log house and met the same junior forest guard. Knowing them to be special guests of honor, especially after their help in freeing the elephant, the guard gave them free run, accommodated all their requests and keeping their secret from the other park officials. On the full moon night around 9:00 p.m., they took the guard's vehicle and drove into the tiger reserve. This time they were better prepared. And Jai drove. He didn't need navigational assistance, as he knew exactly where to go. The moonlight was enough to see by. He didn't want to switch on the vehicle's lights, which would easily give away their position to any forest rangers keeping an eye on the tiger reserve from other observation posts, not to mention attracting any tigers who might not have been asleep.

Diana and Masako carried long electric wands with enough current to shock an attacking animal when activated by the push of a button. Bill carried a tranquilizer gun.

Just when they thought the drive was going well, it started raining; it was as if their resolve was being tested by a higher power. Soon it launched into a heavy downpour, a serious cloudburst. The dry dirt road turned into mud and the drive became difficult and dangerous.

Jai used all of his Special Forces' skills to keep them straight on the road, as it became more and more treacherous. At one point, the vehicle got stuck in a slurry of mud and refused to move. Jai tried everything to get it out. Finally the vintage model quit and its engine fell silent, as the heavy rain drowned the motor. The friends remained calm, while being drenched to the skin, as thunder and lightning danced over their heads.

Diana yelled over the storm, "How far are we from the no-man's land?"

Jai studied the laminated map with a small flashlight. "About a kilometre."

"*Damn it,*" said Bill, "now we'll have to go the rest of the way on foot. We don't have any other choice."

Masako spoke up. "Do you think the man-eater will be around?"

Jai smiled and reached into his backpack, bringing out a million candle flashlight. He switched on the powerful light, which can temporarily blind a person or animal. "This should keep the tiger at bay," he said confidently. He, along with the others, got down from the vehicle and started walking. Masako and Diana carried the battery-operated electric wands, while Bill carried the tranquilizing gun. Their progress was difficult as they slogged through the mud, straining their energy. With midnight fast approaching, they couldn't afford to miss their window of opportunity which came only once a month.

They were about 200 meters from the edge of the tiger reserve and before the start of the no man's land, when they heard something like a high pitched growl. They stopped in their tracks, straining their ears to hear the sound over the storm. Finally, Jai was able to make out the direction it was coming from. A tiger, a few meters behind them, stood ready to attack.

Jai barked orders. The other three quickly moved behind him, pulling out their respective weapons. Jai turned on his flashlight to blind the animal. When the next flash of lightning happened he clearly saw the wild beast in front of him positioning itself to lunge. The only thing holding it back was the powerful light blinding it. They knew they had little time and still 100 meters to go to safety. They slowly walked backward toward the fence where they had earlier crossed over.

They moved carefully with Jai in front keeping the light in the tiger's eyes. It regularly growled loudly and paced from side to side, trying to avoid the blinding light. When they were about fifty meters from the fence, Jai slipped and fell flat on the ground in the mud and incessant rain, losing his grip on the flashlight. The tiger stopped dead in its tracks and hunched down. Jai shouted, "Tranquilizer!"

Bill could barely hear due to the noise of the storm, but he placed himself between Jai and the tiger and squeezed the trigger of the tranquilizer gun. To his horror, the gun jammed. Jai looked back at Bill as Bill frantically tried to un-jam the weapon. Suddenly, the tiger leapt, and that's when they both saw a huge branch come from out of nowhere and hit the tiger on the head, knocking the beast unconsciousness.

As they turned to see what had saved their lives, they made out a huge animal standing in front of them. It was an elephant!

Masako moved closer and looked at its collar. "Jai, it's the same elephant we helped the other day; see the "G" mark on its collar? It's unmistakable. It's Gajendra!" The friends closed in and gently touched the beast. It seemed more than happy and let out a trumpeting sound.

Jai looked at his watch. "We have less than an hour to midnight and we have a long way to go."

As if responding to his words, the elephant kneeled, appearing to invite them to climb aboard. Masako was the first to oblige. She gave a shrill laugh as she climbed on the elephant's back. Next, it was Diana's turn. Realizing what was happening, Diana spoke. "It wants to help us. I think it wants to return the favour."

Finally, Bill and Jai mounted the animal.

Bill said, "I think this is divine intervention, Jai. Try whispering where we're going into its ear. Somehow, I think it'll take us there, and fast."

No sooner had Jai whispered, *Nagadevata mandir*, the elephant shook its head, slowly got to its feet and started walking toward the no-man's land.

Diana was speechless as this profound event unfolded right before her eyes. She couldn't believe what was happening.

As they held onto each other and the elephant's hide and collar strap to keep their balance, the animal made quick progress, cutting through the vegetation and breaking through one section of the fence with ease, bringing them near to the forest clearing where the temple stood.

Jai checked his watch. It was now twenty minutes to midnight. Gajendra knelt and allowed them to dismount, then stood up and waited, seeming to indicate it was willing to take them back. The friends patted and kissed her before moving toward the temple entrance.

Surprisingly, there was no rain there, and the ground seemed dry; it was as if the thunder and lightning was happening at a distance outside the entrance. The moonlight was bright enough for them to see the ground below. As they walked forward, coming closer to the temple, they could clearly see the numerous termite mounds surrounding the temple.

It was an eerie place, but somehow Diana was not afraid anymore after the close encounter with the man-eater. She felt they all seemed to have conquered their fear. No one spoke aloud, they only gestured to each other. With five minutes left before midnight, the friends stood right below the giant Nagaraja; with folded hands they showed their respect to the deity of the Serpent King. Jai advised, "This is a special place; we need to demonstrate qualities of kindness, magnanimity and peace under all situations, so be prepared for anything."

Everyone nodded.

When the clock struck midnight, there was a great trumpet from Gajendra, seeming to signal both midnight and the arrival of something unknown. Diana understood and instantly sat down with the others onto the ground, chanting *Omkara* in her mind, as Jai chanted it quietly aloud.

The full moon lit up the surrounding area as a slight breeze flowed through the temple, producing an eerie musical, violin-like, high-pitched sound. The elephant stood in the woods, away from the clearing, as huge serpents of many kinds, emerged from the ground all around and entered the temple, undulating in a delicate and deliberate dance-like motion. Inside the temple, Diana and friends turned their heads slowly, only to see serpents moving across the ground, coming closer and closer from all sides. The heads of the snakes were aglow with illuminating jewels. Diana and the others tried to remain calm, meditating on the mantra.

Four, huge, hooded cobras crawled up behind the four friends and simultaneously slithered up their backs, sending shivers along their spines. The friends held their breath as the creepy feeling inundated them. The snakes, as if locked in some magical, rhythmic dance, wove their way around the four bodies and encircled their necks, before lifting their hooded faces and staring straight into the human eyes, as if searching for any malevolent intentions.

Jai looked right back into the serpents' eyes, doing his best to emanate compassion and love. The snake seemed satisfied and slowly slithered down his body and onto the floor without harming him.

Bill, who was trained in jungle warfare and familiar with snakes, though not as deeply in communion with the creature as Jai, managed to keep his control, as Jai had instructed. He tried to look directly into the serpent's eyes, in an open, friendly, and un-fearing way. The snake seemed satisfied and slowly slithered down his body.

Masako had goose bumps. She had impersonated a few animal movements in her martial arts training, but this was too much. She concentrated and looked toward the serpent, as calmly and compassionately as possible, although she could feel the inner vibration of her own heart. The snake slowly uncoiled itself and moved away. Diana was in total horror. She could feel a cold sweat dripping from her brow. She told herself to focus on Arthur's mission and the *Omkara* mantra as much as possible; and somehow managed to regain her composure. This experience was beyond craziness. By the time she decided to look at the serpent, it was already beginning to leave her body.

The four cobras hesitated, looked back, and as if trying to communicate something, opened their mouths, and displayed their fangs.

The four friends slowly stood up and looked at each other, momentary confusion on their faces. Instantly, they became aware of drops of moisture falling from above. They looked up simultaneously to see that the fangs of the Nagaraj Deity were dripping with some kind of liquid. They saw three fangs in the central head and not two as the others had. Looking at each other, they suddenly realized the lower single fang of Nagaraj was not a fang at all, but the Nagamani jewel they had been seeking. At that very moment the cloud cover moved and the moonlight fell straight onto the jewel, making it sparkle into infinity.

Jai signaled, motioning for Diana to climb onto Bill's shoulders to get to the jewel. Bill squatted down and then stood up, holding onto Diana's legs once she was in place. For a moment, Diana thought Nagaraj was coming to life as the stone statue seamed to change in texture. She carefully placed her hands on the sparkling jeweled fang. As she touched it, she was momentary transfixed, as if in another world. Bill nudged her from below, bringing her back to this world. When she snapped out of the spell, the jewel was in her hand. She carefully descended with the help of Masako. The jewel, a bluish-white, was cylindrical, about four inches long and a half inch in diameter. She clutched it in the palms of her hands, and assisted by the others, started walking out of the temple. Realizing Nagaraj was not a mere statue but a celestial deity who had helped her to achieve part of her quest, she felt compelled to offer her thanks.

She turned back and bowed toward the immense deity. As she did so, the numerous serpents, assembled there on the full moon night, made way for her to walk through them.

It was as if the four friends were in a huge snake pit, with thousands of snakes entwined in dances of love all around them.

As they left the temple, they walked quickly toward Gajendra, who upon seeing them, knelt down for them to mount. The Nagamani jewel had a deep indentation around the circumference at one end. Diana removed the black cord from her neck, upon which were strung the tulasi and rudraksha beads, and passed the string around the indented portion of the jewel, tied a knot, and then firmly secured it to the necklace, before putting the cord back in place around her neck.

The friends held onto each other as the elephant stood up, and then began the return journey.

* * * *

Diana held Gajendra's trunk, gave the animal a big hug and thanked her for her kindness. Soon the trunk of Gajendra slipped out of Diana's hand, as the animal moved away and seemed to fade into the night. The four friends waved their hands just as Diana felt a tickling sensation on her face. She immediately scratched at her skin, and it went away. After a few moments, the sensation returned. She swiped her hand across her face and hit something soft, startling her. She tried to make sense of it. Again the tickling sensation returned, along with a strong flow of air and a loud roar. She forced open her eyes slowly.

The sun was directly above her in the sky, and a helicopter was flying overhead. Her friends lay in the grass, next to her, still asleep. As she lay there, the memory of the night before slowly returned. The long grass blew wildly around them in the strong wind. Slowly the others regained consciousness.

Masako spoke first, her voice hoarse. "Where are we? What is this place? It doesn't look familiar."

Diana pointed to her right. "Look! There's a helicopter landing over there."

Jai took out his binoculars from his backpack, which was lying in the grass beside him, and checked more closely. "It's an Indian Army helicopter."

Bill checked his compass co-ordinates and looked at the map. "Seems like we're inside the Indian Army jungle warfare school. How did that happen?"

Diana shook her head. "How did we get here from the Nagadevata temple? I don't remember a thing."

Jai smiled. "Maybe the elephant brought us here. I remember that once we sat on Gajendra, you put the Nagamani jewel on the cord around your neck, and at that instant, some sort of energy field enveloped you."

Bill interrupted, excitedly. "I remember that. We were sitting pressed up against each other on the back of the elephant and some type of light seemed to radiate from the jewel, engulfing all of us, and then I woke up here."

Masako spoke up. "Diana, check and see if you still have the jewel."

"I checked the very moment I woke up. It's here. Everything happened for real." She held up the jewel.

Jai quickly grabbed his satellite phone and made two separate calls, one to Professor Cariappa and the other to Karry. Both were elated with the team's success.

Bill related their current location, and Karry told them he knew the commandant of the army jungle warfare school and would immediately arrange for a military helicopter ride to Chennai, toward their next destination south of their current location.

Chapter 13 - At Sri Rama's Bridge

After having a good rest in Chennai, the four friends began the trip from their safehouse in Besant Nagar, to the southernmost tip of India, Rameshvaram. They left at sunrise in a large SUV. The early morning breeze was enlivening, the road was relatively free of traffic and Jai drove the vehicle at a good speed. After a while, they reached Tiruchchirappalli on the banks of the river Kaveri.

It seemed that nobody had been following them, but still they were careful to keep their important possessions with them, watching them closely at all times. Later they reached Devipattinam, where they stopped for a late lunch before continuing toward Rameshvaram.

At Mandapam, they were greeted by a majestic view of the sea on both sides of the city. In the southwest, it was called the Gulf of Mannar, while to the north-east, it was called Palk Bay. Everyone was in awe of the splendid geography. They finally reached Rameshvaram after ten hours.

"This is the same route Bhagavan Rama once walked," commented Jai reverentially, as he tightened his grip on the steering wheel. "He went to Sri Lanka to rescue his wife, Sita, from the demon king, Ravana."

"Rama must have had very deep feelings of love for his wife," said Masako

Bill smiled. "Of course, Rama is called *Maryada Purushottama*, meaning an ideal human being with 'supreme' qualities. But the rescue of Sita is not just a wonderful story of love and courage, it also contains very deep and symbolic meanings on many levels."

"That's true," said Jai, keeping his eyes on the road. "You know, before proceeding to Sri Lanka, Lord Rama installed a famous Shiva lingam that is still present today at the Sri Ramanathaswamy temple. The present temple super-structure was built later on to commemorate that particular event. You can see the temple...there," he added, pointing at a massive, yellow, pyramid-like structure that was visible even from a good distance.

"Let's visit the temple and perhaps we can get his blessings," Diana suggested. Everyone nodded enthusiastically.

"How long was Rama's bridge?" asked Masako.

"About fifty kilometres," replied Jai. By the expressions on the others' faces, he could tell they were amazed.

* * * *

After checking into the hotel in Rameshwaram, the four friends visited the temple at dusk, and then spent the rest of the time chatting in the hotel lounge. During the visit they learned that the Shiva Lingam there is one of the original twelve Jyotir lingam. It is said that Lord Rama himself fashioned the original from the sand on the beach. The temple has twenty-two wells, and the taste of the water from each well is different than the others. There is also a huge corridor, almost four-thousand feet long, with richly carved twelve-foot-high granite pillars. On them were statues of ferocious lions painted in yellow. The ceiling was covered in rich pictures displaying various wheels, which denoted the energy vortexes in the human body, as designated in Ayurvedic study."

"I heard rumors there might be some commotion at Rama Setu," said Jai, unfolding a flyer in his hands. "The local people here said there were lots of outsiders, in the last few days, coming from all corners of India, and also some from abroad. They were organizing a rally to protest against the dredging under the Setu Bridge to open a new channel for ship navigation." He flashed the flyer written in English and Tamil. "They've been distributing these here for several days. It seems we'll have company where we're going." He smiled.

Bill picked up the rally flyer and studied it. "Listen to this," he said, "Here it says '...several groups have called for a nation-wide protest movement against this desecration by the Indian Government of a Ram Setu bridge monument that is not only a sacred place for over one billion Hindus worldwide, but is also a world archaeological relic of enormous importance. It's much more ancient and unique than the Buddhas of Bamiyan...' you know the ones destroyed by Taliban extremists in Afghanistan."

Jai jumped in. "The present Indian government wants to break the Ram Setu at any cost to create a shipping channel. They are going against the wishes of Hindus who consider it as sacred, environmentalists who are worried that the natural barrier the Setu is providing against the effects of a tsunami, which if removed will expose the communities living along the shore to greater danger, and the economists who consider it as a wasteful expenditure of people's money to fill the coffers of some dubious industrialists."

Masako seemed annoyed. "It's unfair and unacceptable by any human standards."

Diana was visibly outraged. "The United Nations should do something!" she exclaimed.

"It will not happen in today's India," retorted Jai, angrily. "The so-called secular Indians, educated in the British system established by Macaulay, are very much prejudiced, and are still being conditioned by the inferiority complex instilled by colonial rule. For them, nothing that is connected to Hinduism can be of value, what to speak of being worthy of respect."

"And some obviously don't care for the environment, either," said Bill, still reading the flyer.

Early next morning, the four friends checked out of the hotel, got back in the SUV, and left for Dhanushkodi, the first section of the semi-submerged Setu, or bridge. Before long, they began to see the crowds assembling, and noticed unprecedented security all around. There was a full battalion of special State Police barricading the road, and since there was no secondary option paralleling the highway, it was impossible to proceed.

Jai stopped the car on the side of the road to go and talk with the police officer, and when he came back he didn't look very happy. "No way to go today," he said shaking his head. "And probably not even tomorrow or the day after. The police don't know when the protesters will leave, and they have orders to remain here as long as there is a security risk."

"What'll we do?" asked Diana.

"I have a backup plan," Jai replied. "I think we should go back to Devipattinam and get a boat from there; it'll be a longer route but it'll get us to the Setu."

"Okay, sounds good," said Bill. Masako and Diana nodded in agreement.

Jai turned the car around and they headed back. There were still several hours of daylight left, and Jai, determined to salvage the day, drove directly to the dock. There, his contact showed them a few motorboats. There was one that looked more solid than the rest, and contained diving gear suited to their purpose. Bill made sure the boat had extra fuel tanks and a tool kit; then he examined the engine. Finally, he declared it was good enough and didn't seem to need any repairs. All of this preparation was necessary but took considerable time; it was late afternoon before they finally moved out into the open sea.

Keeping a good distance from the coastline, they sped outward, first travelling east, then southeast, hoping to avoid problems with the Coast Guard patrols. A few hours later, they reached the Setu.

Jai slowed the boat and gestured toward the limestone shoals, as they cruised toward them. "See, this is the Rama Setu, the bridge of stones built by Rama. It's still visible." After peering through the binoculars, he handed them to Bill.

"I've never seen anything like this before," whispered Bill, his voice full of awe. "Professor Cariappa showed us the satellite images, but it's difficult to relate them to reality on such a scale. The direct experience is really something else."

He handed the binoculars first to Masako, who then passed them on to Diana.

Not far away, a large ship seemed to be stationed in the middle of the sea. Surrounding it was a modest fleet of smaller motorboats,

some of which were Coast Guard, and others—
with their slogan-filled banners—obviously
carried protestors. There was also a Greenpeace
boat, accompanied by a dozen inflatable rafts
positioned right in front of the large dredging
ship, risking the lives of the people sitting on
them. Each raft carried a large banner.

Several thousand were crowded along the
narrow strip of land near Dhanushkodi, but were
too distant to be clearly visible even with the
binoculars, although several banners could be
seen.

Jai pushed the engine throttle forward; then,
keeping a good distance from the center of the
action, sped past the protesters' boats and
eventually reached the dredging ship. He didn't
slow down until their motorboat had reached a
clear area, a few kilometres beyond the ship.
There, they approached the semi-submerged
limestone shoals of the Rama Setu.

It seemed that the Coast Guard was busy
with the protesters and not interested in
pursuing them. Jai cut the engine.

"I guess we're on the edge of Sri Lankan
territorial waters; we can't go any farther," Jai
said confidently.

"So much the better," added Bill. "If we stay
here, we might have a more peaceful dive. What
about sharks? Any man-eaters around?"

"No," said Jai. "I haven't heard of attacks in
this area; the water's too shallow for them."

Everyone looked visibly relieved. Bill opened the large bag to extract the scuba diving equipment.

Jai looked at the girls. "Ladies, I think you should stay in the boat and keep an eye out for unexpected company."

They both nodded in agreement.

Jai produced two very long, thin nylon ropes. "We're going down with these. If anyone comes along, yank on the ropes and we'll come back to the surface immediately." He paused. "If nothing happens, and we need to go farther to search for the crystal, we'll surface and pull the rope from our side, so you know we need you to bring the boat closer to us. The ropes are only one hundred meters long, so we can't swim very far."

"All right," said Diana, staring at the guys, her face a reflection of worry. "I know how to operate the engine and drive the boat, but I think you'll soon need to use your headlights, because the sun's going to set."

Smiling, Bill and Jai strapped their headlamps on, and then adjusted their masks and mouthpieces before sliding into the warm waters. They swam quickly and soon were near the bridge rocks, about one to three meters under water.

Jai was in total awe, as if in the presence of Rama himself. As with any sacred object, he respectfully placed his right hand on one of the stones, then brought his hand instinctively to his forehead before placing it on his heart. Hovering right behind him, Bill watched Jai's actions and was powerfully reminded of the sacredness of the place.

The two friends covered their one hundred meters of submerged rocks without noticing any particular geological formation besides the limestone. Their re-breathers afforded them invisible diving time, as they produced no surface bubbles. Plus, because the closed circuit of the tubes drew the carbon dioxide air through a scrubber that regenerated it before sending it back to the air tank, with experience in using the system, they would be able to stay under for an extended length of time. Still, they didn't want to be run over by their own motorboat, so they pulled their ropes, resurfaced, and remained floating alongside while Diana slowly maneuvered the boat nearer. In the meantime, Masako wound up the rope to prevent it from getting caught in the blades of the motor.

"No luck yet, but we'll go on," said Bill, while treading water—his mask perched on the top of his head when the boat was close enough for them to talk.

"Very well," said Diana, nodding in agreement, as she switched off the engine.

We're okay," Jai called out, smiling reassuringly when he saw Masako's worried face. "Don't worry; we know what we're doing."

The two young men disappeared again under the quickly darkening waters. The sun seemed to suddenly sink below the horizon, and the two women began to grow anxious once more. They didn't want to use any light on the surface of the sea for the fear of being spotted by the patrol boats. Each of them held several coils of rope, and they were somehow comforted by the idea that the ropes kept paying out at a steady pace. This meant the men at the other end were swimming regularly and everything was going well.

The two girls took turns using the binoculars to watch the area where the dredging ship was stationed. Soon after sunset, they noticed that all the patrol boats and the protesters had cleared away.

Around 8:00 p.m., Bill and Jai decided to call it a day. After tying the boat to the rocks of the Setu and pulling it out of the water, they climbed back in to get dry and rest up. Jai lit the LED lamp, and used the infrared binoculars to gaze around. He soon declared that nobody seemed to be watching them. Indeed, the air was eerily quiet, and the sea surface still, as Diana and Masako extracted snacks and drinking water from their luggage. And yet, they had to be on their guard. As soon as they had eaten some food and arranged their blankets and inflatable pillows for the night, the lantern was switched off.

* * * *

At dawn, they awoke rather tired and cramped, but it was a small price to pay for the extraordinary quest they had embarked upon. They did their best to smile at each other and Bill even tried making some feeble joke about taking a morning bath, getting some sympathetic giggles from Diana and Masako. Jai, who had been through extensive diving training at the Valley, checked their equipment, making adjustments as necessary. Everything was soon ready for another immersion.

After a quick breakfast, Diana and Masako insisted on having a dive as well. Bill and Jai agreed as they learned both were skilled in the activity. The women started where the fellows had left off the previous day. Meanwhile, Bill and Jai took turns watching the dredging ship.

After some time, Jai lowered the binoculars and stared into the distance. "It's really moving—I mean the dredging ship—but very slowly. I think they're laying down nets or something. Moreover, there are no protest boats today."

"I think we should try to follow the dredging ship," urged Bill, as he made small tugs on the ropes to alert Diana and Masako. "Probably they've resumed the dredging and this means they might use low-intensity plastic explosives to blow up the rocks and change the current flow. If this is the case, they won't use nets, but strings of small bricks of RDX or IED with some kind of time trigger that leaves the ship time to get away without being damaged by the explosions."

"I think you're right," said Jai.

Almost immediately, Diana and Masako surfaced and climbed back into the boat to remove their diving gear. Bill and Jai told them what they'd seen. The four agreed to carefully follow the dredging ship, watching out, of course, for any underwater explosives. Keeping the engine at its slowest and quietest setting, Jai pulled the boat right into the dredging ship's blind spot and followed its trail at a safe distance. Once in range, Jai and Bill dove in and swam underwater toward the ship, seemingly undetected. Upon reaching the hull, they approached the net that was being laid and carefully studied it. Jai figured the trigger was a rudimentary electronic signal traveling through the cable that connected the plastic explosive bricks. He signaled and Bill followed, rightly assuming that he was going to sabotage the cable as soon as it was released from the ship. That would give them sufficient time to swim away without getting hurt.

The two reached the vicinity of the ship's hull just as a new, long row of plastic bricks, all connected by a cable, was being released. They grabbed the cable and quickly cut it off where a small red light was blinking on the timer. They then routed the signal backwards, in such a way that the resulting trigger would short-circuit the firing mechanism within the ship itself. The ship would not be laying or detonating any mines for quite some time. After completing their task, they swam back to the boat.

They returned excited and elated, and when they climbed back on board they could not stop laughing, imagining the puzzled faces of the ship's engineers. Today it was just a few strings of explosives, and undoubtedly the ship would eventually fix the problem, but they felt like they had valiantly fought against the forces bent on desecrating India's native heritage, and they had won this battle of the war.

Resuming their search at a safe distance from the dredging ship, Bill and Jai noticed there appeared to be a huge abandoned plow stuck in the sea bottom. It was most likely from the dredging ship, which may have been somehow broken off and got stuck when they were trying to wreck the barrier by displacing the stones, before they could start dredging. Now both understood why the ship was trying to use mines—the Setu was built strong. Due to the ramming of the plow, several rocks seemed to have been cracked or shattered and their internal core was exposed. At some point, Jai had a glimpse of a faint light twinkling from among the rocks, and he signaled to Bill. Swimming close together, they reached a cluster of badly damaged rocks and saw that, in fact, a small stone emitted light, a sort of fluorescent, pinkish hue.

Jai picked up the stone and pulled his rope, followed by Bill. They surfaced and swam toward the boat without waiting for it to come closer. Diana and Masako realized that something important had happened.

Climbing back onto the boat, Jai showed the stone to them. Forgetting the ropes and everything else, they all stared excitedly at the extraordinary find. Its light was faint and the daylight proved a hindrance to seeing its full luminescence, but their hearts were still racing. They pumped their fists into the air triumphantly.

"I don't know much about minerals," Diana said, rubbing her hands together in excitement, "but I've heard there are some fluorescent substances that absorb the sunlight and glow in the dark. This rock must be like that, only I thought that the glow was green or yellowish. I wasn't expecting reddish-pink."

"Well, I guess if it's a 'fire' crystal, it should be glowing red," commented Bill, smiling, "But it's a nice color, for sure."

"We need to have it examined by some laboratory to ascertain what it is," said Jai, apprehensively. "It might be radioactive, and then we would have exposure problems if we're not careful."

"I don't think it is," said Diana confidently. "I have a good feeling about this." She smiled and carefully wrapped it in a cloth, placing it inside a protective, lead-lined container—provided by Jai—to contain any radioactivity.

The return journey went faster, as they traveled at full speed and without detours. In a mere two hours, they reached the dock. The boat owner was very happy to see his vessel back without any damage, and even happier to be paid a good sum of money. He informed them that the Director of Police—and a stooge of the Chief Minister of Tamilnadu—with Dravidian supremacist ideological roots—had encouraged his two hundred police officers to ruthlessly attack the more than 9,000 protesters, including women and children. All had gone through the security blockade and it had been ascertained no one was a threat and none carried any weapons. The police charge had caused panic and several people had been seriously injured; some had even died in the resulting stampede. The police also arrested several Greenpeace activists and Hindu protesters who apparently tried to defend the women and children from the police.

Jai called Karry on his secure line and reported the events of the day, including their encounter with the dredging ship, and the police action. Karry said he would speak with Balaram and make sure the Prime Minister and President of India knew exactly what was going on. Thankfully things moved, and the government temporarily halted dredging to take stock of the situation. In the meantime, the Indian Supreme Court stopped all dredging activity till a committee of experts could reassess the situation.

* * * *

It was a much needed breakthrough for Professor Jawahar. The last two weeks had been very hard on him, and he had developed a sort of automatic jerking movement in his arm that annoyed him even further.

He had pulled all the strings he could at the Intelligence Bureau. He'd convinced a mid-ranking officer, Mr. Masoom Singh, that the British woman and her friend, the black American, were dangerous spies on a mission. They had caused him much frustration in these last few days; the two foreigners seemed to periodically disappear, as they were not using public hotels and guesthouses. They showed up near a place where a large political rally had been disturbing the peace and several other foreigners had been arrested for obstructing the duties of local law enforcement, and endangering the operations of a government-approved project. Also, between their arrival at Guwahati, in the eastern part of India, and their subsequent appearance at Rameshvaram, in the south, there had been no record of them traveling by air, railroad or hiring a vehicle. There was obviously something fishy about their motives.

"I'd not be surprised if drug smuggling is involved in this, as well. There could be a huge promotion in this, for sure," Jawahar had said, and in the end the officer agreed to help him, albeit reluctantly.

Jawahar successfully tracked the identity of the Chinese girl who had fought against his men the night of the wedding party. Masoom had notified him of her home and movements. As the daughter of a cultural attaché from the Chinese Embassy in Delhi, not much could be done about her. If his political contacts or the other members of SEPS found out he was harassing a Chinese national, a family member directly connected to the diplomatic corps, he could get into serious trouble. Jawahar became uneasy merely at the thought, and quickly rationalized the girl must have been there by some strange coincidence. *SEPS and Dyer be damned. In the end, the treasure will be for Jawahar Katju, and Katjuooooooooooo alone.*

The identity of the Indian man who had fought to defend the two foreigners was still a mystery, and Jawahar was enraged by his inability to find out anything about him. He felt impotent; he could not even achieve a hard-on and so could not screw the fresh, new prostitutes his henchmen provided. All this made him think he would go mad. In the end, he was left hoping that the *bastard* Indian would show up again, be recognized and properly punished.

It would only be a matter of time.

* * * *

Instead of traveling back to Chennai, the four decided to go straight to Bengaluru, where Jai said he had a contact at the IISC, the Indian Institute of Science, who could help them in identifying the stone and determine if it would have any effect on their mission.

The Vajra Team had a safehouse there which the four friends reached without harm. Their next move was a meeting with Professor Adarsh Srivastava, a specialist in Metallurgy and Geology, working at the institute. It was decided Jai would meet with the professor while the rest stayed put for a much needed rest.

The professor was about to head to his university lab when Jai arrived. "I am surprised to see you here, Jai," Adarsh said with a beaming smile. "But it's a pleasant surprise. How can I help you?"

Returning the warm smile, Jai replied, "Professor, I have found a very peculiar stone while traveling, and I'm hoping you can tell me what it is. It seems to be fluorescent, but with a reddish-pink glow."

Professor Srivastava was startled. "My dear friend...how interesting indeed. These are rare materials, and there are few opportunities to examine them. Come with me to the lab; we will work there."

Once they were inside, Jai produced the fluorescent object, removed its protective anti-radiation cover and placed it in a glass shield, while the professor, clearly intrigued, switched off the light.

"It is a beautiful piece and seems to be a composite formation," he said, reaching out to take the specimen. "The bright red roeblingite is certainly the most notable of its components. It is a very rare and valuable mineral. And I can also see small crystals of clinohedrite that give the orange hue, and smaller quantities of manganaxinite and calcite cleavage, again red and orange." He moved the rock to catch the light. "The shimmering is caused by tiny particles of hematite and mica embedded inside the aventurine feldspar, and rather common quartz stone also called sunstone; plus the activator element is most likely manganese."

The two sat on high stools close to the test bench while the professor launched into his scientific explanation. "Phosphorescence is a phenomenon of delayed luminescence. When an electron is kicked into a high-energy state, it may get trapped there for some time. In some cases, the electrons remain trapped until some trigger gets them unstuck. This triggering energy source kicks an electron of an atom out of its lowest energy ground state into a higher energized and excited state; then the electron returns the energy in the form of light so it can fall back to its ground state."

"I must say the stone is glowing now much more than it was when I found it," noted Jai.

"Yes, indeed. This is perfectly normal. This means that it is simply phosphorescent and not radio luminescent—which would imply a relative health hazard due to radiation exposure for those who handle it."

Jai looked visibly relieved. "So there's no danger in handling it?"

"Not at all. It's a beautiful thing, and harmless as well. It is certainly valuable, but the mixture of the components in such a complex formation makes the extraction of the roeblingite impractical, so you can definitely use this nice object as a paper weight in your office," the professor concluded jovially.

"Can we polish it a little, so that it can glow even more?" asked Jai.

"Of course. By the way, polishing can also show if this particular formation is triboluminescent, that is, if the phosphorescence is enhanced by mechanical action. Some minerals glow more when they are hit or scratched. We can also test the specimen with pulsed laser excitation, for calcite is well known to react to it. LIF red bands are usually observed in the range of 685 to 711 nanometers." The professor smiled. "You know, once shined, this beauty will glow like a living fire...like something from another world."

Jai smiled in enthusiastic agreement.

A couple of hours later, he triumphantly returned to the safehouse to show the wonderfully glowing fire crystal to his friends. They were speechless in amazement. The stone had been shaped into a prism, smooth and polished, and when kept in the dark, it truly resembled a living fire.

"When it is subjected to pulsed laser excitation, the crystal glows even brighter," explained Jai. "I am sure that in ancient times they used mantras and biomagnetic fields to create laser-like effects, using sound instead of light. There have been several experiments on the physical effects of sound modulation, a science of vibrations called Cymatics. I read that a German Professor, Ernst Chladni, made some experiments back in the 1780s, yet it seems he was neither the first nor the last to study the effects of sound on matter. I have always believed that these particular studies could confirm the great power of mantra described in ancient Sanskrit texts."

Diana spoke up. "I think we should go see our friend, Professor Cariappa, again, and show him the jewel and crystal. What do you think?"

"I think it's a great idea. We can also introduce Jai and Masako to the Professor. We should just be careful not to bump into those 'septic' people..."

Diana and Jai took a few seconds to take in the humorous allusion to SEPS, the Society for the Eradication of Pagan Superstitions, nearly forgotten in their amazement over the wonderful find, but they soon started laughing.

After meeting with Cariappa, they were to drive on to Mumbai, which was a thousand kilometres away. During the meeting, Cariappa warmly welcomed them, and was very happy to meet the two new friends of Diana and Bill. He was totally in awe, after seeing the jewel and crystal. He repeatedly held the four friends' hands and pleaded with them to complete the search for the benefit of humanity. After reassurng the professor that they would, they drove on to Mumbai, on their way to Dwaraka, where they hoped to find the mystic symbols, the third clue left by Arthur in pursuit of the treasure.

Chapter 14 - The Submerged City

Jawahar Katju, Professor at Jawaharlal Nehru University, Delhi, and the all-India Director of the Society for the Eradication of Pagan Superstitions, had a problem.

His problem was serious, and had become increasingly difficult to tackle, in spite of all his good efforts and the full mobilization of his best contacts. Actually, there were really two problems, and their names were Diana Warwick and William Johnson.

It had all started on March 7th, when Ormila Naukar of the Indian Council of Historical Research in Delhi had called him to report that a young, white, British woman had appeared at her office looking for information about her ancestor, Arthur Warwick. The odds that such a person would innocently approach one of his closest associates were ridiculously small, and yet the same, apparently naive and helpless girl had thwarted all his attempts to monitor her movements, her motivation, and intercept the information she had collected.

Five days later, on March 12th, the situation had become much more complicated, with the appearance of that black American guy, William Buford Johnson. Since then, they had been jumping here and there like rabbits, all over

India—although apparently without finding anything.

Another eight days, and the rabbits had totally escaped his clutches, in spite of his arrangements. In fact, the problem seemed to have compounded exponentially, with the appearance of the daughter of a Chinese diplomat and a mysterious young Indian man. He had joined them in their travels, registering under the name of Srikanth Khare. It was a false name for sure, and impossible to verify, for no identity document was given at the hotel register in Rameshvaram. Unfortunately, the hotel owner had no idea that writing down the license plate of the vehicle would earn him 5,000 easy rupees; otherwise he would have surely done so. All the sorry hotelier had to offer were the names and passport numbers of Warwick and Johnson, the diplomatic passport of the Chinese girl, and the description of the four of them.

"Thanks for nothing! That is something I already had from my own stupid people in Delhi. What good is the IB if they can't get real info on the Indian," Jawahar growled under his breath while on a call with Masoom.

Enlisting the help of the IB field officer, Masoom Singh, had been quite useful in tracing the two foreigners. He had used a lookout circular to all IB branches, to watch out for the suspects, requesting top priority in monitoring their movements, and combing through the data.

All hotels in every town were ordered to report all names and passport numbers immediately. Without that lookout circular, he would never have known about their visit to Rameshvaram. *Yes, yes, Masoom is useful. I'm sure there will be further use for him in the future,* ruminated Jawahar, as if chewing on a tough piece of grass.

A few nights earlier, he had finally succeeded in meeting Chote Nawab, the son of a Bade Nawab, and leader of an influential political party in the National Government, having its roots in Uttar Pradesh state. Of course, these were nicknames used by their followers and cronies, but they were catchy names, and they had become famous through false family lineages, thus creating a fake dynasty to keep power for themselves. Everyone knew about this, but for fear of quick and heavy retribution, they kept quiet and let them loot the country through corruption done with impunity. The meeting had been rather rough, as Chote Nawab, the perennial bachelor, had insisted on asking what would be the benefit for his party— and especially for himself—if he allowed his own name to support SEPS. Jawahar had no choice and was thus compelled to reveal something about Arthur Warwick's treasure, just enough to ignite the light of greed within the eyes of Nawab. It wasn't long before Nawab asked for his mobile and called the Assistant

Commissioner of Police, Masoom Singh, to confirm that ensuring Professor Jawahar's success was the right thing to do, even though it was not official. Jawahar sneered. *Finally, the guy with low IQ has succumbed to my superior wit, stupidly believing he will share the booty.*

Back in his university home, Jawahar tried to relax by watching sports on TV, but he was still feeling nervous and distracted. The two foreigners had briefly been in Rameshvaram, where they had given the slip to their tails, yet again.

There were those completely blank periods, in which they could actually have gone anywhere and met with anyone including "...the most dangerous terrorists, or exchanged drugs, or accessed the most delicate secrets of the nation," as he had told IB's Masoom Singh. Working IB for information which would help Jawahar was the primary goal of the relationship. "Information about getting to that treasure is mine! Screw the nation!" Jawahar grimaced sourly to himself. *As for my quarry...normal people do not disappear into thin air, once maybe, but never days at a time. Normal people need to sleep in places where you can find them. Normal people have the decency to allow themselves to be followed and controlled.* He scrunched his face in seething anger.

He poured himself a double whiskey, then downed it in one go. It was time to call for a SEPS summit. He dialed the private telephone number and had a brief and unpleasant conversation with Lord Dyer. Dyer informed him that the black man, Bill, was an ex-army major from the U.S., supposed to be on a spiritual quest in India. The info did not help much, except that he now knew why his guys had gotten beaten badly. After he caught his breath and settled his nerves with the whisky, he took out a list of names and phone numbers from his secret safe, and started calling them one after the other.

* * * *

On Saturday, Jai exchanged vehicles and loaded the Valley's specially modified Toyota Tundra—which was temporarily stationed in Mumbai—with all the necessary equipment, before they sped off north, toward Valsad, Surat, Baruch, Vadodara and Ahmedabad.

Jai and Bill took turns driving so they were able to travel throughout the night. In the morning, they stopped to refresh themselves in the Ahmedabad safehouse, had an excellent breakfast of *puris, dokla* and hot milk, and then the four friends drove along National Highway 8A toward Rajkot, and on to Jamnagar in the state of Gujarat.

Just before arriving in Dwarka, they changed into traditional Indian clothing—Jai and Bill into *dhotis* and *kurtas*, and Diana and Masako into *saris*—transforming into perfect Hindu pilgrims. On the insistence of Jai, Bill shaved his head, which made his appearance much more Indian. In that guise, the four of them visited the famous Dwarakadisha temple, a truly magnificent five-story building. On top of the 235-foot-high structure sat a proud, eighty-four-foot-long multicolored flag which exhibited the symbols of the Sun and Moon. After they had paid their respects to the main temple of Krishna in the city, they retired for the evening.

Next day, at a tranquil bit of coast, they parked their truck. Jai procured a motorboat from a local contact within the fishing community. It was the high seas again, venturing out toward the area which Professor Cariappa had indicated as the site of recent submarine archaeological discoveries. Meanwhile Masoom Singh's team was searching for them in the main cities, not knowing they were in a remote part of the country where his agents were unlikely to find them.

The sea here was much deeper and rougher than at Rameshvaram. Jai and Bill took the first turn, and as the sunlight and visibility only reached to a depth of about thirty meters below, they decided to continue using the ropes and headlamps. This time, however, Diana and Masako would use paddles to keep the boat moving behind the divers so they would not be snapped back when the rope reached its full extension. Down below, Bill and Jai were immersed in a deep blue, silent world, where corals of all colors and other marine life grew over immensely ancient, stone structures at the bottom of the ocean. For a long time they swam along beside what seemed to be the fortified walls of a big city, extending for more than five kilometers on each side, searching for a gap that could have originally been an entrance gate. It was not easy. In some places, the wall disappeared altogether under a mass of aquatic plants and corals; at others, the sand of the ocean floor had almost completely covered the structures, perhaps carried there from the beach by return waves during some ancient storm. This was also an area where sharks had been sighted several times; they come to feast on the numerous fish that live in the cool, deep waters.

Around noon, Bill and Jai climbed back into the motorboat to rest while Masako and Diana continued the exploration. Keeping an eye on the thin nylon ropes, the two young men munched on chips, peanuts, and crackers, ate *samosas*, and drained the small amount of tea from the thermos bottle, leaving the coffee for the girls. They had abundant rations for a few days.

Two hours later, refreshed by their leisurely swim in the beautiful and scenic seawater, the two women happily returned to govern the ropes and engine.

By 6:00 p.m., the afternoon sun had softened into a golden globe, and the waters darkened. Jai and Bill, now back in the water, were startled by frantic tugs on their ropes. They looked around and in the distance saw a shadow approaching which resembled a large shark. It was so huge they could only see its bulk blurred by the distance, as it headed directly toward them. The girls had obviously seen it and were trying to alert them. They immediately dropped their ends of the ropes.

Quickly calculating the distance, Bill decided it would be impossible to reach the relative safety of the boat in time; the shark was closer to them than the boat and less than thirty meters away.

His mind shifted to searching for cover in the middle of the coral formations; there seemed to be a depression large enough to allow their bodies and gear shelter. The access to the depression was too small, though, and they needed to break off some of the coral. Bill pulled his knife out of the sheath on his leg and started to pound on the edges with the blunt, hammer-like end. Jai understood what he was doing and joined his frantic efforts with his own knife. The great white shark was less than eight meters away and clearly visible when Bill and Jai finally succeeded in squeezing themselves into the coral cave. In a matter of seconds, they had the truly frightening experience of watching the huge creature—almost five meters long—sliding past their hiding place. Its cold eye watched them a few inches from their faces, and its jaws were open in expectation of a bite that was now impossible. Its jagged, razor-sharp teeth filled its mouth by the hundreds, all designed to rip, rend, and tear the flesh of its prey. The shark circled the place and slid back past them again, visibly frustrated. Bill and Jai signed when the shark left. As they came out of the hiding place in relief, Bill noticed that his right hand was stinging a bit, and to his great horror he saw a thin vapor of his own blood slightly tingeing the water around him; probably his hand hit some sharp coral edge when they were making room to hide. Jai followed his eyes and saw it too. In the silent depths of the blue ocean, the pumping of their hearts became an unbearable noise in their ears.

It was only a matter of time; the huge shark would become more and more impatient for the close presence of a bleeding prey, and if there were other sharks in the area, they would surely appear very soon. With a chill, Bill remembered he had read somewhere that great white sharks can sense blood in water with as little as one part per million.

When he looked at Jai, he saw his friend's face mirrored his own fear.

They were stuck there in the coral cave, barely safe. The predators might even try to break in if they were hungry enough. Jai twisted around to let his headlamp reveal more of the narrow depression in which they were sheltered. He saw that directly under them there seemed to be a larger cave, totally dark; it could possibly accommodate them better and maybe confuse and discourage the sharks.

He twisted around again and used his heel, protected by the rubber flipper, to pound the coral growing there. Bill got the idea and quickly joined in, and soon the coral mass collapsed, giving way into a submerged cave. Relieved, the two friends pushed themselves into it and for a moment the view in front of their eyes made them completely forget the sharks stalking them. In the light of their headlamps, they saw that the cave was not really a cave but a rather wide open area of stone walls. A swarm of very small fish stormed out, apparently disturbed by the unexpected visitors. The walls were about seven meters apart, and there were large steps on one side, like stairs rising to a watchtower. Excited and feeling safe from shark attack, Jai and Bill proceeded to explore the ancient observation post, finally finding a metal door fifteen meters below that was in amazingly good condition. They pushed and banged on it, with absolutely no effect. Awed by that astounding product of ancient metallurgy, the two friends finally gave up and decided to go back to have a look out of their cave and see if the sharks were still around.

At the surface, the girls had seen the huge shadow underwater, then the dorsal fin of the white shark approaching the boat. After circling a couple of times, the big fish had apparently decided that the boat hull was not palatable and moved on. At first they were seized with fear for their own safety, but then they realized the danger for their two friends below. The shark was going in the direction where Bill and Jai had been swimming! Diana realized the ropes had become loose and got busy winding them up into the boat, following exactly the same logic that had prompted Bill and Jai to release them. The women breathed a sigh of relief when they saw that the ends of the ropes had not been cut, nor severed by a bite. Masako left the ropes to Diana and started rummaging in her duffle bag.

"What's the matter, Masako?" asked Diana biting her lower lips anxiously, while she kept quickly re-winding the ropes into two irregular heaps.

"I have it somewhere, somewhere..." babbled Masako nervously, and then she let out a triumphant cry and held up a canister of shark repellant.

Diana smiled.

Masako moved forward, started the engine and began following the dorsal fin of the shark, and then his shadowy mass underwater after he dove deeper. When she saw him circling down below, she stopped the boat. Diana let out a scream of terror and warning. At least four more sharks were approaching fast, but they did not even stop to examine the boat like the first one had done, they already knew where they were going.

When they were directly above the place where the white sharks were circling, Masako unscrewed the cap of the canister and started pouring its content into the water, she even dropped two of the opened canisters in. She turned to Diana, inhaled a sharp breath and said, "Jai gave it to me and explained how to use it."

Diana watched as the repellant dissolved in the water around their boat. Then, after a few minutes she yelled in amazement as she watched the sharks giving up their hunt and swiftly moving away.

They sat down, looked at each other and began to laugh.

* * * *

When Bill and Jai surfaced and climbed back into the boat, they found the girls laughing almost hysterically so they momentarily put aside all other news and stared at them, waiting for an explanation.

"Well, thank God for the shark repellent," said Bill, shaking his head, after they heard the entire story. "From now on, I'll never go for a swim without this magic liquid. Good thinking, ladies. Let's call it a day."

It had been a stressful time and none of them could wait to get to dry land. With Jai at the helm, they sped off back to shore, to a point where they had earlier parked the Tundra. In the meantime, Diana attended to Bill's wound with loving care.

Once they docked, they headed for the truck to relax and get something to eat and drink. As if by unspoken agreement, no one talked about the fright they had experienced. They just enjoyed each other's company, happy to be safe and whole. Their friendship was getting stronger and deeper with every adventure they faced together, evidenced by the comfortable silence they now enjoyed.

When the sun finally set, the four of them climbed into the truck, locked the doors, and rolled the windows halfway down. The cargo bed contained modified sleeping quarters, like an RV. Jai impressed his friends by activating a tiny radar screen on the dash. "It'll beep loudly if anything gets within twenty meters," he assured them, smiling.

"We're all set now," said Masako, sitting up attentively. "Who wants to start talking first?"

"You won't believe what we found," said Bill, his eyes reflecting his joy. He launched into an enthusiastic description of their adventure and the amazing discovery of the hidden chamber. Every now and then he would gesture to Jai, who filled in more details. The shark encounter was also discussed in detail.

"Tomorrow we'll go back out there," Bill concluded, confidently. "I'm sure we're going to find some pretty amazing stuff. We'll tie one of our nice yellow flotation pillows above the entrance, then we'll go exploring."

"We need to take some heavy tools to remove the door hinges," reminded Jai.

"We'll be better equipped than today. And I have more repellent!" Masako laughed.

"Thank God!" agreed Bill, patting her on the shoulder.

Masako smiled, before looking at Jai, who flushed.

"All right, guys, let's wrap up the party for today," said Bill, setting the food basket aside on the front seat before turning off the lights. "Lights out. Nighty night!"

For some time they all lay there silently, each wrapped in their own separate thoughts.

* * * *

Early next morning, everyone was ready for another day at sea. It wasn't too difficult to find the marine cave, but before going inside, Bill and Jai carefully studied the surrounding area to ensure no surprises awaited them. Bill tied the nylon rope with the inflated yellow pillow to the coral just above the cave entrance, keeping it tight then he and Jai dedicated themselves to a second day of exploration.

They used various tools to attack the metal door at the bottom of the fifteen-meter-high watchtower, until finally they were able to remove the bolts keeping the hinges in place. The entire door came off. Jai gestured forward before diving deep into the cavity, closely followed by Bill.

There was a horizontal corridor about five meters wide, and they carefully swam along it for several minutes before reaching a grilled door. They put their tools to work again, and soon the second door had been removed. Bill and Jai entered a vast hall of ruins with many windows partially covered by an outgrowth of coral and other marine organisms. It was difficult to see clearly in that scanty light, but they could tell that despite being covered by underwater plant-life, the walls were intricately carved and the floor, very smooth.

On the opposite side of the hall, there appeared to be a raised platform made of stone; beside it was a door-sized opening. Venturing inside, Jai discovered a maze of large rooms connected by short corridors—possibly a temporary residence for the guards of the fort's outer walls. All the rooms were in rather good condition, and were built with massive precisely-cut stone blocks.

Bill and Jai kept swimming within the silent rooms until they reached a circular hall with many pillars supporting a vaulted domed ceiling. On the wall opposite them, they saw something glittering, and moved toward it as quickly as possible.

Jai gently passed his hand over the plant-covered wall, removing the outgrowth, and soon a large symbol, about one foot wide, came to light. Both friends immediately recognized it—it was the six-pointed star, the original Yantra of the Mother Goddess, the Star of Devi, and known in the West as the Star of David. Bill came to Jai's assistance, and soon the symbol, made up of a strangely lightweight but bright metal, was detached from the wall. Both men immediately began searching for other symbols and before long they had found a Vedic swastika, made of the same material. Soon after, a bright crescent moon was uncovered. Bill and Jai looked at each other, their eyes widening behind their masks. They had found what they came for. They were many of each, however they only picked one of each symbol.

On the surface, Diana and Masako patiently waited, anxiously scouting the water to spot any danger. It was nearly two hours later when they finally saw some glittering shapes emerging from the dark cave about twenty meters below.

The women watched as the shapes grew larger and clearer, not daring to breathe until they were sure it was Bill and Jai carrying them.

When they leaned out of the boat to grab them, the artifacts seemed wonderfully light. Their majestic and radiant beauty had remained untouched despite the possibly thousands of years they'd been immersed in salty water.

"Mission accomplished," gasped Bill, removing his mask. "I deserve a vacation."

"Not at the seaside, I hope." Diana grinned broadly, elated by the splendid success.

"Nope, next time I'd like to go to the mountains for a change," said Bill.

"Be careful what you ask for, you might just get it." Diana laughed.

"All right then, if your mountains are just like your seaside, I think I'll go for the Medal of Honor instead." Bill leaned back into the side of the boat with a sigh. "Back home?" he asked.

"Back home!" Jai replied triumphantly, and started the boat engine.

* * * *

That evening they camped on the beach again, and had a long conversation on speakerphone with Professor Cariappa, so everyone could participate.

"I think you have found the military quarters for the garrison, at the external wall of the fort," said Cariappa thoughtfully steepling his fingers in confidence. "The opening where you entered must have been a window into the guard tower."

"Without that shark attack we would have probably never found the access, because everything was thickly covered by coral and plant life," said Jai.

"This is probably why the previous expeditions did not find any entrance, but just stone walls," remarked Cariappa. "You have been very lucky. God is making things happen for you, even if he is putting you in some danger." He paused. "As they say, 'No pain, no gain.'"

"I'd say so!" admitted Bill.

"The room where you found the symbols was circular and the dome was supported by pillars, correct?" inquired Cariappa.

"Yes, Professor," replied Jai. "It must have been a prayer room."

"Now, I don't need to tell you that you must keep the symbols well hidden, and especially from SEPS." Cariappa spoke with a cautionary tone. "From now on, if you need to travel around with the artifacts—which will be required when you get to the next phase of the expedition in the Himalayas—you cannot carry them on commercial flights or keep them in hotel rooms."

"Very well, Professor. We've already decided to keep traveling by road," explained Jai.

"Excellent. I am very happy to hear that. Keep me informed, my friends. The science of archaeology, the faith of billions of *yogis*, and Hindus, and the future of mankind will be deeply indebted to your work."

After, the four individually used the vehicle's secure phone to speak with their families, and reassure them of their safety.

They talked for a long time that night, discussing the next phase of the hunt and deciding what each should do.

"I need to go back to my other pending assignment," said Jai apologetically. "My team has been working on a very serious, security problem, and my presence is now required." He paused for a moment for the others to digest the information. "Since we have found the jewel, fire crystal, and the three symbols, you should lay low for a while, so Jawahar totally loses track of your movements. In the meantime, I hope that my work will be completed so that I can rejoin you."

Diana smiled understandingly. "I think it's a very good idea, Jai. I can't really see you having much success with the difficult task of just staying put," she teased him. "You're a very dynamic man and I'm sure your team misses your energy, intelligence and companionship."

"We'll really miss you, too," said Masako, quietly.

Jai smiled affectionately before pressing Masako's hand. "I'll be back soon, I promise. And you also need to go back to your parents and show up around the Embassy—otherwise we'll all have the Chinese Secret Police sniffing after us!"

Masako slightly bowed her head, reverentially. "It is true. It's part of my duty."

"I have another surprise for you, Bill," said Jai, before stretching his hand to the dashboard, turning a lever and pulling out a very thin desktop computer which was wired into the car's electrical system. "This beauty has a built-in secure satellite internet connection, active 24/7, a RAM memory of 100 Gigabytes, a scalable hard drive of 100 Terabytes, plus a number of interesting software programs and applications, including social media stuff which can't be tracked easily." Jai smiled at the astonished faces. "Amazing, eh?

"The vehicle has two ways to provide you with constant electricity, as well. It has an automatic solar generator; plus a second, more conventional method. You just need to let the engine run for about thirty minutes a day, with this lever in this position, to channel all the kinetic power directly to the dynamo, so charging of the battery will be much more efficient. Needless to say, the battery is custom-made and much more powerful than ordinary car batteries; it won't run down so easily."

Jai pointed at a button on the dashboard near the desktop slot. "This button deploys a telescopic antenna that goes up two meters, so make sure you don't have anything up top when you operate it." He looked at Bill and Diana, their faces wide-eyed with surprise.

"I'll drive with you all the way north to Srinagar, Kashmir," assured Jai. "Enroute we'll drop Masako in Delhi; then I'll fly back to join my team, and leave the truck in your custody. You'll need it more than me."

He paused a moment, thinking. "Remember, laying low is your first priority. Srinagar is an extremely dangerous place; the Jihadis are on a rampage and there is a large army presence to keep order. Everywhere there are check points and I'm sure it will be full of spies. Make a wrong move and SEPS will have your home address in their pockets within the hour."

"Understood," said Bill, coming to attention. "We'll try to avoid trouble, Sir."

Jai smiled. "I'll take you to Rasul, our contact in Srinagar. You can trust him and he can run errands for you."

"Cool!" said Bill, enthusiastically, "I feel like James Bond, right now."

"You outshine him any day, without even trying," whispered Diana softly, a bright smile lighting up her face.

Then they were off, driving fast and furious to Srinagar, the capital of Kashmir state.

Chapter 15 - The Conspirators

Professor Jawahar was having trouble sleeping. There was no good news from Officer Masoom, and tomorrow afternoon the SEPS summit was to take place at his house.

He had discussed the matter with Lord Dyer, and it was concluded that Jawahar's house was still the safest place because of his personal influence at the University, as well as his good contacts with the Government.

He tossed and turned in his bed, mentally reviewing the plans for the meeting. He would send his car to pick up the mullah, and had already arranged to hire private vehicles for the priest and pastor. The others would come in their own vehicles; they didn't trust anyone else to drive them.

Food, drinks, seating arrangements— everything was ready. They would conduct the meeting in his drawing room which had been cleared for the occasion, although he had rented two good tables and one single tablecover to give the space a more official look.

He would draw the curtains and keep the lights on. The vehicles would be parked off-campus and return to pick up their passengers, only, when the meeting was over.

Everything was indeed in order. Yet Jawahar was tormented by anxiety. He was in the unenviable position of exposing himself to the acidic remarks of the other SEPS members regarding his failure to monitor Diana Warwick's activities. After announcing the summit on April 3rd, he had suggested the afternoon of the 8th for the meeting. Everyone had agreed, as this gave them sufficient time to arrange for their travel. Those had been very anxious days, and the only news from Masoom was the return to Delhi of the Chinese girl. The IB had no specific instruction to tail Masako. Yet, Jawahar was feeling very uneasy. He finally fell asleep around three in the morning, helped by a generous dose of whisky.

The next day he was especially grateful his guests would not be arriving until later in the afternoon, for he was still feeling the effects of his overnight alcohol consumption. At two o'clock he decided to take a pain pill, as the cars would be arriving soon and he needed to get rid of his throbbing headache.

The first to arrive was Mullah Omar Angrez. Because the man spoke English, his nickname was Angrez, the Hindi word for English. He belonged to the Sunni Salafist movement and had forewarned Jawahar not to invite any Shia leader, as he considered them heretics. He shot an intense look at Jawahar before accepting a glass of chilled mango sherbet, probably trying to decide if his host was a true friend of Islam or not, and if the drink was Halal, meaning lawful under Islamic law, or Haram, meaning unlawful under the same. Then he sat at the table, gathering his long black robe around him, and, after fixing his glassy gaze at a distance, he started mumbling devotional prayers.

After about ten minutes, the two private cars with the priest and the pastor arrived. Father Francis Xavier Montero, a secretive Jesuit activist from the State of Goa, and the notorious Pastor Joseph Isakson, from the State of Gujarat, met at the door, and shared a few seconds of uncertainty as to who should enter first. Each man made a show of humility, inviting the other to go ahead, until Pastor Joseph apparently decided he was more important than the other and therefore entitled to priority. Like Francis Xavier, Pastor Joseph was a descendent of Indian Christian converts; one of whom was a personal friend of the Superior General of the Jesuits order, while the other had established a Protestant mission with a large center in Ahmedabad called "The Sacred Mountain".

Just after them, two middle-aged men in casual clothing arrived on a battered motorcycle and parked it just outside Katju's gate. They looked rather unassuming, but Jawahar knew better. They were none other than Paagal Majumdar and Prachanda Sanyal, two extremely powerful and ruthless leaders of Maoist factions from the states of Orissa and Jharkhand. They quietly entered the house and sat at the table next to the Christian preachers, oddly at ease with them. Jawahar discreetly approached, and a few minutes later served them alcoholic drinks in plain glasses.

The mullah's indignation at the sight of alcohol was distracted by the arrival of an American-looking, middle-aged woman, dressed in an informal, black pantsuit, suit jacket, and black sneakers. Professor Katju hurried to offer her a seat next to Pastor Joseph, and to get her a sizeable glass of red wine, similar to the one already in front of Father Francis.

Soon afterward, Lal Salaam, Member of Parliament of the Indian Communist Party from Kolkata, reached the gate together with Roger Farsight, a businessman of Anglo-Indian descent, from Simla. The MP promptly walked in first. Jawahar was ready to welcome them, then he quickly went to give instructions to the boy in the kitchen, and in a few seconds he was able to serve a sizeable cup of hot, thick, milk tea, and a chilled, lime Perrier to his last two guests.

When everyone had comfortably settled in their seats, Jawahar sent the boy out on an errand, locked the entrance door, walked over and stood behind his own chair at the head of the table.

"Welcome to you all, delegates of the Society for the Eradication of Pagan Superstitions," he started confidently, his hands clasped behind his back. "As is customary, I would like to urge each member to address the summit and briefly describe, in your own words, who you are, what you represent, and why you are here, so that we can better understand each other and create a cohesive plan for moving forward." Jawahar flashed a phony smile.

"All of you are extremely important and powerful personalities, therefore I will not presume to assign an order of business to this meeting," he said in a modest tone.

"Should it become necessary to extend the meeting for a longer period of time than originally suggested, please know I will be honored to provide anything you need to make your time here comfortable and memorable."

Everyone around the table nodded in silence and Jawahar sat down, like a school boy.

The Mullah, obviously considering himself superior to the rest and feeling he had the divine right to go first, resolutely raised his hand, and all heads turned toward him. Without waiting, he proceeded. "My name is Omar Sheikh Sâmî al-Mâjid bin-Fayyed. I represent the Voice of Allah and his messenger, the holy Prophet Mohammed, peace be upon him," thundered the Mullah in an Pashto accent. He had been a noted member of the mujahedeen guerrilla fighters during the Soviet occupation of Afghanistan, and received his training from the Pakistan army and the ISI.

The faces of the others remained impassive. The MP and the Jesuit nodded, while the two Maoists shifted slightly in their chairs.

The Mullah didn't notice anything, or pretended he hadn't. "The world today needs order and morality," he cautioned, for this was something all the delegates could agree on. Even Jawahar, a strict secularist, was favorably inclined to have a world population regulated by a rigid moral code, under a religious law…as long as he was included in that small number of those who always remained above and beyond the law.

The Mullah correctly sensed he had the backing of the others in this matter. "The Pagans are the enemies of order and morality," he asserted forcefully. "The majority of Pagans remaining in the world today are the Hindus, followed by Buddhists, and even the atheists, who for all practical purpose we consider Pagan."

The body language of the delegates clearly expressed their agreement and relief to see the discussion was going in precisely the right direction. The Mullah was good; he had perfectly grasped the point and was not beating around the bush.

"It is therefore our holy duty to guard ourselves against this greatest obstacle of our times. Unfortunately, the Hindus are overcoming the inferiority complex imposed on them over the last few centuries. Before that happens, we need to work together to discredit them in all possible ways, once and for all!" He lifted his chin in contempt. "At the same time, we will bring the fear of God into their hearts and minds, so that they will understand there is no other way but to surrender to the Almighty Allah and to follow his laws faithfully and obediently." He clenched his jaw in anger.

It wasn't long before the Mullah seemed to sense that some of the audience was cooling to his viewpoint, so he quickly changed his direction like a chameleon changes color. "We, the Muslim Ummah, are prepared to work together with all of you, for the establishment of a pure world order, where each of us can share the power after getting rid of the Pagans," he said in a conciliatory tone.

Katju could feel the tension easing in the room. This was something they could digest. He smiled benignly, an expression of reassuring friendliness spreading across his face. He reached out for his glass, pouring himself some fresh water from the pitcher on the table. He watched the Mullah look at Lal Salaam, nod in appreciation and smile, knowing that he, the Mullah was the face of more open and direct

Jihad, whereas Lal Salaam was the real hand behind the stealth Jihad. They knew perfectly well that it was an age-old gameplan played by the two to confuse, and then destroy the non-believers. One would play the violence card and the other the peace card, outflanking the enemy from both sides. However, they were part of the same team, using different strategies to establish global Islamic Kalifah, under Sharia rule, by any and all means.

Pastor Joseph rightly interpreted the interlude as a signal indicating the end of the Mullah's preliminary speech, and he stood up, addressing the meeting in the firm tone of voice he used on his TV shows.

"We are all natural friends and allies, and we must trust each other, and cooperate very closely, as there is no other way to get rid of the Pagan menace." He paused to see if everyone was listing. Seemingly reassured, he continued with gusto.

"Today we are facing a very critical time. The ascent of relativism and ideological anarchy, and the proliferation of the so-called New Age delusional idea that anyone can be the master of his own life and destiny, have favored the resurfacing of the ancient superstitions— witchcraft, worship of demons, snakes, idols, *yoga*, and all that hocus-pocus and fairy tales. Although we have all done our best to discredit and ridicule Paganism and uproot it every time it's surfaced, it has gone underground and somehow survived, waiting for a favorable moment to raise its ugly head again. And they are doing this now, by using the very same English education we have given to these people. Why, since 2003, Halloween has become the second biggest holiday of the year, right behind Christmas! It's a no-brainer that Halloween is a Pagan festival. And the Christmas tree and Santa are now more famous than Jesus.

Americans and Europeans are shelling out more money for *yoga*, witchcraft and astrology than ever before. Harry Potter's books and films have been a serious blow to Christian values, as well."

The Jesuit nodded, but didn't speak. Pastor Joseph continued his hostile speech. "Such is the gravity of the situation that even respectable universities have started to listen to the Pagans and accept them as legitimate teachers. This has increased the interest of the general public toward their abomination. In fact, many scholars, and even general members of the public, have begun studying Pagan texts as if they had some intrinsic truth or validity," he said, twisting his lips sarcastically. "This is happening because our own people of all denominations are not interested in supporting SEPS' cause, instead they are supporting the Pagans, and that is the crux of the problem. We need to do something spectacular to wean them away, that way we can destroy Paganism; it's SEPS' primary duty."

The Mullah and the Jesuit slightly shook their heads in agreement with Pastor Joseph's views, but the other members remained still, immersed in thought. The businessman, Farsight, seemed more absorbed than concerned, but didn't say a word. Pastor Joseph continued. "This, we cannot allow. Our Mission Ministry, the Sacred Mountain of the Message of the Christ, is ready to cooperate closely with anyone who shares our goal, to control and eliminate the Pagan menace once and for all."

He looked at the Jesuit and the two Maoists, smiling, and acknowledged the smiles he received in return. Father Francis slightly raised his hand as if to interrupt, but Pastor Joseph hesitated to sit down. His face reflected that he realized he had made a mistake by standing as he spoke. It was a habit developed during his preaching, both in church and during his television programs, where his imposing figure would hold the attention of his audience. Now he would have to sit down like a schoolchild, because Francis certainly did not seem inclined to stand to speak. Joseph quickly found a way out of his predicament. He raised a hand to ask for a pause, then approached the window and peered out from behind the curtain, as if to verify no one was listening outside. Then he turned back to the meeting with a smile. "Everything is in order."

The Jesuit smirked, while patiently waiting until the Pastor had comfortably seated himself, at which time he raised his hand again as if nothing had happened. "I hail from Goa, but I am in charge of our Order here in Delhi. The Holy See is worried, too, and we have received special instructions. Let's hear the details, and then we'll chalk out the strategy." His lips moved slightly into a tight-lipped smile.

The two Maoists seemed taken by surprise at the brevity of the Priest's speech, but they didn't waste time. "I speak for the People's Liberation Army of India," said the shortest, but fiercest looking, of the duo. "My name is irrelevant, as is the name of my comrade here. You may address me as Prachanda. I can say I was trained in China and I am now leading the Revolution from Nepal. But that, too, is not so relevant.

"What *is* relevant is that we are tired of the oppression enforced upon us by the high-caste Hindus and their low-caste Hindu stooges. These parasites, and all those who stand in the way of the justice of the people, will be physically eliminated." He spoke in an annoyed tone with his lips pressed tightly together.

"Very well said, Comrade!" cheered the MP Lal Salaam of Kolkata, as he loudly applauded the short and intense speech of the Maoist Naxalite. "We happily assume the burden of sitting in Parliament and working hard to legitimize your campaign in the name of the Communist ideology, and to convince people that the only way to avoid violence is to give the oppressed people sufficient power."

The two Maoists grinned. "Thank you, Comrade Salaam. We are frontline revolutionaries, but we greatly appreciate your backing. Our cadres keep growing by recruiting disenchanted youths who are introduced to the glorious communist ideals by your ICP activists. You are the 'respectable' legal arm of our Revolution. Hail Mao! Hail Stalin! Hail Fidel!"

Roger Farsight, the patient businessman with an East-India company mindset, took advantage of the disruption to speak. "My family is of Anglo-Indian descent, and we enjoyed privileged status during the Colonial era, but left the country at the time of India's Independence out of fear of reprisal from the natives. The mission of our company of multinational investments is to bring prosperity and an enjoyment of the good things of life to those who have been kept in a backward state of stagnation, and deprived too long of a progressive and higher quality of life because of the oppressive nature of medieval superstitions, such as Hinduism, Buddhism, Tribalism and Atheism." He curled his lips in indignation.

Currently, Farsight was working on breaking the Ram Setu Bridge with his company's dredging ships, even if it meant the complete destruction of the sacred place—to the utter dismay of Hindus and environmentalists. Even as he rejoiced over it, he would call it a 'Crusades' moment.

He also paid protection money to the Maoists—who controlled certain areas in the hinterland—which was then used to procure arms to overthrow India's legitimate democracy. The money also went into the coffers of the two Christians sitting at the table who were involved in active proselytization of the natives.

The American woman had listened to the various speeches without showing any sign of impatience; she also didn't seem uneasy about the less-than-warm attitude from the other members, especially the Mullah and the Pastor. She was used to that. In her long and brilliant academic career, she had repeatedly faced gender prejudice and all kinds of fanatics, but had always left the arena a winner. Her strategy had been refined over time and during innumerable debates. She worked like the patient crane standing still in shallow waters, relaxed but extremely alert. And like a crane, was able to catch her fish, while keeping her prey, unaware. Wendy Wetzel, Professor of Religious History at the University of Denver Divinity School, Department of South Asian Languages and Civilizations, was able to instantly spot a *faux pas* made by an adversary, and nail them. She could sit motionless for hours during endless lectures, and notice and remember every single word anyone had said. It was easy to underestimate her, but usually her adversaries never made the same mistake twice. She was the Director of SEPS in America.

After everybody had finished talking, Wendy Wetzel straightened her back in the chair and remained silent until Katju addressed her.

"Professor Wetzel, thank you for joining us. Would you like to address the meeting?" He timidly folded his hands.

Wendy cast a long, cold stare around the room, squarely facing off with the eight men at the table.

"Thank you, Professor Katju," she said, with a deep, resonant voice. "I'm sure we can work very well together. We know what our organization stands for. Dyer said you had a serious problem on your hands and you needed help. Let's hear about it."

Everybody adjusted their sitting position, appeared extremely attentive, and turned to Katju. Now the *real* meeting was starting.

Katju cleared his throat nervously with two or three annoying coughs, excusing himself immediately thereafter. "We have successfully put an end to most Paganism in Europe, America and Africa, albeit for a few pockets, through forced conversions and violent jihad; however we failed to do the same in Asia, on any size or scale. For this reason, Hinduism, Buddhism and Tribalism have survived, and as we all know, one of the greatest dangers we are facing today is the voluntary conversion to Hinduism and Buddhism by many Westerners coming from non-Indian families. Also, there are many who—even if they are not converting—are actively sympathizing with the Pagans and befriending them. Surveys have shown that these men and women are educated and generally white, thus immune to the inferiority complex created by the Colonial racial conditioning of the indigenous peoples. More importantly, they are choosing to convert because they are intellectually and ideologically convinced that Hinduism and Buddhism have better answers. They feel it is more satisfying than the Christianity under which they were born and raised, and the industrialized society they have experienced fully, and now they are taking up civil, environmental, and animal rights issues with a disturbingly Pagan flavor." He wrinkled his nose in apparent disgust.

All the members of the summit expressed their grave concerns for these serious problems, and for a moment, there were several attendees speaking simultaneously. Jawahar had the uncanny ability to allow them to spontaneously return to silence before barging in.

"This fundamentally undermines one of our best arguments, the very rationale that

Paganism, especially Hinduism and its sister, Buddhism, are at best curious antiques, good only for the museum, or perhaps fairy tales valued only by the backward and awkward, under-developed and illiterate, who have never known anything better." He waved his hand dismissively in contempt.

Here it was. He was about to drop the bombshell. The silence in the room was deafening. Now he really had their attention.

"I am sure you have all heard about the case of Arthur Warwick, the British aristocrat who came to India during the Colonial period and who had the audacity to publicly convert to Hinduism. He undermined the very foundation of the educational work started by our esteemed founder, Sir Macaulay, for development of social and political stability, as well as the development of a qualified secular ruling class that was going on at the time." He looked around, seeing all the faces had the same stern, yet puzzled expression. *Very good. They are ready, now. There is no other way.*

"About one month ago, a woman claiming to be the direct descendent of Arthur Warwick arrived in India, determined to follow in the footsteps of her ancestor, and to retrieve a treasure he was rumored to have found. She first visited the Indian council of Historical research inquiring about Arthur, then she went to the Gora Baba Ashram, and then I personally met her. I clearly saw in her eyes that she knows something about the treasure.

"If my hunch is correct, we must get to this treasure first! I fear that such a treasure might consist of considerably valuable artifacts, and jewels of immense antiquity.

"The discovery of certain artifacts could compromise ancient original texts whose discovery could be compared to the discovery of the Dead Sea scrolls and the Qumran documents, thus disturbing the historic narrative of the world civilizations," He inhaled his breath sharply, suggesting fear.

Horrified whispers ran around the room. Jawahar savored the tension he had created with his carefully engineered speech before continuing to illustrate the problem at hand. "Yes, indeed. After all the efforts that we and our predecessors have made to eliminate or confuse and distort the documents and testimonies of the ancient Pagan superstitions, we are now facing the disastrous possibility that a hitherto unknown and pristine copy of such knowledge will be distributed freely, and on a global level, to an ideological market that has already seen the exponential multiplication of the adepts of Wicca and New Age doctrines, the madness of Gurus and religious sects of all denominations, and a variety of individuals free-thinking eclectic nothingness. Even conspiracy theories are being converted into virtual forms of religion," gasped Jawahar. He was putting on a good show and he enjoyed every minute of it.

Everyone's attention was heightened to an almost painful degree. Jawahar held back a smile.

"For one month, this woman has been running around India under the pretext of a sentimental family interest. We have reason to believe she has secretly found many important clues to locate and retrieve this treasure from its secret hideout; a treasure that has remained undetected until now—in spite of our most determined efforts—for almost two hundred years." He paused took a sip of water and continued.

"And what is even more worrisome, it is evident that this woman has established contacts with a number of other agents who work against us. Apparently there seems to be a very organized and wide network that spans from the USA to China, with potential safehouses here in India. This woman has often disappeared for days at a stretch, subtracting herself from the legitimate monitoring of the Government authorities, and even baffling the most qualified and powerful officers of the Investigating Bureau." Katju smacked his palm theatrically into his forehead in apparent utter shock. He knew his performance would do the trick.

He sat back in his chair, exhausted, and allowed the delegates to express their personal emotions and concerns as they saw fit. His job was done. The ball was in their court. Now they had to mobilize their own resources to help him find the treasure.

The distrust and spite they felt for his allies was kept well hidden behind diplomatic appearances. These were allies of convenience. Their divergent personalities, motivations and agendas were put aside temporarily to face this very real and present threat. The focus was now on the common hostility of all toward Pagan Hindus.

Jawahar waited until the commotion subsided, and then brought their attention forward to the strategic planning phase. They would deploy all the powers and resources behind the executive committee of the Society for the Eradication of Pagan Superstitions. Jawahar was pleased. The meeting was going well. Rather than a blundering fool, he was now recognized as a valued source of information and even as the leader in the effort. The meeting went far beyond his expectations, and long past its scheduled time.

* * * *

1859

The prison guard screamed in anguish, "The Baba is dead...the Baba is dead...Gora Baba has taken Samadhi!"

The act of Samadhi was the last stage of evolution on the eightfold Ashtanga Yoga path, when an individual's consciousness can connect to the Supreme consciousness by self-endeavor, thus leaving behind the mortal body. The other guards rushed to see the spectacle. Gora Baba, as he was affectionately called, was sitting upright in the lotus position.

The jailers tried touching and pinching him to bring him back to consciousness, but it was to no avail. Gora Baba's body was radiating a luminescent color; he was clad in only a loin cloth. His face was beaming as if he were still alive and filled with joy. For the prison guards it was an emotional shock; their loving friend was gone. It took some time for the English doctor to arrive; he checked him thoroughly, before walking over to the prison warden, a fellow Englishman, to inform him of Arthur Warwick's death.

The stress was too much for the warden. He never expected this to happen, especially not on his watch. He was a devoted Christian, and appreciated Arthur's devotion to his faith, in spite of the hurdles put up by the organization, SEPS. He immediately called the governor and informed him of the unfortunate event.

The message was relayed back to SEPS President Macaulay, who was very happy indeed that he was finally able to neutralize his sworn adversary; he was in a celebratory mood.

The local Bishop and Macaulay initially conspired to deprive the members of Warwick's ashram of access to Arthur's body. But to their displeasure, the low-ranking police, comprised mostly of Indian Hindus, had a soft spot for Arthur, as he had talked their language of freedom and respect. Somehow things got out of hand, and the media became involved. It was too late to cause any interference, and so they reluctantly agreed to the warden's recommendations to hand over Arthur's body to his ashram to complete his last rites. At least, since the Baba had chosen Samadhi, no one would suspect foul play on the part of SEPS.

The Bishop, Macaulay and the Governor relished the thought of having finally made an example out of Arthur Warwick. Now, they hoped no other Englishman would ever dare to cross their line. They still didn't know how the Baba had actually died; as they didn't believe someone could happily choose death. Their only regret was they had missed an opportunity to torture him.

In 1857, during the first war of Indian Independence, Gora Baba was one among the many who inspired the Indian revolutionaries. However, the revolution failed when the English ruthlessly crushed it. Finally, in 1859, the English got their chance to illegally arrest Gora Baba on the pretext he'd met with a group of young Indian freedom fighters. He had, in fact, only inspired them to peacefully fight for their rights to be free and independent, but the

English contrived to make it sound as if he had incited them in an uprising against the British government and their revered Queen Victoria. He was charged with treason, a crime punishable by death.

The irony was Arthur never considered himself an Indian freedom fighter; his only mission had been to raise the consciousness of the enslaved people in order for them to gain freedom on their own, in a peaceful manner, just as Moses had done for the enslaved Jews in Egypt.

When the Bishop confronted him as to why he was betraying his fellow Englishman's cause, Arthur replied he would have done the same if it were the French instead of the English. He went so far as to say that if England was ever occupied by India, he would inspire the English to fight for their freedom, He would do this, he said, even if he were Indian. This successfully silenced the dishonorable Bishop. Arthur's fight was for the principle, not for any attachment to a particular nationality based on birth prejudice. He said his fight was for Dharma, the righteous path, and that he was ready to pay any price for it.

After his arrest, there were numerous attempts to talk him out of his path. Gora Baba was an ascetic and had taken the renounced order, so he kept his long beard, long hair and saffron clothes. SEPS made plans to thoroughly humiliate him before torturing him. They forcibly removed his saffron dress, scoffing at him and calling him a fake sadhu. Then they shaved all his hair, and just gave him a loin cloth to wear. They spit on his face and gave him meat, which he refused to eat; instead he chose to fast. All this was done in an underground dungeon of the organization, away from the law and the population. Arthur was lucky that one of his admirers, the wife of the Governor, intervened, and had him placed in a proper prison.

When those methods did not succeed, they tried to divide his disciples by threatening them and their families. Baba was not afraid of torture; he was brave enough to withstand it, believing the Mother Goddess would help him. But the thought of harm coming to his disciples rattled Arthur's gentle and compassionate heart. However, he still could not give up a cause he knew to be just; it was his life and soul. The only option before him was to leave the world peacefully and gracefully, and the best way to do was take Samadhi. Once he had left the world, he hoped his disciples would not be harmed. So he made the ultimate sacrifice.

Arthur was just thirty-eight when he took Samadhi, forever engraving his name in the annals of human history.

The truth could not be hidden, once his act of sacrifice became known and the general population rose in support; thereafter, it became much more difficult to harass the members of his ashram. The location of the hidden treasure was lost with him, a development that the British Empire deeply regretted. Arthur took the secrets to his grave and no one else even knew where to begin looking. No one knew that Arthur had in fact passed the clues to the treasure on to his descendants, hoping that someone among them would one day find it. He trusted the treasure would be found at the right time, when India was independent and in a better position to use his gift for the benefit of the world.

Gora Baba made sure he anointed his best disciple, Amitananda Sarasvati, as the natural successor of the Ashram before he took Samadhi. This was done smoothly.

In the fifty years that followed, SEPS managed to fully remove the memory of Arthur Warwick from the minds of the people of India. Of course, there were those who had kept the knowledge alive secretly, but it was mostly those whose reach was minimal. Until now, that is, when Warwick's descendant, Diana, came to revive his memory for everyone to acknowledge. It was truly a divine moment in time.

Chapter 16 – The Entrapment

On the 18th of March, while Jai, Masako, Diana and Bill were in Bengaluru, Major Babur, head of the Pakistan inter-services intelligence ISI station in Hyderabad, India, left for the Maldives. Before his departure, he instructed the local members of the Islamic Students Movement to have the bomb moved from Hyderabad, in Telangana State, to Malegaon, in neighboring Maharashtra state.

A few days later, Tej and Ranil of the Vajra team arrived in Hyderabad, carrying British passports that identified them as Akbar and Jahangir of Manchester, in the U.K. Nila and Lilavati traveled with them as their loving wives, Razia and Salima.

According to the plan, the young men rented two adjacent rooms in a hotel in a Muslim neighborhood. On their first day of exploration, the girls stayed behind. They had all changed into conservative Muslim clothing, with Nila and Lilavati donning black *burqas* over their comfortable tunics and trousers. Before leaving on their preliminary investigations, Tej and Ranil went to get some food for the girls and saw to their safety in the hotel.

The city of Hyderabad was known for its exquisite cuisine. Visiting the local food shops, around the famous Charminar, also gave them a firsthand idea of what the local Muslims ate and drank, and their mannerisms.

They reached the mosque in the neighborhood of the address of Fatima, the woman whose name popped up when the Vajra team was monitoring Hakim Kutty's phone contact in Hyderabad. He had received the bomb from the Maldives when it arrived in India. The Vajra team members blended in quietly, listening as much as possible, speaking only when required and eagerly looking out for an opportunity to glean more information. When the *namaz* prayer was completed, Ranil humbly approached an elderly member of the congregation and introduced himself as a Muslim brother from the United Kingdom. He had come to India for business, but was also searching for moral and religious edification.

The two polite, well-dressed, and apparently wealthy visitors were invited to the house of the hopefully gullible old man. They sat in the living room with him and his three sons, enjoying sweet, chilled sherbet and homemade snacks.

"We have recently attended the International Islamic Soft Drinks conference in Mashhad, Iran," Ranil explained, in a typical Manchester accent, while rubbing his hands together in excitement. "Delegates from forty-five countries participated, and they are all interested in developing newer technologies and making international investments. There are between three and four million Muslims in the United States, and upwards of forty-four million in continental Europe. Their purchasing power has been calculated by the New York based Center for American Muslim Research and Information as upwards of 125 billion dollars annually in the U.S. alone, and is expected to reach globally over 2.55 trillion U.S. dollars by 2024.

"Muslims of all kinds, from Shiites to Sunnis, and Gulf Arabs to Southeast Asians, are becoming increasingly sensitive to the necessity for serious adherence to religious laws, and they are ready to make their consumer choices accordingly." He paused for his hosts to digest the information he was sharing.

"It's a huge business, with great room for expansion. Today, soft drinks are an inseparable part of many families' diet; it's not only a question of excess refined sugar and artificial additives, but sometimes these additives are unclean and unacceptable for Muslims, as they may contain alcohol—which is used as a solvent in natural flavors—and even gelatin, which can be derived from pigs.

"But natural and artificial flavors can be made without alcohol by using a non-alcoholic solvent such as Propylene Glycol," he paused, this time, to make sure he was on target. "Also, we believe that American firms already dominate too much of the market, and much of their profit goes to support anti-Islamic wars and the occupation of Palestine by the Zionists.

Various alternatives have started to appear, not only locally, but also at a global level. In the United Kingdom there are at least four million Muslims. The first Muslim pub has already opened, not far from where our families live in Oldham, Greater Manchester, and patrons are served only non-alcoholic drinks in a clean entertainment environment. But we want to expand."

Ranil sensed the four men were getting confused, so he brought the conversation to a platform that could be more easily understood. "There are plenty of funds. The HSBC Investment Bank has created a Global Islamic Finance Department and there is a Dow Jones Islamic Index with mutual fund programs. As we naturally feel affinity for the Muslim community in India, we are making a survey to gauge the potential for investment here."

The eldest son of their host, a pale young man who had introduced himself as Asad, suddenly leaned forward. "Elder brother," his eyes sparkled with anticipation, "do you mean to tell us there is money to be made in the industry of recommended Halal beverages, and investments can come here from abroad?"

Ranil was glad the message had reached home. "Precisely." He nodded, smiling.

Asad looked at his father, and then turned to his brothers. All of them had starry eyes, except for the old man whose gaze was somehow clouded by an incipient cataract, but was able to show his own excitement nonetheless.

"We will certainly be happy to help you," the second son, Jamaluddin, said enthusiastically. "The happiness and development of our community are greatly important for us. What would you like us to do?"

This was the opening Ranil was eagerly waiting for. "We would be greatly honored and grateful if you could help us to meet the learned and authoritative members of your community. We need to get their suggestions and blessings for our business plan. Also, we feel we and our wives can learn so much from such a traditional and ancient Muslim community as yours, here in the old city of Hyderabad. We wish to be instructed by you in matters of religion and faith, so that we will get inspiration to purify and perfect our personal lives."

Their hosts were ecstatic. What an opportunity for their family! They immediately started to talk among themselves, picking out the names of the most respected and active Muslims of the old city. After only a few minutes, Asad was on the phone with the first of the contacts. The old man explained patiently, "We are requesting that our honored leader, Razakar, receive your first visit, and Asad will also accompany you. Thus, you will be introduced to our foremost members and you will be able to interview them as per your wish.

"Regarding your wives, each day there are special meetings in the home of Razakar, where, in the ladies' quarters, the women study the Koran and the sacred laws. You can accompany them there and they will have the opportunity to ask all the questions they want and learn the Islamic etiquettes."

Tej and Ranil responded with big smiles. "Thank you. We are deeply indebted to your kindness."

The old man smiled back.

"We can go right now to meet the honored Razakar," said Asad, putting his phone away. "He has kindly given his permission."

The two members of the Vajra team bowed to the old men and his sons, touching their foreheads with their hands in a sign of respect before leaving. Tej and Ranil handed the men a hundred-thousand-rupee check as a goodwill gesture, causing numerous expressions of joy from the family, and thus securing their loyalty.

* * * *

In no time, they reached the palatial home of Razakar, who was there to personally receive them. Asad eagerly related the main points of the business discussion that Ranil had outlined earlier at his own father's house, before he let the two businessmen present their proposal.

Razakar seemed satisfied and impressed. It appeared that he too needed money for his political activism, and free money in British pounds seemed very attractive, as recently he had become a kind of monetary beggar after the federal government had suddenly removed high-value denomination currency bills from circulation to prevent corruption. His politics had depended and thrived on it.

A program was organized for the young men to meet a number of important families in the following days.

After settling the schedule, Tej and Ranil were escorted back to their hotel by a happy Asad, who was apparently convinced he had already earned the position of official assistant to the two.

Over the next few days, they would undoubtedly have to navigate their way through many meals loaded with meat. Though Vajra members had strict vegetarian upbringings, they sometimes had to behave differently in the line of duty; and in this case, to prove they were good Muslims, the role they had temporarily adopted.

They kept careful count of the times of the traditional Muslim prayers, and as a first stop in their day's work accompanied their two female team members to the house of Razakar for 'religion and morality' classes. At the end of each day, the women would be driven back to the hotel in the private vehicle of the Razakar family, as a special favor to the wives of these important men.

* * * *

Nila and Lilavati had already met Fatima, herself, at the classes, but at first it seemed that Fatima did not know much except for juicy gossip about her family and the other families of the community. At least this could help their 'husbands' to avoid false steps when interacting with others in the group.

The women received intense instruction on how they should constantly fear for their sanctity and honor, and to take particular care not to mix with men under any circumstances.

Luckily, no one seemed to frown on the mixing of women with women, and during the breaks, Nila and Lilavati chatted animatedly with the younger ladies. They soon became friends with Fatima, who behind the exterior of a shy and timid woman was very interested in what Muslim girls were allowed to do or not do in the United Kingdom. She had been married at the early age of twelve to a seventy-year-old Arab man. The marriage was a sham, with her husband abandoning her after a year, claiming she could not bear children. He moved on to marry another teen in a different locality. Unfortunately, this was quite normal in the Muslim community of old Hyderabad, which treated Arabs as demi-gods, wanting to appease them at all costs. In return, they would get high-value currency for giving their daughters in marriage, helping them to overcome their poverty. Finally, with nowhere to go, Fatima had been allowed to return to her father's home to help the wives of her brothers with their children.

Vajra team agents, Nila and Lilavati, were careful to stick to their *husbands'* story. And they were equally careful to avoid the sharp ears of the elderly lecturer. They consoled and entertained Fatima with the "strange habits of the British," quickly winning her confidence and trust.

After a few days, Fatima confided she was contemplating the possibility of becoming a *shaheed,* or holy martyr. She wanted to blow herself up, maybe in some railway station, or airport, and kill as many people as possible. It's not that she was keen on doing it, but her brother had been preaching to her, telling her it would make her own life truly glorious. "In other cultures," she told them, "people kill themselves over depression, romantic loss, even economic deprivation. At least, I would have a glorious path sanctioned by Allah." It appeared she was trying to convince herself more than the others.

Fatima was obviously afraid of saying too much, but her mind was torn between the need to pour out her feelings, the desire to feel worthy in some way, and the hope for friendship, validation and support.

Her despair of a life going nowhere was palpable. Nila and Lilavati—continuing in their roles—reassured her that indeed it was a brave and saintly decision, and that they, too, were ready for such a sublime choice if the opportunity were to arise.

"You know, Fatima, I can't believe they demean such an act of martyrdom with the term *suicide bombing*," Lilavati stated.

"That's right," Fatima confessed, "My brother says the doctrine of Jihad never calls it suicide, for it is not a waste of life, but the gift of life to God."

Perverse as the logic seemed, the team members realized it drove the Jihadis to ignoble action.

Soon Fatima started to spill the beans. She couldn't hold back anymore. Fatima's cell phone was always with her brother Jafar, and he was an adherent and admirer of, and blogger for, the Islamic State. Nila and Lilavati had given Fatima their 'home numbers', as she had said she wanted to make friends with their UK relatives. Shortly thereafter, Jafar discreetly called the Manchester, UK phone number, and Karry's contact there confirmed the entire story. This served to dissipate the doubts that some people in the community had raised about the strangers.

* * * *

Finally, on Day Five, Jafar agreed to meet Tej and Ranil. Banking on the information and suggestions supplied by their female team members, Tej and, especially, Ranil engaged all their attention and intelligence to win the trust of Jafar, and convince him that their greatest aspiration was to serve Islam and atone for the callous attitude of their own families toward religion. They expressed feelings of shame. They even let slip the idea that sometimes they had contemplated the possibility of joining some Jihadi cell in the United Kingdom, or going to the Middle East and joining ISIS. When asked as to why they hadn't joined, they said it was fear and a lack of solid support from true Muslims like Jafar. Also, that their parents might find out and inform the police. They explained that as westernized, 'moderate', secular Muslims, they had already attempted several misguided efforts to save their own families.

Jafar had tears in his eyes as he listened to how difficult it was for Akbar and Jahangir to get along with their parents. They recounted that they had almost given up eating meat altogether because their families did not care if the animal was *halal* or not. They were often scolded and ridiculed because they refused to participate in

453

the alcohol-fueled parties their families organized for wealthy business partners and customers. The only thing keeping their parents from constantly fighting with them, Ranil had said, was the decision of the two young men to engage in business, marry, and have a 'normal life'.

After much praise to Allah and his Messenger for rescuing Akbar and Jahangir from such a difficult environment, and bringing them to meet with real Muslims, away from the prying eyes of such insensitive families, Jafar confided to them that he was most fortunate, for his own family was very dedicated to the glory of Islam. He also recounted a conversation he'd had with his sister Fatima. She told him the good wives of his new foreign friends were also faithful Muslims who aspired to the glory of martyrdom. Indeed, he was grateful to them for encouraging his little sister on that path. Tej and Ranil did not push by asking more questions, but continued in the glorification of the Jihadis and the establishment of a true Dar-el Islam in India and the world at large.

After lunch, Jafar offered to take his two new friends around town. They visited the important places in Hyderabad, starting with the Mecca Masjid, the Charminar, Golconda Fort and the Taj Falaknuma Palace.

Tej and Ranil showed the appropriate enthusiasm for the ancient glory of Indian Islam, and expressed a desire to see such grandiose times once again, recounting that glory and power for Muslims was the glory of Allah.

By dinnertime, Jafar was completely taken in by the Vajra agents. Sitting on the rooftop of his house, away from the rest of his family, Jafar confided in his Muslim brothers. He poured out his soul as to how the Indian government did not respect Allah nor the Muslims. "Something drastic must be done to awaken the collective conscious of the Muslims of India," said Jafar, and he urged them to join the glorious Brotherhood of Islam as the "power of the true and faithful Muslims would soon be obvious to the entire world."

This was the time; it was now or never. Ranil actually shed tears of love in praise of Allah, praying to be blessed to see that day. Tej scowled (something that was not very difficult for him at that time) demanding the infidels be punished for their arrogance and put in their place.

After saying prayers and taking a few more minutes to give thanks and praise, Jafar revealed "the glorious secret" to his two new confidants to lift them out of their despondency. His group was involved in a very significant operation that would change everything for the good. A single, low-intensity nuclear bomb would soon be detonated, in a place and time guaranteed to "shock the entire world!" Encouraged by the awe and admiration of the two, Jafar boasted of his part in the drama. In a fit of zeal and self-importance, he gave the two agents all the information he had regarding the movements of the device and its possible present location. He also mentioned things they did not expect him to know.

"We also know that there is an informant in the Pakistani Intelligence Services," Jafar said, with visible disgust. "Our leaders have responded by circulating false information about the movement of the device. So, my brothers, the bomb is not going to Nagpur, as suspected by them, but has gone to Malegaon from here!" He jumped up and pumped his hands in the air victoriously, bragging about the rest of the plan in detail.

It was obvious there was no doubt in Jafar's mind that the happiness he saw on the faces of Ranil and Tej was based on their joy of fooling the infidels, and he barely listened to their confirmation in that regard.

The young man was almost delirious in his relief at being able to confide in such trusted friends. He soaked up their admiration and support. Tej and Ranil knew this was the most delicate moment of their mission. They could not bail out suddenly, otherwise they would be suspected; they needed to show just enough enthusiasm to reassure Jafar, but not overdo it;

to be two dependable Muslim men who knew how to keep the matter confidential.

Ranil spoke kindly to the young man. "Our dear brother, Jafar, we are honored by your confidence, but we think you should not talk about these things so openly. Someone could overhear and who knows what may happen as a result." He bit his lips in a display of anxiety.

Tej nodded and comforted the confused Jafar, who was starting to realize he had been somewhat imprudent.

Ranil pressed on. "Be assured we will keep your secret; we will not tell it even to our wives. This is a very delicate plan and many things could go wrong if we are not careful. But rest assured, we will certainly not tell anyone; it will be kept deep inside out hearts."

Tej nodded gravely in agreement.

Jafar smiled, reassured.

Ranil continued. "Now, my dear brother, let us return downstairs, so that your good family will rejoice in your company. We are also eager to see our wives and enjoy celebrating this glorious day with them."

Before leaving the Osaivi house, Ranil gave one thousand pounds to Jafar, as their contribution to the cause; Jafar was elated by the generosity and appeared enamored by the look of the British Pound bills, flipping them back and forth multiple times.

The next few days would be crucial and require all their attention and energy. The schedule was wrapped up with a last grand assembly after the Friday prayer meeting at the mosque. There, the "brothers from London" announced the completion of their investigation and that they were returning to the United Kingdom via Delhi to finalize the report.

Tej and Ranil did not dare send the information to Karry through email or phone and decided to return to the Valley first, and there, brief him in person; it was too important to be left to chance.

They reached the Valley on March 27th. In the meantime, there had been other developments.

Chapter 17 – The Mongoose

When Balaram had met Karry and Jai in Room 721 at the Tivoli Garden Resort, during the marriage of Priti, he had been unsure of how much to disclose in front of Jai. A need to know basis is a rule for any Secret Intelligence Service. Information has to be protected by compartmentalizing; therefore if one agent is compromised, or captured and subjected to torture or drugs, they would be unable to reveal what they truly did not know.

Balaram had smiled when his friend joined him in his car in the hotel parking lot after the marriage party. At that time of night, they could be alone and informal, talking more leisurely than during their official communications. Balaram had looked pleased. "I like your Jai. If all your agents are like him, we are in good hands." He had lifted his head, smiling, in confidence.

"Thanks," acknowledged Karry. "I saw you wanted to tell me something more in private. What's new? What do you think about this new development with Katju and SEPS?" He had leaned toward his friend.

Balaram looked around cautiously, but there was no one in sight. It was very late, nearing midnight, and practically all the guests had already left. "I chatted with the Mongoose

459

yesterday. It seems Hyderabad is indeed an important connection. According to the operational plan of the Pakistani ISI, the device was expected to move from Malappuram in Kerala, to Coimbatore in Tamil Nadu, and then to Hyderabad in Telangana." He rubbed his eyes as fatigue set in due to the lateness of the hour.

"I knew it!" exclaimed Karry, trying to contain a strong yawn. "Something is going on there in Hyderabad, something big. It could even be the heart of the entire operation."

"All right, Karry, now listen to me. We cannot be one hundred percent sure about anything here. There can be plans inside the plans inside the plans. It's a war of wits and deceit, and it is possible the official information has been engineered specifically to send any onlookers on a wild-goose chase."

"We can manage that. This is the reason why we have organized the Vajra Team the way we have with individuals who can operate alone and in small groups, switching tasks and multi-tasking."

"It seems the Pakistan ISI is trying to send the bomb through a meandering route with many stops, trying to complicate things, and hoping we will lose track of their movements."

"I understand. Is there any other information?" asked Karry.

"In fact there is. And that's what I'm so excited about. Mongoose said that according to the ISI plan, from Hyderabad, the device will go to Nagpur, Gwalior and Aligarh. Again, this could be a decoy, and the route might be different altogether, or just partially modified in order to confuse us. We may end up in the right place at the wrong time, leaving the terrorists even greater freedom of movement."

"Yes, of course."

"Very good. About Katju and SEPS, I think it would be a good idea to send Jai with these two foreigners to protect them and to find out more of their story. Run the regular profile checks on them just to be sure. They probably have no idea what they're dealing with, but if Katju and SEPS are so anxious to steal their luggage and have been tailing them for so long, the stakes must be high." Balaram stroked his chin thoughtfully. "This could be *really* big. They spoke about a treasure, right? If SEPS is so interested, it can't be just about money, gold or ordinary antiques. It must be something that has great ideological value; even possibly involving some extraordinary historical evidence; something which cannot be ignored or hidden from the masses."

Karry smiled thoughtfully. "I think you're right. Baba, my Guru, once told me something like that was going to happen. He spoke specifically about the hidden treasure of the Pandavas, and the help of people who one, otherwise, would not expect."

Balaram looked amazed. "Really? Wow, so if it's connected to this treasure of the Pandavas, it's big! Okay, that seals the deal. You definitely need to ask Jai to stay with the two foreigners, help them in their search, and watch out for SEPS as they go along. Please return home or to the Valley as soon as possible, and let's keep in touch to coordinate the entire operation."

Just then, as Balaram was about to start the car, they heard shouting in the distance. From the window of the passenger seat, Karry could see some commotion in a corner of the parking lot. "Wait for me here, Balaram. I'm going to see what's happening down there. It'll only take a few minutes."

"Alright. I'll stay out of sight, but if there's any serious trouble, shout, and I'll drive up and rescue you."

Karry briskly walked away.

Fortunately, there had been no need of a rescue, and within a few minutes, Karry was back and Balaram had dropped his friend a short distance from the safe house. During the ride, to his amusement, Karry briefed him on the fight in the parking lot. They both shook their heads.

* * * *

The next morning, after talking with Diana and Bill at the safe house in Delhi, Karry instructed Jai to remain and help the couple find out more about the treasure, and then he boarded the first flight back to Mumbai and traveled to the

Valley in the evening. There he was briefed on the developments. Avinash, Vikram and Satish had just returned from the Maldives and Malappuram, and passed on the information they had gathered.

Tej, Ranil, Nila and Lilavati had been sent to Hyderabad. Karry met Ganesh, who had been staying at the Valley to take care of communication and coordination, and Mahendra, who had returned there after a meeting with the nuclear scientist in Mumbai, leaving Lachit with Professor Sarabhai.

In his office in the Valley, Karry met with Ganesh and Mahendra. "I want you two to head out on a very crucial investigation. We have received information that Nagpur could be the next destination of the Scorpion Egg, but we cannot rule out a decoy. After that, if everything is in order and your cover still holds, you should proceed to Gwalior and Aligarh, for these are the next target locations the device is supposed to reach. We have information it will be detonated in a densely populated area, ideally the city center, for maximum destruction and psychological impact; we can only hope we'll have the time to find the device before it's too late.

"Mahendra has seen the sketches of them, so he can recognize one if you're lucky enough to find it. We're hoping you might be present when the device arrives, and are able to steal it back before it can be activated. I know you're ready for this mission, so let's get going." Karry smiled reassuringly.

"Certainly, sir," Ganesh and Mahendra replied immediately, each giving a sharp salute. "We look forward to this task."

* * * *

The two young men reached Nagpur by air, before settling into a modest hotel. Presenting themselves as geology engineers from a reputed university, they claimed to be researching natural emissions of noxious radon gas which creates health problems. It made sense, especially after the Cobalt-60 leak in Delhi. Armed with a very sensitive radiation detecting device, able to identify material within twenty meters, the two members of the Vajra Team decided to examine several important schools and public buildings in the city center within a one-square-kilometer zone.

While talking with local residents, two men approached them with a rather unusual degree of excitement. The volunteers offered some general information about the city and told them that in a Bharatiya Vidya Bhavan private school nearby, there had been some children who had fallen sick with strange symptoms.

From their descriptions, it seemed the sickness could have been caused by radiation exposure. Mahendra and Ganesh expressed a polite interest and asked to visit the school.

They ran their tests, assiduously accompanied by the same two men, but without finding anything. Their guides apologized loudly and said they must have been mistaken; that it should have been the local government school and not the private one. They escorted the two 'researchers' through an area of about ten blocks, going from building to building. As there was no perceivable threat, after about three hours search, Ganesh and Mahendra thanked their helpers and said they needed to break for lunch.

"Something's wrong," said Ganesh, looking at the computer screen during the meal in their hotel room. "Our cover story is very good, and we shouldn't worry too much about being exposed, but I find it strange those two guys were so anxious to help us. Nagpur is a big city; it almost seemed like they were waiting for us. Plus their facial expressions give it away; see— take a look."

"Hmm," said a puzzled Mahendra. "You'd think concerned citizens would refer us to some municipal office, or a government hospital. Why bother spending an entire morning taking us to those other places? It might be a trap. But it won't be too difficult to find out."

They visited the District Medical Officer, Dr. Patil, and offered the same story, introducing themselves as students preparing a thesis on the accumulation of radon gas in urban areas and its effects on the health of the general population.

"After some preliminary inquiry, we have been told that recently there was a report of several students exhibiting symptoms of radiation exposure," said Mahendra. "With the permission of the local residents, we've examined various school buildings but didn't find any trace of radon or other radioactive material."

"I am happy to hear that," commented Dr. Patil, with a frown that clearly disproved his statement, "because I had no report of any such events."

Ganesh shot Mahendra a meaningful look.

"Maybe it's because the school principal didn't want to have any trouble," Mahendra offered, "or they were unable to recognize the symptoms."

"It is possible," commented the doctor, dryly.

"We would be very grateful if you could kindly keep us informed about any such occurrence in your city in the near future. We are planning to complete our thesis before the end of April, because our exams are coming up between April and May. Here are our e-mail addresses," Ganesh added, smiling.

Dr. Patil graciously took the card Ganesh offered him and thanked the two students, but he didn't seem completely convinced.

And neither were Ganesh and Mahendra. That evening found the two surfing the internet, in the privacy of their room, searching for the best form of transportation to Gwalior

"Okay, Ganesh. There are only two flights a week from here to Gwalior, and we are not in luck—unless we want to wait another day,"

"Listen, Mahendra, before moving in with the Agarwals, I spent my first nine years in the Bhindi Bazaar, in Mumbai. I can smell danger. This is not a good place for us to stay. Let's pay the hotel bill, and tonight we take a bus to Bhopal."

"Alright. I think you're correct. Let's pack."

Gwalior was not very different from Nagpur. On March 26th, they'd already gone through the routine of students searching for radon gas in the city center, with a strikingly similar pattern of three local people immediately volunteering to take them around, claiming there had been some recent episode in some schools, and with the exact same time-wasting and disappointing results.

Once again, Ganesh said he felt uncomfortable, as if he were being watched constantly; it was no more a mere coincidence, but a sure trap.

Mahendra was not surprised. "You're right. They're taking us for a walk around the park. They've been watching us all the time, and they know we're not just students. The situation is getting more dangerous at every step. Should we abort the mission?"

"Yes," said Ganesh, frowning. I think we'll have to skip the last place on the list, Aligarh. Almost certainly, they've prepared a final trap for us there."

"I think you're right. However, I don't think they're actually following us all the time; it's more likely they have a few contacts here and there watching out for us, alerted by the previous cell."

Mahendra was about to put the laptop away, when Ganesh pulled it toward himself to send an email to Karry. "Dear Father, the marriage was cancelled; the groom came to know the girl had lied about her place of origin. We are coming back home straight away."

They quickly went to the railway station and purchased tickets to Aligarh, but at the last moment boarded a train to Jaipur in the opposite direction.

During the journey, they received a confirmation text from Karry. "Good thinking, Kids. Marriage was not worth the effort. Neighbor informed me it was a scam." They understood Karry was in agreement to abandon the radon search, as he had received intel from Ranil & Tej that their route was indeed a trap. They felt a great sense of relief. Without spending any time in Jaipur, they flew to

Mumbai, and then on to the shelter of the Valley.

* * * *

When he read the email, Karry was worried. His fears had been confirmed. It was a decoy, and certainly the trap would have closed on his brave boys if they'd lacked the foresight to abort the mission. Luckily they had avoided the worst danger at the last minute, and were coming back safely.

However, this was not the greatest disaster. When Ganesh and Mahendra reached Gwalior, they unfortunately confirmed to their enemies that they had a list of cities, and this could mean one thing only, the Mongoose had been found out and was now in immediate and mortal danger. He quickly sent an urgent text to Balaram's personal cell phone. "We need to talk."

He hurried to his office and climbed the ladder into his secret communication center.

It was four in the afternoon when Karry switched on the equipment in his hideout. His friend and ally in the fight against terror was already there, just as anxious as he was.

"Is it what I think it is?" asked Balaram.

"Yes. The route was a trap. Our boys have managed to get out in the nick of time, at least for now. But it's almost certain Mongoose is in extreme peril."

"I understand. I'm leaving immediately. Over and out." He closed the communication channel swiftly.

Balaram only stayed in his office long enough to send a message to the Mongoose. "I am coming for you. Take the Friendship Bus to Amritsar tomorrow." Then he explained what Mongoose should look for to identify him.

* * * *

Pakistan ISI Chief, Lieutenant-General Aurangzeb was pleased with himself. The trap had worked. The Indian Secret Services had sent two young agents posing as students preparing a thesis on radiation exposure from radon gas. They had gone to Nagpur and Gwalior. It would be time to pull the net over the two birds, as soon as they reached Aligarh. Major Babar's men would be waiting for them.

Now he also had a pretty good idea who the mole was in his team.

Aurangzeb had prepared a number of different fake lists and sent them to a small group of insiders. The list followed by the two Indian agents was the one given to Air Vice-Marshal Azad Balochi. He was not likely to be the mole himself, but he had a strange wife, who worked in the Culture Ministry of the civilian government of Pakistan, on a program called Aman-ki-Asha, a peace initiative between the warring countries, which the military despised.

Wagah is a village that was divided in 1947 by the famous Radcliffe Line, when India gained independence from the British Empire. The eastern half of the village remains in India, while the western half is in Pakistan. The Wagah border is sometimes called "the Berlin Wall of Asia", and it is in this very place every evening where the lowering of the flags, by the Border Security Force (B.S.F) of India and the Pakistani Rangers, is carried out in a ceremonial display to manifest their respective patriotism through carefully choreographed, and openly hostile marching maneuvers.

The two nations tried to improve their diplomatic relationships through peace initiatives, including the establishment of the Samjhauta Express, a train service between Lahore and Delhi that passes the border twice a week at Attari, five kilometers from Wagah, and the regular bus service, called the Friendship Bus that was inaugurated between Lahore and Amritsar. Balaram arrived at the border about one hour before the bus was due to cross.

On the bus, Mrs. Shabnam Balochi, the wife of Air Vice-Marshal Azad Balochi sat next to her friend and confidante, Ms. Waheeda Sindhi. Although Mrs. Shabnam was married and had children, she had developed a very intimate relationship with Waheeda, and sometimes they would travel together to Amritsar, where they would stay for a few days and enjoy the wonderful freedom; freedom that seemed to her like fresh water after crossing a desert.

She deeply admired Waheeda, who was bold and daring, even in her personal life. Waheeda had not married and was not interested in men. She preferred women and had taught Shabnam many tricks that had changed her life.

Shabnam looked at Waheeda. She appeared strained and worried. Shabnam immediately felt a surge of affection and concern. "Are you feeling well, my dear?" She put her arm around Waheeda's shoulders.

The woman seemed to snap out of her deep thoughts before turning to her friend and lover. Looking into her eyes possessively, she said, "I'm all right, dear. I'm just tired. I hope I can have some quiet days away from the oppressive atmosphere in which we live."

"Of course, Waheeda. We can stay a few more days, if you like. We'll have at least one week of freedom." She smiled in anticipation.

Waheeda seemed to be lost in thought again. "Freedom..." she whispered. "How long will this freedom last?"

She seemed to be talking to herself. Suddenly she looked around. The bus was partially full and they were sitting in the back, alone. "Yesterday, when I suggested you could arrange some meetings with the Ministry of Culture in Delhi, you were saying that we should not go to Delhi. Why?" she asked deliberately.

"I shouldn't be speaking about this," replied Shabnam timidly, bowing her head in embarrassment. "Azad was talking to someone on the phone about something that will happen in Delhi soon. I think they're going to blow something up on the occasion of a big celebration or event."

Waheeda looked very interested, so Shabnam continued so as not to disappoint her. "Azad mentioned a ...."

* * * *

Back in Rawalpindi GHQ, Aurangzeb confronted Air Vice-Marshal Azad Balochi over the absence of his wife.

"Do you realize what is going on here?" he raged. "This is a matter of national security, and your wife is a traitor. You should have kept your mouth shut and watched her more carefully!"

Balochi, understanding the gravity of the situation, trembled in fear and shame. "I am deeply sorry, sir. How could I know, sir? She is just a woman."

"Precisely! And as such, she should have no freedom to go around as she pleases, especially without your direct control. Where is she now? When did she leave?"

"I'm not sure, sir. She left this morning; she said she was going away for a few days."

"Find out where she's gone! Now!" The ISI Chief stormed out of the room with his fists clenched in anger. "If we don't stop her, prepare yourself for a Court Martial."

Sometime later, information arrived that she had left for India, along with a cultural delegation, as part of a peace initiative.

The Lieutenant General was seriously worried, as he flicked his fingers through his hair for the third time. *First of all, we must close the border. If she gets into India, it won't be easy to catch her,*

He immediately called the garrison at the Wagah border, ordering them to stop the bus and apprehend Mrs. Balochi immediately. "As a dangerous spy and a traitor, don't hesitate to shoot to kill, if need be," he shouted.

* * * *

When the call came, Captain Abdali of the Pakistani Rangers went into deep anxiety. The ISI Chief had allowed a spy to get away and now all the responsibility was on his shoulders; he was just the subordinate officer in charge of the gate. He looked at his watch. The bus must have arrived already. He ran out and saw the border gates on both sides were open and the bus was crossing through the no man's land in between, which was about one hundred meters wide.

Quickly gesturing to his rangers, he rushed toward the bus, shouting and waving his hands. The bus driver, confused, stepped on the brakes.

The large vehicle screeched to a halt to the great discomfort of all the passengers.

Captain Abdali was almost faint when he reached the vehicle, and needed a few seconds to catch his breath before he could give the necessary orders.

"By order of superior command, I am to arrest Mrs. Shabnam Balochi, wife of Azad Balochi," he screamed out, not knowing Azad Balochi was the Pakistan Air Force Vice Chief.

He regained his composure and stepped onto the bus. "Please show your documents," he announced loudly to the passengers.

Shabnam and Waheeda, in the back of the bus, clearly heard the captain's orders. Shabnam stood up immediately. Waheeda instantly tightened her grip on her friend's hand.

"I am here," said Shabnam. "There must be some mistake, but I am ready to come with you, Officer."

Captain Abdali looked up, relieved, and immediately forgot the documents of the other passengers. "Please come forward, and keep your hands high and well visible. I have orders to shoot if you resist arrest." He brandished his gun menacingly.

Disturbed by the sight, Shabnam let go of Waheeda's hand and obeyed the Captain's orders. Waheeda followed her, also keeping her hands high.

The Captain rolled his eyes, annoyed at what he perceived to be a challenge. "And who are you?"

"I am traveling with my friend. I want to know what is going to happen to her," demanded Waheeda.

"All right," scoffed Captain Abdali. "You can get off the bus, too, and come to my office at the garrison post. "Slowly! Go ahead, I will follow you both."

Shabnam was immediately afraid and confused, not seeming to understand what was happening, but Waheeda knew very well what was going on and about to occur. She could not afford to just let it happen.

Beyond the strip of no man's land, Balaram stood near the Indian border post, thinking quickly. There was one thing they could do.... He spoke to the Officer-in-Charge. Balaram jogged toward the bus, together with the head of the Indian border security force, Assistant Commandant Zalak Gujjar, and a column of soldiers.

Captain Abdali was just descending the steps of the bus and getting ready to take the two women into custody, when he saw the Indian group approaching at a fast pace.

"What's happening here? What do you want?" he asked, his eyes filled with anxiety. It seemed he was about to become the scapegoat for an international border dispute.

"Why have you entered the no man's land without permission," challenged Assistant Commandant Zalak.

"These two women are Indian citizens," bluffed Balaram. "They are being unlawfully arrested by the Pakistani Government. We demand to check their identity and also that of the other passengers on this bus," he blustered.

Waheeda immediately recognized Balaram by the clothing he was wearing, as had been agreed upon.

Captain Abdali broke his silence and screamed, "That's a lie! These are Pakistani citizens, and they must be questioned by the authorities for suspected anti-national activities."

"We demand bilateral verification!" shouted Balaram, and the Indian Commandant nervously gestured to his men to get ready for a potential fight.

Waheeda took her chance and sprinted off toward Balarama and the accompanying soldiers. Captain Abdali opened fire and all hell broke loose as both sides started to shoot. In the confusion, Shabnam also ran. Both women were hit and slumped to the ground. Others, from both sides, were also hit, but soon the officers began shouting and the firing stopped, and silence returned.

Balaram's shots had flattened the bus tires; he wanted to make sure it didn't move out of the no-man's land. Captain Abdali verified Shabnam was dead, by poking the barrel of his gun into her fallen chest. Just to be sure, he fired another shot into her head at close range, knowing that the Indian troops would not leave without the bodies. In the heat of the moment, he scornfully turned to the Indian border security force and jeered, "You may have the bodies, if you like. And, after all, I guess they *are* Indians."

On the orders of the Commandant, a few men put down their weapons and picked up the bodies of the two women, then carried them as carefully as possible to the Indian side of the border gate. One of the two women was obviously dead. The other, although seriously wounded, was still conscious and trying to speak.

Balaram leaned closer to try and reassure her. "Hold on, we are getting a doctor," he placed his hand over the wound and pressed firmly, trying to stop the flow of blood.

Waheeda struggled to speak, as blood oozed from her mouth. She gasped, trying to breathe. "Mongoose," she gasped. "I am Mongoose."

Balaram was thunderstruck. He had expected a man to appear from the stranded bus. He sent the officer to get the doctor quickly, and knelt at the side of the wounded woman. She tried to smile, but was obviously suffering terribly.

"The Scorpion Egg, ah...bomb, is going to Delhi...and will be detonated by a Bollywood celebrity called Lion...probably an actor...during a public event...with many important people attending." She struggled as she swallowed her own saliva mixed with blood. Waheeda was bleeding profusely from a bullet wound in her back, and getting weaker and weaker by the moment, but still trying to bravely communicate. She held onto Balaram's shirt tightly. He tried to give her water, but she pushed it aside. It was a race against time.

"There is a mole in the Joint Intelligence Committee...the other bombs are going to the United States...to European Union, Russia....China and Israel...." At these final words, she lost consciousness, her grip loosened on Balaram's blood-soaked shirt and her hand dropped down to her side.

Minutes later, a military doctor arrived, followed by paramedics carrying a stretcher. The woman was carefully moved into the ambulance. After a quick exam, the doctor said, "She was hit in the back, at the top of the left lung. There is an exit wound. I think that's the most serious one, but we need to have a better look in the hospital."

"I'll come with you," said Balaram, his eyes glistening with emotion as he climbed into the ambulance, and the door was shut. They drove away as other emergency personnel and vehicles arrived to care for the wounded soldiers.

They reached the Amritsar Military Base Hospital, and Balaram watched as Mongoose was carried, unconscious, into the emergency room. He sat outside, waiting, hoping and praying for a miracle.

* * * *

Pakistan's ISI Chief received the news of Mrs. Balochi's death with a limited amount of satisfaction. *She should have been taken into custody, and properly punished for her crimes. A quick death was too good for her. But at least the traitor has been eliminated, and now we can proceed with the operation without being tracked by those filthy good for nothing, Hindustani bania bastards.*

The Wagah border incident, of the 29th of March, instantly became international news. For the first time in its seventy-plus-years history, gunfire had been exchanged resulting in death and injuries on both sides. The media jumped on the story and all the government and non-government agencies expressed outrage and indignation. Foreign governments and peace activists appealed for calm on both sides.

Pakistan blamed India for firing upon their security personnel and civilians without provocation, and also unlawfully taking away two dead Pakistani citizen's bodies. India angrily protested it was the Pakistani Rangers who started the shooting that killed two Indian civilian women on their way home to India, and injuring many soldiers.

The Friendship Bus service was canceled, the Samjhauta Express train service was suspended, the "peace process" was put on hold, and the gates and ceremonies of Wagah were closed indefinitely.

Though reported as dead, Waheeda's surgery was successful and her condition stabilized, although she remained in intensive care for a number of weeks. Balaram arranged later for her to be discreetly moved to Patna under a new identity and admitted into a private nursing hospital under the direct care of one of his personal contacts. Shabnam was given a secret burial as per Muslim rites.

As soon as he returned to his office in Delhi, Balaram contacted the NSA director, Dr. Modi, who promised to inform the Secret Services of the other countries about the bombs. The NSA director asked Balaram if he had any information about the device destined for India. Balaram informed him they'd lost track of it, but were still following some intel, hoping it would lead them to its location.

* * * *

It was ten in the morning when Karry switched on the equipment in his communications room. He found Balaram already onscreen and ready to discuss the latest crucial developments.

He relayed the vital information concerning the Scorpion Eggs and the danger connected to an upcoming event in the capital, Delhi, with the astounding news that the suicide bomber would be a big name from Bollywood. Karry was astonished.

"This is big news and very bad." Karry rubbed his tired eyes with his palms.

"Yes it is, and more surprising is the discovery of a mole inside the JIC itself. As IFA, we cannot conduct official investigations against members of the government without prior clearance from the president, but nobody can stop *you* from doing so," said Balaram. "You take care of the politicians; we will look into the others."

"I understand. Who's the politician?"

"There are three Members of Parliament who sit on the Joint Intelligence Committee, and get regular updates from the IFA. They are Jagdish Dutt Tiwari of the Indian National Party, Keshav Mahajan of the Indian Peoples Party, and Lal Salaam of the Indian Communist Party."

"That definitely narrows it down considerably. Very good. I'll update you as soon as we've confirmed the identity of this enemy collaborator. We're getting close to tackling this horrific conspiracy," thundered Karry confidently.

"I am surprised that the Pakistani backed jihadis want to attack China, their all weather friend, it does not make sense" added Karry.

"Jihadis are supremacists; they do not care for anyone and might want to extract revenge, for what Communist China is doing to the Muslim Uyghurs, in Xinjiang"

Karry nodded and the converstion ended.

Chapter 18 - The Bollywood Lion

The Vajra team wasted no time following the leads they had received from the Mongoose.

Vikram, Satish and Avinash left for Delhi and settled into separate rooms, in very modest accommodation, with new sets of identities. In order to avoid suspicion, they kept in touch only by phone, text and email, never meeting in person. They also avoided the safehouse.

Then, with great discretion, each agent began to stalk his quarry. The details of particular political parties were gathered, and target groups infiltrated. Posing as volunteer social workers, they were welcomed into these groups and soon given tasks in the main offices; money played a big role in the successful operation. Appearing to be sincere, albeit slightly ambitious activists dedicated to serving the nation through party affiliation, they quickly made friends with other volunteers; even spending their spare time with their new comrades.

It wasn't long before Vikram learned of a job opportunity in Lal Salaam's residence. The previous chauffer had been sacked over some petty theft, and Vikram volunteered for the post, professing that even a small salary would be of great help to his family. He got the job, having convinced the individual hiring that he had the necessary skills required.

Satish, however, was less fortunate in finding employment with a local politician. For unlike Lal Salaam, whose family lived in Kolkata, all of Jagdish Dutt Tiwari's contacts were right in Delhi. His family had lived there for several generations, so there was a long line of local applicants who had some kind of personal recommendation. Any job openings in the house of the famous and powerful politician were hard to come by.

But Satish was undeterred. He located the phone exchange for the area, and early one morning went and loosened a few wires serving Tiwari's home. He bided his time before showing up to fix the damage.

He rang the bell of the villa. When a frowning manservant answered the door, he explained that after receiving some complaints of phones not working in the area, the telephone company had sent him to check on the problem. As he was guided through the various rooms of the residence, including what looked to be Tiwari's private office, Satish surreptitiously planted listening devices within each of the telephones in the house. Most importantly, he placed one in the office.

Although the bugs were not actually connected to the phone lines, they would capture every sound—including phone conversations—within a few meters. Under the suspicious gaze of the sour-faced manservant, Satish made a good show of checking each phone before going outside to tighten the wires. Afterward, he smilingly declared everything was now in order and exited the property.

During the next few days, the young agent spent most of his waking hours sifting through the recordings from the equipment he'd planted. Yawning with boredom, he listened to the usual instances of bribery, professional incompetence and questionable dealings, including a couple of private parties with underage sex-workers. He fast-forwarded carefully, trying not to lose anything important, but it seemed that other than the usual shortcomings which often characterized the ruling class, the old politician was not conspiring against the nation. Though several acts were highly criminal, these crimes did not represent the clear and present danger he was investigating, and were not part of his official mandate. The evidence would, however, be made available to his superiors at the appropriate time, if and when they decided to take the man down.

Avinash gained entry into his quarry's home by completely different means. Keshav Mahajan's son was a drug addict, and happy to provide information to anyone who supplied him with excellent stuff at reasonable prices; and Avinash offered home delivery. He soon was in the intimate confidence of young Harish, and the father was pleased his wayward son had finally found a decent friend who dressed with some taste and didn't raise hell in the house. If Avinash had a good influence on the man's son, it could go a long way to reassuring his supporters in Mumbai that his own house was in order. Avinash was given full run of the place, but all he learned was Keshav was a clean and credible politician; he didn't use drugs or engage in sex parties as other politicians often did.

Luckily for Vikram, Lal Salaam made a lot of phone calls while traveling around in the car. He seemed to appreciate the loyalty of a young chauffeur, who was constantly at his beck and call, and who sat quietly outside his office ready to serve him at any time; he did not at all suspect who Vikram really was and what he was up to.

It was only the third day on the job when he had a fantastic stroke of luck. Lal Salaam asked Vikram to drive him to the JNU campus in Delhi to attend a summit. He pulled the car up to campus security, glad Lal Salaam could not see his face when his boss directed him to continue to the home of Professor Jawahar Katju. Vikram struggled to look uninterested as he watched a number of strange assorted characters leave their limos and disappear into the house. One of them was unmistakably a fundamentalist-Islamic Mullah, and Vikram noted that the man had been picked up by Jawahar's personal driver. Another, a short Indian-looking guy in a black cassock, was certainly a Catholic priest, and the third man was most likely a protestant pastor. Two other Indians appeared to be something like youth club activists, but had a dangerous air about them. The penultimate individual definitely looked like a businessman, the way he dressed and carried himself. The last to reach Katju's residence was a Western looking woman.

After dropping off Lal Salaam, Vikram parked the car far away from the house as directed by Katju's personal chauffeur. There he waited for a couple of hours, then lazily walked over to Katju's car and offered a cigarette to the driver. The two young men struck up a conversation, and as soon as he learned Vikram was new to the job, the driver assumed the role of mentor. He instructed Vikram on how to deal with important employers who have private and confidential contacts.

After befriending the man, Vikram decided it was time to put some surveillance equipment in his boss' rooms, and did so at the first opportunity.

* * * *

Meanwhile at the Valley, Ranil, Tej, Ganesh and Mahendra were working on a list of possible hideouts for the nuclear device that was making its way to Delhi.

The general meeting of the Vajra team was scheduled for the 12th of April, *Rama Navami Day*. Jai arrived on the evening of April 8th and joined Lachit at the Valley. Lachit had just returned from his meeting with Professor Sarabhai who'd taught him how to neutralize a mini-nuclear device.

Simultaneously, Lilavati and Nila had been tasked with researching Bollywood VIPs with any history of sympathy toward terrorism, or fundamentalism, radical character changes, or symptoms of mental breakdown. On the second day of their search, Lilavati struck gold. The famous actor, Zalim Khan, fit the character profile. She contacted Karry, who immediately agreed with her conclusion.

"Look at this, sir," she said. "About fifteen years ago, Khalil Hamad—you know, the journalist from *Good Afternoon Mumbai* who had connections with the Mumbai Mafia— interviewed young Zalim Khan about his successful debut film. This is from the beginning of his career."

Lilavati ran the digitized file of the broadcast on the computer screen.

The journalist asked the actor many questions, including one about his recent love-marriage to his college sweetheart, a Hindu girl, for whose sake he'd had a Hindu wedding ceremony.

"We are secular, and humanity is the greatest religion; we celebrate both Hindu and Muslim festivals in our home," he explained to the journalist, his face a mask of joy. "We pray together and we are very happy about that."

"Now that you are married, is it true you are contemplating the idea of becoming a vegetarian?" asked the interviewer.

The young actor smiled convincingly. "Yes, indeed. I have discussed this matter with my wife, and I must say, she has convinced me totally. There are many health benefits, and the environment certainly needs a more sustainable way of producing food for all."

"But many in our own community might feel offended by your decision; they may feel you're betraying your tradition," pressed Khalil.

In the video, Zalim looked directly into the camera with the captivating, childish smile that had made him famous. "I think you mean that as a Muslim I should rather show the example of eating meat. Well, I have the greatest respect for all religions, and I don't want to disappoint or hurt anyone, but I really think eating meat is not good for human beings." He paused to make the point before raising his eyebrows passionately and continuing. "What's the problem for God if I don't get some innocent animal killed to make a curry? There are so many other excellent things we can eat. After all, God is supposed to be the merciful and loving father of all creatures, right?"

The video stopped. Lilavati said, "Now look at this, sir." She ran the second file.

A visibly older Zalim, in his early forties, was again interviewed by a similarly aged Khalil, on a similar subject, but with very different conclusions.

"Let's come now to your recent campaign in support of the beef-producing mechanized slaughterhouse located near the Hindu holy town of Pandarpur. Several environmental and animal rights groups, along with several Hindu organizations, have protested against it. What would you like to say to them?" asked the journalist.

This time Khan's expression was far from captivating. He frowned, visibly annoyed. "I would simply tell them to *go to hell*. I am a Muslim first, and eating Halal beef is my birthright. Not even my wife can stop me." He paused to make sure his audience heard him clearly and precisely. He then continued. "Islam is the *only* true religion, and Mohammed, peace be upon Him, is the last prophet. He has shown us the way through the Quran and Hadiths, which take care of all the needs of the human being who surrenders to the only true God, Allah." As he spoke, he stared into the camera like a maniac.

Karry's hand involuntarily went to his forehead in shock. "Of course!" he growled. "This is so obvious. A change of heart would be an understatement. This is a complete U-turn."

Lilavati spoke. "Sir, I'm pretty sure he's the 'Lion' we're looking for. There's also another disquieting piece of news. Take a look at this." The screen showed another interview, this time on MDTV. Raj Desai of *My Delhi Television* was sitting with Zalim Khan, who appeared to be in his early thirties.

"And what astrological sign are you, Zalim?" he queried jovially.

"Leo," replied the actor with a smirk. "And I've always liked lions. I remember once in some inter-school art competition, I won the first prize, and my painting was of a lion."

The journalist politely raised his eyebrows. "That's interesting. Why do you like lions?"

"Well," said Zalim, lifting his chin superiorly, "you know the lion is the 'King of the Jungle'. I like that. If I was to be reborn as an animal, I would certainly choose to be a lion."

Karry looked at Lilavati's face and smiled. "I think we've got our big cat in the bag. Very good job! However, I also think you should continue your search, and don't disregard other details which might be important. Try to find out the schedule for Khan's upcoming public engagements and events, with a focus on Delhi. We are at the most vital crux of the game."

Lilavati nodded in agreement.

* * * *

The next day, it was Nila's turn for action. She came up with the idea of publishing a provocative article in a leading newspaper. The article alleged some very famous Bollywood personality was closely connected with the Mumbai Mafia Don and was getting his support and protection, while honest actors like Rishi Mehra and Vinod Shetty had faced assassination attempts. Karry introduced the new journalist to the newspaper where he often published his own writings, and Nila's article appeared under a pen name.

The bait worked. The article raised flutters in Bollywood circles, with most actors giving scathing interviews about the questionable motives of people who launched unfounded allegations to defame celebrities. They even suggested Mehra and Shetty were using cheap publicity stunts to boost their sagging fortunes. The entertainment media went into a feeding frenzy, and it seemed like every star had something to say on the subject.

Only Zalim Khan remained absent from the public debate. For the past ten years he had fiercely protected his privacy and perhaps he was not about to change his policy now. Not just yet, anyway.

Behind the scenes, however, Khan was furious over the insinuations that questioned his self-reliance. His personal relationship with the Mumbai Don, who financed nearly eighty percent of Bollywood productions, had simply helped him to attain a success that was actually due to his own talent and hard work. But he certainly was not going to allow anyone else to walk all over him.

Nobody had challenged his influence and position in the movie capital of India for at least a decade, and he'd be *damned* if they were going to start now. He was the Bollywood Lion King, and his authority had to be preserved and affirmed. He had to do something to prove it.

He called his good friend Lal Salaam.

The Member of Parliament was in his car, on his way to the Lok Sabha, the Parliament House in Delhi, when his mobile phone rang. "Hallo," the politician said laconically.

"It's Zalim Khan, Salaam." The actor's voice was stern.

"Ah, Zalim, how are you? I was going to call you."

"Have you seen that outrageous article about me? It's terrible! What are we going to do about it?"

"Yes, I've seen it. It's very offensive but does not say your name specifically, so why bother?"

"Whether my name was or wasn't stated is not the point, you know it was directed against me. I hope you do something about it quickly, because this story could harm my reputation. I have a new movie coming out next month, and there's not much time to turn this bad press into good publicity," snarled Zalim angrily.

"Zalim," Salaam said firmly, "No panic, okay? I have a plan. I'll call you later."

* * * *

Although Vikram was only able to hear Lal Salaam's part of the conversation, the following chain of events was enough to point the Vajra Team in the right direction.

On the 9th of April, a press release announced that the famous Bollywood actor, Zalim Khan, had received an anonymous letter threatening to kill him. The style of the accusations and the threats were typical of the Mumbai Mafia.

"Mr. Khan has reported the matter to the police for further investigation," the media reported, "and has requested personal protection in view of the impending danger to himself and his family."

This was exactly the kind of press Khan wanted, for it deflected blame from him, and the attention it generated reaffirmed his status as a national treasure.

The star graciously granted several interviews, a story in and of itself, since he had rarely spoken to the media for the past decade.

MDTV went all out and put the report at the center of their news updates for an entire three-day period.

Suddenly, the media was flooded with twisted stories about Islamophobic sentiments and the marginalization of minority communities, especially Islamic. Islam was actually a religion of peace and brotherhood, these stories said, and was being vilified and misrepresented by bigots, and people should learn about Islam for their own benefit and come to respect it. However, the question was: why was religion injected into the discourse, when it was just a mafia criminal issue? But the Vajra team knew exactly why. This gave extra protective cover to Zalim Khan, as if he were being deliberately victimized.

Balaram followed this turn of events closely. Karry asked him to contact the Officer-in-charge at the Bandra police station, in Mumbai, to gain his insights regarding the entire affair. When he did, he learned the actor had been requested by the police to keep the threats out of the media glare. Such attention obstructed police work, but Khan insisted his fans and the public needed to know the truth. He even tweeted on the subject, and his zealous fans re-tweeted his words, and some even began a Facebook campaign to support their hero and demi-god.

While the Vajra team was happy, they'd successfully baited the Lion to come out of his den, and would hopefully be able to catch and cage him soon; by the time Nila was to write the second article, she had to use all of her 'womanly charms' to convince the editor to overcome his fears of retaliation from the Mumbai Mafia Don. This follow-up article suggested the threatening letter was a phony, merely a clever trick to gain sympathy; not to mention cheap publicity. The controversy deepened into a new wave of media frenzy, in which the 'scam hypothesis' started to gain credence among serious journalists.

Angrier than ever, Khan immediately stopped granting interviews, hurt by the deductions. His next phone call to Lal Salaam was not overheard by Vikram; nor was it recorded, as the politician sat in his garden, out of reach of the microphones. But the ensuing move was spectacular.

* * * *

On the 11th of April, Zalim Khan participated in an annual function at his daughter's school. The stage was set in an open-air auditorium, where many seats had been arranged for the parents and public. Seriously concerned about the star's safety, the police provided an armed escort.

Once the children's performance was over, Khan was invited by the school principal to distribute the awards to the best students.

Smiling broadly, he climbed the steps onto the dais.

After he distributed the third and second prize, his smile deepened as he heard the first prize would go to his own daughter, Alisha. This was the condition on which Khan had agreed to participate in the function. It was also his idea to have the program out in the open. His wife then joined him on the dais to help him present the award medals.

Suddenly there was the sound of gunfire. After the first bullet was fired, Zalim was found screaming and clutching his left arm. A second bullet hit at a bad angle on the stainless steel frame of the backdrop and ricocheted, biting deeply and painfully into his left buttock. Zalim shrieked again and fell to the ground as pandemonium broke loose. The police constables assigned to his security detail drew their guns and looked around, trying to locate the sniper, as hysterical parents grabbed their children and ran for cover.

One of the policemen, who had closed in to protect the actor, was felled by a third shot to the chest. A fourth shot came from the opposite direction. The officer in charge divided his confused men into two teams and sent them to search the nearby buildings, but their movements were hampered by the panicking crowd trying to escape. By the time the ambulances arrived, two police constables were dead and Khan was on the floor, bleeding and moaning. The medics attended to a number of other people with lesser injuries caused by the debris and stampede.

The news of the mafia attack added yet another twist to the raging controversy, and tilted the balance of public opinion in favor of Khan.

The actor was rushed to the hospital, where he was immediately taken into surgery. A few hours later, the doctors gave a brief press conference, announcing the bullet had been removed from his buttock and he would fully recover. His arm had only been grazed and was no cause for concern. Khan would have to remain in the hospital for medication and rest, but he would be able to attend the premiere of his new film on the 18th of April, one week away.

Lal Salaam was furious with the snipers for the additional buttock wound; it was not part of the plan, and Khan would no doubt call him in a rage as soon as he could lay his hands on a phone. Somehow, Salaam would have to reassure him that the proper steps had been taken to punish the snipers for the mistake.

* * * *

The actor was indeed in a leonine rage. He had envisioned the most glorious day of his life in a more dignified manner. How was he supposed to walk onto the main stage of the stadium holding the nuclear device, with a limp? He had pictured himself stepping onto the stage with the grace and might of a true lion, his face illuminated by the saintly smile of the noble Shaheed martyr, in ecstasy from a glimpse of paradise that awaited him on the other side; now those bastards had ruined everything with a bloody bullet in the butt. Every small movement was causing him a very unsightly grimace of pain, so how was he supposed to keep a stern, yet serene face?

They had screwed up big time and they would have to face his wrath. As expected, his towering temper exploded at Lal Salaam. Salaam tolerated the outburst, probably knowing he could not contradict the golden boy of the mission, the man who was actually going to blow himself up for their cause. Soon enough, however, Khan discovered his popularity had not suffered as much as his rear-end. The media instantly turned him into a 'real life' hero, from the mere, 'reel life' star he had been all these years. He rejoiced in his glory.

* * * *

Khan lay face down, relaxing on the bed in his private room at the Juhu Apollo Hospital. Two policemen were stationed at the door.

Khan didn't know that on the day after his admission, the delivery man who had carried in flowers and other get-well presents had stuck a few micro-transmitters behind the nightstand, in a place where they were unlikely to be removed by the housekeeping staff. He had lazily watched as Jai, dressed in a uniform with the embroidered logo and name of a large and famous florist; had arranged several baskets around the room.

After the shootout at the school, Jai moved to Mumbai and into Karry's house. There he spent hours in the tiny communication center examining the recordings from Khan's room.

Khan's wife visited her husband each afternoon and remained until evening. There was not much conversation at that time, mostly angry mumbling by the injured actor which changed to moaning every time the nurses changed his bandages. Clearly, the relationship between the man and his wife was rather strained.

In one of the recordings, on the afternoon of the second day, as soon as the attending nurse had left the room, Zalim called his friend, the Communist MP from Kolkata. Lal Salaam must have asked him about his health, because the actor exploded. "How do you think I am doing? *Fucking lousy!*"

Jai paused the sound, then switched on the recording relayed by Vikram in Delhi to go overtop and in sync with this one. Now he could listen to a continuous complete conversation.

"I know you are angry, but please try to understand, it was an accident. The bullet ricocheted. It was a chance in a thousand, ten thousand, maybe—nobody could have foreseen that. The two men have been severely punished, and I can assure you they are extremely sorry."

"Yes, but that's literally my ass on the line!" raged Zalim. "You guys should have been much more careful. You know how much it hurts, and even worse it takes away my dignity!"

"You said yourself, it needed to look real. We could not get more real than this; don't forget the first bullet just clipped your shoulder as planned."

Zalim exploded into an interesting collection of foul words, and Jai realized the Lion's enormous ego had been more wounded than his body.

The politician apparently decided it was time to change the topic. "Have you heard from the mullah already?" asked Lal Salaam.

At the mention of his spiritual mentor, Khan seemed to instantly calm down. "Yes, he usually calls me in the early morning just after his *namaz* prayer. He's been a great support and inspiration for me in these days."

"Well, I'll tell him to call you more often, Zalim. It seems you need some more motivation for your mission."

Zalim remained silent for a moment, and when he spoke, his voice was almost humble. "I am motivated. I will do it. Don't doubt even for a moment. It is my glory in this world, the guarantee of eternity of my name and fame, and my reward in paradise."

When the conversation ended, Jai quickly copied the file onto a flash drive, then climbed down the ladder and returned to Karry's office below.

Karry looked up. "Got something?"

"Yes, sir, I certainly do."

Karry breathed a sigh of relief after Jai replayed the conversation he'd recorded. "We have nearly all the pieces to this puzzle, except for one. Tomorrow morning, we'll go to the Valley and have our general meeting. Time's getting short; we need to find the Scorpion Egg before it reaches the venue on Wednesday. The two operational words now are: 'Locate' and 'Defuse'."

* * * *

Tuesday, April 12th was celebrated at the Valley as *Rama Navami*, the day of the appearance of Sri Ramachandra, the ideal King and Dharmic warrior of ancient India. All the members of the Vajra team—except for Vikram, who needed to remain in Delhi to monitor Salaam—returned to meet and review the entire situation in the garden next to the temple. Now began the most crucial phase of their mission.

"So, let's begin with the good news," Karry said. "We know who the Lion and Mole are, and we've got them bugged and being monitored." Karry paused a moment for the team to absorb and rejoice at their first major success. "We know there's only one small, low-intensity nuclear device destined to explode in Delhi during a top-level government event; however, we still don't know what event and date. We really need to concentrate on how to locate the bomb and defuse it." He gazed around the room; his steely eyes meeting those of each member of the team.

"There's more bad news. We've lost track of the bomb, but by now it shouldn't be too far from Delhi. It may even be there already."

"The information we collected from Jafar, on March 27th, is that the device reached Hyderabad from Coimbatore, and from there has gone on to Malegaon. After that, it will head to Godhra and Ajmer before reaching Delhi.

"We checked the route leaked by the ISI, and it nearly cost us the lives of two good agents and of our informant in Pakistan. But I think there may be no time to verify the other routes. Does anyone have any suggestions?"

Jai spoke up. "I think we should keep a close watch on the Lion here in Mumbai, and the Mole in Delhi, as they're our best bet and could easily lead us to the bomb at any time."

From the nods and grunts in the affirmative, it was clear there was a consensus among the team.

"I think you're right, Jai," Karry said, "We need to keep a watch on Zalim. Without the

The Treasure of the Pandavas

Lion there will be no circus, and since our Bollywood star seems to be rather passionate, there may be some chances he'll unknowingly give us more leads in the next few days.

Lilavati raised her hand, and everybody turned toward her. "Sir," she said rather stiffly, "I believe Nila and I could infiltrate Zalim Khan's inner circle."

Karry frowned. "I can't deny our desperate need may require desperate actions. And I trust you're both fully capable of handling yourselves."

Lilavati and Nila responded with almost tiger-like smiles. "You bet, sir. Anything in the service of Mother India."

"All right, then, I'll join you boys in Delhi and leave Avinash & Satish to back up Nila and Lilavati in Mumbai, just in case."

"Yes, sir." The team replied in unison.

* * * *

While Karry traveled to Delhi with the male Vajra team members, their female counterparts began attending the same luxury fitness club where Khan's wife spent her mornings after sending their children to school. They easily befriended her, as the poor woman seemed to be very depressed, and starved for affection. They learned she had no extended family to support her emotionally. At the end of the second day, Nila had only to ask whether something was wrong and the woman broke down. She told the

505

story of the shootout and how scared she and the children had been.

The two girls consoled the woman and offered to go to her house to give her some company. Mrs. Khan eagerly agreed and said she was lucky to have found such friends in her time of need.

The very next day, Nila and Lilavati found themselves inside the Lion's den. The children, Alisha, seven, and Umar, four, were still in shock after the shootout and seemed to need extra attention. The two young women quickly won their confidence, and gained their interest through drawing, painting and telling amusing stories. When Zalim returned home two days later, after being discharged from the hospital, the two agents had already become family friends and bonded deeply with the children. Zalim had no reason to consider the young women as any sort of threat. Moreover, he never ever concerned himself with his wife's friends: it was always about him and his own activities.

When Nila arrived with some special amulets, called *taviz*, for the entire family, Mrs. Khan gave one to her husband, too. All the talismans had listening and tracking devices embedded into them. No one seemed to suspect anything as Nila and Lilavati were wearing identical ones. They told a very interesting story about the famous peace-loving Sufi Saint from Ajmer, Hazrat Khwaja Moinuddin Chishti, who was revered by Muslims and Hindus alike. These blessed talismans came from his tomb. After successfully 'collaring the cat', Nila and Lilavati remained in the close circle of the Khan family.

On Monday, the 18th of April, the Khans attended the premiere of Zalim's latest movie, and the actor was extremely happy to see his popularity seemed to have grown exponentially since the shooting. He was nice to the crowds and paparazzi, and adoring journalists filled the channels with enthusiastic comments. Lilavati and Nila spent the night at the Khans' to take care of the children, and when the actor and his wife returned home, the women were the first to get the news of his imminent journey to Delhi for a special awards ceremony at Talkatora stadium. That night, Nila sent a coded text to Karry saying, *"Arrival tomorrow & E-day Talkatora."*

The next day, Mrs. Khan went to the airport to see her husband off, and when she came back her eyes were red and puffy. The girls volunteered to stay overnight for a few days, saying their families wouldn't mind. After the children had gone to sleep, the three women sat together in silence for some time, holding hands. Finally, Mrs. Khan was able to open the dam of her despair. Zalim had been very cold and distant for the past two years and had told her he didn't know when he would come back to Mumbai. She was tired and afraid, and had no idea what to think. The only concession Zalim had given her was the address of the place where he would be staying in Delhi.

The young team members exchanged worried looks before hugging the distraught woman. Lilavati relayed the coded message to Karry: "Zoo animal near Jama Masjid."

The Jama Mosque was an enormous square complex, with a large central dome and smaller domes on either side. There were three entrances leading into the central courtyard: the east gate known as the 'royal' gate, for the entrance was once used by royalty, and the north and south gates for everyone else. On the west side, Chawri Bazaar Road was choked with hundreds of small shops trying to attract customers with interesting offers. The Vajra team immediately identified the house where the Lion was staying by decoding the phone number Khan had given to his wife. It was a stone's throw away from the mosque; this was not the usual place a Bollywood actor would stay. Vajra team knew exactly why, but the locals hadn't seemed to notice, otherwise there would have been a stampede to see their beloved 'demi-god'.

Karry, who had joined the group, was carrying a black backpack. Inside the nondescript bag was a portable specialized ultrasound device which could detect the exact locations of the underground tunnels he knew ran beneath the complex—it once having been an ancient Hindu temple, before it was destroyed by Muslim invaders and the masjid built in its place. Attached to the device was a small earpiece which resembled what would be connected to a cell phone; in this way, no one would hear the soft beeps guiding the team.

They started from the southeast corner and walked along the east wall of the mosque, talking innocently as if they were taking a casual evening stroll. There were not many people around, but Karry was still extremely cautious. Mahendra, Jai and Ganesh walked and talked alongside him, while Lachit, Ranil and Tejinder kept close watch from nearby shops to see if anyone was approaching. About halfway, not far from the main entrance, the sound changed. Karry slowed down, then gradually turned away from the mosque and moved along a slightly oblique line, carefully monitoring the sound. After a few minutes, the group reached the maze of buildings and alleys of the Meena Bazaar, opposite the Jama Masjid complex; Karry kept walking slowly to avoid losing the location of the tunnel.

The beep changed tone again as they were walking past a particularly old and decrepit building. This time Karry did not stop, but led the team to the corner of the road and explained it all.

Victor Cosmos

* * * *

That night, around 1:00 a.m., Jai, Mahendra and Lachit walked silently to the marked building in Meena Bazaar, followed at a short distance by Tejinder and Ganesh. They carried small bags filled with a variety of tools for the next—and most dangerous—phase of the mission. Not far away, Ranil sat at the steering wheel of the getaway van. Unobserved, they approached the building and picked the lock, then noiselessly slid inside. They paused in the first room, which was empty and rather decrepit. It appeared to be an old reception room, but was now cluttered with boxes. They waited silently for a moment, listening for any signs of life; a soft snore could be heard down the corridor. Looking carefully for any stairs descending underground, the team crept carefully past the many doors of the hallway, helped by the dim light around them. As they passed each one, they rolled a soft small ball into each room from under its door. In two minutes, the vapors would send anyone inside into a very deep sleep for several hours.

Luckily, the stairs to the basement weren't far away. They tiptoed down them as swiftly as possible, listening for any noise. Nothing stirred within the building, so after some time they risked switching on a flashlight. The first thing they noticed was they were in a large space with no doors. It was obviously a storage room

Ganesh ran the ultra sound along the wall. After a few minutes, he found what he was looking for: a hollow space in the west wall, just to the right of the stairs.

Mahendra loosened a brick from the wall with the help of a flat blade; then he very quietly slid in two long, thin, steel rods, each with a small hook at one end, on either side of the brick. While the others worked around him, Mahendra carefully pulled his brick out and gently deposited it on the floor. Ganesh then carefully inserted his hand into the hole and felt the size of the opening behind the wall. For a few moments, they continued to remove bricks. Finally, Ganesh stepped forward, grabbed the flashlight, and slid into the opening of an underground tunnel, gesturing for the others to follow.

Tejinder stayed back in the cellar to watch out for any sign of danger, while the others walked on cautiously, switching on more flashlights, tool bags in hand. After about fifteen minutes, the smelly, rat-infested tunnel ended in front of an old iron-grilled door; from it hung an ancient but sturdy-looking lock. Ganesh and Mahendra quickly removed the door's hinge, and then silently placed it on the ground. Another grilled door at the opposite side of the small corridor was similarly removed. The agents found themselves in another old cellar, very similar to the one they had left a few moments before, but with one important difference: this one was furnished with a wooden door. The place had a horrible stench, as if it had been used as a toilet. Their face masks helped them avoid inhaling the toxic gases.

This door was also locked, but they easily picked it, and soon they were climbing up the inside stairs of the east gate of the mosque.

The mosque itself was closed for the day. Most of the doors to the rooms in the inner courtyard along the stairs were unlocked, and again they heard light snoring coming from the inside, which they dealt with as before. Finally Ganesh found yet another locked door, this one with a modern combination lock. He signaled to his teammates, and Jai took out his bolt cutters and cut it off. In just a few seconds, they slid the door open. Their hard work had paid off: in the middle of the room, on a low table, lay a large black bag. They knew what it was. They had done it! They communicated their joy through gestures to maintain the silence.

* * * *

Lachit moved in quickly and unzipped the bag, while Mahendra brought up their gear, and Ganesh remained at the entrance as lookout. During the four weeks he had spent in Mumbai with Professor Nathuram Sarabai, Lachit had studied all possible models of miniaturized nuclear devices, but this one was rather strange.

It looked like a medium-sized briefcase, and had a numerical combination lock. He paused a moment, then pulled a tiny electronic notebook from his bag and switched it on. He attached a super sensitive microphone to it, and then cautiously started to move the combination lock on the 'briefcase'. One by one, the nine dials stopped at the right place, forming the number 786786786. Lachit drew a long breath, and pushed the release button. The briefcase obediently opened, revealing a screen and keyboard. With a start, he realized that by opening it, he had activated the device; the screen lit up almost instantly, showing a pop-up window with two slots. Apparently, the ID and the password had to be inserted there to log into the computer interface.

Lachit wiped the sweat from his brow. He knew he had to act fast, for it was very likely that too long a pause between the opening of the case and the entering of log-on data could set off a disastrous chain of events: it might either block the entire device or, worse, send out some silent alarm, perhaps even back to Pakistan. For all he knew, it could have an automatic default set to explode once it had reached Delhi!

Let's think; Zalim Khan is supposed to remember the ID and password, so it can't be too difficult, can it? He smiled, in spite of the seriousness of the situation. He typed: LION.

513

The cursor jumped to the password slot, and blinked.

Now the password. Lachit wiped his forehead again. He typed "2004", the day and month of the event at the Talkatora indoor stadium. He pressed the enter key, but instead of "access granted", the pop-up window showed the message he feared most: "wrong password." His heart stopped.

These types of programs usually gave only three chances to successfully log on. At the third incorrect entry, the silent alarm would probably go off. *How foolish I am!* he chided himself. *When the password was set up, they didn't know what day the event would take place.* This was bad judgment on his part.

He controlled a wave of panic and felt Jai place his hand upon his shoulder. Lachit took a deep breath, prayed to the Almighty and connected his own laptop to the bomb; this meant more time, and therefore, more risk. The USB plug was recognized, and a new window opened. Lachit launched a special file scanning program, and in a few seconds the prompt appeared on his own screen. He typed the ID "Lion" and hit the enter key. The password slot flashed for a few seconds, and then it read: "06Aug1966."

Right, mouthed Lachit silently. *It's the actor's birthday and he's a Leo.* Quickly, he typed in the new password, and instantly, a different window popped up: "Access granted."

It had only been his second attempt. With a sigh of relief, Lachit searched the program menu for "deactivate for internal inspection," then, greatly relieved, gave the command.

The screen shut down. He looked for a sliding cover through which he could access the device itself. Lachit was acutely conscious of the time passing and of the constant danger; he had to complete his mission as quickly as possible. Jai and Mahendra were watching him intently.

Here it is! Lachit's finger found the sliding cover of the compartment and he opened it. The device was a relatively simple one: a basic, gun-type A bomb, with two pieces of fissile material, each at two-thirds critical mass and at opposite ends of a tubular device. He remembered the explanations of Professor Sarabhai: the two spheres of active material would be brought together very rapidly, by a propellant consisting of a high explosive, to form a single super-critical mass. He cautiously unscrewed the tube and removed the tampers protecting the small spheres. From his bag, helped by Mahendra, he extracted a radiation-proof container, where he deposited the active material, and wrapped it in a special piece of hard cloth.

From another container, he took a piece of clay and formed two small balls, slightly smaller than the spheres of active material, and wrapped them in just enough cloth to cover them, then inserted the two clay pieces inside the device.

After closing the casing, he switched the computer on again. He then selected the menu option "reactivate", and waited to see if the computer could be fooled into believing that clay could be radioactive material.

A pop-up window appeared: "Device activated and ready."

Jai, Lachit and Mahendra exchanged smiles. The team silently moved out along with Ganesh, leaving everything as they had found it. Mission accomplished!

Another minute and they switched on their flashlights and replaced both hinged doors, and then they rushed back to the cellar in the building of the Meena Bazaar.

Tejinder seemed extremely relieved to see the others return safe and sound, their faces lit up with smiles. The team quickly replaced the bricks, and then piled some empty boxes up to hide the damaged wall. This time they didn't hear any snoring; it was obvious the gas was still working. Without further ado, they slid back upstairs, through the reception room of the old house, and into the street.

Walking briskly away from the neighborhood, the team members were elated by their good luck and success; yet they remained cautious as they moved toward their vehicle. By this time, it was four in the morning, and the air, crisp and light, reminded them of the many early mornings when they had trained for this exact moment.

They jumped into the vehicle where Ranil was waiting, and then rolled quietly onward to the Delhi safehouse.

Chapter 19 - Terror at Talkatora Stadium

"All right, guys," began Karry, smiling and thrilled by their success. The Vajra team, consisting of Jai, Ranil, Tej, Ganesh, Mahendra and Lachit, had gathered back at the safehouse in Delhi. Even Balaram joined; he wanted to hear the good news first hand. "Thanks to your excellent work, the main danger has been averted, a second win for us. Please give yourselves a very well deserved pat on the back."

He turned to Balaram, who added, smiling, "Great job, everyone. No amount of words can express my deep gratitude."

Lilavati, Nila, Avinash and Satish joined via a secure satellite video link from Mumbai. Only Vikram was missing, as he had not gotten a chance to leave Lal Salaam's. He would be briefed later.

"Lachit," said Karry, "let's hear the details of the Scorpion Egg."

"Well, sir, the device apparently appears functional. It should fool the Lion for sure. As we suspected, it looks like this is a joint team effort of Pakistan and North Korea. We believe the Pakistani scientists must have been working in a nuclear facility in North Korea. Nobody else would have used the number 786786786 as a code."

The others nodded, for they all knew the significance of this number. It had long been used as a holy number by many Muslims on the Indian subcontinent. The Arabic letters of the opening phrase of the Qur'an add up to 786 in the system of Abjad numerals; 786 is a substitute for the phrase *bism illāh ir-rahmān ir-rahīm, which* translates as: in the name of Allah, the merciful, the compassionate.

Lachit explained the tense moment when he had typed in the wrong password and how they fooled the computer with balls of clay.

"Very good," said Balaram, as he exuberantly shook Lachit's hand.

As soon as the conversation stopped, Jai stepped in to explain the rest of the plan. "We still need to keep an eye on the mosque, the Jama Masjid. It's unfortunate the terrorists are using religious places to hide bombs. By doing this they are endangering the entire Muslim community. Anyway, the conspirators must not suspect their mission has already failed, they must expose themselves and their accomplices in public." Jai looked at Karry, who nodded for him to continue. "We need them to demonstrate directly, by speech and deed, their purpose and motivations. The public would never believe it if we simply denounced them, they need direct proof. To most people, Bollywood actors are like demi-gods. Given the number of corrupt police officers and magistrates, they often walk away from their crimes, scot-free. It has happened before and will happen again. With their money, political contacts and media support, even a full-scale investigation often increases their popularity and procures them publicity for their latest films. Our government's appeasement policy only makes things worse. They will never acknowledge the truth regarding home-grown terrorists because they are afraid of losing the minority vote."

There was a moment of silence, and then Jai continued, raising his head in confidence. "But if Zalim Khan tries to detonate the device in the presence of thousands of people, the truth will be irrefutable, and all the doubting Thomases will have nowhere to hide."

"Precisely," said Karry, leaning forward. "People need to see the Lion's dance, hear its roar and make their own conclusion. So are we sure we haven't done anything that might make our quarry suspicious?"

"Don't worry, Sir," said Ganesh. "We carefully covered our tracks—nobody saw anything."

"Now we need to focus our attention on the last phase: E-Day." Balaram commented. E-Day was another name given by Vajra team for the feared 'Explosion Day'.

Karry nodded. "In a few days, there will be an award presentation ceremony for the youth of India who have distinguished themselves with acts of bravery and excellence. They are to be honored at a gala on the 20th of April, at the Talkatora Indoor Stadium, not far from the Presidential Palace. That's where Khan is planning to detonate the nuclear bomb for maximum impact."

"It is the perfect plan for the terrorists, for in addition to the President and the Prime Minister, many honored guests, including several scientists, scholars, judges, military generals and police officers will be in attendance."

"It is certainly an ideal target which could terrorize the nation and decapitate the government," Balaram interjected, "not to mention demoralizing our youth. Our own installations under the Buddha Jayanti Park would be seriously damaged, if not destroyed. Luckily for us, you have averted the main danger. The whole country will be forever grateful and proud of the Vajra team."

"We already knew the IFA's work could be jeopardized," Karry reminded him, "and now we know exactly who has been leaking the information—Lal Salaam. Now that we have him under constant surveillance, the danger is hopefully under control."

Jai spoke up. "Zalim Khan is here now, living near the mosque, itself. Nila and Lilavati have been holding their own in Mumbai at Khan's house, and were able to plant a bug on him in the form of a talisman. Avinash and Satish are keeping track of his every move and also backing up the girls. The first person Khan saw back home was his cousin Jinnah. It seems he is bringing along a special cricket team, composed of new and promising young talent. We have reason to believe this new promising talent will be part of the plot."

Satish frowned. "Jinnah is a cricket bookie and is known to be deeply involved in betting and match fixing."

"That is not the half of it!" exclaimed Jai, "During the private conversation between the two cousins, Zalim's bugged talisman enabled us to hear Jinnah had placed an order for six signature cricket bats—which are twice the length, breath and width of a standard bat—to be given as souvenirs. He received the shipment yesterday."

At Satish's quizzical look, Jai explained further. "These are not ordinary signature cricket bats, but have been supplied courtesy of the Pakistani Secret Intelligence Service. Instead of being made of solid wood, like the ordinary bats, some of them have been hollowed out and fitted with a new series of AK assault rifles, preloaded with special bullets. This weapon is one-half the weight and size of a standard AK-47 Kalashnikov, but just as lethal. From what he explained to Zalim, the handle of the bat can be easily unscrewed and the covering pulled away. Two of the bats have the stock; two have the barrel and the other two, the action assemblies. These can be quickly put together to form two assault rifles. It appears the terrorists are posing as movie extras from the sets of Zalim Khan's new film, 'Chak de Cricket'. Zalim has been working on this film at the Feroz Shah Kotla cricket grounds. I guess he's been maintaining his cover as the 'dedicated Bollywood icon'.

"And that's not all, they will also be carrying a small box of similarly special cricket balls, each fitted with a mini hand-grenade; the stitching is fake and the covering can be removed easily. Their plan is to keep security at bay while Zalim carries on with his terrorist act, which means even without the nuke, considerable damage could be done."

Karry wearily passed a hand across his forehead. "Any other relevant information? Aside from the President and other government officials, do we have a specific guest list?"

Nodding, Jai pulled out a piece of paper and began calling out the names of some of Bollywood's biggest stars, top Indian cricketers, and famous politicians.

Balaram looked at them, his raised eyebrows knotted in fear. "There is another problem. On the same day as the event, there's also a special session of Parliament scheduled, and the sole agenda concerns efforts to combat homegrown terrorism. It has been officially requested by...guess who? Our very own Lal Salaam. Most of the Members of Parliament will be present, and it is very likely many of them will participate in the award ceremony at the Talkatora. That's the reason the session was planned on E-day to begin with; now everything is falling into place."

He paused and stroked his chin in thought before continuing. "Of course, there will be heavy security, both in uniform and plain clothes. As stated earlier, we want this to play out within the public arena. Otherwise, nobody would believe the cricket bats are actually guns, or that Zalim Khan's briefcase is actually a nuclear bomb. It just sounds a bit too crazy."

Karry nodded in agreement. "Last thing we need is to make sure the conspirators carry on seemingly undetected until the final moment. So, ironically, our job is to make sure Zalim, his briefcase bomb, and Jinnah's fake cricketers all enter the venue unchecked."

Balaram winked playfully at the team. "You mean get the bad guys in place for the final ambush? That we can do."

"We'll need to be there as members of security as well," said Jai.

Karry looked at Balaram, who immediately nodded.

"What about Nila and Lilavati?" asked Jai anxiously.

"I think they should remain in Mumbai and take care of Zalim Khan's family. After Zalim has exposed himself and his plot in such a public and horrific manner, his family will need serious security," cautioned Balaram.

"Yes," agreed Karry. "They are innocents in all this. We cannot abandon them to a mindless mob of vigilantes. They need to evacuate Mrs. Khan and her two children to a safe location, preferably incognito. Anything else?"

"I was wondering," Jai said, hesitantly, "who is Mongoose, and how are they doing? That shootout at the Wagah border crossing was quite dramatic."

Balaram smiled. "Mongoose is safe, although still in Intensive Care in a private clinic, and under a new identity. The damage to her lung was serious, and although she regained consciousness yesterday, she still has a number of chest tubes in, and the doctors have prohibited her from being stressed in anyway until the tubes can be removed. The prognosis is good, but healing will take a very long time. When she gets well, we will, of course, offer her a position as a consultant to IFA."

"The Mongoose is a *she*?" Jai asked in surprise, raising his eyebrows, then added, "Thank you, sir. Everyone will be happy to hear that. We all know how crucial she was to this mission. You know, I'd like to meet her. The first question I'd ask is why a young Pakistani Muslim sister put her life on the line to help us Kafirs."

"Intriguing, indeed." Karry nodded. "Sad to say that her partner, Mrs. Shabnam, died in the incident."

He noticed Jai's surprise look. "Now Jai, and the rest of you, listen. Lesbian identity is not a factor here. What matters is who stands up for what is right. History teaches us that Bhishma, Drona, even Yudhisthira, sat silent as Draupadi was assaulted by the evil Kauravas. Heroic Shikandhi, though born transgender, helped the Pandavas win the Kurukshetra War! And as India now faces a worse crisis, it is these two Pakistani ladies who saved the day for India. I salute them."

There was a moment of silence as Jai and the others considered his words, then Balaram brought the discussion back to the present. "We also can't forget this is part of a global Jihadi power play. According to our intel, the other five bombs landed in Somalia and were retrieved from Ibrahim Jr.'s yacht. Luckily, a few days ago, the Americans successfully intercepted the device on the New York docks—it was destined for the U.S. capital of Washington, DC. The bomb meant for Brussels was found yesterday in a storage facility in the Antwerp harbor. Clearly, the terrorists' aim is to take out the world's most important cities and their people. Unfortunately, there is no information yet about the bombs that were destined to hit Russia, China and Israel."

His words were greeted by a deep silence. "There is a good chance one of them will blow up," Karry said sadly, "and unfortunately we can't do anything about it. However, if the E-day plot is exposed with sufficient impact at the international level, it's possible the global public opinion will shift, and suitable measures can be taken by the affected countries and the Security Council of the United Nations. This is why our work here in Delhi is so important."

"Well, everyone will have to listen now," said Jai. "All our media efforts are in play. The Bollywood Lion's 'big moment' will be covered by the international press."

"Finally, we'll get a good performance out of that phony Khan!" smiled Karry. "All right then, let's wrap-up this meeting." He gestured to Jai. "You and I will be official guests at the event, so we'll have a front-row seat to better keep an eye on things; the rest of the Vajra team will be snipers."

The meeting ended.

With most of their preparations complete, the Vajra team found the hardest part of their mission was the waiting. The tension in the air was palpable. When E-Day finally arrived, it was almost a welcome relief.

* * * *

At noon, sharp, Karry and Jai arrived at the Talkatora Indoor Stadium, located within the Presidential estate in the heart of New Delhi. The special guests had already started entering, amidst heavy security. The less important invitees were also starting to trickle in. After presenting their invitations and credentials at the door, they headed inside toward the lavish buffet to get something to eat before settling into their assigned seats.

At 12:15, Karry received a phone call from Mahendra confirming that about an hour earlier, Zalim Khan had entered the Jama Mosque, only to re-emerge a few minutes later, accompanied by a small group of associates. In his right hand, he clutched a black briefcase.

According to plan, Mahendra and Lachit were following him at a safe distance.

At 12:30, the children who were to be presented with the National Awards for Bravery arrived at the venue. It was a group of about twenty boys and girls of various ages, led by officers from the Ministry of Women and Child Development, and from the Youth Ministry.

At 12:45, Vikram called, saying that MP Lal Salaam would not be attending the event, as he had suddenly left his house in Delhi and flown to Kolkata "to take care of urgent family problems."

What a coward! Karry thought when he heard the news; *at least the Jihadis were willing to die for their mission! This guy wants to be around to take advantage of the power vacuum created by this attack. He is definitely the most dangerous opportunist.*

Karry instructed Vikram to head to the stadium and join the other members of the team.

Just after that, Lilavati called to confirm she and Nila had arranged a safe location for Mrs. Khan and her children in Colaba, Mumbai.

At 1:00 p.m., Jinnah's car pulled into the parking lot of the Talkatora Stadium and parked in the appropriate space. He was dressed in a long blue tunic when he emerged from the car, along with his cricket team; they all walked calmly toward the Stadium entrance. At the same moment, Zalim Khan, along with his associates, and dressed in a long black tunic, emerged from his SUV carrying the black briefcase. No one checked or stopped him. The listening device, implanted within the talisman, was not giving out any more info; no doubt the Mullah had objected to the 'heretical' Sufis and their superstitions, and had it removed at the mosque. The Vajra team was not concerned, however, for its work had been done.

The Vajra team within the security detail made sure these particular VIPs were not searched: this included Zalim and his ordinary, albeit large, briefcase. Jinnah and his cricket team, with their bats and balls, were ushered through as well. Zalim was a little perplexed by the seemingly negligent security, but thought it was due to his star stature that he was not checked. At the same time, Jinnah smiled, knowing he had bribed several important officials within the security team.

* * * *

After issuing perfunctory greetings to a few people, Khan went to sit in his assigned chair. Then, in plain view of everyone, he opened what appeared to be his briefcase. Secretly, he was enjoying the irony of the situation, as well as the rush of adrenaline and feeling of danger.

Keeping the device on his lap, he unlocked the case by rolling the number 786786786 on the nine mechanical levers which he double-checked before pressing the release button. The computer automatically switched on. He offered a prayer to Allah, thanking Him for the unique opportunity to become a holy martyr. *I will soon be in Paradise, with its eternal life of pleasure and happiness. All these infidels will soon be blown into hell to suffer for eternity, their just reward for refusing to surrender to the only true religion, Islam. Surely, blessed is the true believer, entrusted with such a task by all-mighty Allah Himself.*

He finished his silent prayer, then typed his user ID and password, and when prompted, chose the "set trigger clock" on the menu. He paused, calculating how long it would take for all these useless nonbelievers to finish their blabbering speeches. Finally, he set the clock for two hours and gave the "enter" command. The numbers started running backwards: 1:59:59...1:59:58...1:59:57. The countdown had begun. He closed the briefcase, locked the levers again, and smiled. Two hours till Paradise.

At 1:15, Karry's own guru, Gokarnath Swami, arrived and was offered an elevated seat of honor, a *vyasasan*, on the dais. Karry and the Swami exchanged smiles from a distance. A few minutes later, the Prime Minister, the President, and their assistants, reached the venue, and the program officially began.

Khan smirked to himself as the national anthem began to play. *Last time I will have to hear this bloody song.* He forced himself to clap as the Master of Ceremonies, presidential secretary, Mohini Jhadav, gave the welcome speech.

"Her Excellency the President of India, our honorable Prime Minister, our special guest Guru Gokarnath Swamiji, and other distinguished guests, thank you for gracing this occasion and making our event a success.

"I also want to thank our panel of judges, led by the former Director General of Police, Kranti Negi, and our special guests of honor, Li Wang, cultural attaché to the Chinese Embassy in

Delhi, his good wife, Hangaku Murayama, and daughter, Masako.

"It is my good fortune to welcome you all to this special event, the National Bravery Awards, to celebrate the younger generations of our glorious nation."

Everyone clapped enthusiastically.

"Now I would like to ask our special guest, Guru Gokarnath Swamiji, to say a few words."

The Swami, sitting cross-legged on the *vyasasana,* smiled graciously and waited for the microphone to be brought to him. Then he began his speech by melodiously chanting a few Sanskrit verses.

"Om sahana bhavatu, saha nau bhunaktu, saha viryam karavahai, tejasvi navadhitamastu ma vidvishavahai. Om Shanti...Shanti... Shanti....

"May we be united. May we learn together. May we walk bravely together and be enlightened together. May we never be divided by quarrel or selfishness. Let there be peace...peace...peace...."

His eyes closed, the Swami paused for a moment. Then he opened his eyes and serenely addressed the crowd.

"A true *yogi* automatically acts for the benefit of others, as it is said, *para upakara,* and is ready to sacrifice himself for the benefit of others. Selflessly working for the benefit of all is also called *Dharma,* the eternal duty of all living entities, as shown by the example of innumerable great personalities in the history of our ancient nation, India, also called *Bharata Varsha* or Hindustan. These children here have shown by their personal deeds that they have instinctively understood the real meaning and purpose of *yoga*. They did not see any difference or separation between themselves and the others they saved with a brave act of self-sacrifice. Indeed, they are great souls, and I salute them as true *yogis*. They are the real heroes of *Bharat* and humanity at large. *Hare Krishna Hare Krishna, Krishna Krishna Hare Hare. Hare Rama Hare Rama, Rama Rama Hare Hare.*" Thus, with this final *maha mantra,* the Swami concluded his short speech.

The crowd was delighted. Zalim Khan looked around, smiling like a clown, all the while mentally envisioning blowing everyone up. Observers assumed the 'Bollywood Lion' liked the speech. The Swami smiled at the children, returned Khan's smile and humbly bowed his head with folded hands as the crowd erupted with sincere applause. Caught off guard, Zalim gave a sheepish grin and joined them once again.

"The Honorable President and our esteemed special guest will now present the awards to the children," Mohini Jhadav said, as soon as the room was once again quiet.

The first boy climbed up onto the dais and the Master of Ceremonies introduced him

"This brave child, Jinji Onge, comes from a village near Adi Basera, Port Blair, and he is a member of the largest native Jarawa tribe there. When the frightful tsunami hit the islands for the second time in known history, as the only survivor of his family, Jinji saved himself by clutching onto a tree. When the wave had passed, he swam in the flood waters until he found a dry place, then tied together some wood for an emergency raft and paddled back to his devastated and flooded village to search for survivors. In this way, he found and rescued fifteen people, both children and adults, who otherwise would have died. He worked tirelessly until dark, ferrying them to safe grounds and assisting them to the best of his abilities until the rescuers arrived."

This was followed by huge applause.

The Swami affectionately took Jinji's hand, while the President pinned the Medal of Honor on the boy's chest. She then presented his award for bravery, and the prize money cheque, and finally, shook his hand. Beaming proudly, the young boy offered his respects by bowing his head and returned to his seat.

Jhadav introduced the next child; a girl from Kashmir named Farida Wani. "Last year, Farida stepped forward and helped the Indian military locate the hideout of a terrorist group in the thick forests of Kashmir. Their bloody attack on an army base had resulted in the deaths of ten people, including soldiers, women, and children, and the serious injuries of five others."

The crowd applauded again.

Zalim Khan, who had remained quiet, albeit stone-faced during the speeches, was suddenly filled with rage. *These stupid fanatics are really crossing the line with their offensive blabbering. A foolish and rebellious girl betrayed her own Muslim community and challenged her own parents and relatives to cause the killing of the good and faithful Jihadis! This is intolerable. I almost feel like detonating the bomb now, but no, I can't do it before giving my message to the world.* Zalim uncomfortably twisted around in his chair, clutching the briefcase. He looked at his companions, two rows of seats away, who were also scoffing and scowling, and then looked at his watch; less than one hour remaining. A smile came back to his face. Farida Wani received her medal, prize money and award certificate, offered *pranams* to the crowd and walked down from the dais, while the next child was announced by the Master of Ceremonies. The award ceremony continued.

Zalim was getting super annoyed and impatient with all the rhetoric about *stupid children saving useless lives.* Didn't they understand that life only has value when it is sacrificed to the order of Allah? He looked at his watch again: only twenty minutes left on the countdown clock. Suddenly he realized it was time for his own speech. The moment for which he had been born and had waited for!

The Bollywood star suddenly stood up and gestured to the Master of Ceremonies. She hesitated for a few seconds, and then announced that famous movie star Zalim Khan wanted to address the audience. It was not part of the plan, but if the most famous Bollywood actor wanted to speak, how could she object?

Zalim's face reflected a dark smile as he walked to the microphone. He tried to bring the grace of a Lion, but his butt was still hurting, and so he moved with a slight limp, which he hated. This was the moment he'd been waiting for; the moment that would give glory to his entire life and people.

The audience buzzed with speculation. From his seat in the second row, Jinnah motioned to his fake cricket team and they too walked to the dais. A restless murmur went through the crowd. Was the much beloved movie superstar going to present some wonderful surprise for their entertainment?

Zalim's companions from the mosque also rose from their seats and approached the dais and positioned themselves to the left of the dignitaries. At the same time, Jai and Karry quietly got up and approached Balaram. The other members of the Vajra team, Tejinder,

Vikram, Ganesh, Lachit, Mahendra and Ranil, moved into position behind the screen, wearing their balaclavas. Each one of them had been assigned a target to be felled at the proper time. Balaram approached the officer-in-charge of security detail and reaffirmed that it was now time to follow his command. He quickly explained the situation and the police snipers discreetly moved into position.

Zalim Khan grabbed the microphone and addressed the audience.

"Assembled guests, witnesses to history, I also have a great gift, not just for these youngsters, but for the leaders of the Indian Government, for the people of this nation, and for the people of the entire world!" growled the Lion lustily.

Despite his odd choice of words, some people from the crowd applauded, believing this sudden turn of events to be some Bollywood stunt. The media people rushed up to the dais to record the speech. This promised to be a good scoop.

Suddenly, the eleven members of the fake cricket team unscrewed their bats and pulled out their assault rifles. The crowd immediately fell silent. What was going on? What kind of prank was this?

"It is a gift that I have prepared for all of you, with the help of my good friend MP Lal Salaam." Zalim waited for Lal Salaam to stand up and be counted and come to the podium to share his glory, but he did not see him.

The first hint of doubt crept into his mind. *That Commie bastard! He must have fled somewhere and plans to pick up the pieces in the aftermath. No matter, I can do this alone. And my Muslim brothers have long ago developed a plan to take out the Communists, all avowed unbelievers, and thus, kaffirs. No matter; this is my hour; my moment of glory!*

"Power! What is true power? This, my foolish friends, is power! This, in my hands, is a nuclear bomb." Khan triumphantly held the closed briefcase high up for everyone to see. A shiver ran through the crowd, and the journalists froze. An Hiroshima moment! The dignitaries on the dais shifted in their chairs. Only the Swami and the brave boys and girls looked unperturbed.

Balaram motioned to the head of the security detail to keep his men quiet; they needed Zalim to expose himself and the plot completely before he and his accomplices could be taken out. The man nodded and signaled to the police snipers to hold their fire.

"This is not a joke. We will all die in fifteen minutes. Yes! It is a mini nuclear device So what? Everything within a radius of one kilometer will be vaporized, and everyone will be affected by it, so there's no use running away." Zalim jeered at the plight of the audience who were trying to get up from their seats and attempting to run. As the significance of his words settled in, everyone fell back into their seats terrified and confused. Some took shelter in prayer, and others hugged their neighbors in fear.

Each of Zalim's companions from the mosque moved forward to stand behind a dignitary; in their hands were machetes, which they placed at the necks of their victims, ready to behead them in the standard ISIS Daesh style.

The Bollywood actor smiled. Even he knew this was his best role yet.

"No one move now. If anyone moves, these people will be the first to die, and in a painfully graphic and horrible way."

Everyone froze. He had their attention.

He began his long lecture. "Listen very closely to what I am saying; these are the last moments of your lives. They are the last minutes of my life, too, but there is a big difference between you and me. You are probably thinking I am a suicide bomber, but you are very wrong. I am a holy warrior, a sacred martyr, acting in the name of God.

"My companions and I are going to Paradise, while you are all going to hell. Unless, of course, you immediately repent and subject yourselves to the one true God, Allah, to the supreme message of the Quran, and to the only true last Prophet Mohammed, may he always be blessed and may peace be upon him."

He paused to judge the audience reaction; it was his birth trait as an actor. He smiled broadly, trying to seduce his audience. "Let me know now, who all are ready to convert and die to reach Paradise. It's your last chance. Raise your hands so that I can clearly see you. I will read the *Kalima* for your conversion, and you can repeat if after me."

When he saw no hands raised, he shouted in anger, "You *Kafirs* all deserve death and hell!"

Comprehension and horror started to dawn on the dignitaries and the others in the stadium.

Suddenly, a well-dressed Muslim man, wearing a Nehru cap, stood up; it was the Vice President of India. "Zalim, listen please! I speak to you as a brother, a fellow Muslim. How can you be sure this is the will of Allah? I know you do not agree, but killing anyone like this—especially fellow Muslims—is just plain wrong, it is *takfiri*. It is by the will of Allah there are many people of faith in this audience. Clearly you must desist from this transgression. You cannot justify the act of killing us in the name of our own faith. Surely this is against the spirit of Islam!" pleaded the VP.

An expression of astonished wonder appeared on Zalim's face. "Respected Elder, pray, open your eyes to this moment of glory. My Muslim brothers and sisters, hear me! I am your most welcome friend and your very key to Paradise itself! Can you not see I am gifting you with that most precious gift of all? This is an instant ticket to Paradise. Soon you will be in the gardens of heaven, rejoicing in the company of the pure and faithful. I salute your great and good fortune."

He looked at them, wide-eyed, in a frenzied jubilance. "Rejoice, O ye faithful, for Allah, God Himself, awaits you!" He suddenly looked up, his eyes rolling back in ecstasy.

As agreed earlier, Zalim's accomplices kept a professional and icy focus on their victims and did not become swept up in his 'devotions'. There would be time for such and more, once they had arrived in Paradise.

Among the journalists, there was a low but obvious buzz of panic. Many vowed that if they got through this alive, they were changing their professions.

The head of security glanced over at Balaram, alarmed and anxious. Balaram just shook his head and offered the smallest hint of a smile. The officer-in-charge looked at him as if he had gone mad, but remained still; orders are orders, and you can't disobey a senior officer.

The eleven 'fake cricketers' suddenly pointed their weapons at the helpless crowd.

"There is nothing you can do," Zalim commanded calmly. "Anyone moves, shoot them. At the smallest movement from security, we will slit the throats of the President, Prime Minister and all the others...and the bomb will explode anyway." He chuckled cynically. "Just ten minutes only. You have no time to dispose of it safely; the only thing you can do now is hear my words of wisdom. Amongst all of us, I alone shall stand in the presence of Allah, it's guaranteed!"

* * * *

From the Jains' family home in Colaba, Mumbai, a faint and speechless Mrs. Khan sat watching her husband's horrendous actions on the TV. Viewers throughout India and around the world, who had tuned in for the live ceremony, were similarly stunned by the magnitude of the threat and the horror of the situation. Within seconds, TV and Radio channels began screaming headlines: "Terror in Delhi." The breaking news interrupted all scheduled programming.

Zalim's rant continued. "Some of you may be wondering why a successful movie star with my money and fame would suddenly become a dedicated martyr. Well, I am going to tell you all; listen carefully.

"For years, I lived uselessly and without purpose, enjoying petty pleasures and rejecting the call of the one and only true religion. Then, by the merciful blessing of our venerable Mullah Omar Angrez, I was awakened from that slumber of ignorance and complacency. I have seen the truth. We must all surrender to Allah and do his bidding alone, without any other consideration. The reward is eternal happiness in Paradise! We must destroy the evil idols and either convert or destroy the idolaters. There is no place for nonsensical delusions like secularism or patriotism or nationalism. Only Allah is worthy of being worshiped, and all other forms of worship must be stopped by any means.

"All true Muslims must immediately stop worshiping the false goddesses, like 'Mother India' and 'Mother Earth'. The worship of the tombs of those so-called dead Sufi saints, who are in fact *kafirs*, must be immediately stopped, and their tombs destroyed. It is not prescribed in the *Koran* or the *Hadith*. The Sufi dancing, and singing, in the form of Qawwali, is abhorrent to Allah. Sufism is in fact a cancer on Islam; the same goes for the deviant Shias. Root them out now and forever!

"Only Allah is great; and only Allah must be praised, and no one else; for even his prophet, though appreciated, is not to be praised!"

Zalim stared around the room, his eyes shimmering feverishly. The audience sat frozen in their seats, terrified, as he continued his blustering.

"It is time the true believers took control of the world as is proper and just. Enough with living on the alms or salary of the *kafir*, or playing the clown to amuse them. Once India belonged to us, before the British came in and took it away from our hands. It is now time to take it back; it's non-negotiable.

"Our true brothers in Pakistan are ready to support us and protect the resurgence of the ancient Kalifates. The sufferings of the Kashmiri and Palestine people will come to an end instantly, and the divine Shariah law will bring peace, order, and true faith to the entire region. Once Greater Pakistan, the land of the Pure, is established here in India, it will lead the way for all the other nations. Faithful Muslims have already positioned themselves for many years, waiting only for this blessed moment. Now is not the time to fear. It's a time to rejoice, for Allah's plan is perfect!"

He leaned his head back, his eyes wild and yelled, "*Allahu-Akbar! Allahu Akbar! Ash-hadu alla ilaha ill-Allah, Ash-hadu anna Muhammad-ar-Rasoolullah Hayya 'ala-ssalah. Hayya 'alal-falah, Allahu Akbar, Allahu Akbar, La ilaha ill-Allah.*"

In India and around the world, people sat transfixed in front of their televisions and computer screens, hearing the message of a super terrorist. In Rawalpindi, Lieutenant General Aurangzeb sat glued to his TV screen. The Indian military went on Red Alert, the highest level of alarm intended for imminent war-like situations. Foreign embassies erupted in chaos and the Delhi telephone exchange network overloaded and collapsed.

Emergency lines switched on and the National Disaster Management sent out directives to its action squads. All the guards in the Presidential estate rushed toward the Talkatora Indoor Stadium, but no one knew what to do once there.

The stadium security detail remained in position, waiting for a command that wasn't coming. Balaram smiled again and discreetly motioned to his watch. The security officers seemed puzzled, and then they looked at their own watches and understood. The time set for the explosion had passed, and nothing had happened.

Zalim Khan, in his madness, had not yet noticed. He was too worked-up in his glorious speech. "So you ask me," he continued, "is it right that Muslim brothers and sisters will die in this explosion?" His face twisted viciously. "I will tell you now that secular Indian Muslims have become lethargic and complacent, wasting time in enjoying and making friends with the non-believers, forgetting their duty and their pride, and betraying their cause.

"In the eyes of Allah, they are not true Muslims, but merely false leaders practising 'taghut', and they deserve to die. Now that's the real answer to you fake Muslim bastards! If you were true Muslims you would have joined in my calls to prayer. You would have rejoiced at the news of your soon-to-come ascension into Paradise." The actor looked around triumphantly, for the bomb would go off at any moment. He met the eyes of his companions and they all smiled.

"You might want to ask me whether I have any compassion or love for my wife and children," he continued. "I tell you now that he who does not love Allah more than his parents, what to speak of children and wife, is not worthy of being considered a true Muslim. Moreover, I am tired of a wife who refuses to surrender completely to the orders of Allah. I don't know how many times I caught that stupid cow murmuring Hindu mantras!" His face fumed at the betrayal.

In front of the TV in the Mumbai house, Mrs. Khan became pale, passed her palm across her forehead and lost consciousness, slipping down from the chair. Her friends immediately attended to her. Fortunately, her children were playing in another room, closely watched by Priti and Dhiraj.

Lieutenant General Aurangzeb watched impatiently, checking the clock on the desk, wondering why the clown had not yet set off the bomb. Didn't Zalim know the mission could be aborted by the Indian Secret service at any time? He yelled out, "Come on Zalim, act fast and finish them off! Stop this stupid annoying speech!"

Mullah Omar, on the other hand, watched the TV with an amused smile, clapping at his protégé. This long speech was not part of the plan, but was no surprise, given Zalim's huge ego.

The crazed actor continued, forgetting the time. "When the Martyr meets his Maker, all his sins are forgiven from the first gush of blood. He is exempted from the torments of the grave; he sees his place in Paradise and marries seventy-two dark-eyed virgins. He is a heavenly advocate for seventy members of his family. On his head is placed a crown of honor, one stone of which is worth more than all there is in this world."

"You might want to ask me if I have no gratitude for the people who have befriended and supported me in the past." He smiled wickedly. "You think that because I was born in a slum and made my way up to the highest levels of Bollywood royalty, I should be grateful to all those who gave me the crumbs off their tables." The Lion roared at the memory of humiliation he had felt in accepting help from non-believers. "I tell you now they had no right to possess the wealth and resources of which they shared only a few drops. Only the true believers can rightfully possess the wealth of the world and enjoy it to please Allah. So what they 'shared' with me was already mine! They were actually giving to me that which is already mine in the service of Allah!'"

It is time, thought Zalim, so he stopped speaking, closed his eyes, raised his hands like a prophet, and waited for the blast to occur. Everybody else was frozen. Each second seemed to stretch into an eternity.

Slowly, the actor seemed to realize that something was wrong. He opened his eyes and looked at his watch, shook it, as if to check whether it was working or not. *It should have exploded more than ten minutes ago! What's wrong with this stupid North Korean piece of shit!?* He rolled his eyes in annoyance and helplessness for he never thought that it would come to this; he hadn't planned for this situation, and didn't know what to do next.

* * * *

From that moment, everything shifted to lightning speed. Zalim saw Balaram signaling to the Officer in charge of security, and quickly turned to his henchmen, screaming, "Kill them all!" But the initiative was with the police. Before the terrorists had time to pull their triggers or slice the necks of their hostages, the Vajra team, backed up by police snipers, took each of them down. Those terrorists who had a chance to pull the trigger did too late, and their bullets hit the ground and ceiling, sending debris flying, hitting a few people with non-lethal results.

The shots seemed to break the spell. Chaos erupted all around, with people screaming and trying to escape from the huge hall.

The guards of the Presidential estate and the action squads of the National Disaster Management barged in to contain the crowd. Fortunately, there were only a few hundred people, and order was soon re-established.

In the meantime, the President's bodyguards shot Zalim as he tried to attack Swami Gokarnath with the useless briefcase. He was once again hit in the buttocks—this time a direct hit to the right one—as well as several shots to his legs. Now, with both his kneecaps shattered, he lay on the floor, bloody and moaning. All the fake cricketers were down, lying in thick pools of blood. Jinnah, who had joined Zalim on the dais at the time of the shooting, also lay seriously wounded on the floor. The grenades, he had never had a chance to throw, were safely out of his reach.

Still wearing his balaclava, Lachit stepped forward and retrieved the briefcase from the floor. Putting it on the table where the dignitaries were still sitting, he quickly opened it by rolling the levers in place. Everyone watched, wide-eyed with fear, and the crowd threatened to erupt again.

Balaram intervened. Grabbing the microphone, he explained that the device had been deactivated the day before and there was no threat. They had allowed Zalim to move forward with his plan so they could capture all the key players, and that the attack was masterminded by Pakistan's secret intelligence services, ISI. Everyone nodded in a big sigh of relief. The presidential guard's safely removed all the guns and grenades.

The tension immediately broke. Slowly, the President started to clap her hands, and was soon followed by the other dignitaries and the rest of the guests. Within seconds, the entire stadium had exploded into applause and cheering, creating a tangible wave of relief.

When the applause finally died down, Lachit opened the case to reveal the gun-type nuclear device. The conventional chemical explosion, which was meant to be a detonator, had taken place at the time set by Zalim Khan, but it had been contained within the case. Lachit remembered the case moving violently, but Zalim, in his indulgence, had failed to see it. During the conventional chemical explosion, one clay ball smashed into the other clay ball, crumbling into pieces. Had it been the fissile material, none of them would have been alive. All the TV cameras zoomed in on the device, as Lachit showed the crumbled pieces in his hand.

The Treasure of the Pandavas

The ovation began again and continued for several minutes. Lachit finally bowed and managed to slip away without further fanfare. The rest of the Vajra Team quickly retreated and moved out. Anxious to keep their anonymity for the sake of future missions, they melted into the woodwork and were gone.

In the privacy of his office, Lieutenant General Aurangzeb, Director General of ISI, felt a strong pain in his groin, and growing fast. It had come on suddenly, from nowhere, and he bit his lip and vomited violently, soiling his immaculate uniform with his hastily eaten lunch. The sense of loss and failure was too much. He almost blamed Allah, but checked himself at the last moment, for he did not want to go to hell for blasphemy. Meanwhile, Major Babar was dismayed: how could those Indian *Bania*s unearth his superbly laid out plan, and why did Allah not help them?

In Mumbai, Zalim's wife had regained consciousness and was in Lilavati's arms, sobbing uncontrollably. The TV was switched off and her children had joined her in the room, frightened and confused. Their mother embraced them, speechless.

Lilavati did what she could, wiping the woman's tears and comforting the children. Nila joined in, and Mrs. Khan seemed to find strength from the solidarity of her new sisters. Most importantly, she and her children were safe. When the angry mobs assembled at the Khan's residence to seek revenge, they were especially unhappy to find out no one was there to kill. Instead, they stoned the walls of the opulent house, shattering its windows, ransacking it, and taking away whatever valuables could be found. Later, the house was set on fire.

In Kolkata, the home of Parliamentary member, Lal Salaam, was attacked by an angry mob and burned to the ground. The Salaams were not as lucky as the Khans. The crowd trapped the MP, blocking his escape, and he and his entire family perished in the fire. Riots broke out in several cities across India, and many offices of the Indian Communist Party were broken into, ransacked, and even burned in some cases. Mosques were also attacked, and in turn, bands of Muslim fanatics raided the commercial areas and attacked temples and churches in retaliation. Hundreds of people died, and thousands more were injured. It was madness all around. The Prime Minister had to quickly deploy the army to save the situation.

All over the world, various Heads of State, ambassadors and diplomats frantically communicated on secure lines.

The President of the United States, the Presidents of Russia and China, and the President of the European Parliament, as well as other world leaders, all demanded an explanation from Pakistan.

After a few hours, the Pakistani Government issued a very brief press release, declaring Pakistan had been wrongfully accused, and the entire event was a trick organized by anti-Islamic and anti-Pakistani forces who wanted to discredit their innocent religion and country.

The media was in a frenzy. Newspapers and magazines sold out all their special editions. The internet was overloaded with people logging-in to check twitter, read blogs and participate in chat room discussions. Then came the announcement that similar nuclear devices had been found and neutralized in the United States and the European Union. However, the bombs destined for China, Russia and Israel had not yet been located.

* * * *

The morning after E-day, all the Vajra Team members assembled in the Delhi safehouse for a debriefing. They, along with Karry and Balaram, recounted the days leading up to and including the attack, in exact detail.

They were interrupted by a knock at the door. At Balaram's invitation, Uttam Chaudhary, who was in charge of this particular safehouse, hurried into the room, a terrified look on his face.

"Sir, I think you all should see this," he said, in a faint voice. He motioned to the TV set on the opposite wall, and Karry clicked the remote. What they saw sent a chill up their spines.

All the channels were filled with the same horrible news: the nuclear bomb destined for Israel had been successfully detonated, pulverizing the city of Tel Aviv and bringing death and destruction to the relatively small nation. International military experts who had examined the satellite video footage established that the bomb had been fired from Gaza, apparently from a hidden Iranian-made mobile missile launcher.

Horrified journalists gave sparse and emotional comments, repeating the frightening news and calling the new disaster the worse terrorist attack in human history.

The Vajra Team members sat frozen, watching as the scanty footage of the explosion was played again and again, with footage of reactions throughout the world. It seemed the Islamic extremists were celebrating in the streets. Jihadis brandished their Kalashnikovs in one hand and Korans in the other, shouting and cheering the destruction of Israel.

At about 6:00 p.m., there was more shocking news. Russia and China had declared a state of emergency, in view of the attack on Tel Aviv. Martial law was declared, as the police and military enforced new drastic measures of total control. All forms of Islamic expression were outlawed, and mosques and Islamic clerics were put under strict surveillance. Movement of Muslims across those countries was stopped indefinitely. Extensive searches were immediately carried out by the armed forces of both countries, deploying all contingents. Unfortunately, innocent Muslims were punished for the acts of the few fundamentalists. By 10:00 a.m. the next morning, the remaining two bombs had been found and deactivated: one in a Moscow mosque where it had just arrived from Chechnya, and the other one in the Xinjiang province. It had been brought in by the Uyghurs and was headed for Beijing.

Europeans urged the EU to take drastic steps along the lines of what Russia and China had done, and not be content with symbolic *burqa* or *minaret* bans. It looked as if humanity was being put to a test.

While the Security Council of the United Nations sat in an emergency meeting, riots started in various countries spearheaded by Islamic fundamentalists who considered this dramatic turn of events to be the actual signal for a global holy war, the *Al-Malhama Al-Kubra*, especially after their successful attack on Israel. The fierce Jihadi platoons were met by equally fierce opponents from all sides. The Police and army had to intervene en masse to bring back a semblance of peace and order. Several countries called national emergency meetings, and desperately considered adopting the same drastic measures taken by Russia and China. Islamic State leaders in hiding released a statement taking credit for the nuclear attack on Israel and promised more to come. They encouraged their followers to take the law into their own hands and not allow any restrictions by their host countries.

* * * *

Zalim Khan underwent neurosurgery for the severe head injury he sustained at the Talkatora. A few days later, he woke up from his brief coma to see a beautiful woman standing in front of him. Smiling lustfully, he mumbled something about all the female *houris* in paradise who wanted to have sex with him. He wondered why the woman was not smiling back.

As his vision cleared, his face twisted in horror. For the woman was no *houri*, but a uniformed policewoman, flanked by armed guards. "What have I done?" he screamed, "O merciful Allah!"

He sunk into a deep state of depression. Now and then he exploded into terrible rages, and the doctors needed to keep him restrained and sedated so as not to hurt himself or others. Sometimes, he addressed a doctor, who was dressed in a white uniform, as "Almighty God," and asked why he had failed him, and where he had committed any wrong.

The Treasure of the Pandavas

Arunmathi was a so-called peace activist, known more for her political grandstanding than any real peace work. Not surprisingly, she jumped to the defense of the Bollywood Lion. Her spin: "The Vajra team has openly admitted to the setup. If there had been a real threat, they would have and should have taken care of it before any public drama took place. But no! They set the poor man up. There is evidence he was baited into participating in an 'anti-terror drill' organized by the office of the Indian Presidency itself. We have seen this happen with the peace-loving people. The police constantly kill their own, and then in turn, blame those activists struggling for freedom and democracy in Kashmir, Palestine and elsewhere. Now look at this Zalim Khan incident. As we all know, using hapless members of a minority community has long been a trick of the Indian State. Poor Zalim is just a beloved actor who tried to serve his people at the bidding of the government. And now they've framed him for terrorism. There is no real proof against him. Time will show he is an innocent and well-intended man and he is being framed."

Watching Ms. Arunmathi refer to Zalim's attempted martyrdom as an act of servitude to the Indian government, drove him to outrageous depths of rage. He felt like raping her repeatedly, and then beheading her over and over again for her insolence. How dare the bitch demean his acts of valor!

The doctors increased his doses of medication, and the Bollywood Lion slowly slipped into a state of oblivion where he could escape from his unpleasant reality. He wore a childish smile, as if he had found his paradise. At other times he cried and moaned in the night, tormented by the inner demons in the hell of his own making.

People often heard him repeatedly yelling, but to no one in particular.

"I am Khan! Am I a terrorist?" He would laugh hysterically and yell, "No, I am Khan and I am a martyr! I am a *shaheed* and I am ready for Paradise!"

One night, he managed to extricate himself from his restraints. He could hear voices all around, calling him to wake up and come to them. As he opened his eyes, he found himself standing on the top edge of a mountain, and in front of him was a white cloud floating in the distance, on which scantily clad women, whose beauty was beyond description, raised their hands, calling out his name for sexual union. Zalim's face lit up like a lusty young *jihadi* in anticipation of the *houris*; paradise was in sight and he had to but leap to reach the white cloud. Jump he did—out the hospital window which was open—falling six stories to the ground below. No one could stop the Bollywood Lion in life and no one could stop him in death. He fell straight down like a stone and was killed upon impact.

It was the final act in the tragic life of Zalim Khan, the Bollywood Lion. Rather than a roar, he had gone out with a whimper. And rather than an admired hero, he died mourned by few and despised by many. The *Jihadis* had lost one more battle, but the war was not over for them yet.

Chapter 20 - The Shankara Hills

In Port Blair, in the Andaman Islands, two thousand kilometers far away from mainland India, Professor Katju sat comfortably with a whiskey in hand, and fried salted fish on his plate. Jawahar was a self-hating Hindu and a self-serving person. As part of his DNA, every bad thing that happened he always blamed on the Hindus; even if they were the victims and not the perpetrators.

He had been watching the live TV broadcast of the explosion-day events, and was flabbergasted when that Bollywood clown suddenly decided to publicly name Mullah Omar and Lal Salaam. Two important members of SEPS, compromised and sure to be eliminated! Katju was terrified the authorities would connect them to him. Although he'd had no actual knowledge of the terrorist plan, he had, nevertheless, stationed himself far away from Delhi on the advice of the Mullah.

Struggling to come to terms with the unexpected turn of events, he arranged a brief consultation with Lord Dyer, and a new cunning plan was hatched.

On the 23rd of April, he returned to Delhi, and backed by the financial and political resources of SEPS, sent around a press release via the friendly and sympathetic news anchors.

In the release, he accused the Englishwoman, Diana Warwick, and the American, William Johnson, of being Zionist agents. He alleged they had come to India to mount a hate campaign against Muslims, which was to culminate in multiple bomb attacks in densely populated areas of Indian-Muslim communities. Their aim, the release stated, was to exact revenge against the Jihadis who had targeted Israel, and to destabilize India's religious harmony.

This 'news' was regurgitated everywhere, and within a few hours, it dominated the Indian airwaves. Priti and Dhiraj were outraged. They called Balaram and flew in to Delhi to meet with him, along with Karry and Jai.

"We need to do something to help Diana and Bill," said Jai, worried not only for the safety of his new friends, but also for the repercussions of such a smear campaign. It was bound to create confusion and jeopardize their true quest.

"We certainly will," replied Karry seriously, after which he began to chalk out a strategy with the owners of WIN TV, briefing them about the story of the Pandavas' treasure and Arthur Warwick.

By the early hours of April 24th, Balaram and Priti prepared and sent out their own press releases, and WIN TV had announced exclusive interviews with the core Vajra team members: "Meet the Heroes Who Saved India!"

The Team members were interviewed, but their identities were protected by blurring their faces and distorting their voices. All the relevant details of the mission were disclosed without compromising the Vajra team's safety and security. Jai also described his experience with Diana and Bill, explaining how they were following the historic trail of Diana's ancestor, Arthur, checking out where he had gone and how he spent his life as a Hindu monk upholding *Dharma*, and eventually attaining *Samadhi*. They also discussed the existence of the rogue organization which was trying to stop them. For all intents and purposes, SEPS was outed, and its centuries-old secrecy destroyed. WIN made sure not to disclose the names of the members of SEPS, to keep the surprise element intact and make it easier to catch them red-handed.

Diana's hunt became official as the Indian President and Prime Minster approved the mission, and Jai and Masako prepared to join them in Srinagar, Kashmir.

Professor Cariappa flew in from Bengaluru and gave extensive interviews to any journalists who were willing to listen. And there were many.

Professor Jawahar Katju had not realized that Warwick and Buford had made such strong alliances in India. When the couple effectively retaliated against his smear campaign, the pressure became too great. He stopped answering the phone and started drinking more heavily than ever. Some of his stooges, seeing his plight, offered him *hafeem* or opium. It gave him momentary escape from his misery, and his boys a chance to raid his stash of booze and cash.

WIN TV continued relentlessly and fearlessly with its counter-campaign, getting official support from Balaram as the highest ranking officer of IFA.

On the 26th of April, the UN Security Council called for an international conference on religion and democracy. In the meantime, Interpol issued an international arrest warrant for Mullah Omar Angrez, but the Mullah was already in a safe house in Karachi, Pakistan under ISI protection.

The Himalayan Mountain Range separates the Indian subcontinent from the Tibetan Plateau, and is home to the world's highest peaks, which include Mount Everest and K2. The main Himalayan range runs west to east, from the Indus River Valley to the Brahmaputra River Valley, forming an arc 2,400 kilometers long, which varies in width from 400 kilometers in the western Kashmir-Xinjiang region, to 150 kilometers in the eastern Tibet-Arunachal Pradesh region. Some of the world's major river systems arise from the Himalayas, and their combined drainage basin is home to some three billion people in eighteen countries: literally half the world's population. The Himalayas have profoundly shaped the cultures of South Asia; many Himalayan peaks are sacred in Hinduism, Buddhism, Jainism and Sikhism. The range has many peaks and valleys, and one such valley is in Kashmir, where the Shankaracharya Hill stood.

On April 9th, Jai left Diana and Bill in Srinagar, but they were not alone. They had been entrusted to the care of the local army veteran, who was a JCO in Karry's unit, when he served in the Army. Subedar Rasul Hangal lived on the bank of the famous Lake Dal. Diana and Bill kept a low profile; Katju was surely on their trail and was the last person they wanted to see as they embarked on the final leg of their quest.

Rasul was a true seeker of grace. A 'liberal' Sufi Muslim. He would often say, "Religion is an individual personal matter based on one's direct relationship and experience with God, a merciful and loving Father who equally loves all his children. This all-loving God has innumerable names by which He can be glorified and prayed to."

He liked to tell fascinating stories about the Sufi saints whom he venerated, and had many friends among the Hindus, openly saying he preferred their association than the bigotry and aggressiveness of the radical Islamists. He believed that among the three sects of Islam, the Sufi's gentle and peaceful philosophy resonated more with certain aspects of Hinduism.

Rasul held a deep conviction toward 'sacred nationalism'. For him, there could be no separation of his love and devotion to Allah, from his love for Mother India. He felt it was Allah's will he'd been gifted with not only birth, but with a beloved birthplace as well. Allah was the Father, and India, the Mother.

Rasul also believed in freedom of expression, and pluralism, as a healthy function of society. From his last name, 'Hangal', he came to know his forefathers were once Hindu. He was deeply saddened by the turmoil causing so much destruction and suffering in his home region of Kashmir. He was really worried about the looming future he could foresee for his people. Yet he had immense hope Allah would one day correct the situation for everyone. For him, Allah was the same as Shiva, Rama, Krishna, the Buddha or Yahweh.

At Jai's request, Rasul selected from his fleet a very large, strong boat. When Jai arrived with Diana and Bill, they drove the special valley vehicle onto the boat, where Rasul positioned their vehicle in the middle of the hull, and quickly built a temporary room around it, completely hiding it from view. He also had the boat thoroughly cleaned and freshly painted. The room had a skylight, which could be opened, allowing plenty of space for the fresh air to come in.

On Monday, April 10th, they moved into their temporary home. "Kashmir really seems a paradise on earth," commented Bill, his gaze lost in the majestic misty mountains, as the sky began to fade in the last rays of the afternoon sun.

Rasul sighed. "Indeed. Srinagar literally means 'the City of Lakshmi'. Lakshmi is the goddess of beauty and prosperity. But in the last few centuries, and especially since the partition of India in 1947, this beautiful and fertile valley has seen much horror, violence and suffering, especially with the unnecessary interference of Pakistan. In this 'Paradise', it is easy to find oneself in 'Hell'. Unfortuantely, China has teamed up with Pakistan and creating trouble for us in Ladhak, by grabbing our historical lands." He remained silent for a few minutes. Then turned to Bill and Diana and started to speak about the history of his homeland.

"My forefathers, who were Kashmiri Hindus, first began to flee the valley in the time of Sultan Sikandar Butshikan, the seventh Muslim ruler of Kashmir, who reigned from 1389 to 1413. He killed several thousand Hindus and forced more to convert or choose exile, all the while destroying hundreds of Hindu and Buddhist temples and monasteries, and converting many of them into mosques. Once again, in the late-1980s, the Jihadis started another wave of violence, driving out the remaining Hindus from their ancestral homes, by killing, ransacking and other intimidation tactics. The total scale of this ethnic cleansing is staggering. We want all Kashmiris to live as brothers in one united India."

Rasul's sad expression made him look much older.

Bill looked sadly at the darkening mountains. "I think I understand India much better now…" he paused in reflection for a moment, "and what I've learned has helped me to understand the world better, as well. Perhaps one day soon, sanity will return to this valley. I pray for such a day."

He turned and smiled. "And I believe there is still hope. Now please tell us about Shankar Acharya and Kashyapa Muni."

"Certainly, my friend. Jagad Guru Adi Shankara was here. He came to rest in Srinagar on this very hill before returning to Badri, where he finally left his body and where his *samadhi*, his burial place, is at present. On Gopadri Hill, now also called Shankaracharya Hill, there is still a temple dedicated to him."

Rasul continued. "The very name of Kashmir comes from our great and famous ancestor, Kashyapa Muni; he too meditated on that Hill."

They had a long and healthy discussion on many similar aspects between Kashmir and

Hinduism. No one noticed the time until Diana began to yawn uncontrollably, at which point they called it a day. At the request of Diana, Rasul promised to take her to the temple the next day.

* * * *

By the time Rasul showed up the next morning with his car, Diana was neatly dressed and ready with her camera. She wore a *pashmina* shawl over her head, and a *phiran*, the typical Kashmiri loose tunic, used by both men and women. Rasul smiled as she climbed in, for she could now pass as a native; her fair complexion easily melted with that of the locals. Bill decided to stay back as he was too identifiable due to his coloring and height.

The drive was pleasant, with an awesome view of the snow-capped mountains all around.

"In the good old days, this place had thousands of visitors," commented Rasul as they cleared the temple's police checkpoint at the base of the hill.

Slowly, the car journeyed the few kilometers to the peak, 1100 feet above the Karapura plain where the city of Srinagar sat.

The view was impressive. Diana marveled at the large Dal Lake—eight kilometers long and two kilometers wide. A few people who came stood on the massive walls taking pictures. Diana looked up at the temple, not quite able to believe she was really there.

The Treasure of the Pandavas

The stone and brick structure was constructed on a high octagonal plinth; to get there they would have to climb a steep flight of about one hundred steps. As they moved on, they passed below a simple stone arch decorated with a brass bell. Devotees rang the bell while passing through the arch, announcing their visit to the Deity.

Two small side flights of steps united at the door of the circular inner sanctum, where the large Lingam sat. In a corner were the images of Adi Shankara and Kashyapa Muni, the great Hindu Acharyas. A nearby sign read Adi Shankara had "attained spiritual knowledge" in this particular place before establishing various Maths—or schools—around India. Also Kashyapa Muni was the first preceptor of Kashmir. That matched the reference to Diana's third clue.

Some loudly chanted *mantras* while approaching; the most popular seemed to be *Om namah Shivaya;* but there were also others, such as *Hara Hara Mahadeva, Bam Bam Bhole,* and longer ones she was unable to distinguish or remember. Like the other pilgrims, Diana bowed down to the Deity, and then returned to the car along with Rasul. She would have loved to stay longer to find clues to their quest, but something inside told her she should wait for Bill, Jai and Masako. It wasn't the same without them; besides, the palm reader in Prayagraj had

569

said she would find the treasure with the help of three friends. Not wanting to jeopardize the mission, she decided she would just have to wait patiently until the four of them were together again.

Later that day, after Rasul had helped them load the boat with fresh provisions, Diana and Bill sailed to the middle of the cool, clear lake. They stopped in a solitary area surrounded by sweetly-scented lotus flowers already blooming with the first warm days of summer.

Diana showed Bill the photos she had taken from her excursion then they rested and enjoyed the much needed down-time. Finally, talk turned to the clues. It was a true relief for them to be able to speak openly between themselves and sleep fearlessly, with nothing to do and nowhere to go. The small radar in the vehicle gave them a sense of security as well. They turned in early and soon fell into a deep, peaceful sleep.

That night, Diana had a strange dream. She found herself walking over the Shankaracharya Hill, beyond the road and into the forest trails, where she came across a King Cobra. It reared up to eye level, but instead of being frightened, she was more curious, knowing instinctively it was the same one which had been sitting around Lord Shiva's neck in tranquility. Still, she was unnerved by the creature, and part of her wanted to scream and run away. Suddenly, she had an inspiration to chant the Shiva mantra she had heard in the temple. The energy of the mantra became visible. It manifested into a vibration of pure, multicolored, effulgent light emanating from her own heart. The eyes of the cobra began to reflect a soft, deep, all-embracing luminance; then he bowed his head, turned around and began tilting it toward a very narrow path among the trees.

Instantly freed from all fear, Diana followed the snake, as it slithered in front of her, to a beautiful little pond filled with lotus flowers of many different colors; there were white, pink, deep red, purple and blue ones filling the air with a beautiful fragrance.

The snake seemed to smile—*oddly enough*, Diana thought, *but it's just a dream*—then he silently slid away.

She heard the sound of bells, and suddenly two identical, beautiful, white, black and brown cows appeared from the bushes. They came to the bank of the pond and drank of the crystal-clear water before walking to a cave nearby. Diana followed them and saw they had positioned themselves over a hole in the ground and were releasing their milk there. Then they touched the ground with their foreheads and left.

Approaching the cave, Diana saw some inscriptions at the entrance. She passed her hand over the writing and the letters began to glow. She stared intently but could not recognize the alphabet. Then she heard a deep voice pronounce the names: *Bhumi, Jala, Agni, Vayu,* and *Antariksha.* As they were named, the inscriptions glowed with a beautiful light: first green, then blue, red, snowy white, and finally, jet black. Then another light, golden yellow in color, started to pulsate from the rock wall itself, but there was no inscription in that location. Finally, all the inscriptions vanished.

The voice spoke again. This time it was in English, or at least Diana was able to understand what it said. "This heavenly map has been drawn on the order of Emperor Vikramaditya, and only the worthy and pure of heart can find and claim it."

In the dream, Diana felt reassured and safe. She walked on, entering a tunnel into which the cave had been the gateway. Time had no meaning there. The tunnel opened into another similar cave, and finally a lush green valley filled with trees and flowers of banyan, Tulsi, fig, ashoka, jasmine, lotus, marigold, and scented grasses blowing gently in the breezes. It was home to beautiful birds and small animals. Startled, she walked on, discovering a spring from which a creek flowed. Steam rose gently from the water. She touched it with her fingers and found it very warm.

She awoke with a start. It was the most lucid dream she had ever experienced. She had *been* there. She looked at her hand. Warm water dripped from her fingers.

She immediately woke Bill, anxious to tell him what had happened.

"You know, Diana," he said excitedly, when she had finished recounting her strange experience, "this might not have been just a dream. I read that not only do we have physical bodies, but we have subtle bodies as well. These subtle bodies experience reality on different dimensions or frequencies, specifically during the dream state. So you could have really gone to this place, but in your subtle body. It's kind of like what's known as 'remote-viewing'. Both the American and Russian military—and who knows who else—have carried out remote viewing projects over the years. Basically, a team of psychics band together and focus their awareness on a certain person or location. Their observations are recorded as they watch their target...and they can do this from anywhere."

Diana stared at him blankly for a moment, not quite sure she was ready to accept such a notion. Bill smiled, shook his head and looked at his watch. It was still the middle of the night. They turned out the light and tried to get back to sleep.

Diana had no sooner drifted off when the dream began again, like a film that had been paused mid-scene. In the distance she saw an elderly lady, clad in orange-colored robes, sitting under a large tree. Her eyes were closed and she had a peaceful smile on her distinguished face. Diana walked over to her and sat instinctively at her feet.

The elderly woman opened her eyes. She did not move her lips, yet Diana heard the woman's quiet voice in her mind. *"Welcome, my child. My name is Bhairavi Brahmani."*

Diana felt a sudden urge to prostrate herself in front of the *sannyasini.*

The woman nodded in approval. *"I was waiting for you, my child. I told Shivananda you would come. Like Ramakrishna, Shivananda became my disciple after passing the test that I will now present to you. Are you ready?"* The lady smiled.

There was no fear in Diana's mind. The affectionate woman was certainly not bent on harming her in any way. "I am ready," she uttered calmly, confidently lifting her head and looking the woman directly in the eyes, not knowing how she could muster such courage.

Bhairavi stood up and, taking Diana's hand, led her into yet another cave and another tunnel; both of them were floating, their feet not touching the ground. Then she motioned for Diana to go ahead. *"I will watch over you,"* she said in Diana's mind, *"but you need to face the test alone. Do not turn back. I will always be near you."*

Definitely not a dream, thought Diana.

She moved through many tunnels, finally reaching what appeared to be a small island of black rock, supported by a large black pillar, which was occupied by five young boys dressed in white robes and sitting peacefully on the ground. Moving nearer, Diana realized they were not young boys at all, but dwarves with large faces and pointed ears, like the leprechauns or goblins of Celtic lore.

The five dwarves smiled at her, as if reading her mind, and one of them spoke. "Welcome, daughter of Shivananda. We have been waiting for you. We know that, like him, you come from a place where our people once lived free and were respected by the human beings. Sometimes our two peoples even made friends and alliances. Few recall those days amongst the humans, but nay, we have not forgotten. Right now we have a test for you, and if you pass, we will help you in your mission. If you fail, you will fall down into this abyss, which is deep like space, and end up in a very different place."

It is a test of intelligence and wisdom, thought Diana.

"Are you ready?" The friendly face flashed dangerously for a moment, revealing a glimpse of a terrible dark power.

Once again, Diana fought the urge to run. Instead, she gathered her courage and replied, "Yes, I am ready."

"Very well. We have some questions for you.

What is the fastest thing in the world?"

575

"The mind," replied Diana instantly.

"What is the greatest vehicle you've ever driven"?

"The body," said Diana.

"What is the greatest miracle for the mortals?"

"Birth."

"What is certain in life?"

"Death."

"What is it that does not die?"

"The soul."

Diana had no idea how the answers were coming to her, yet she felt some deep pool of confidence. She suddenly realized this was based on her past-life learning experiences and something else, as well.

Somehow, she could feel the voices of her ancestors within her. Diana remembered something Bill had told her about the Indian Hindu epic *Mahabharata*, where the virtuous king, Yudhishthira, found himself in a similar situation.

The five dwarves looked at each other, smiling. "You have done your homework, child. Now, answer this, what is the greatest wealth?"

Diana thought for a moment. "Knowledge," she replied.

"How can one attain greatness?"

"By perseverance and effort."

"Who is the most helpful companion?"

"Intelligence."

"What is the best happiness?"

"Contentment derived from appreciating what we have."

"What is cleanliness?"

"Purifying the mind from all unclean desires."

Still smiling, the five dwarves stood up and bowed to Diana. "You have passed our test," they said in unison. One by one they introduced themselves as the Yaksha, guardians of the five elements—earth, water, fire, air and space. "Now you have our blessings and we will protect you and your friends when you return here, very soon. But you need to do some *sadhana* meditation, thus purifying yourself before entering these caves; this same advice will apply to your friends."

At that, they moved aside, allowing her to proceed over the stone bridge and beyond. She bowed to them. "I am very grateful for your kindness."

The five dwarves smiled and waved their hands, encouraging her to continue her journey.

Stepping into the next tunnel, she found herself on the threshold of a vast illuminated cave filled with treasures. Bhairavi Brahmani was there, waiting.

"There are still other tests, said her sweet voice in Diana's mind, *but you will find out in the future, when you come here with the three companions I have chosen for you. Now it is*

time for you to return to your body." The elderly lady moved closer and touched Diana's forehead with her warm hand.

Suddenly, opening her eyes in the dark room, Diana wondered what had happened. She was completely disoriented and confused. The last part of the dream had been especially vivid, so much so that the room on the houseboat almost seemed an hallucination.

Her body felt very heavy, cold and stiff, and did not respond well. She tried to sit up but her head was reeling, so she decided it was better to lie down and stay quiet for some time. On the other bed, Bill was sleeping on his side, snoring lightly. The houseboat was almost still on the quiet lake, and the thin sliver of the waxing moon gave only a feeble light. Still a little dizzy, Diana finally got up silently and went to the car, switched on the computer, and typed out everything she could remember about the sequential dreams.

* * * *

The next day, Diana described the rest of the mysterious dream journey to Bill and told him what she thought it might mean.

"It all seemed so real; I'm confused. I think this means we have to qualify in some way, some spiritual way, before we're allowed to find the treasure."

Bill nodded. "I think so too. This isn't a normal treasure hunt. It's a quest, a spiritual journey, like the stories we read about those knights of the ancient times who went to seek the Grail."

Diana chuckled. "Indeed. Like a Knight of the Round Table, Sir Perceval, coming all the way to India...." Suddenly, her eyes went wide. "It was precisely like that! Sir Arthur Neville Warwick, a knight from the old kingdom, actually came all the way to India and found the cave himself."

Bill was quiet for a moment, his mouth open in shock.

"Bill, did you hear what I just said? Arthur actually found the treasure all those decades ago!" Diana couldn't understand why she hadn't seen it before. "He obviously decided it was best to keep it secret, because SEPS and countless others would either have had it destroyed or looted! So he preserved the secret by keeping it in the care of his spiritual descendants, then he left the clues for me, his physical descendant. But he most definitely found that treasure...and he wants us to rediscover it at the right time in human history!"

Her excitement was contagious.

"You said the old lady mentioned Shivananda. Wasn't that Arthur's *sannyasi* name? This means that Arthur passed the test and was *allowed* to find the treasure," interjected Bill.

Diana smiled. "It does indeed."

579

* * * *

The computer in the Valley vehicle had secure phone capability, and Diana used it to call Professor Cariappa's secret phone. On the video call, she described the dream, the treasure hidden in the hill, the orange-robed *sannyasin*, the dwarves and Arthur Warwick.

Cariappa, thoughtfully listening to every detail, asked several questions, and seemed to contemplate the answers. When Diana finished the entire story, he remained silent for a few minutes.

"Bhairavi Brahmani," he said finally, in a voice filled with awe, this is indeed great news. Do you know who that lady was?"

Diana and Bill shook their heads, surprised. "No"

"Ever heard of Ramakrishna Paramahamsa?"

"Yes," said Bill, "he was a great saint from the 1800s, who worshiped the Mother Goddess Kali."

"She mentioned a Ramakrishna?" said Diana, in a faint voice.

"In the 1860s, Bhairavi Brahmani, an orange-robed, middle-aged female ascetic, appeared at Dakshineshwar temple," said Cariappa, in a solemn voice. "It is said she was thoroughly conversant with the Hindu texts of Shaivism, and Vaishnavism, and practised Tantra. At the time, Ramakrishna was experiencing a phenomenon that accompanies *mahabhava*—the supreme attitude of loving devotion toward the Divine—and quoting from the *Bhakti Shastras*. She told him other faith figures like Chaitanya Mahaprabhu had similar experiences.

"Bhairavi initiated Ramakrishna into *Tantra* and *Kundalini Yoga*. Ramakrishna considered himself to be a son of hers."

"It is believed that she is actually an earthly expansion of Kali Ma, who manifests from time to time to teach the transcendental knowledge, *Vidya*, and the intimate personal *bhakti* to the Mother Goddess, whenever there are deserving disciples who are ready to carry this priceless jewel. She gives her instructions and initiations for a very short period of time, and then disappears, only to reappear again at an appropriate time later. We should be thankful, for she has reappeared to help the *Dharma* cause."

Diana smiled. "Well, my great-grandfather, Arthur, was a real knight of the old code, pure in heart and soul. He went on a sacred quest to find the truth, and shared it with all his strength and dedication. He also protected and preserved it for future generations."

The Professor spoke in amazement. "Then, I believe you are his worthy descendent, Diana. We have been blessed by your coming here. I realize now that your name is also special; in Sanskrit *dhyana* means 'meditation'."

"No, no," chuckled Diana, "it is I who need help from you. But that's very intriguing about my name's Sanskrit meaning."

"In one word, you are the chosen one, meaning you are already eligible. However, I would suggest you both start doing *yoga* to achieve a purifying effect and gain the necessary qualifications to pass the tests ahead of you. May Mother Goddess give you the determination and strength to succeed."

"Yes, Professor, but can you give us some more details? I think we will need them," suggested Diana.

"There are four most important kinds of *yoga*—you already know about them—which can help your body, mind and soul to connect to the Supreme: *Asthanga, Karma, Jnana* and *Bhakti.* You can choose any one or combination and be sure of success."

Bill interrupted. "Given our short timeframe, which one would you suggest is easier and fastest?"

Cariappa smiled. "If I were you, I would choose *Bhakti Yoga*, as it is suitable for the Kali Yuga and preferred by Mother Goddess. Most importantly, you must do it seriously and sincerely, and be fully dependent on the Supreme for success."

"Got it." Bill replied.

Diana nodded her head in agreement.

Cariappa suggested important *mantras* and scriptures to be considered.

After multiple thanks, the call ended.

Diana and Bill remained up late into the night, discussing the wonderful things they had learned and experienced together. Per the Professor's advice, they decided to follow the *mantra* meditation of *Bhakti Yoga*, to purify their existence on the physical, mental, emotional and spiritual levels. The next morning, after rising early and long before sunrise, they bathed, sat cross-legged on the floor, and began *mantra* meditation, chanting the *Hare Krishna mahamantra* and the *Gayatri mantra,* for several hours. Later in the day, they read Vedic scriptures from the *Bhagavad-gita* and *Srimad Bhagavatam.* Before having their meal, they prayed to the Supreme to accept the food they had prepared, and thanked Him. In the night, they focused on the *Mahamrityunjaya mantra* and the *Narasimha* mantra for protection. As days passed, their confidence increased. Finally, they began to experience a state of bliss during meditation, giving them the necessary clarity to change their lives and complete the mission.

* * * *

On Friday morning, they received a call from Jai. He was fine; the mission had been successful, and he was planning to join them as soon as possible. He would be arriving the next day with Masako to help with their search. He asked if they had seen the news yet.

"No, we haven't," said Bill. "We've been a bit busy doing nothing."

"Well, check the news online, and see what happened on Wednesday, the 20th of April in Delhi, and afterward in Israel. When I come, we'll be able to talk in detail. Gotta go now. Thanks."

Intrigued, Diana and Bill turned on the computer as soon as they hung up. They were relieved to read about Zalim's foiled terrorist plot, and shell-shocked to learn of what had happened in Tel Aviv. It was *deja-vu* all over again for Diana, after her own experience with the bomb blast in Israel.

They felt like they'd fallen off the face of the earth after only a few days in this secluded place of Srinagar.

They also came across another frightening story: the smear campaign launched against them by Jawahar the Jackal. Diana gasped when she saw their passport photos flash across the screen like they were wanted criminals. They also saw how WIN TV was countering the false propaganda against them by effectively nailing SEPS' lies.

Their hunt was now an official mission; they didn't need to worry about the Indian government, but for sure about SEPS, who would be desperate to lay their dirty hands on them and the treasure.

Masako and Jai finally arrived at five the next day.

That night, Jai recounted the events of April 20th in great detail. Masako, too, spoke of her terrifying experience, as she hadn't known the mini-nuke had been deactivated. In turn, Diana explained her dreams, completely mystifying the others.

They awoke very early in the morning and drove up the narrow road inside the Shankaracharya Hill complex in the Valley vehicle, accompanied by Rasul.

The temple *pujari* was pleasantly surprised by the visit of the four friends.

"It is as if the whole world has come to the feet of Lord Shiva," he observed, his eyes calmly moving from Bill, to Diana and Jai, and finally Masako. "You seem to represent all mankind today in this holy place, and I am sure that your mission is blessed. I am fortunate to have witnessed this portentous day. How can I help you?"

"We need to remain on this hill for a few days, and we need the freedom to explore unrestricted—with your permission, of course," said Jai. He pulled out his credentials and presented them to the man.

"Usually a special permission from the police and army is required, but I see you have all the blessings of the government." The *pujari* looked at the fax Jai had produced. "Please come with me."

They went into the temple, waiting for Jai while he offered his obeisances to the temple deities, surrounded by the magical atmosphere of flickering *ghee* lamps, sweet incense and the sound of chanting *mantras*, then they returned to the vehicle and packed their backpacks with supplies Jai had brought from Delhi: water bottles, food, a compass, flashlights, first-aid kits and Swiss army knives. Still, they managed to keep the provisions to a minimum, not wanting to be burdened by heavy packs.

The *pujari* and Rasul, the boat owner, offered to accompany them to the small lake where Diana wanted to start the search. The *pujari* had immediately recognized the area from her description.

She happily accepted their offer and the six set off along the wooded trail. They left the main path, heading deeper in amongst the rocks and vegetation. Soon they reached a beautiful clear pond where they drank the water, and then sprinkled their heads in an act of self-purification. At this point, the small group split up to look for the cave. It was Diana who found it first. Unlike the one she had seen in her dream, this one was hidden behind thick bushes and creepers, but luckily, she recognized the shape and called to the others. Bill and Jai gently cleared away the plants covering the entrance while Diana looked for any inscriptions. They were difficult to find because of the mud and moss that had accumulated over the years.

After scraping them clean, Jai was able to read aloud the *Devanagari* script: "*Bhumi, Jala, Agni, Vayu, Antariksha.*"

"That's it!" cried Diana, triumphantly. "This is the cave entrance! Let's go!"

The *pujari* was startled by the sudden turn of events. The cave where Kashyapa Muni and Adi Shankara were said to have meditated during their stay on the Hill had long been lost and had become somewhat of a legend. Many people had looked for it, but unsuccessfully. It seemed to have appeared from nowhere.

"Do you...mean to go inside now?" he asked, stammering slightly.

"Sure, why not?" replied Bill, a little surprised. "This is the reason why we came all the way here, and there's not a moment to waste."

The elderly *pujari* looked at him intently.

"Sir, did you see the news on TV?" Bill asked. "We need to find this treasure now, as soon as possible."

The *pujari* stepped back, biting his lower lip in obvious anxiety. "The legend says that some people, in the ancient times, went to search for the cave's treasure but never returned."

There was a moment of intense silence.

"So be it," said Jai, determination on his face. "If it is our destiny to die trying, so be it. But you should pray for our success, because more than Kashmir is at stake."

"I have faith in them," Rasul added. "May Lord Shiva protect you."

"As you wish," said the *pujari*. "My blessings are with you, also."

The four friends offered *pranams* to the *pujari* and to Rasul, and then walked into the depths of the cave.

* * * *

At the same time, not far away, the morning flight from Delhi was landing in Srinagar. The security measures had been upgraded, and it was over an hour before Jawahar Katju and Father Francis exited the airport.

Earlier that day, Jawahar had turned on the TV and flown into an immediate rage when he learned his smear campaign against Diana and Bill had failed miserably. His mood improved, however, when CBI officer Masoom Singh informed him that the two had been spotted in Srinagar; they had gone to the Shankaracharya Hill accompanied by a young Chinese woman and an Indian man. Masoom also told Jawahar that going forward, he would have nothing more to do with the case, as the foursome's mission was now officially supported by the IFA, an agency of the Indian Government.

Too bad for Masoom, but the rabbits are finally popping out of their hole! Jawahar quickly got into his car and rushed to the airport. To his surprise, he found the Catholic priest checking onto the same flight. At first he tried to pretend he hadn't recognized him, for the Jesuit was dressed in plain clothes, but the man caught his eye and Jawahar had no choice.

"Ahh, Father. You are going to Srinagar, too?" said Jawahar, anxiously, his eyes darting back and forth as if he were constantly checking his surroundings. "We are going to travel together, then?"

The Jesuit did not seem particularly enthusiastic about the idea, but gave an oblique smile. "Yes, Jawahar. I believe we are going to the same conference."

"Ah, yes, yes," said Jawahar with a slightly perplexed look. *These Jesuits have a stronger network than I have, it seems.* "Where are you going to stay?" he asked, "Do you have a hotel?"

"No, our Order has a house in Srinagar. If you like, we will be happy to have you as our guest," winked the Jesuit playfully.

Right, and keep me under constant surveillance. "Of course, it will be an honor for me," he replied aloud.

The journey was mostly silent, with each man lost in his own thoughts. Apparently, no other member of SEPS had decided to follow

Diana and Bill, probably because they didn't have sufficient backup in the area, especially after the exposure of Lal Salaam and Mullah Omar. It was only the two of them, and they made an odd couple indeed.

The black station wagon which picked them up at the airport drove smoothly to the Jesuit house. The Priest and Jawahar sat in the back seat, while the front seat closest to the driver and the seats in the rear luggage area, were occupied by four local boys, dressed casually, but wearing voluminous jackets. Jawahar was willing to bet that under those jackets there was a lot of firepower.

Upon arrival, Katju was assigned a guest room, and after making some private phone calls on his cell, had lunch with his host. He was not disappointed—there was plenty of red meat and fine wine.

Chapter 21 - The Treasure

"Bhumi...Jala....Agni....Vayu....Antariksha.
These are the names of the *Pancha Bhutas,* the five primary material elements: earth, water, fire, air and space." Jai re-read the Sanskrit inscriptions.

Jai's and Masako's flashlights further brightened the area, and a series of seven symbols became clear. Miraculously, their colors were still bright after more than several centuries of exposure: a plain circle; a green triangle pointing upward, with a double line at the base; a blue triangle, also pointing upward; a plain red triangle pointing downward; a white downward triangle with the double line at the base; a black square; and a yellow Star of David inside a circle and a square. They were all inscribed on the stone.

"There's writing here, Jai," Bill said, lowering his flashlight.

Jai bent a little to decipher the ancient Sanskrit letters, and then translated the writing for the others. "This heavenly map has been drawn on the order of Emperor Vikramaditya, and only the worthy and pure of heart can find it and claim the treasure."

With a start, Diana remembered her dream—the words were the same!

"This should be the map!" she exclaimed.

591

"Then what are the meanings of these symbols?" inquired Masako.

Bill spoke first. "I think the plain white circle represents the pure white light of the soul; the *sattvic, dharmic* person who is walking on the path of this sacred search. There are layers and layers of meanings in this map. It's not just a map to find a treasure by following geographical directions, it's a map of the journey of the soul through the five material elements of the universe, to reach the completion of life's mission, by the attainment of sacred knowledge, and is symbolized by the *Sri Yantra*—what we call the Star of David."

Diana looked at him, once again amazed at how much he had learned since arriving in India.

"Something tells me we're going to find some missing links in this place; also the last symbol seems to be the combination of other symbols like the circle, square and triangles," observed Jai.

"Indeed." Diana nodded her head quickly. "But now I think we should go on and actually find them. "Okay?"

Bill smiled. "Yessiree, Sarge," he teased.

As Diana started walking, she observed Jai look at the wall one last time, before taking some quick photos; she was sure he would message them to Karry.

The ceiling was high; even Bill could easily walk without bending his head. They kept their flashlights on, proceeding diligently one after the other as they followed Diana through the dark tunnel.

As he moved, Bill began to softly chant the *omkara mantra*, and Diana joined in, thinking how surreal it was that she was here in Kashmir, hunting treasure, and opening her heart to *Yoga Dharma*.

Soon Jai picked up the words and joined in, quickly followed by Masako.

The fourth symbol, the OM, is also appearing in our midst as foretold by the swami at the ashram, thought Diana. *It would have made Arthur happy.*

The floor of the tunnel was smooth, and they were able to walk briskly, and luckily without encountering any snakes or scorpions. After some time, they saw a light which gradually brightened, and soon found themselves in the lush green and warm valley Diana had seen in her dream. *This could well be the Green Earth depicted by the green triangle.* She looked at Bill and knew right away that he was thinking the same thing.

"Green Earth!" he exclaimed happily.

Masako cried out in surprise and delight. "But this is Shambala! The secret golden valley described by the Tibetan Buddhists!"

"I thought it was called Shangri-La?" said Bill.

Masako smiled, "That's just another name. I'd bet there are many."

"Yes," Jai said, nodding. "It is also called Kailash, the abode of Lord Shiva. This must be Nanda Kanana, the enchanted gardens where Lord Shiva sits with his retinue." Jai looked around, his face a mask of wonder. "Different people call it by different names, but the proof of its existence is here; right in front of our eyes."

Diana looked at him silently. If he was right, they had left their earthly dimension and entered into a different one. Somehow this did not strike her as odd anymore.

As they walked into the green valley of glowing sunlight, it was obvious to Diana that they all felt an indescribable sense of joy which reflected on their faces. Jai knelt on the soft grass surrounding a pool of water, where two different springs, one warm, and one cool, poured out. He touched the two gushing streams before taking some water in his cupped hand to drink. "It's very tasty," he announced, "and refreshing."

The others joined him around the pool and tasted the water, marveling at how there were springs of two different temperatures at the same location.

The four of them spent some time experiencing the beauty of the wonderful garden, looking at the colorful birds, and smelling the sweetly-scented flowers. An overall sense of well-being stirred within Diana, and as she regarded her friends, she realized they were all experiencing a strong sense of contentment.

Jai remarked, "Moments like this remind me of why Vajra team fights for *Dharma*."

"Such sweet beauty is a reflection of a joyous life lived in harmony," Masako mused. "Yet all this beauty combined together presents a perfect creation. Something unique has been created out of all of the various elements involved, and that is what we call Mother Nature. It is of unequaled beauty and beyond any of the economic or socio-political constructs of the human mind."

"That's some deep wisdom there, girl," Diana said, chuckling softly. "So, basically what you're talking about is real beauty. It is so true; the most beautiful things in this world were indeed created without a price tag or copyright in mind."

Everyone was silent for some time, soaking in the energy of the place. "Yes, you can really feel it. There is a tangible presence here..." Bill seemed to briefly search for an apt metaphor. "It's a feeling of home...of that comfort you can only get from Mom."

"Well, this is as close to Mom as we can get, anyway," remarked Jai. "The Earth really is Mother to every single thing on this planet, both technically and spiritually. Hail Mother Earth!"

"Where to now, Diana?" Bill asked.

"This way." She walked straight ahead, and up to another tunnel in the mountain side.

* * * *

In the meantime, after lunch at the Jesuit house, the car was ready to take Father Francis and Professor Jawahar Katju to Shankaracharya Hill. Actually, there were *two* cars, and the second vehicle was even more closely packed with young men in big jackets.

Father Francis showed no surprise when Jawahar was joined on the way by two jeeps filled with similar young men but wearing scarves which could easily cover most of their faces. The entire party of twenty-two exited their vehicles at the Hill. Arriving at the top, the search party dispersed into the forest, while Jawahar and Father Francis went to interview the *pujari* in charge of the temple. Meanwhile, Rasul had already returned to his family in the city, and the *pujari* was alone as usual.

"*Namaskar, ji,*" said Jawahar Katju. "I am a professor from JNU in Delhi. I've come with my students on a research project about the holy place of the meditation of Kashyapa and Shankara."

The Treasure of the Pandavas

The *pujari's* face lit up with enthusiasm. "Oh, but this is the most extraordinary coincidence! Just this morning the entrance to the ancient cave was discovered. It's indeed a momentous day," he said excitedly.

Jawahar grinned like a joker. "Wonderful, indeed! We are anxious to see this amazing discovery. Could you please take us there?"

The *pujari* seemed thrilled to be able to illustrate the wonders of the temple, but Jawahar and Father Francis insisted on going to the cave immediately. He appeared to be a little perplexed when he saw twenty-some young men accompanying them, all wearing heavy clothing. They probably didn't look much like students, nor did they seem at all friendly.

In his innocence, the *pujari* led them to the cave. Upon reaching it, Jawahar's heart leaped and he thanked the man pretentiously with folded hands. In no time, to the *pujari's* utter dismay, the young men rushed past the two ring leaders and into the cave.

* * * *

The four friends eventually came to a large passageway Diana recognized as the place where she had met the lions in her dream. "Watch out, guys," she said, "We may find some wild animals here, but don't be afraid. Empty your heart of any fear and hate and they'll let us go unharmed."

The others looked at her, worry on their faces, but said nothing. As they walked across the cave, they saw tiny low caves in the sides of the rocky expanse. Golden-yellow eyes glinted in the dark, and suddenly a tawny form emerged from one of the openings, and stood watching them. The four friends stopped right in their tracks, waiting to see what would happen next.

The lion shook his mane and yawned, then continued to just watch as if he, too, was waiting for something. Diana repeated the *omkara mantra* in her mind, quickly whispering to the others to do the same. She instantly felt a calming effect on her emotions and heart. More lions appeared, but didn't seem threatening. Finally, one large lioness stepped forward and walked right up to Diana. She sniffed Diana's hand before licking it with her coarse, warm tongue. Diana laughed a bit shrilly, and the lioness looked up at her. After a few moments, the huge cat seemed satisfied and proceeded to sit down, watching the friends intently with her intelligent amber eyes.

Other lions approached to greet them, and soon the animals were licking their hands and letting them pet and scratch them. Finally the four resumed walking. They were followed for a while by the pride. After a long time, they reached the semi-dark lake which occupied the entire space between the tunnel walls. It was there, that the friends realized the blue triangle symbol was for water.

Diana stared intently at the wall, looking for something, as if recalling her dream. "Search for a small place on the wall where a symbol could fit and be unlocked," she stated. "I think we need to release the floating stones here."

They all began examining the wall, and soon Jai found a depression that seemed to match a crescent moon he was carrying. Sure enough, the symbol found in Dvaraka fit perfectly into the depression. As Jai pushed and turned it a little more, the spot in the rock seemed to yield. He heard a click and signaled to Diana. She turned to the lake and saw a number of flat stones come up to the surface, rising one after the other and stopping a few inches above the water.

"Careful now," she said. "Not all of these are stones. I expect there will be a few crocodiles as well."

Masako, who was just about to step onto what seemed to be a particularly rugged brown stone, froze. It silently emerged a little more, revealing two yellow-green eyes and a long snout. Masako stifled a cry and rapidly chose a smoother one.

Quickly, but cautiously, they crossed the lake without incident. Jai retrieved the crescent moon before catching up with the others.

"It seems the stones will keep floating," said Bill, looking back at the lake.

"I think so, especially in the 'unlock' position," said Diana. "We will need them when we return. Let's keep going."

The passageway grew increasingly warm as they continued their trek. It was hours before they reached the next obstacle in their path: a river of molten lava, glowing red in the darkness, and a few hundred meters below them. At the edge, the heat was very intense, despite the distance. Smoke and hot vapor rose constantly. It was the Red Triangle zone.

Diana immediately looked around for the place she had seen in her dream. She called Masako, who was carrying the Sri Yantra, and guided her as she fit it into a depression in the wall. There was a click and a stone slab bridge slid into place, allowing them to cross in relative safety. The tremendous heat caused the rubber on the soles of their shoes to begin to melt, but fortunately the stone slab was very large and stable, and their crossing was swift.

Masako stowed the symbol in her backpack and was the last person to cross, the slab remained there in the unlock position; they continued trekking into the depths of the mountain.

"Mind your step," Diana said. "Now if I remember correctly, there should be some deep crevices in the rock along the wall, with a number of stairs climbing up."

That was an understatement. The stairs seemed endless, and there were deep splits in the rock floor of the passage. Diana thought it had probably happened in some ancient earthquake. The four discussed that they could have been created by the people who had hidden the treasure there, so as to make its retrieval possible only to those who were able to overcome the difficulties on their path. They realized some of the splits may have been illusions; the Yaksha dwarfs were perfectly capable of creating them.

* * * *

In the meantime, a motley crew, for whom the treasure was never intended, made its way into the sacred caves. Professor Jawahar and Father Francis had entered the first cave together in the company of their thugs. They soon found the first tunnel. The professor scowled at the inscriptions on the wall. *Stupid Hindu pagan superstitions! What's the meaning of these idiotic drawings?* He took his compass out and checked the direction, then told his men to switch on their flashlights and keep their guns ready: the place was probably filled with many hidden dangers.

Egged on by an increasingly impatient Jawahar, the entire party moved ahead. Trying

601

to stick together, they at times hampered each other's progress through the narrow passage.

When they reached the wonderful valley, they stared at it in amazement like schoolboys on their first field trip. The simple-minded wonder of the hired goons was quickly squelched as the priest began yelling, "All this is devil's work and enchantments! Stop gawking, Fools, and let's move!"

Jawahar chuckled cynically. "He's right. If you really want to be amazed, wait till you see the treasure. So yes, let's move on!" In his heart of hearts, he hoped that the pagan treasure was real, otherwise his life would be ruined.

At the insistence of the two ring leaders, the thugs were convinced to continue on without exploring the area.

Jawahar and the priest pushed their henchmen up front, not only to keep up the pace, but also so the goons would be the first target in any possible danger. As a result, they were alerted ahead of time when they reached the second cave.

"Lions! Lions!" someone shouted.

Lions? What nonsense. But Professor Jawahar didn't move to the front of the line. *There is not enough space in the passage,* he told himself. When his boys had fanned out into the open area of the cave, he heard and saw firsthand that there *were* lions, an entire pride of them, pacing up and down, roaring threateningly. The sound filled the cave and reverberated all around the men. He felt the need for his flask.

The sound and movement was too much. Jawahar panicked and yelled, "Just shoot them!"

Father Francis agreed. "Shoot them all!"

The *gundas* didn't need much convincing. They opened fire, and wasting an awful lot of ammunition, they felled the first three animals in the front of the pack. That was a mistake, for instead of running away in fear, the others, enraged, attacked them before they had time to reload their guns. Within seconds, four men fell screaming. They struggled in vain against the powerful jaws now tearing them apart.

Leaving their fallen comrades to keep the lions busy, the rest of the group fled into the next section of the dark tunnel. The few who dared look back saw many more lions coming out of their dens to join in the slaughter.

No one needed encouragement to keep a fast pace, and this time Jawahar found himself at the front of the line as the men tried to put as much distance as possible between themselves and the angry cats.

When they arrived at the lake, he was the first to see strange things floating in the water. They were arranged in a path, except for a few off to the side.

Jawahar cautiously tested one of them, but was unable to tell what material they were made of. They seemed to be like stones, strong enough to support a man's weight, so he slowly ventured onto the next one and further into the lake.

Father Francis was right behind him and the others followed. The panic started when one of the crocodiles began to move with the thug still standing on its back. The man lost his balance, and fell into the cold, neck-deep water. His loud swearing and the sniggering of his companions soon turned to screams of pain and terror. The crocodile had bitten into his leg and was now pulling him down into the black, away from the others. He struggled ferociously, kicking and punching the reptile, but to no avail. Gripping its victim with its front claws, the crocodile firmly clamped down on the man's leg and began a spin of death. The struggle lasted less than a minute, but long enough for the man to drown and the crocodile to begin its feast.

The others watched, frozen in terror, as their companion disappeared beneath the murky waters. They flew into a panic, jumping quickly from one floating 'stone' to the next. Six more lost their balance, slipped and splashed into the lake. They immediately started swimming as fast as they could toward the opposite bank. The men who had not fallen tried to rescue their comrades by shooting indiscriminately into the lake. They killed many of the crocs, but also shot several of the men in their panic. Only three of them made it out alive of the six who had fallen into the water.

Panting and gasping and scared as hell, the now depleted group of *gundas,* or thugs, must have been wondering what type of disastrous misadventure they had gotten themselves into.

"This is blessed work, my friends," Father Francis asserted when the men started talking about abandoning the mission. "Have no doubt the good Lord Jesus, is watching over us."

"Screw you and your holy babble!" one communist thug snarled. "Jitu didn't look very blessed when that crocodile ate him! Where was your Jesus then?" The man advanced on the priest, fists raised. But another man immediately came to the Father's rescue.

"If you touch a hair on his head, so help me God, I will blow your head off right here and now!" Suddenly the group was divided, with the professor's boys on one side and the priest's on the other. Father Francis and Jawahar looked at each other for a moment, and if by some unspoken agreement, decided it was best to keep the status quo...for now.

Jawahar put a hand on the shoulder of the boy who had threatened the priest, to calm him down. "I'm sure the esteemed Father agrees with me when I say we must stick together if we want to succeed. Be it the Lord's work or just a great opportunity for all of us, we must continue."

He also reminded them that anyone who turned their backs on the mission would still have to get through the crocodile lake and the lions' dens on the way out. Besides that, what if he and Father Francis didn't make it out? How long would it be before the police questioned them? No one would believe the *gundas* story.

The thugs looked at each other, clearly having second thoughts about quitting. Then the priest observed that it would be better to face any difficulty as a group rather than alone. "'O ye of little faith!' If you don't have faith in Almighty God, at least have faith in the treasure! What we seek is of enormous value. Some may die in its pursuit. So what? Great saints have died for less!"

He pointed out that with every man who was down, the survivors would have a larger share of the reward. That settled the matter; greed overtook common sense. The men were still angry, but they had to agree with what the priest had said. Still fuming and resentful, they, nevertheless, gathered their wits, guts and guns, and marched forward.

A few minutes later, however, the situation grew significantly more perilous. The tract of the tunnel ended in a rocky ledge, a kind of rail-less balcony over a chasm, peering deep into the inside of a volcano.

"You are a bunch of whiners," cried Jawahar. "Look, there is a nice solid rock bridge here.

True, it's a little hot in this place, but there is no immediate danger. I think the worst is over."

Mumbling and shaking their heads, the men lined up under the priest's orders to navigate the bridge one at a time to avoid any excessive load; they cautiously crossed over without any further casualties. This time Jawahar and the priest remained at the back of the group to make sure everyone made it safely over without delay. They also had a chance to see whether there were any cracks in the rock before their own turns.

After passing the lava river, the morale of the men received a significant boost, and they started feeling invincible once again. However, they clamored for a rest and a drink in the overwhelming heat. Their leaders were also exhausted and thirsty, and their legs were starting to hurt. It was difficult to calculate distance in these tunnels. Jawahar glanced at his watch; it was already five in the afternoon, so they took a break.

When they resumed their march they realized that walking had become more tiresome and even dangerous, as the tunnel started ascending in a series of steps. They needed to be very careful where they moved, as there were deep fissures along the walls, some wide enough to swallow a man. Jawahar and Father Francis walked cautiously, keeping their flashlight beams close to the ground as they pushed the men to forge ahead as quickly as possible. They needed to catch up to their quarry.

Four times one of their men screamed in that dark tunnel, but somehow they managed to grab a companion and were pulled up in time. In the fifth occurrence, however, the gap was too large and one of the *gundas* fell in too quickly for anyone to help him. His scream of terror reverberated for ages in the tunnel and only died out very slowly: evidently the chasm was extremely deep.

Jawahar took a good swig from his flask. *One less claim on the treasure,* he thought, hiding his smirk behind his whiskey-induced grimace.

* * * *

Many kilometers ahead, Masako suddenly froze in her tracks so abruptly that Jai crashed right into her back. "Did you hear that?" she asked the others. "It sounded like a scream."

They had all heard it. Diana felt the hair on the back of her neck stand up. She thought for a moment about what Arthur Warwick had had to face—persecuted and chased by his enemies—and she shivered. They were being pursued by SEPS.

Their party reached the end of the dark tunnel and found themselves staring at a frail-looking rope bridge swaying in the now freezing wind; it was the White Triangle zone. It was suspended between two tall mountains, from which white crests of frozen snow were being blown up by the rising air currents. The height had to be more than 3,000 meters; the air still had some oxygen, but breathing had become more difficult.

She looked down but couldn't see any green valley below them, only barren, snow-covered and jagged rocks all the way to the bottom. Now and then, the view was obstructed by wisps of fog, or maybe—Diana was suddenly struck with the realization—clouds.

Shivering from the sudden drop in temperature, they dug into their backpacks and pulled out sweatshirts, scarves and gloves that Jai had insisted they take "just in case". Then one by one, they slowly ventured onto the old wooden planks, tied together with what seemed to be rotting rope made from some rope-like fiber, and walked the eleven hundred or so meters to the other side of the bridge, waiting until the person ahead had completely crossed, before beginning their own arduous trek across the swinging bridge. In spite of the poor conditions of the structure, they all reached the other side, half frozen, but safe and sound. A few eagles soared below them, but left them be.

As soon as they were all across, they hurried into the tunnel to escape the biting wind, rubbing their hands and faces to activate their blood circulation and warm up. Walking briskly, but carefully, in the bright tunnel, rare golden shafts of the setting sun shone upon them, and the four friends found their warmth and good spirits begin to return.

It was six in the evening when they finally stopped. They sat on the floor of the tunnel, took some high-energy snacks and drank a little water; just enough to keep them going. Yet, strangely, none of them was particularly hungry or thirsty or needed to answer nature's call.

"Guys, this is weird," Diana said, looking perplexed. "We have been walking since seven this morning—eleven hours—yet this is our first stop. I'm not feeling particularly hungry or thirsty, or tired. It's like the needs of my physical body have somehow been suspended here."

No one answered for a moment. Finally Jai spoke up. "Diana, you said that in your lucid dream you met five Dwarf Yakshas, right?"

"Yes," said Diana, nodding her head.

Jai smiled. "Well, if I remember correctly, Yakshas are a very powerful race who are naturally capable of controlling the mind and senses through the practice of *Tantric Yoga*. This same practice enables one to partially control the mind and the senses of others as well. And you know, I've been thinking that the Yakshas you described, sound to me like they are important personalities, not just ordinary individuals. Perhaps they are in charge of this place, endowed with some higher power to protect the treasure," he elaborated.

"Now, you met five of them," he continued, "so I suspect each one of them was the guardian, not only of one of the five material elements— the *pancha mahabhutas*—but of one of the material senses as well, the one that is connected to that particular element. As you know, we have five senses, as well as five organs of perception, and five organs of action, all connected together. Our bodies, too, are made of the same elements."

Bill stared at him incredulously. "So you are basically saying that those five little guys are controlling our bodies, and suspending or slowing down some of our feelings and functions to help us on our mission?"

"Precisely. There is no other logical explanation." Jai smiled. "I think that without the blessing of the five guardian Yakshas, no one would be able to reach the treasure without suffering hunger, thirst and much greater discomfort than we are. From what Diana has told us, I can easily conclude that this special protection is given to us because our mission is worthy and blessed by higher powers."

"I agree," interjected Diana. "I was tested, and told that I would be protected." She paused a moment to reflect. "But I was also told that more tests would be awaiting us. I don't know

611

what they might be—although I hope we'll pass them as a team."

"I'm sure we'll get help and guidance," added Masako.

"Right," said Bill, thoughtfully. "I think, though, we should be more careful from now on; we need to keep a closer watch on what we do and think, and be ready to help each other. I feel that something else is coming."

"Whatever comes, we'll face it together," said Jai solemnly, reaching for the others' hands.

"I value our friendship and the trust you've shown in me. It'll be a great honor for me to fight by your side," Masako said, slightly bowing her head, "No matter what it takes." She spoke firmly like a samurai warrior.

Diana was startled by a tingling sensation in her head.

"*The test of unity*," whispered the voice of the middle-aged woman in her mind.

Diana laughed, eliciting curious looks from the others. "The test of unity," she repeated aloud for her friends. Everyone smiled.

They resumed walking, with Bill in the lead, and made their way along the passage, knowing they would be going toward the zone represented by the Black Square. After some time, Diana touched Bill's shoulders and he stopped abruptly. She pointed down.

The Treasure of the Pandavas

Bill called out, "I can't see the ground ahead of me."

The others closed in around him.

Bill swung the beam of his flashlight ahead, and the others joined in with their own. The lights just dissipated, and nothing could be seen.

Diana smiled. "Okay, let's just wait a moment. It's here, in my dream, that I met the Yakshas. We should stop and thank them for helping us so incredibly in our mission."

"You're right," said Bill. He thought for a moment, then with palms clasped, he said, "Thank you, sirs! We offer you our deepest gratitude, and seek your forgiveness for any mistakes we might have made."

Jai added, "O friends of *Dharma* and protectors of the treasure, we offer you our humble respects. We are very grateful for your kindness and will never forget you."

"Without your help and guidance, it would be impossible to reach this point, and I hope you'll continue to assist us until we achieve our goal," Diana said humbly, her hands folded in prayer.

Masako bowed her head respectfully. "We salute you, O venerable monks, and we offer you our gratitude, and recognize that without your help we would have had no hope of completing our mission."

Diana laughed again. "The voice just said, 'The test of gratitude.' I think we have all passed the tests for now."

The others looked at her, in awe of the messages she was receiving;

Jai pointed toward the vast opening in the passage. "This is definitely the great abyss; we will have to use the third symbol to cross it."

Diana quickly found the depression on the floor, perfect for the sacred Hindu swastika emblem. There was no sound, as if they were in a vacuum.

Masako moved forward to the edge of the passage. She directed her flashlight into the vast opening and as the beam hit a particular area next to the edge, they could see the bridge appear and disappear as the light moved. It seemed to be made up of some kind of fluorescent material. Masako moved her beam forward along the bridge revealing that it was a lengthy one; where it ended wasn't visible from their location.

"That's the bridge we need to use," said Diana; she then removed the sacred key and started walking toward it. When Diana had moved forward just a few paces onto the bridge, she felt as if she was in some kind of energy field. Her flashlight helped her navigate as the beam fell on the energy wave. The rest quickly followed her.

After about ten minutes of carefully making their way, they saw the entrance of a new passage. Once inside, Masako looked back and checked for the energy bridge to see if it was still there, thus reassuring their safe return journey.

The next few hours passed as the previous ones: comfortable and without mishap. Diana chanted the sacred OM mantra, feeling happy and contented in her heart; she felt they had already accomplished their mission.

* * * *

Behind them, their pursuers struggled and fumed. They were desperate for rest, food and water. Jawahar and Father Francis were thoroughly exhausted—their feet sore with blisters, and their legs painfully cramped. There was a near mutiny when they reached the end of the tunnel in front of the rope bridge, and so at that point they finally allowed their men to stop and rest. Everyone retreated into the warmth of the tunnel, away from the sharp wind and swirling flakes of sleet and snow. This time the priest produced two bottles of whiskey and some packed food from his bag. There wasn't enough to go around, and fighting soon erupted as the tired and hungry men fought each other for the scarce bits of food and drink. They were too exhausted to do any real damage to each other. In the end, both Jawahar and the priest imposed order by rationing out what was left of the supplies, if only to shut the men up.

They slept uneasily on the hard rock floor of the tunnel, their dreams haunted by memories of the dangers they had already gone through, and the fear of those to come. When the cold light of morning began to filter in from the outside, they awoke even hungrier and thirstier than before, with pain and cramps throughout their bodies, along with stiff legs and backs, and ulcerated feet. Still, they were all so cold, the idea of staying there any longer seemed worse than moving on. At least then, they would warm up a little from the exertion.

The rope bridge proved to be a dangerous obstacle. The first two men who attempted to cross were too heavy, and a few wooden planks cracked. One of them broke completely through, causing him to plunge toward the rocks. His scream faded as he fell, and then ended with a sudden awful finality. The other man remained frozen for some time, grasping onto the ropes of the swinging bridge, until the shouting of the others convinced him to move forward to the opposite end.

The next men who crossed the bridge were more cautious, but still two more stepped on the wrong planks. With fingers numbed by the sharp wind, they were unable to grab the ropes. The eagles, disturbed by all the noise, began flying dangerously close and eyeing the terrified men. When the frightened thugs began shooting at the birds, they retaliated, viciously attacking with their beaks and talons, causing two more men to fall from the bridge. With that, it was decided they should stop for a while before resuming their mission. Eventually the remaining men were able to cross.

Jawahar and Father Francis did a headcount. Of the original twenty-two, only eight remained, including themselves. They reached the next tract of the tunnel, frostbitten, miserably tired, and lightheaded from lack of food. They walked slowly and without enthusiasm toward the next unknown danger.

By the time they reached the edge of the abyss, one man, angered at being stopped abruptly, pushed the man in front, cussing loudly to keep moving, but he was shocked as the man he had shoved slid screaming off the rocky ledge and into the darkness below. Ridden with confusion and fear, the ring leaders moved to the front, found the energy bridge and directed the gang to cross.

As the men walked on the bridge, they were startled by sudden peals of raucous laughter that seemed to come from nowhere.

Suddenly one of the man yelled, "Make it stop! Make it stop now!"

The laughter became louder and more sinister.

"I can't take this anymore! Get me out of here!" He ran back along the bridge and suddenly, in mid-scream, he just wasn't there; he had lost his balance and fallen into the abyss. Supernatural entities were obviously acting against them, together with ferocious animals and the elements of nature. The thought of evil spirits on the trail terrified everyone, including Jawahar. He had always been a confirmed atheist and usually refused to believe in what he could not see, but now, as things unfolded before his eyes, his fear was palpable. Father Francis, though equally terrified, ridiculed it as black magic, as his own belief in God began to waiver.

Some of the men cried out about some evil looking dwarves hiding in plain sight; other were shocked by things they saw looking up at them from the black nothing. These visions were unique to each individual, so they only contributed to the thick atmosphere of mistrust and hostility amongst them. Eventually, the six pursuers entered the last tract of the tunnel in an almost desperate state of mind, maddened by the urge to get out of that horrible place, and angered by their long ordeal. Their rage focused on the people they were pursuing; they were now more dangerous than ever.

* * * *

Masako, Bill, Diana and Jai had been walking throughout the night. Now Bill, who was in the lead, came to a sudden halt. The others, lost in their own thoughts, looked up to see what had caught his attention.

The tunnel was blocked by a stone wall. The four stood, perplexed for a few minutes, trying to figure out what was to come next. They focused their flashlights all around.

Suddenly, they were startled by a huge cobra the size of an anaconda, that slithered out of the darkness from the right side of the tunnel. The four made an effort not to cry out, and managed to stay still. The cobra did not attack them, rather it remained quietly poised at a distance, sitting on its own coils and watching them intently. Diana remembered her dream; this was the same snake who was wrapped around Lord Shiva's neck, resting in peace.

Diana whispered, "This is not an ordinary snake. It's waiting for us to do something."

"I think it is the guardian of this door, wherever the door is," said Jai. "I think we need to pray here. Why don't you try asking your guide, Diana? She has been helping us all along, and she wouldn't have brought us here unless she wanted us to reach our goal."

"Yes," Diana said, "I think this is the 'test of prayer'."

They all stood silently, with slightly bowed heads. Then, clasping their hands together, they concentrated in prayer on the benevolent powers who had helped them to reach this point. They expressed their desire to complete the mission for the benefit of the world, not for personal advantage.

This time, everyone heard the words in their minds. *"The test of self-sacrifice."* It had come from the cobra!

They all looked at each other, more than a little alarmed. What did that mean? Would they have to kill themselves? How could this help them recover the treasure?

"I think the self-sacrifice we are required to do here is not something very drastic," suggested Jai. "I think a few drops of our own blood will do." He took the Swiss army knife from his hip pocket and scratched his left forearm, letting a little blood ooze onto the ground just in front of the rock, just as the ancient Kshatriya Hindu warrior Kings of India had done before them; it was an ancient noble tradition.

The big snake nodded. *"Very good,"* the voice in their minds said.

"It's a statement," Bill added. "Yes, I'm ready." He stepped forward to the rock and added a little of his own blood to Jai's.

Diana and Masako followed suit, then stepped back while the snake slithered to the bottom of the rock wall beside the blood. It remained still, as if wanting something else. Diana remembered the Nagamani Jewel; she took it out of her necklace and placed it near the cobra.

"Your blood is pure and of great value," said the snake. *'Your toll is paid, you may proceed."*

The reptile absorbed the jewel onto its head where it began to glow. It touched its head to the rock at the edge of the wall. Suddenly, the entire wall started to slide open, revealing a dark, enormous cavern which seemed to be the heart of a mighty mountain.

When the tunnel access was completely opened, the four stepped into the cavern, flashing their lights around the inside, the sound of their steps echoing loudly. The door was ajar. The snake was nowhere to be seen.

They walked a few hundred meters toward the center of the immense cave; there, a raised stone platform led to a small pyramid that appeared to be made of solid stone. The four stood for a moment, completely mystified. A pyramid was the last thing they were expecting to see. Just above the small pyramid was an eerie light, glinting down as if the rays of the stars and moon were filtering from some hidden shaft in a distant ceiling.

In the top of the small pyramid was a circular hole which Bill studied intently from the inside. Slowly, he walked toward it, as if inspired, removed the fire crystal from his backpack, and inserted its base into the cavity. Something inside the pyramid clicked into place, and a great number of mirrors, made of polished silver, appeared around the walls of the cave. They were all facing the fire crystal and reflecting its light. The entire cave became fully illuminated.

They could now clearly see that the mountain itself was shaped like a pyramid, with four walls tapering toward the top in perfect lines, and another small opening at its crown. The small pyramid before them was just a replica of the mountain.

In the light, magnified and reflected by the mirrors, the cave presented them with a sight both astounding and marvelous. There it was, surrounding them, the vast treasure of the Pandavas! Diana looked around, her eyes bright and her face effulgent. She thought about the struggle of the past months, the many things she had learned and the incredible people she had met. She thought about her ancestor, Arthur, and what he had given to protect this place. She thought back to King Vikramaditya and to Emperor Yudhisthira.

Now she and her friends were standing in the same spot as had these incredible souls. It was overwhelming and humbling. Who could have imagined they would have a role in such magnificence and history? Diana looked at Bill and saw her thoughts reflected on his face.

"Incredible," he said breathlessly. "From the battlefields of Iraq, to the treasure caves of the Pandavas."

Masako and Jai seemed lost in awe as well. They wandered around, examining the vast and long lost treasure.

"I have never seen so many jewels in my entire life, I know about the Kohinoor diamond, but here there are millions of diamonds much larger than it." Masako reached her hand out to a huge pile of rubies, diamonds, emeralds and other precious stones that sparkled with a thousand colors. "Actually, I couldn't have imagined there were this many in the whole world."

Bill examined an array of golden garlands, all fashioned in the same style, yet slightly different from each other, with large delicate flowers of gold filigree and beautiful leaves made from thin sheets of pure gold. The workmanship was incredible, with each leaf artistically carved and including what looked like the veins of natural plants.

Close by, Diana found a number of solid silver caskets, each measuring roughly one foot high and three feet wide, and stacked in fours. Behind them were stacks piled higher and higher, and arranged in steps, all the way to the walls of the mountain. Opening the one on top, she found it filled with exquisitely crafted necklaces of various styles, made of pearls and all kinds of precious stones, and bound together in gold or silver. They formed wonderful designs of mango leaves, plants, stars, moons, and suns. There were also flowers of all kinds, and animals like peacocks, parrots, dolphins, doves, butterflies, bees and exquisite dragonflies. Some of the necklaces seemed to be made with glass beads, but the sparkling, beautiful light emanating from the tiny elements of the designs reminded her more of some special type of transparent material; perhaps crystal or something she had never seen before.

Dazzled by such splendor, Diana opened the trunk on top of the next stack and found an even greater variety of bangles made of gold, silver, ivory, shell, coral, and the same type of shining colored glass she had seen in the necklaces. Next to them, were a number of bracelets and armlets, anklets with tiny silver bells, elaborate turban ornaments, brooches and clips, earrings and ear pendants, and finger and toe rings of all types.

A third trunk contained crowns and coronets of all sizes, and a fourth was filled with adjustable belts made of gold, and embedded with various jewels, of many shapes and styles.

A few feet from Diana, Jai concentrated his attention on an amazing collection of worship paraphernalia including containers of various sizes made of copper, silver and gold, gild conch shells, golden wick-lamps, incense holders of many shapes, brass bells of various sizes, gold, silver and copper plates, small spoons for *achaman*, sacrificial ladles, tall lamp stands, and many other objects he could not recognize.

All this while, Diana was facing the east side of the large cave which was filled with similar treasures. When she turned toward the south side, where Bill was facing, she saw heaps of weaponry, including swords, daggers, bows with arrows neatly contained in quivers, spears, maces and clubs of various sizes and shapes, as well as many tools and instruments for various types of crafts and agriculture. These were not made of gold, but of a shining type of metal, heavy but extremely strong, that showed no sign of decay even after the many centuries had passed. Gold and silver had been used for the gilding and handles, and there were pearls and precious stones on the hilts of the swords and daggers, and beautiful golden bells at the upper extremities of the large bows. Some large war conch shells were decorated with inlays of gold, and the horse harnesses were exquisitely wrought with what seemed to be the finest silk ropes with golden thread and decorated with many bells and pearl pendants.

On the west side of the cave, several shelves held a number of golden jars of various sizes, tightly capped and sealed. Diana saw Jai carefully opening the seal of one of the smallest jars, and after smelling the contents he announced they had found a container of ancient herbs and spices.

"There must be all types of medicines here," he said, "health tonics and extracts that would make any naturopath happy and some doctors, too." In other jars, there were seeds of vegetables, fruits and various plants labeled in Sanskrit; this included many which had been extinct for many years. "I'm thinking this might have been a doomsday vault."

The north side was stacked with ancient manuscripts, maps, scrolls, paintings and engravings. Some of the painting appeared to move and change with the angle and perspective of the observer; some others seemed to be in relief, although the canvas was two-dimensional. There were also many beautiful statues and sculptures of various sizes, cast in gold and various alloys. Upon careful observation, one of the paintings showed the actual faces of the Pandavas along with Lord Krishna; it was stunning! Other paintings showed many of the important personalities of the *Mahabharat*.

There were statues, strikingly lifelike, and delicately finished and polished, painted with joyful and serene expressions. They had inlaid ornaments of various kinds, as well as ornate clothes that were surprisingly soft to the touch. They were no ordinary statues, but life-size representations of great Vedic personalities from antiquity, that even Jai could not recognize.

Their exploration was interrupted by the sudden appearance of an elderly woman dressed in saffron clothes—Bhairavi Brahmani. Diana immediately recognized her and rushed to her feet, just as she had done in her lucid dream. The other friends followed in awe, for they knew this must be the woman Diana had spoken of.

"My dear children, you have finally attained your goal," said Bhairavi emphatically. "But your mission is not yet finished, it has only just begun. Sunrise is coming." She lifted her hand, and a ray of golden light shot down from the ceiling through the fire crystal on top of the pyramid. The cave grew even brighter than before, almost celestial-like. Now they were able to see even more treasure than they had originally; ten times or one hundred times, they were not sure. A price tag would have been impossible.

"The world is in grave danger. You need to return and take with you the best hope for mankind," she said. Standing next to the small pyramid in the center, she spoke: "Bring me the three keys, children. They will unlock the mystery."

Diana, Masako and Jai took the three objects out of their backpacks which they had received in Dwaraka; they seemed to be made of some unknown alloy and were about sixteen inches square but very smooth and light. They headed to the pyramid. In the radiant light reflected by the crystal and the mirrors, they saw indentations on three faces of the small pyramid which resembled the objects they carried. Stepping closer, Diana, Masako and Jai carefully placed the three into their respective cavities. The fire crystal already shone at the top of the structure. The fourth face of the pyramid bore the outline of a human hand, and after some hesitation Diana placed her own hand there.

Bhairavi smiled. "Well done, child. You are very clever; may my blessings be with you."

Another click came from inside the small pyramid. Slowly, the four sides slid down into the floor, leaving only a thin and elegant frame made of a shining metal that supported the fire crystal. In the middle, there was something that certainly looked like a stack of books.

The *sannyasini* nodded, and Diana reached out and lifted one large bundle from out of its protective cage. It was strangely light.

Bill, Jai and Masako also moved closer. Diana passed the bundle into Bill's hands. She opened the cloth covering and found a neatly tied stack of extremely thin sheets of a strange material; neither metal nor cloth nor paper, but something in between. It was covered in small uniform writing.

Jai looked closer. "It is Sanskrit!" he exclaimed.

"It is," confirmed Bhairavi, smiling. "*Maharishi Vedavyasa svayam likhita mula grantha*: the original scripture compiled by Vedavyasa Rishi himself, before the Pandavas retired from the kingdom. Maharaja Yudhisthira personally carried this original copy to this cave when he and his brothers made their last journey to the Himalayas, together with Queen Draupadi."

The four friends were astounded by the historical validation.

"What is this material?" asked Bill inquisitively, pointing to the pages.

"It's called *vanda*, and the secret of its manufacture is contained in those manuscripts down there," Bhairavi replied, indicating the northwest corner of the cave. "It is a special metal alloy to which molten crystals are added, and it can be hammered very thinly.

"Molten crystals," murmured Masako. "Stone, glass, fire and light, clearly a perfected art."

"Venerable lady, please help us to understand," inquired Jai, his palms pressed together. "What is this place? What are these treasures? Who are you, and how can we serve you?"

Bhairavi smiled again. "This mountain is called *Hiranya-shringa,* the 'Golden Horn', while the next mountain is called *Mainaka.* We are north of the Kailasha peak, where Mahadeva Shiva resides on his earthly sojourns. This is also the place where Nara and Narayana Rishi celebrated sacrifices in the presence of Brahma and Yama for the benefit of the entire universe. It is here that Lord Krishna and Balarama performed a great *yajna* to honor Kuvera, before starting to build their capital, Dvaraka. Here King Bhagiratha performed penance for many years in order to bring Mother Ganga from the heavens to this earth."

She looked at them sympathetically and understood that more explanations were required. "To make it simple, the universe has three kinds of human-like beings, called by the names Devas, Manavas and Danavas. The Danavas are an ancient people, or race, akin to the Manava human beings; but not quite human. They have great mystical powers, being able to change their shape at will, and to interact with matter in a subtle way. They have their own planets, but they like to visit the Earth to interact with humans, and have done so for a very long time during ancient astronaut expeditions across the galaxies. It was Maya Danava who perfected the art of making *Vanda*, many thousands of years ago.

"The Rakshasas are usually the most violent and cruel of the Danava sub-races. They are man-eaters and always on the prowl for more humans to satisfy their indomitable hunger. One would not dare cross their paths even in one's dreams. There is another sub-race of Danavas that you will find here: the Nagas, who usually live in water reservoirs, and are expert in shape-shifting, often taking the form of great serpents or dragons. For example, the large cobra you met at the entrance is actually a Naga called Vasudha, son of Takshaka. The city of the Nagas, Bhogavati, is also hidden beneath one of these mountains, and they travel by moving through the waters of the subterranean rivers. They are friendlier to the human beings and sometimes fall in love with them, but they are still very dangerous, and it is better to keep a respectful distance from them. Kinnaras are another sub-race."

Bhairavi looked at Diana. "You have already met the Yakshas, the friendly Danavas. Some of them are short of stature, like dwarves, and others are tall and stout of body, like Kuvera. They also have red or blond hair, a white complexion and sometimes grey, green or blue eyes.

"Yakshas are kinder and they do not enslave or mistreat human beings. They often intermarry and have children with humans, and groups of their descendants have settled in various places on the Earth, excavating tunnels under the ground and into the mountains, where they like to live and hide their treasures."

Bhairavi Brahmani looked around at the cave and also at the astonished faces of the four friends. "The Yakshas have been guarding this treasure for more than 5,000 years now. Before you, Shivananda was permitted to enter this place; however, he did not want to retrieve the treasure as the time was not ripe, so instead he chose *samadhi*. Before him, Emperor Vikramaditya was permitted to enter and take whatever he needed to establish and defend his empire for the sake of *Dharma*.

"However, the most valuable treasure of all is contained in these books. These are the original manuscripts compiled by the great sage Vedavyasa, who summarized the eternal and universal knowledge in a suitable form for the people of Kali Yuga, this current age, also known to you as the '*Iron Age*'.

"Vyasadev prepared three versions of the *Vedas*: a complete one destined for the Devas who are in charge of the administration of the planets; an almost complete one for the Danavas, and finally an abridged version. This one was prepared specifically for the limited understanding of the human beings or Manavas. To give you an idea of the difference of scope, I can tell you that the version given to the Devas is six million verses, while the one for the human beings is only one hundred thousand verses long. The Devas are people with extraordinary powers, they take care of universal administrations; they are obedient, and well-wishers of all. A few races among them are the Siddhas, Gandharvas and Adityas.

"In your world, even the abridged version has been a target of mutilation and distortion by ill-intended people whose goal is material domination and human control. Here you can find a copy which has been preserved, together with Vyasadev's personal instructions for the dissemination of this knowledge.

"These books contain the answers to all the problems the world had faced before and is facing today, and will also face tomorrow. We have decided it is time to bring them back to the human race; thus a new age of higher consciousness and evolution can be inaugurated. Otherwise, the planet will suffer a major catastrophe and all lands and people will have to be purified in a much more agonizing way. As usual the choice is left to humans, as are the consequences."

The *sannyasini* paused, her noble face saddened by the thought of the billions of people who would perish in such destruction, and of the many millions who had already died and suffered because of ignorance and illusion, unable to achieve liberation in this life.

"These books contain the philosophy and the ethical rules needed for human beings to live in peace and harmony, the knowledge of the purpose of life, the structure of the universe, and the history of every conceivable race scattered throughout the various planets of this universe; but they also have the answers to the necessities of protective or defensive warfare, energy production, transportation, communication, and every other field of knowledge, including medicine and the environmental sciences. These books contain a summary of the entire body of universal knowledge; these are eternal.

"By studying them and applying the knowledge to your current scenario, your scientists will be able to reverse the damage inflicted on this beautiful planet in the name of technological progress and prosperity. Humanity can then placate the cosmic forces controlled by unearthly beings, and thus bring true happiness, real peace and sustainable living to all. We are ready to help you understand these treatises and apply this knowledge. The Devas from other planets are ready to help you. You may simply call them by following the instructions contained in the section about interplanetary communications and travel."

Bill's eyes opened wide. "Interplanetary

communications and travel? You mean there are aliens who are waiting for us to call them?"

"Of course, you are not alone in this immense universe, nor is 'mankind' the most advanced race of all." Bhairavi smiled. "Human beings have been the students of other ancient races a long time before the beginning of what your scholars consider the birth of civilization. For millions of years, and until a few thousand years ago, the higher beings called Devas regularly visited this planet and guided many, considering the human beings or descendants of Manus as their younger siblings. Truly, they cannot be considered as alien either, for there has been a massive interchange between these beings and humanity from the very beginning of time. Please know that Manu is your first human forefather, through whom all of you have come; thus the word 'mankind' is used interchangeably with 'humankind'.

"The Devas have become quite concerned about the children of Manu. Ever since your race learned how to disrupt the balance of the universe by splitting the atom, great danger has arisen. This power has been unleashed using very crude methods, and with the development of extremely destructive weapons. In response to this danger, through a subtle action on the energy field of the human brain, the Devas have inspired the development of a higher level of consciousness. By suggesting new ideas and concepts, and positively reinforcing the good intentions of various receptive individuals, we have created great strides toward a global awareness. The actions created by ill-motivated beings are very strong. There are negative forces at work who intend on total domination of both the physical and metaphysical realities. And they are very determined, as they work stridently toward their dangerous goals.

"What has been happening in the world during these last few centuries is a genuine disaster. Serious consequences in the form of natural disasters and wars are repeatedly visiting your planet. Have no doubt, my friends, the knowledge contained in these books can halt and reverse the damage done. But this will only occur if enough people are willing to commit themselves to truth and harmony, and thus become capable of absorbing the wisdom contained within them."

The four looked at each other, amazed. Never had they imagined Diana's quest would be of such magnitude. "Can you please give us more precise instructions?" asked Bill respectfully.

Bhairavi looked at him with compassion, and then his companions. "First of all, my dear ones, this vicious cycle of violence plaguing the world must end. It is primarily fueled by unnecessary wars based on unwarranted anger, the massive slaughter of innocent animals due to lack of mercy—especially cows & bulls—the termination of the innocent unborn in the womb due to lack of sensitivity, indiscriminate felling of trees and misuse of machines, thus polluting the Earth's air, water and land. All this must stop immediately! Going forward, one should not gamble with nature's resources, or one's life with drugs or money. We need more love, and the courage to say no to all forms of lust. Humankind must accept this basic premise or you will be unable to avail yourselves of this knowledge. The guidance of the illustrious beings is the key to understanding this knowledge, and its wisdom can only be understood and effective with those who are rooted in *Dharma*."

Again, Bhairavi studied each of their faces.

"I see you have all come here for different reasons. Diana—searching for treasure; Jai—to overcome the troubles in his mission. Bill is seeking knowledge, and Masako is here out of inquisitiveness. These are the four motivations that inspire good-hearted people to approach God. You are truly blessed.

"My friends listen. You are the chosen children of the four races. I see your unspoken question: 'Chosen for what?' Well, beloved ones, you will present a plea at the Great Assembly in the Palace of Glass on Kurmadvipa, or Turtle Island, in that land now called America. Take Professor Vivek from Bengaluru, and Madhava from Prayagraj, with you; they are needed in this mission. You must go and implore the world leadership to wake up before it's too late. If you can convince the rulers of the planet to take the side of *Dharma*, humankind will still have some hope to solve the problem by itself—which is always the best option. If they will not fix this issue then you will need the help of your elder brothers from the higher Deva world of the Siddhas, Gandharvas and Adityas."

The *sannyasini* paused a moment, placed her palm behind her ear, as if listening. "But now, we will have to take care of more imminent danger. You have been followed, and they are coming to loot the jewels and destroy the scriptures. They are wicked people, frightened, hungry and angry. They will attack you. After a great many losses, they have still been allowed passage. The Yakshas have let them pass swiftly, urging them on to their final doom." She fell silent, and closed her eyes. Now the four friends heard them too: the footsteps of several men, resounding from the tunnel entrance.

* * * *

A moment later, Jawahar the Jackal and Father Francis burst into the room. This time, the professor and the priest were at the head of the small group of six. They crossed the entrance of the huge cave and, seeing their quarry in the middle of the hall, extracted their weapons.

638

The Treasure of the Pandavas

The four friends turned toward the entrance but remained still and silent, waiting. The *sannyasini* stood with her eyes closed.

The hunters cautiously walked toward them, glancing greedily over the heaps of treasures stacked everywhere. Smiles lit up their faces as they called to each other. "We are rich, super rich!"

"So," Jawahar snarled at Diana and Bill upon seeing them, "you weren't looking for any treasure, were you? From the very first day, I knew you were trouble, lady. But you have been useful, actually very useful, and now you have finally been outwitted. What irony. All your foolish efforts and those of that freak 'Grandpa Arthur' have now guided me here. After it's all said and done, in the end, I win."

Jawahar eyes flickered over Masako like she was a non-entity, and then settled evilly on Jai.

Before he could say anything, Father Francis spoke. "Jawahar, I think we should just shoot them where they are. Then we should return to town and get the necessary equipment to recover this loot."

Wisdom from the mouth of a fool, yet wisdom it is, thought Jawahar

The priest quickly lifted his gun and aimed it at the *sannyasini*. He pulled the trigger, but the gun clicked without shooting.

* * * *

639

Bhairavi Brahmani, who had been silent all this while, opened her eyes, and an immense power began emanating from her being. High above her head, she gripped a long staff, something Diana did not remember seeing before, and murmured a few words, a *mantra* unknown to them. The four friends repositioned themselves behind the woman. This was no ordinary confrontation. They couldn't stop the bullets, but it was evident that powers greater than their own were about to be called upon.

Jawahar, the priest and the thugs frantically tried to shoot their guns, as well, but with the same poor results. The bullets seemed to have magically vanished, their weapons had become useless, and for all practical purposes, they were now unarmed.

The thugs panicked, screamed and turned on their heels to flee the cave. It was obvious they were more afraid of this woman than they had ever been of the lions and crocodiles, or the scary dwarves. But their movements slowed down as if they were caught in some kind of invisible net. Soon they were immobilized. Arms pinned to their sides, they crashed rigid to the ground like felled trees—all of them, including the professor and the priest. They lay on the floor, their eyes bulging with fear and rage.

"In the end, Jawahar the Jackal gets no treasure and now lies impotent, unable to reach even his own flask," murmured Diana.

"Yeah, I almost pity the fool." Bill chuckled. "All that effort of his and SEPS could never counter the commitment of your Grandpa Arthur. I think we knew it all along though."

Fifteen dwarves with pointed ears suddenly walked in, as if on cue, chuckling and smirking. They bowed to the *sannyasini*, smiled at the four adventurers, and then lifted the thugs and carried them away without a word.

Masako looked at Diana, who had a slight touch of concern on her face.

"They will not be harmed," said Bhairavi with a knowing smile. "But your concern for these horrid people is direct proof of why the four of you have been chosen. This treasure is clearly in the right hands. These opponents of yours will be told and shown many things for their own edification, and for some time they will be out of commission, so your work will be easier. They have done enough damage. When they are released back into your world, they will have lost their credibility. They will be unable to explain where they have been without admitting the existence and superior power of the 'objects of pagan superstition' they dedicated their lives to disproving. I do not think you will hear from them again anytime soon." Then, unexpectedly, she laughed a crystal-clear ringing laughter reminiscent of the sweet sounds of a silver bell.

"Now, now, my children," she said affectionately, "worry not. You have passed all the tests successfully, and you have nothing to fear. Now you are all ours, members of our sacred family. We will watch over you and care for you always. Take these books. Keep them with you for a while and let them be your guide, your beacon of light in these troubled times." She motioned her hand, and the bundles of texts which had been preserved inside the small pyramid, came floating in the air toward the four friends.

"These are the most important ones. Make copies, study them, act on them, and then return this treasure to the cave. In the future, you may return to this place in a much easier fashion. You are the ambassadors of the four races. And especially you, Jai, for you will become the future Bharat."

The four friends nodded. They didn't totally understand the meaning of Jai becoming the future Bharat, because he was already a Bharat, Jai Bharat, but they all had the same thought: whatever would happen in the future, they would have to wait to see it.

"Now it's time to go back to your world," commanded Bhairavi. "You shall leave from the opposite gate." She pointed her hand toward the southeast corner of the cave, and all of a sudden another tunnel appeared out of nowhere. "Go now; we will meet again soon." Her smile reached into their very hearts.

The four respectfully bowed to the *sannyasini* then shouldered their bags with the Vedic and Puranic books in them and walked into the new tunnel. Soon they found themselves in a cave very similar to the first one they had entered at the beginning of their journey. Sunlight filtered through a thick growth of bushes and plants in front of the cave entrance; they pushed their way through the vegetation with little difficulty.

* * * *

As soon as the four friends exited the cave, Bhairavi floated up toward the opening in the apex of the mountain and disappeared. The fire crystal was the first thing to fall from its location in the ceiling, immediately losing its shine. The small pyramid retracted to its original shape and the mirrors folded back into the walls, drowning the mountain cave in pitch darkness. The cave door, which had been kept ajar, swiftly closed. Next the energy bridge over the abyss, the rope bridge across the mountains, the slab over the lava river, and the floating stones over the water all retracted and disappeared. Both the cave entrances at Shankaracharya Hill and the one they were leaving now were closed-in by dirt and foliage which appeared out of nowhere.

It seemed as if the cave had never existed. When the four friends turned around to take one last look at the cave entrance, it had vanished. They were not really surprised.

They found themselves in a small forest on the slope of a great mountain. Elated and lightheaded by their very powerful experience, they made their way to the green slopes below. An ancient Buddhist monastery sat next to a glimmering stream. The many colorful flags of the monastery proudly flew in the wind, inviting them to the sacred place of prayer.

They had almost reached it when they came upon a monk. He, too, was walking along the forest path, carrying a load of pinecones wrapped in a net. The young man was so startled he almost dropped his load, but then smiled in a friendly manner before gesturing with his free hand toward the religious center. The friends nodded and followed him.

Lama Norbu, the leader, was just as surprised as the young monk. The valley was practically inaccessible and the eighteen monks who lived there, very rarely had visitors. It was surrounded by very tall and ragged peaks that kept it hidden and protected.

Although the Tibetan monks had almost forgotten about the external world, they were still very hospitable toward their unexpected visitors. They spoke an old local language and were also conversant in Pali, but not even Jai

The Treasure of the Pandavas

was able to understand them or to make himself understood, so only sign language was used. The monks showed their guests to an empty room and provided four thick mattresses and plenty of blankets for their use. The bathroom was not far and they all took turns visiting it to freshen up. Jai used his satellite phone to call Karry and brief him on the events which had transpired. Karry was elated by the recent developments, and said he would arrange their transport right away.

The next day, around 3:00 p.m., they heard a large helicopter flying low over the monastery. As they waved, they saw Karry climbing down a rope ladder from the aircraft that hovered above: no landing was possible on that rugged terrain. The chopper flew off and Karry walked happily toward Jai and his friends.

"Good job, Son!" he cried out as soon as they were close enough. He actually embraced Jai, who stood there embarrassed, but happy. Karry's enthusiasm was contagious. He shook hands with all the others, including the monks who had come out to see what was happening.

"Not to worry, not to worry," said Karry, as the monks returned to the monastery. "This place is officially within the Chinese borders, but India's relationship with China has improved considerably after the failed terror attack in Delhi and the discovery of the nuclear device destined to detonate in Beijing. In fact, it

645

was our intel that neutralized the threat. The Chinese, needless to say, are grateful, at least for the moment, so we have a window of opportunity to get things done quickly, before hostilies breakout again, as Communist China cannot be trusted and will soon be back with their bullying tactics. He turned to Masako. "Your parents were a great help. Thank you, Masako."

Masako smiled happily in response.

"We're not far from Manasa Sarovara, but this valley is not on the pilgrimage route. The nearest peak is 22,028 feet high. It is considered the actual Kailash, or Sumeru, because of its extraordinary shape. It looks like a nine-storey *svastika*, with four sheer steep faces marking the cardinal points of the compass, and around it are the sources of three great rivers, the Sindhu, the Brahmaputra, and the Ganga. The two lakes at its base, next to each other, are the Manasa Sarovara, a round freshwater lake, and the Rakshasa Tal, the highest saltwater lake in the world; it is shaped like a crescent moon."

The four friends smiled, listening to Karry's enthusiastic explanations. The man's obvious happiness and excitement were contagious.

"When I saw the satellite map showing where the signal from your satellite phone was coming from, I practically shouted for joy. I would never have believed you had gone about seven-hundred kilometers inside the mountains in just about five days! But here you are, and it's not a dream or a fantasy. It's a miracle! These are great and powerful holy places!" He laughed happily.

This was a Karry no one had ever seen before, not even Jai.

"I was sure you would make it, guys, but I was not expecting something this momentous. And you say Jawahar and Father Francis are out of the game? Well, I have another piece of good news: the American drones have taken out Mullah Omar in Pakistan's Quetta. Also Maoist Prachanda was killed in a police encounter in Orissa State a few days ago. For all intents and purposes, SEPS capabilities have been partially neutralized. Oh, this is truly wonderful!"

Karry's happiness was spreading, and soon they all found themselves laughing and recounting tales of their incredible adventure.

* * * *

After the others had finally gone to sleep, Karry approached Jai, his mood once again serious. In a hushed voice, he asked, "Can I see them?"

Jai sat on his mattress and gently pulled the books out of his bag. Karry was now silent and seemed in awe, almost afraid to breathe. Setting the book on a table, he delicately opened it and turned the pages. Admiration lit up his face as he saw and felt the exquisite artistry of the ancients. The small letters shone brightly. The two of them sat in silence for a long time.

Chapter 22 – The Last Warning

The morning broke with a brilliance of spectacular colors. As the guests prepared to leave the monastery, a soft glow infused the air of the hidden Tibetan valley. They went one more time to thank their hosts, and sensing the importance of these strange and sudden visitors, the Buddhist monks performed a blessing ritual to see them on their way. Then Lama Norbu gifted them with a large bag of dried berries which he called *goji* and seemed to value very much. In return, the four friends offered the only things that could be useful to them in this secluded land: the special flashlights they had carried on their mission; the flashlights had special built-in batteries that could be recharged manually or with sunlight. Lama Norbu was very pleased by the unique gift and thanked them most enthusiastically.

They heard the chopper a few minutes before it appeared. Karry climbed into the suspended rescue basket first, helping the others, one by one, as they too were lifted into the copter. They waved to the monks from above as the steel bird left on its way to Delhi.

A few hours later they arrived at the President's Residence where an enthusiastic hero's welcome awaited them.

They learned that, in their absence, WIN TV had maintained ongoing and steady coverage of their story. Thousands had joined in a major support campaign for Diana and her friends. When they arrived in Delhi, both Priti and Dhiraj were there waiting with their TV crew.

For years, compromised news anchors had been accepting bribes from Jawahar Katju. Under Jawahar's direction, they had been maligning Diana and Bill; however the directors of these channels now found themselves under intense scrutiny. Their credibility and stock plummeted when the truth, as presented by WIN TV, was officially endorsed and confirmed through repeated broadcasts on State TV channels.

The media directors frantically tried to contact Jawahar for his side of the story, but without much success. Jawahar and associates seemed temporarily reduced to silence. Suddenly, there were no more brief calls to invite the journalists to highly profitable luncheons. And no one else stepped forward to offer any financial incentives for continuing the smear campaign against Diana and company.

The directors of these news agencies quickly calculated the ramifications of the new scenario, and turned coats without a second thought. A splashy new campaign was a hard-hitting exposé on Professor Jawahar Katju. They came out with a new special edition exposing the slanderous campaign against the four heroes, organized by "a radical Delhi professor. This shady and dubious character spread false information for political gain. As an ardent admirer of Marx, Mao, Stalin and Hitler, he was dedicated to sabotaging India's relationships with the West in general, with the United States and Russia in particular." According to "groundbreaking revelations" from Jawahar's personal driver, the stations revealed they had not actually been duped by Jawahar, but had been working for the benefit of India all along. They claimed they had taken a cue from the Vajra team, playing along with Jawahar's plot and giving him room to hang himself. They then joined the general chorus glorifying the great achievement of Diana, Bill, Jai and Masako in order to white-wash their own blunders. To top it off, they offered handsome rewards for any personal interviews from the four "heroes and treasure hunters." People were not fooled, however, and their attempt to legitimize their actions and steal WIN TV's thunder failed miserably, and they had to suffer loss of face and finance due to peoples' boycott, leading them to a meltdown, and the eventual closing of their operations forever.

Professor Cariappa and his wife flew in from Bengaluru. Diana and Bill were invited by the President to stay at the palace as her guests. After meeting with the President, Professor

Cariappa was guided to the library, where he nearly fainted after seeing the texts they had brought.

He dove into reading, forgetting everything else. Emerging a few hours later, he explained that he needed help—the sheer size of the texts was overwhelming; it was impossible to go through them all by himself.

"This is a most miraculous discovery," he said excitedly. "Many texts that had been lost are once again available to bless and help mankind. As soon as possible, we will translate and publish the complete set in all the languages of the world, and soon this treasure will be human treasure, accessible to one and all, without any copyright issues. Universities, scholars and others can now use this ancient science to reverse the chaos and catastrophes now plaguing the planet. These, my friends, are indeed momentous times. My friend, Madhava, has come to help, but it's not enough. I have called a number of my colleagues—Sanskrit and History professors from various cities—and we will work around the clock in shifts."

"Professor," said Jai, giving him a double handshake in earnest, "we need you to come with us to the United States...tomorrow night."

"Huh?" Cariappa seemed too sleepy and dazed to understand. "What are you talking about?"

Diana stood up. "Professor, Bhairavi Brahmani told us we need to go to the 'glass palace' and speak to the world assembly. She specifically mentioned you and Madhava. We believe she meant the United Nations. Please come with us and help us prepare a speech."

Cariappa's tired eyes went wide. "Are you serious?"

"The Security Council of the United Nations has already called an international conference on religion and democracy," said Diana. "We must go there with the books." She gazed at the horizon for a moment, her eyes momentarily aglow. "This knowledge is the reference for all religious traditions because it establishes the universal and eternal principles of religion."

"You are right," the professor replied promptly. "I'll pack a copy of the entire collection."

With the help of Balaram and Karry, and many others, the books were quickly but carefully photographed, scanned and catalogued, then distributed in sections to the various scholars, who had been arriving for an impromptu symposium at the Presidential Palace. Their work began immediately.

The President herself had expressed a keen interest, and would frequently check in on their progress. The ongoing research and investigation was given highest priority, for this was, in the President's own words, "the greatest discovery in recorded human history."

"Your flight leaves tomorrow at midnight," Karry urged. "Jai, we had a talk with the President of India: you are now officially the special Indian delegate to the United Nations, and your friends are your consultants appointed by the Indian Government."

The four responded with shocked looks as Karry passed the official letter to Jai. "Now *we* all know you are actually the emissaries of the Divine beings, the Devas and Rishis and the authors of these texts, but we cannot present you as such to the United Nations. So you will go as officials from the Indian delegation. However, to be clear, the message you bring does not come from the Indian Government, rather this is a message from the ancestors to all humanity."

"We will do our best, sir," said Jai, giving a half salute with a wave of his hand.

Cariappa trotted away to pack a complete copy of the text, and his exit signaled the end of the meeting. Everyone got up to make final preparations before the long journey overseas.

"Strange, leaving India like this to go back home," commented Bill, smiling. "Things will not be the same, even back there. The world has changed. I have changed."

"We have all changed," said Diana smiling, as she reached for his hand. "Change is not bad in itself. Now it's up to us to make it better."

He took her hand and gently squeezed it.

Jai met with the Vajra Team, drawing accolades for his successful heroic mission. He spent some quality time with them. Masako went to see her parents, who had been anxiously awaiting her return. Bill and Diana took the opportunity to call home to let them know they were safe and confirmed the events their respective families had watched on TV and the Internet.

Priti, Dhiraj, and the WIN TV crew had remained close by to interview the four whenever possible. They recorded several hours of exclusive interviews regarding the journey to date, as well as their upcoming trip to the United Nations General Assembly. Although Diana and Bill had already been exonerated from the allegations spread by Jawahar's journalists, people were still very eager to learn more about the treasure and the special mission. That week and for several weeks afterward, WIN TV received the highest ratings in the history of Indian television.

* * * *

After the sixteen hour direct flight, their plane landed at New York's JFK International Airport at 6:00 a.m. The special delegation from India was welcomed by officers from the Indian Consulate, and then escorted to the Millennium Plaza, a hotel a few blocks from the UN's 46th Street headquarters. At the hotel, they checked in, to stay on the 29th floor. It had a fantastic view of the Empire State Building, the Chrysler Building, the East River, and the eighteen-acre site of the United Nations.

Soon their limos arrived. It was a very short trip, barely ten minutes, as the tall building was already very visible from the hotel. The vehicles passed the row of flags, and finally stopped right in front of the entrance. Walking into the General Assembly Hall, they were struck by the vast space, the dramatic lights, and the tall, golden panel with the logo of the United Nations behind the table.

The special session was still going on, now in its third day, and the Secretary General was rocking in his chair with a dejected face, barely listening to the speech presently being delivered by the delegate of a small nation.

An usher led them to a row of seats in the back, and then proceeded to the central table where he gave a note to the Secretary General, who looked up and glanced over to where the four were sitting.

After the small nation's delegate had finished his talk, the U.N. General Secretary switched on his microphone. "I have an announcement to make. The special delegation from India has arrived to bring an important message on the issue we are discussing. I am requesting our members hear their spokesperson."

The four friends and two professors looked at each other. They had not anticipated the possibility that just one of them would be allowed to speak. Jai made a quick decision. "Diana, you should go. You are the one who was entrusted with the mission of finding the treasure in the first place. Try to stimulate their interest, so suitable action can be taken by all." The rest nodded in agreement.

* * * *

Diana looked toward the central table where the Secretary General was sitting. Her eyes went wide. Bhairavi Brahmani was standing there, but nobody else seemed to see her. Diana straightened her back, looked around at her friends, then stood up and nodded to Bhairavi. She smiled back.

The Secretary General spoke again. "Will the spokesperson for the special Indian delegation come to the podium, please?" An usher hurried up to escort her.

Diana calmly walked between the aisles of chairs and down to the middle of the huge hall, then to the podium facing the assembly. She had no idea what she would say. She silently prayed, *Let me be an instrument of God.*

She closed her eyes, and the words started flowing from her mouth, effortlessly.

"I wish to thank the Secretary General and all the members of the Assembly for allowing us the opportunity to deliver this message." She opened her eyes and looked up at the last row of chairs, where her friends were seated.

"We have witnessed a failed terrorist attack in Delhi, the successful discovery of nuclear weapons—in the nick of time—in the United States, Europe Union, Russia and China, and the most unfortunate nuclear missile hit on Tel Aviv. Much has been said already about global terrorism, religious fundamentalism, weapons of mass destruction, and even vested interests, political pressure, and interference in matters of national self-determination.

"I do not need to remind you about the purpose of the United Nations, or to make long speeches about international rights and security, ethics, integrity and earning the trust of the people."

Diana realized the delegates had been taken by surprise by her candid and straightforward approach. She turned around: Bhairavi was not visible anymore, but somehow she felt her presence in her heart and mind, comforting and supporting her.

This was the crucial moment. There was no other way to put it.

"The message that I am bringing you is actually not from the government of India."

Diana paused for a few moments, allowing the members of the assembly to digest this last crucial statement.

"This is a message from a people who do not have representatives sitting in this assembly. We have been requested to act as their emissaries. The Indian government has generously agreed to be their conduits, because this message has a global relevance. We can certainly shed light on the present dilemmas facing mankind, and surely that is reason enough to be here. The message comes from what is, for all intents and purposes, an independent nation that has been living hidden within the boundaries of what we consider Indian Territory. Their culture is extremely ancient and wise, and they have much to teach us. They have entrusted us specifically with the mission of delivering this message, or call it 'the last warning'."

After the first moments of amazement, the members of the assembly started murmuring quietly, putting heads together with their neighbors for hushed comments, and carefully looking around to check the reactions of their colleagues. Many looked like they were wondering who had let this crazy woman into the room, let alone allowed her to speak.

"The message of this people is that the leaders of mankind, sitting in this Assembly, need to recognize and uphold the truth. What is that truth? It is that freedom can only be granted to those who do not misuse freedom and do not rob others of their freedom, thus strangling the human spirit.

"On one hand, no individual, or group, has the right to violate the rights of others, under any pretext, even by passing religious blasphemy laws, or non-religious totalitarian laws.

"On the other hand, as every action has a consequence, the exercise of freedom for the wrong reasons can have disastrous consequences, not only for humans but for the entire planet—for Mother Earth and all her children—including the ones who have sent this message. We are now at a critical juncture."

Many delegates started clamoring. Diana turned around to look at the Secretary General, but his expression was inscrutable. She continued, speaking louder. "I am simply a messenger, and you may like the message or not, and choose to abide by it or not, but you must listen to it, at the very least."

The tumult gradually subsided, but several delegates still looked outraged.

"The people who sent this message are not asking for a right to vote in this Assembly, and they do not want to impose their will on anyone. They simply want to inform the Nations of the Earth that wrongful actions will naturally bring a reaction according to the intrinsic laws of the universe, which we call *karma*. This planet is in very serious danger, and the way to save it is explained in the texts that we have here with us today. These texts are written in Sanskrit, so we have with us Professors Vivek Cariappa, and Madhava Gupta from India, who have studied this ancient language and are conversant in it." Diana gestured to the two professors, who stood up from their chairs, and slightly bowed to the assembly.

"Oh great!" grumbled a Pakistani delegate to a colleague. "So the Indians are going to save the world? Not bloody likely!" The other theocratic delegates shared in the glares and grumbles of their Pakistani allies. The British delegation hurriedly whispered amongst themselves, mortified that a fellow countrywoman was causing such an uproar.

"This is all we needed to say," Diana continued. "If the assembly wishes to hear more about how we met these people, what we know about them, our opinion or our suggestions, we will be glad to cooperate. Thank you very much for giving me the opportunity to speak."

A few brave open-minded delegates clapped their hands, and the sound echoed hollowly in the huge hall. Diana turned to the Secretary General, gave a little bow, and walked back to her chair, to a hearty welcome by her friends, who hugged her and shook her hand.

"I think we have finished our work here, at least for now," announced Jai.

Suddenly, they realized that the Secretary General was speaking about them. "...deliver the texts you spoke of?"

This time, Diana walked to the central area, along with Cariappa and Gupta, who carried the copies of the texts. They approached the table where the Secretary General was sitting, and set the books on it. The man's eyes glistened intently behind his glasses.

"Thank you," he said. "We will examine these. I will be in touch."

Diana left as the Secretary General was speaking with the two professors about how they would work together. At the podium, another delegate started his speech.

* * * *

They arrived back at the hotel to find Bill's family waiting for him. Desmond, Vivian, and Shirley Buford stood awkwardly in the lobby, a little intimidated by the luxury of the hotel, as well as Bill's new found status as an international celebrity.

For his part, Bill was beginning to feel some reservations about having introduced Diana to his family, especially since Shirley kept giggling like a child, and his mother, Vivian, was scanning Diana from head to toe with a certain maternal scrutiny.

Diana, however, seemed to take no notice, and was the picture of charm and friendliness. Within a few minutes, she had easily won the hearts of Bill's family.

When his sister turned to him with a wink and a smile, Bill felt his face growing hot. He didn't know what was going on, but suddenly felt his world was moving very fast. He had not really contemplated the idea of having a romantic relationship with Diana, and despite the fact they had often slept in the same room, they had never been intimate. *We are very good friends*, he told himself. *Just very good friends.* Then he caught Diana's eyes, and saw that they were sparkling with happiness. The radiance of her face struck him, and he could no longer deny the truth of his feelings. How odd, he thought, that his family was able to see in five minutes what he had not recognized within himself.

Suddenly, he realized his father was talking to him, and shook his head, slightly dazed. "Sorry, Dad. I was thinking about something else. Can you say that again, please?"

Desmond Johnson smiled. "I was asking about your future plans, Bill. Are you staying or are you planning to travel some more?"

Bill glanced at Diana, Jai, and Masako who were sitting in the comfortable armchairs of the lounge, before answering. "I don't think our work is quite finished, yet," he said. "I could not explain the entire story to you by phone, but I'm sure that in the next few days we'll have time to sit down so I can bring you up to speed."

* * * *

On Wednesday morning, they received a courteous note from the Secretary General, asking them to return to the U.N. for a meeting with the Chair of the Committee assigned to the texts. They eagerly agreed to be there that afternoon.

When they arrived, they were led into the office of Kurt Weissmuller, a tall square-shouldered, tired-looking man with a hint of a German accent. With him were Cariappa and Gupta.

"Thank you for coming. Please, have a seat. I have been discussing the texts with the professors, and there is something I must ask you before we send a summary report to the Secretary General." He stared at Diana, and then shifted his gaze to the others. "I was told that the four of you actually met these people who sent the messages and the books; but now, am I to understand that they are not *people* at all? Is that true?"

Diana straightened in her chair, readying herself, for she had expected this. She wouldn't have believed it either, if she hadn't seen it with her own eyes. "You may call them whatever you like. It is a fact they are not part of mankind as we know it; they are not even from this planet. They are genetically more capable of utilizing their psychic abilities than humans are."

"Aliens or mutants, then?" blurted out Weissmuller. He looked a bit nauseous.

"I don't know if alien or mutant is the right word, either," Diana said, crossing her arms, protectively. "But the important thing is the message. Human beings are not alone in this universe. Others are here and they are watching over us. Presently, mankind is threatening not only this planet, but the balance of life in the entire planetary system. Man needs to correct himself, or face the consequences; we are behaving like a rogue species and they don't like it. Those who gave us this message can help us avert disaster, using both the knowledge already in our hands, as well as the knowledge contained in the texts they have entrusted to us.

"If mankind wants to clean up its act, the people who gave us this message are ready to help. We just need to make contact."

There was an embarrassed silence before Weissmuller spoke again, his voice calm and controlled, as if he were speaking to a lunatic. "Several delegates have been enquiring about the identity of this mysterious nation and its connection to India."

He picked up a list from his desk. I am not sure I want you to tell them officially in the General Assembly, that you got this message from aliens." He put down the paper and frowned.

Jai shifted in his chair. "There is an intrinsic value in the message. What does it matter where it came from?"

"We lose credibility," said Weissmuller sharply. "We cannot afford that; we have already very little of it. These types of ideas are usually circulated by crazy conspiracy theorists who are considered a laughingstock by the media and academia. We are the secular bastion of mental sanity and humanistic values. And we can't speak of outlawing or expelling member nations on the advice of some little green men, out there." He seemed to be coughing up sentences in a sort of instinctive reflex.

Diana sighed. "Dear Sir," she said, "there is more. We don't need to tell the Assembly, but we are kindly requesting you to please give this information to the Secretary General. If human beings remain stubborn and unable to substantially improve the situation very quickly, those you call aliens or mutants will have to intervene directly to save the planet and chastise humans, because Mother Earth is very important to them as well."

"Pardon?" Weissmuller gasped, his blue eyes bulging.

"Yes," said Diana calmly. "These beings are fully capable of controlling the very elements of nature, and I believe they will give some demonstration soon, if they consider it necessary."

"What do you mean? Is this some kind of threat, Ms. Warwick?" blurted Weissmuller, his face turning red in anger.

"You might call them 'natural disasters'," said Diana, suddenly inspired as if Bhairavi Brahmani was prompting her to speak. "But they will happen simultaneously on one chosen day. I will return to India and speak with those who sent the message. If it's an exact 'date of doom' you want, I will ask them for it. If it's a demonstration of their capabilities you want, then get ready for one. I will soon let you know exactly which day that will be."

Weissmuller, no longer bothering to hide his feelings, looked at her with a mixture of annoyance and pity, as he pressed his lips together into a thin line.

"In any case," Diana continued, "we believe the United Nations should take a firm stand against the politicization of exclusivist religions and totalitarian ideologies that practice overt or covert imperialism, Also abject materialism, under the grab of capitalism or communism, is also affecting human consciousness and destroying Mother Nature," said Diana. "Such ideologies disrespect Mother Earth and lead to excessive exploitation of her children in the name of religion, and her resources in the name of development, causing a serious imbalance, and wreaking havoc all around."

Weissmuller leaned back in his chair, and stared at her. "You cannot be serious."

"I am. Are you?" retorted Diana, who was starting to lose her patience; she was not going to mince words anymore. "Religion should be a matter of individual personal faith; for freedom of religion to mean anything, no system of religious beliefs should be enforced by any government, no matter if they have been elected or not. Persecution of those who dissent, especially in the matter of religion, violates the very purpose of the establishment of the United Nations Organization. We demand that membership in the UN be based upon a commitment to freedom of religion and basic human rights. Any and every member is beholden to respect these basic rights, or they must be expelled."

Weissmuller lifted his head with a challenge. "Now listen to me, young lady. You are speaking radical theory and I'm talking about political reality. Your policy negates our ideal of engagement among nations, regardless of their political systems at home. Do you think it's so easy to solve these problems?"

"Easy or not, it's supposed to be your job. And it's quite a lousy mess you have made of it," Diana said angrily, her flushed face.

Jai spoke up. "We know it's not easy, sir. But there is no other alternative. There are other dimensions to be considered, which have not been talked about by Diana. If the United Nations does not take a strong stand which is legally binding, the problem will lead to World War III between different groups desiring global domination—call it a war of civilizations or cultures: Allah vs. Jesus, or believers vs. non-believers, haves and have nots etc. If it comes to that, the result will be disastrous, total and complete.

"We have defused a few nuclear devices, but how many can we stop? Now that Israel is nearly crippled, religious fundamentalists on both sides have become emboldened. They are rallying for Armageddon, the final battle, even now, as we speak."

Weissmuller sighed. "I will report your suggestions to the Secretary General," he said curtly, then offered to shake their hands, signaling the end of the meeting. "He may decide to pass them to the Academy of International Law and the International Court of Justice. Thank you for your sincere effort."

* * * *

A few days later on Friday, to the delight of the four friends, the General Assembly of the United Nations bravely passed the bold resolution by a margin of just two votes, with none of the five permanent members vetoing. The historic declaration condemned the politicization of exclusivist religions as a violation of fundamental human rights. In order to fight it, they expressed the need for religious pluralism and religious tolerance, followed by the removal of all blasphemy laws and all anti-religious laws, and the strict separation of church and state. A call was also made to strengthen and expand democracies around the world. The second part of the resolution took a strong stand against non-sustainable development, and the indiscriminate exploitation of Mother Earth's resources: especially the misuse of land for animal farming rather than for food crops; the hoarding of food by rich nations thus causing worldwide hunger; water shortage due to construction of huge dams diverting water from previously fertile areas of land, and lastly, climate change caused by deforestation and fossil fuel use.

The response of those affected member nations was fierce, immediate and predictable. Certain radical fundamentalist Christian denominations publicly called for a prayer vigil for the salvation of the atheists and pagans. They argued that the imposition of religious pluralism was a direct attack against evangelization, their religious canon, and the establishment of the proper morality in society. And the legalization of the rights of the planet itself, of inert matter, was an outrageous challenge to the instructions of God, who had given man full dominion over the animals, the plants, and the land.

Around the world, some political parties, along with many environmental groups, celebrated the successful passage of the resolution, while others expressed outrage. The breakaway faction of the Organization of Islamic Countries, the OIC, aligned with the Islamic State, twisted the meaning of the resolution and thundered against the imperialistic western countries that controlled the United Nations and had practically declared war against the Ummah, the collective Islamic community. They were outraged the UN was trying to introduce concepts and practices that were against the basic tenants of Islam, at least their version of it.

Many Third World Countries cried foul, but for a different reason. They accused the rich countries of trying to stop their progressive development, which they saw as a political ploy. In their eyes, this was a move to keep the West dominant over them, both politically and economically. Chaos erupted around the world.

The Indian Consulate arranged for the return of the special delegation to Delhi, as the Indian government was feeling responsible for their safety and security. Bill decided to fly back to India to accompany Diana to Prayagraj. She wanted to go there to honor the request of her ancestor Arthur. Professor Cariappa, on the other hand, decided to remain in New York to continue working with the UN Committee.

The journey back to India was much more subdued. Everyone dozed off comfortably in their seats, and although they woke up for meals, they barely ate anything. They spoke little, because all knew what the others were thinking.

After reporting about the UN mission to the President of India in Delhi, they continued on to Prayagraj, accompanied by Professor Gupta and some members of the Vajra Team disguised as *brahmacharis,* young and single male devotees. At Gora Baba's ashram, they received a warm welcome by Shukananda Sarasvati, and the resident *brahmacharis* invited them to stay for a few days. The 8th day of May was the appearance day of Adi Shankara, and a great celebration had been planned.

On Sunday morning, still a little dazed from jet lag, the foursome got up early to participate in the *mangala arati,* the prayer ceremony before dawn, then sat with the Swami and his students for the *homa* fire sacrifice and a lecture on the life and works of Adi Shankara Acharya.

It was around noon when Diana, accompanied by all her friends and the members of the Ashram, solemnly carried the vessel containing the ashes of Gora Baba to the bank of the river, and climbed into the largest boat. When the three large ferry boats were filled, the last journey of Gora Baba started with the accompaniment of sweet melodious *bhajans,* slowly ascending the current of the mighty river to the Triveni Sangam. There, at the confluence of the three sacred rivers, Saraswati, Ganga and Yamuna, Diana spread the mortal remains of her ancestor into the water, amidst the loud sounds of cymbals, conch shells, and joyous *mantras*. She had fulfilled her ancestor's wish and he could now move forward on his journey, taking up another life, or hopefully, going back to the Supreme. Lifting her eyes, Diana was startled, but not very surprised, to see Bhairavi Brahmani standing in the distance. She was not sure anyone else was able to see the smiling *sannyasini*, but her perplexity was dispelled when Swami Shukhananda turned in that direction as well. It looked like Bhairavi was swiftly walking on the water toward them.

The Swami greeted her respectfully, and Diana bowed to touch her feet.

She then officially introduced the holy woman to Swami Shukhananda, and to the surprise of everyone present, the elderly Swami actually prostrated himself on the deck of the boat and touched his venerable head to the feet of the *yogini*.

Then he offered her his own *asana,* and sat down at her feet. The *brahmacharis* of the *ashram*, as well as Bill, Jai and Masako and the Vajra team members, also paid their respects, followed by the guests.

The *sannyasini* gestured to Diana and her friends to sit next to her. When everyone had settled, Diana started to speak, and the spellbound audience eagerly listened to her words and to the translation provided by Madhava, whenever needed.

From their meeting with Professor Cariappa, the encounter with Jawahar's henchmen at Priti's marriage, the journeys to Kaziranga National Park, Rameshvaram and Dvaraka to search for the fire crystal and the sacred symbols, the treasure hunt at the Shankaracharya Hill, the meeting with Bhairavi Brahmani, the return from Tibet, and the travel to New York, all seemed equally wonderful adventures and drew many enthusiastic comments.

The jubilant mood was shattered when Diana received a call from Professor Cariappa. Some countries affiliated with the Islamic State within OIC, and some left-wing dictators among the poor countries, were refusing to implement the UN resolutions. Information also came that some right-wing Cardinals within the Vatican were planning a coup against the liberal Pope for accepting the UN resolutions, which they said went against God's commands.

"I don't think the world is taking the message very seriously," said Diana, wrapping her arms around herself.

"Then there is no other way," thundered Brahmani. "The karmic cup of the Earth is filling up fast with negativity. It is much faster than what was expected at the beginning of the Kali Yuga. Send word to the Great Assembly in the Palace of Glass that Mother Earth will shake her own children to force them to wake up. If they don't wake up, their fate will mirror that of the dinosaurs who became a burden on earth so long ago. "

Diana looked over at Brahmani as she waited for a signal. When she nodded, Diana placed the professor's call on speakerphone.

Bhairavi spoke. "The Earth will split on the western side of America, where many warnings have already been given," Brahmani said loudly and clearly. "The lands of Indonesia, as you call them, now, will spit fire from the bosom of Mother Earth. When the frozen mountain slides into the ocean, the southern shores will see the Great Wave their ancestors have feared in their darkest dreams. The wind will afflict the ancient land of Africa, and space will shower fire arrows on the great northern cold lands of Eurasia. This will be the first great demonstration, and it will happen sixteen days from today, on the seventh day of the waning moon. Warn the people who live in those areas, for Mother is angry with the behavior of humanity, especially their inept leaders, and she will teach a lesson that no one will ever forget, and there will be no discrimination in the execution of punishment."

Those momentous words sounded like a final judgment, and everyone felt the fear and anxiety of the great suffering to come.

Cariappa replied with a tired voice, rubbing his eyes. "I have written it down, and I will plead with the Secretary General to urge the Governments to evacuate people from those areas."

After Bhairavi finished her talk, she nodded to Diana.

Diana spoke. "Nothing else, Professor."

"I will pass on the message. My *pranams* to Devi and everyone," he said.

Diana switched off her phone. There was silence for some time.

"What more can we do?" Diana urged, almost on the verge of tears.

The *sannyasini* looked at her compassionately. "There is not much time left, but you can do whatever possible to raise your own consciousness and the consciousness of the people around you. On the next full moon, the followers of the Compassionate Buddha celebrate his appearance. This is a good opportunity to pray for enlightenment, compassion and peace."

She looked around at the people sitting there. "All of you go back to your homes and take care of your families. Help them to understand the message and what is going to happen and why.

"If you can, speak to the people who live around your home, to anyone who will be ready to listen to the message. The hearts of people can still change, so will their actions and their results."

Masako shook her head in disbelief. "But there must be something more we can do. Can't you help us? Please?"

Bhairavi smiled. "I am helping you already. But I cannot do everything myself. People must become responsible and use their God-given freedom and intelligence to make the right choices, otherwise, they will keep making the same mistakes over and over again. The real purpose of life consists of sincerely learning, accepting the knowledge that has been given to you, and making good use of it. Then everyone in the universe will be happy and prosperous."

Swami Shukhananda looked up. "Human beings have helped the Devas, and Devas have helped human beings throughout the history of the world. Their destinies and histories have intertwined before, and it can happen again. The very fact that the *Pancha Maha Bhutas* are intervening, that Gora Baba's granddaughter had help in finding the treasure, and most of all Devi is sitting here with us, these are powerful signs. We pray to you, Devi, instruct us in this time of uncertainty and danger."

Everyone's eyes turned to the *sannyasini*. She smiled, but fiercely, like a tigress. "Some good people will be protected, but the *pralaya,* the doomsday, is coming. You cannot stop it— the bad *karma* that was created needs to be removed; the good, bad, beautiful and ugly all will be affected, without discrimination."

But Shukhananda Swami would not give up. His head bowed humbly, he continued to speak. "We are your children, Mother. Tell us how we can find shelter and continue to live so we can serve your plan in this world."

Bhairavi's body started to glow, and when she spoke again, her voice was deep and resounding, as if from another dimension. She lifted her right hand, and her smile became affectionate and sweet.

"*Tathastu.* So be it. You have passed the test.

"You will work to preserve and re-establish *Dharma.* The Adityas, Siddhas and Gandharvas will support you. Also the Kinnaras, Nagas and Yakshas.

"I will be with you. You will all have a role to play in this great drama. Here are my instructions: Bill, prepare your family for the times to come. Your land is not safe, so you should be ready to move away to higher locations.

"Masako, you and your family are in danger, too. Do not return to the land of the Red Dragon, because it is presently controlled by people who are against *Dharma*, those whom you call capitalistic communists. You should remain in a holy place here in India and protect your parents. Jai will help you.

"Jai, you and your family will have an important role to play in the future, but you will part ways for some time. Stay away from the ocean and relocate inland."

Bhairavi turned to Diana. "Diana, you cannot return to your old life now. You know that. The big city where you used to stay is not safe, but the house of Shivananda's children will be protected. All of you should go there, including your friend who was born in a cold barren land."

Swami Shukhananda was smiling. Bhairavi turned toward him, pleased. "As for you, my dear child, for now at least, you are free from the persecution of the *a-dharmic* criminals that you termed SEPS. Please bring Arthur Warwick's message to the world without fear, and publish Shivananda's books. Jai will help you. Engage your students in distributing them, giving lectures, and teaching people in all possible ways, thus raising their animal consciousness to human consciousness, and then, hopefully, to Divine consciousness. This is what is needed now: the successful transmission of the *dharma* message throughout the world by word of mouth, and it is the best defense against all evil. *Dharmo Rakshati Rakshitaha*—Protect *Dharma*, and *Dharma* protects!"

"We are your humble servants, Devi," said the Swami, his eyes filled with tears, "and we will carry out your orders."

Bhairavi's body became brighter and brighter, until it looked like it was made of pure light. "I will be with you," she said, and then the light expanded, diluting the form into a diffused radiance which lingered for a moment before fading slowly away, as the boats reached the shore of the ashram.

For several moments, they all stared at the spot where she had been, in wonder and awe. How were they supposed to return to the daily business of living after such an extraordinary experience? But return they must to household duties and relationships that needed to be taken care of, not to mention a mission to take the *Dharma* and *yoga* message to the world. It all seemed like an unforgettable dream.

* * * *

At the airport in Delhi, Jai and Masako said goodbye to their friends before Jai accompanied Masako to her home.

Diana and Bill sat together in the airport lounge. They had found seats on flights back home and called to inform their families of their return. Now there was nothing to do but wait.

Diana's airplane was leaving first, and they both watched the display with growing anxiety. They didn't know what to say. Now and then they caught a few people staring at them; no doubt they'd recognized Diana and Bill from all the media coverage.

Finally, Diana spoke up. "I'll be waiting for you, Bill. I will miss you very much. Just come to Leeds, no questions asked."

"What do you mean, no questions asked?" His eyes searched her face.

"You know what I mean," she said softly, and turned her face away, hiding the tears in her eyes.

"You've got it all figured out, haven't you?" he whispered. "I think you're right, though." He felt a little giddy.

Diana suddenly turned around, and flung her arms around his neck. Startled, Bill found that his own arms wrapped around her, almost of their own volition. She laughed—a silvery burst of hilarity amidst the sparkling tears.

Not much was said, but Diana almost missed her flight.

* * * *

Back in New York, Bill happily reunited with his family, and now, with the newly found clarity in his mind and heart, he was able to answer their unexpressed question.

The next days were among the happiest of Bill's life. He felt more alive than he had in a very long time—probably ever, he realized. He had almost forgotten the warning of the disasters hanging over mankind's head until May 20th, when the TV show he was watching was interrupted by breaking news.

The Treasure of the Pandavas

There was a sudden spurt of volcanic activity at Krakatoa, and within hours the seismic activity around the San Andreas Fault had increased. Reports started coming in that a huge dust storm was forming over the Sahara desert. Scientists were perplexed by the coincidence of these natural disasters. News came in about some space debris moving toward the earth and the imminent cracking of a huge ice shelf off the Antarctic coast.

Realizing what was going to happen, Bill convinced his family and started to quickly move to the West Virginia hill country to live with his uncle; it would be a safer place.

* * * *

At the U.N. Headquarters, Kurt Weissmuller looked helplessly at the Secretary General. The warning from the Himalayan Yakshas was coming true. Fearing it was already too late, they nevertheless alerted the countries with whatever knowledge they had. Some nations took immediate measures; others, confused by the information, put some half-hearted instructions into place; still others completely ignored the warnings, as they seemed to not care about the information, the people or the consequences.

The news of the threats was deliberately leaked to the media by the astute Secretary General, as it was a far greater matter than any one UN mandate could handle. Professor

Cariappa found himself swamped with interview requests, and he accepted as many as he could in order to explain the significance of the predictions given by the Yaksha *'aliens'* on earth. People waited and watched breathlessly as the events unfolded before their very eyes. Many people were evacuated safely, but some unlucky ones were left behind.

Finally, on May 24th, Krakatoa, west of Java Island, exploded. Volcanic ash spread throughout the entire Southeast Asian region. The news traveled fast and flooded the airwaves and the web. The media feasted on the scoop, broadcasting the history of the famous volcano, from its earlier explosion in 1883. That disaster, in which over 36,000 people perished, was the equivalent of two hundred megatons of TNT, and had destroyed two-thirds of the island.

Video clips now showed this latest eruption, which was far greater than previous ones, and continued all through the night and well into the morning. There were toxic gas clouds and pyroclastic flow, the burning fallout of ash and debris reaching the temperature of 900 degrees Celsius. Glowing avalanches incinerated everything in their path. The unstable lava domes, formed by the magma forced to the surface, flowed down the flanks of the mountains, steadily covering more and more land.

The Treasure of the Pandavas

Geologists and volcanologists were having a field day. Some of those interviewed stated that a large scale eruption had been imminent in the region, but it would have been impossible to say precisely when. Moreover, even if it had been correctly forecast, evacuation of the area would have been a superhuman task. Caught by surprise, the survivors panicked and fled by whatever means they could find.

At 10:00 a.m., another devastating update showed satellite images of a giant tsunami hitting Australia, South Africa, India, Argentina and Chile. The massive Antarctic ice shelf had finally fractured, with a large part of it sliding into the ocean. A global tsunami washed away life and buildings alike from the coastlines. Rushing far inland, miles of land was inundated, leaving death and destruction in its wake.

All other TV programming was cancelled. The various channels showed frantic descriptions of the two disasters and a repetition of the video clips recorded from satellites and local reporters; many of whom had lost contact with their offices after sending the films, and were now feared dead or missing.

It was 1:00 p.m. when a new warning was issued. Super tornados had formed over the Sahara Desert, and a huge column of whirling hot air which, according to the satellite measurements, had already reached speeds of three hundred miles per hour, and was moving from Algeria to Egypt in a west to east sweep. Nothing could survive such an assault, and nothing could be done to rescue people in the region until the turbulence had disappeared.

At this point, the TV channels began to broadcast doomsday talk shows with Nostradamus experts, Native American shamans who spoke of ancient prophecies, and the many environmental scholars who never before had obtained the opportunity to speak to the masses. The perplexed scientists did not have a proper answer as to how five major natural disasters were happening simultaneously without them knowing ahead of time. They postulated many theories to substantiate the idea that it was all just pure coincidence; an unhappy incidence of chance; no aliens or mutants were involved.

The loudest and most ubiquitous voices of the media were undoubtedly the crusading preachers of various denominations. They explained how all such disasters had been anticipated in the Bible, and were to be ascribed to the "reign of the Antichrist" that started with the recent United Nations' resolution aimed at legitimizing Paganism, Atheism, and the Earth's own environmental rights.

In the general chaos, the extraordinary shower of meteorites that fell on the entire Eurasian continent went almost unnoticed on the global scene. However, for the people who survived the night of impacts and hellfires, it

The Treasure of the Pandavas

was certainly a most shocking experience. Globally, there was terror, panic and confusion. It was almost expected when the media reported an earthquake in San Francisco at 2:20 p.m., local time. There had been earthquakes before in the region, and the seismic wave was not very powerful, so the emergency services stepped in smoothly and the casualties were limited. However, forty-five minutes later a second and much stronger movement occurred, 9.9 on the Richter scale, and people understood the first shock had only been a preliminary warning. Large and deep cracks appeared in the ground. Panic started. People got into their cars and jammed the highways then started to flee on foot. Airports and railway stations fell into chaos. The San Andreas Fault was finally breaking California apart.

Countries around the world declared a state of emergency, but it was impossible to take effective action in the face of such a large-scale disaster.

In the meantime, on the advice of Jai, Karry's family moved to Pune to live with the Agarwals. The sea level kept rising, and Mumbai was sinking inch by inch. Masako remained at home with her parents in Delhi. Cariappa's interview had become the most talked about program in the world, whereby people around the planet learned it was the work of 'aliens and mutants' who had sent the

685

warning. Some were angry and frustrated about what was happening to the planet because of these creatures, and sought revenge on them. Others requested their governments make peace with these strange beings before the Earth was completely destroyed. It seemed like the world was divided into two rival camps: one supporting the Yakshas, and one opposing them. Finally, the Secretary General requested Professor Cariappa bring the four friends back to Headquarters. The UN had temporarily moved to Camp David in Maryland, due to the rising water levels in Manhattan. In total, the disasters had claimed over ten million lives, or one in every thousand people. This was more than a last warning, it was partial dissolution.

* * * *

When she heard about Krakatoa, Diana was in Leeds. She had already vacated the London flat with no plans to return, as the River Thames would eventually rise. Ana accompanied her.

Her mobile phone rang that night. It was Bill. "We need to talk," he said rapidly, "We have moved to West Virginia. It's happening. I just got a call from Cariappa. He wants us back at the U.N."

"Of course." Diana's voice trembled.

Bill continued to speak. Hearing your voice makes me feel calm and hopeful. "The future is not written in stone, Diana. We can write our future today, and that's what we gotta do."

"I know. And we will do it together." There was a brief silence before she added, "I love you, Bill."

"I love you, too." His voice cracked with emotion. It had been a long journey for them. "You know Diana, I owe you my life."

"It's going to be a new life for both of us."

"With a new love as well."

* * * *

Diana sat inside her parent's library throughout the night. After many hours, as the sky began to brighten, a tinge of pink colored the horizon. Several stars pulsed brightly as the surrounding night sky faded into blue. As she opened the window, a golden radiance began to fill the air as a soft, gentle breeze caressed her face. Morning had broken. Diana stood up from her armchair and walked toward the large glass window. There she remained motionless, mesmerized by the unfolding dawn. A new day had come. She chanted softly in her mind the peace mantra: *OM Shanti...Shanti...Shanti....*

About the Book

I hope you enjoyed reading "*The Treasure of the Pandavas*". If you did!

1. Please write a review at;
   https://www.amazon.com/dp/B08F2ZK87F
2. To contact the author, please email at;
   treasure_of_the_pandavas_108@yahoo.com

About the Author

As a veteran of ten years, he has been deployed to some of the most hotly-contested places on earth. His writing endeavors till now have mostly been within the non-fiction world, creating booklets and press releases for non-profit organizations. Victor has a master's degree in business management and has worked as a professional in a Multinational Corporation for about twenty years. He is interested in serving humanity. *The Treasure of the Pandavas* is Victor Cosmos' first novel. He lives in America with his wife and daughter.

Made in the USA
Las Vegas, NV
20 November 2020

11186121R10380